Maid for the South Pole

DEMELZA CARLTON

Book 7 in the Romance Island Resort series

Cover design by Najla Qamber Designs

Lost Plot Press

ISBN-13: 978-1-925799-11-8
ISBN-10: 1-925799-11-5

DEDICATION

This one's for Opa,
in the hope that he has enough time left to read this.

ONE

Nothing brought a smile to Jean's face like penguins. There was just something about them that could make anyone happy. Here on Heard Island, there were hundreds of them, waddling around Wharf Point without a care in the world. Triumph exploded in Jean's chest. He'd found them! Now, all he needed to do was find a high vantage point where he could see if there were any babies in the colony.

A moss-covered mound looked to be the highest point on this part of the Azorella Peninsula, so Jean scrambled across the dark volcanic rock toward his own, personal grassy knoll. Once he reached the top, he'd see…

The cushion plant beneath his feet compressed under his weight.

Sinkhole.

One word was all Jean had time to think before the fragile net gave way. Falling into darkness. One second. Two. Three? Was it eternity, or did it just feel that way?

The impact jarred every bone in his body, forcing the

breath from his lungs. He lifted his head to watch the cloud of condensation whoosh upwards, a smoke signal to mark his location, but there was no sky to be seen above. The traitorous bush had covered its trap, Jean realised. Damn Australian territory, even if it was part of Antarctica and not the Aussie mainland. Even the plants were trying to kill him.

But he was a goddamn Canadian biologist, and not city-bred, either. He'd grown up next door to the Arctic and he wasn't about to be outsmarted by a plant on the wrong side of the world.

Jean extended his arms, reaching for a wall or a rock or something else to haul himself up on. He couldn't have fallen that far. A couple of metres, maybe. No more than three.

His fingers touched cool, smooth stone. Huh. He must've lost his glove on the way down. Just one, though — he still wore the other one. He ran his bare hand over the rock, looking for a ledge or bulge big enough to wrap his hand around to take his weight. He found a hole big enough to fit his whole hand inside, then another, and that was enough.

Under his breath, he muttered, "One, two, thr…ungh!"

The moment he put weight on his leg, pain knifed through him.

Much like space, in a lava tube on Heard Island, no one could hear you scream.

Breathing hard, Jean leaned on his other leg instead.

This time, he didn't get to scream. The pain was so bad, it stole all of his senses as it knocked him out.

TWO

Audra had never been so exhausted in her life, so naturally, she wanted to dance on the ceiling. She wasn't sure how many people had actually seen the South Pole, but now she was one of them. It felt…exhilarating. Hence the need to dance as soon as she could shut the door of her tiny room, where no one would see. The buzzing in her blood was better than sex. Everyone had sex.

Except…her room wasn't hers. Well, it was, but it was someone else's too. The vacant bunk she'd considered her reading lounge was now occupied by a girl with a round, smiling face. "Hi, hi! Finally we meet. I'm Shelley! You must be Audra. The guys told me it's your first trip and you've already seen the pole. Three winters I've spent here and my first expedition out there, I failed the medical and you got to go instead."

"I'm sure there'll be others. Some of the equipment

wasn't up to spec, so when the right stuff arrives next summer, a team will need to return." Audra couldn't keep the longing out of her tone. Of course she wanted to be part of it. Who wouldn't? But she was only covering Shelley's maternity leave, after all, and it looked like her time was up. "How's your little girl, anyway?"

Now it was Shelley's turn to look wistful. "She said her first word the day before I left: Mum. It killed me to leave her, but Ross and I agreed that he'd get to be a stay-at-home dad with her while I went off to work. God, I hope he can handle it." She waved at their cramped room. "This'll seem like a holiday in comparison, though."

They both laughed.

"Sorry, you probably want a minute to yourself after all that time in the field. Video calls home and such. I'll go take a shower before the boys use all the water." Shelley grabbed her towel and slung it over her shoulder.

"Watch out for the shower monitor. He's a big Russian bloke named Boris. If you try to take a shower even a second longer than three minutes, he'll bust in and carry you off for torture and whatever else Russians do to traitors. Apparently."

Shelley's face fell. "You mean Bruce left? He's the best plumber on the continent!"

Audra couldn't hide her smile. "No, but he did spend a whole day booming at me in a thick Russian accent until one of the other guys ratted him out. I've never forgotten to time my showers since."

Shelley laughed and headed for the showers.

Alone, Audra decided dancing was probably a bad idea, so she dusted off her laptop and woke it up. Calling home could wait until tomorrow, but she could catch up on news and email in the meantime. Hundreds of unread emails awaited her, so she sighed and sat down to sort the spam from the…sixty-three emails from Jay? More?

Huh. She hadn't heard a peep from him since she left Romance Island, and she never expected to, either. Well…okay, for the first week she'd kind of hoped, and maybe for the second one, too, especially after she'd sent him the photo of them together, and the third week…but by the time she'd boarded the *Aurora Australis*, she'd barely checked her email at all. And not because of the restricted internet access, either.

So why on Earth was he sending her thrice-daily emails? Curiosity won and she opened the most recent one.

WHY WON'T YOU ANSWER MY MESSAGES?

Another:

WE WERE MADE FOR EACH OTHER. WHERE ARE YOU?

That popped up a lot, though the wording varied a bit, depending on the day.

After the first couple dozen, Audra skimmed to the first one he'd sent.

I'M HOME. WHERE ARE YOU, BABY? WHY AREN'T YOU HERE?

Had he completely forgotten about her new job? The reason she was leaving the island? Maybe he was drunk. It still didn't explain why he thought she should be at the resort.

Exasperated, Audra typed a response:

"I'm at Davis as one of the Antarctic meteorology team this summer. I just got back from an expedition to Dome

Argus and the South Pole. It was awesome, thanks for asking." She hit send and scrolled through her emails, looking for anything from her family and friends.

Her laptop chimed, signalling that someone wanted to start a video call. Jay, who else?

She hadn't had a shower in days and her hair had been mashed under an assortment of hats and hoods for weeks. One look at her would scare him off for life. Reluctantly, she allowed the call to connect.

"Where the fuck are you really?"

Jay Felix was all charm.

Audra took a deep breath. She'd thought the soundproofing at the resort was bad. Here at Davis, if she raised her voice, the whole building would hear. "Hi, Jay. It's lovely to see you again. It's been months, I'm sure, though I gather you've been busy with your band's tour. I've been very busy, too. First training for my first Antarctic expedition, and then living and working out here for the summer. There are real penguins here, not just a jetty named after one. I must say, the jetty smells better, though."

"Why aren't you here?" Judging by his slurred voice, sobriety had deserted him several hours ago.

"I don't work at Romance Island Resort any more, remember?"

"No. Was it because of me? Did you quit because of me? I told you I was coming back, babe. I own the hotel. Had to come back."

He hadn't known? Then what had he meant that night when they'd... "That last night we spent together. When you answered the door, you said I was just in time and I'd left it until the last minute. You knew it was my last day and I was flying out to Hobart on Monday."

"No, I fucking didn't. You never told me that!"

Audra mulled this over. "So let me get this straight. You spent the night with me, made all sorts of promises you had no intention of keeping, then flew out the next morning to record your new album and go on tour. All the while, not saying a single thing to me. Not a word, a phone call, an email, nothing, until now, when you're demanding to know why I'm not waiting for you with open arms after you deserted me?"

"I didn't desert you! I had to work!"

"And who doesn't? When I got offered the chance of a lifetime, a stint in Antarctica, I took it. I'd have been crazy not to. Especially after dealing with VIPs who threw tantrums, painted the walls with ketchup, and slept with anything in a skirt." She'd never get the image of Jay and Penny out of her mind. It would scar her for life.

"Ooh, is that your boyfriend? Hi, I'm Shelley, Audra's roommate." Shelley smiled and waved over Audra's shoulder before throwing herself on her bed. "Don't mind me."

"Yes, I'm Audra's – " Jay began.

Audra cut in, "No, he's not my boyfriend. Never was, never will be. He used to be my boss." Though it was on the tip of her tongue, she didn't add that he'd once been the bane of her existence. It didn't seem fair to kick a man when he was down.

"What about all the time we spent together?" Jay exploded. "Are you honestly saying everything – the time, the incredible sex – meant nothing to you?"

Audra heard Shelley laugh softly, then whisper an apology.

"It was one night, Jay. One night that you made astonishingly clear meant nothing to you, when you climbed into a helicopter the morning after, then ignored me for months while wrapping yourself in different girls every night. Do you even remember how many? I mean, you did twenty, thirty shows at least, and I know for a fact that you took half a dozen girls back to your hotel room after the Perth concert. Add that all up and I don't need to be a statistician to know you've probably slept with over a hundred women, while you didn't even have time to send me an email saying hi." She drew in a deep, shaky breath. "If it weren't for the other girls, maybe I'd be interested if we were to meet again. But right now, if you showed up in the snow outside my door, I'd kick you right back to the boat that brought your sorry arse to Antarctica."

His eyes got that kicked puppy look that a dog gets when…Audra had never kicked a puppy, but she figured hurt and betrayal and big, wide eyes would feature in there somewhere.

"But…I could fly there now. We can talk about this. I could take you home and…I want to spend the rest of my life with you. How about it? A fresh start with just you and me. I'll marry you if that's what you want. No other women ever again. I swear." That same beseeching look she'd surrendered to before. Never again.

"Jay, you barely know me. Normal people don't marry strangers. Especially not strangers who've slept with a hundred other people in less than six months!"

"Please, baby, give me time to book a flight and – "

Audra's heart nearly broke at the pain in his voice, but somehow she mentally sticky-taped it back together and said, "No. I ship out in a couple of days. Even if you did fly here, I'd be gone, on my way back to Melbourne to finish my training. I told you before, if you want a girl to love you, you have to be more than a rock star. Go back to the hotel library and do some more research. You'll see what happens to guys who cheat. They don't get the girl, that's for sure." She sighed. "I'm sure she's out there, Jay – the right girl for you. But I'm not her. So good night…and good luck." Before he could say anything, she ended the call and slammed her laptop closed.

Shelley whispered, "Was that really Jay Felix?"

Audra nodded.

"And you used to work for him?"

Another nod.

Shelley cleared her throat. "He's always had a reputation for…well, you know. But I've always wondered if it was true or just something the girls made up. What's he like in bed?" In alarm, she added, "I'm only asking in the name of scientific inquiry, of course. Happily married and stored in this fridge and all."

Audra smiled faintly. "Unbelievable."

Shelley inhaled sharply. "I knew it! Wait, in a good way or a bad way?"

"Both."

They both laughed, but Audra's heart wasn't in it any more.

Shelley was sensitive enough to stop. "He seems really into you, despite all his obvious failings. Is there any chance you and him might…you know…reconnect? In some way?"

Audra shook her head. "If he grew up a bit, and maybe turned into a good man instead of a spoiled, selfish arsehole…maybe. But I think hell will freeze over first." She glanced out the window and noticed snow flurrying past the glass, dancing in an evening breeze that she'd never grow tired of watching.

Unseen by anyone, her tears for Jay dropped onto the windowsill. One, two, three, four…the beats of a song that only her heart knew.

"Audra?" The deep voice belonged to Bruce. "I need your help."

Audra wiped her eyes. It was silly to cry over a rock star. Especially if someone needed her. "Mmm?"

"You need to pack your things. The *Aurora Australis* is here early. There was an emergency at Heard Island, so they detoured to pick up a man who was injured. The doctor's on standby at Casey, but they want someone with medical training to travel with him. Seeing as you're shipping out anyway, you just got volunteered."

No time for tears. Audra had a job to do.

THREE

Freezing water lapping at his legs dragged Jean out of the darkness. He was already waist deep and it was rising. Darkness didn't help him work out where he was, until he remembered the cushion plant trying to kill him.

He reached under the surface, feeling far enough down his legs to determine that they were both broken. Bits bent in ways that they shouldn't be capable of being bent.

Up was out, then, if he couldn't use his legs to climb to the top of the sinkhole. That meant he'd have to follow the lava tube to wherever it went. Wherever the water had come in. Quickly, too, because he already couldn't feel his legs. That's because of the water temperature, he told himself, willing his mind away from what else that could mean. More bones broken than just his legs. If his back was broken and he couldn't walk again, there were other bits of his anatomy that wouldn't work, either.

Dairine. She'd never forgive him if he came back and it was his fault they couldn't have kids. He'd promised to give her children.

If he didn't make it home safely, she'd kill him.

No. He'd never broken a promise to her yet, and this wouldn't be the first.

Jean fought to keep his breathing steady. No panicking. He had to get home to Dairine, which meant getting out of this hole.

The camp wasn't far. He'd seen the penguins from the shore, damn it, on the far side of Atlas Cove. All he had to do was get to where the geologists could see him from camp. He was wearing a standard issue, fire-engine red jacket, for fuck's sake. They couldn't miss him.

Now to get out of this hole.

Jean closed his eyes, trying to trace the sound of the waves. He rolled over onto his belly, propping himself up with his arms so his head was above water. Like a seal. He snorted. He wished there was a seal in the cave with him, to show him the way out.

Without a seal, he did the best he could, angling his body so the wavelets broke against his chest. Fuck, but it was freezing. The sooner he was out of the water, the better.

Jean dragged himself along the cave floor, first one arm, then the other in endless repetition until the ground dropped away and a wave broke over his head. He surfaced, spluttering, wishing he'd thought to bring a radio with him. He could've called for help and told the rest of the team he'd run into trouble a few minutes' walk from camp. Sure, he'd be a laughing stock for the rest of the expedition, but he'd be a warm laughing stock.

Another wave topped him and Jean went under. This time, he didn't surface straight away, because he thought he saw light ahead. He squinted, trying to focus, to no avail. It was a light of some kind, all right, but the rock in front of him told him he'd have to swim underwater to reach it.

He'd need a decent lungful of air for that.

Jean lifted his head above the water, paddling with his hands to stay up.

"I'm coming, Dairine," he swore, gulping a huge breath before he dived.

He tried to kick with his legs, but the damn things wouldn't work. He breast-stroked like a man possessed, pushing the water behind him as he paddled toward the light.

Jean's lungs burned, but he swam on. He angled upward, praying he'd reach the surface soon. He could see his hands in front of him now – surely he'd cleared the cave. Was he out, or just in a larger cavern?

Wind froze the water in his hair as Jean's head emerged from the sea. He sucked in a desperate breath, then another, as he took stock of his surroundings.

Oh, fuck. He'd surfaced in the cove, twenty metres from the far shore. He had more swimming to do.

His arms were all he had, so no way in hell was he doing an Australian crawl. The near-freezing water was warmer than the air temperature.

Gritting his teeth, Jean set a course directly across the cove toward camp. He tried not to think of leopard seals and orcas and anything else that lived in these waters. For the first time, he cursed being a biologist who knew this shit. At least there weren't any sharks, unless global warming had finally tempted them south. That would be the ultimate insult for a climate change biologist – to be eaten by something migrating with the warmer temperatures.

"Not today," Jean swore. "I'm coming, Dairine. I'm coming home."

His arms ached, more and more leaden with every stroke, until his hand bumped against something harder than water.

Please don't let it be an orca, he prayed, glancing down. A wave carried him further up the shore until his whole body rested on rock. Sharp chunks of volcanic rock, but right now, it was the most beautiful beach he'd seen this week. He barely felt it through the numbing cold.

Jean lifted his head. The camp was just ahead. All the buildings, where someone should be preparing dinner while everyone else relaxed after a hard day in the field.

The buildings were there, sure, but no one was in sight. Maybe they were all inside, he reasoned. A team meeting, or something. Someone would be out soon. They'd see him and carry him to one of the huts so they could help him.

He counted to five hundred as he waited, but there was no movement at all. Had they decided to sleep aboard the research vessel, instead, then?

Jean groaned as he stiffly rolled onto his back, propping himself up on his elbows to peer out into the cove for the ship.

Which wasn't there.

"Fuck."

While he'd been unconscious in his hole, the geologists

had taken the ship out for a survey. It might be weeks before they returned. By that time, the leopard seals would've eaten his remains.

"Not going to happen," he grunted, flipping onto his belly. He'd crawl back to camp if he had to, and radio those single-minded scientists to come back and get him.

Fixing his gaze on the nearest hut — the decades-old, round, red emergency shelter that they'd dubbed the Apple — Jean stretched his arm out to pull him a foot closer to the forbidden fruit. Two broken legs were a fucking emergency.

One arm, pull, then the other, pull, reach for another handhold, pull, don't stop, reach…

"I'm coming, Dairine. I'm coming," he repeated. His wife's name was his mantra. He had to survive for her.

His fingers scrabbled at the blood-coloured hut. He nearly cried. All he had to do was reach the handle three feet above his head and pull open the door.

Eternities passed as Jean dragged his exhausted body to the side, his arm muscles screaming as he reached up and up until his fingers closed on the handle. When the door swung open, he felt a tear trickle from his eye before it froze on his cheek.

Fucking Antarctica. If it weren't for the penguins, he wouldn't be here.

Jean crawled inside the hut, then hooked his fingers through the vent at the bottom of the door to pull it shut behind him. Out of the wind, but not out of the woods. He struggled out of his coat and all the layers under it until he peeled his soaked thermal shirt from his chest. He was bare for only a moment before he grabbed a musty blanket from the bunk and wrapped it around himself. He turned a second blanket into a cape across his shoulders, hoping to keep in what precious little remained of his body heat.

His sodden pants would be another story, he knew. Once feeling returned to his legs, the agony that he'd felt before would return in full force, and he might pass out again. He had to radio for help first.

Jean dragged the survival kit onto the floor and pried off the lid. He had to rummage through the box until he found the radio, before rummaging some more for some batteries.

His hands shook as he shoved the batteries into the back of the radio. He knew shivering was better than his body not reacting to the cold at all, but it still made it hard to call for help. Finally, he managed to close the little plastic cover. Offering a silent prayer to anyone who was listening that the batteries weren't dead, Jean flicked the switch.

Blessed static washed over him. The best sound in the world.

Jean pressed the TALK button. "This is Jean Pennant on Heard Island. I have a medical emergency and require immediate assistance from anyone who can hear me. Repeat, need medevac from Heard Island. If you can hear me..." He repeated the message and waited.

He eased off his supposedly waterproof pants. Oh, fuck. It looked like he had five knees. Definitely not natural. He wasn't sure if he wanted to peel off the thermals he wore underneath. He couldn't see any blood, which was a blessing, but there still could be internal bleeding. He had to...

Oh, fuck, that hurt.

No response from the radio.

He switched to another channel and tried again.

"This is Jean-Pierre Pennant on Heard Island, requesting immediate assistance…."

More static.

Next channel.

"Hello, this is Jean-Pierre Pennant…"

Another channel.

"This is an SOS to anyone who can hear me. This is Jean-Pierre Pennant at Heard Island – "

The static crackled and beeped. "You're late for your twelve-hourly check-in, Pennant."

Oh, thank fuck. "Yeah, about that. I fell down a hole. I may have broken a few bones."

"You're in luck. We're still at Spit Bay. Dismantling the huts took longer than we expected. There's a couple of elephant seals who aren't helping. Could've done with your help charming them."

Jean coughed out a laugh. "It was a Weddell seal that fancied me, dude. A baby one. It was cute and it was curious, and it liked the taste of my boots. The sort of thing you want to cuddle. Not an elephant seal."

"You're the biologist. Are you sure you're injured, if you're laughing and trying to teach?"

Feeling was returning to Jean's legs now he was out of the cold, and it fucking hurt. "I've got two broken legs, man. It's bad."

Jean heard swearing before it was replaced by static. He waited a few seconds before he ventured, "You still there?"

The crackling ceased. "Yeah. We'll be there as soon as we can. Where are you?"

"The emergency Apple. The one we're not supposed to use."

More static, before the voice came back. "Pennant? One of the guys here said there should be a first aid kit in there. The supplies might be a bit out of date, but it should be fully stocked. He said he saw some of the really good meds in there. Stuff we're not allowed to carry now, but were fine back when the camp was constructed. Should be unopened. Can you check? He says it's under one of the bunks."

Jean felt around in the cavity under the nearest bed and was rewarded by the feel of a metal box. "Yeah, got it."

He flipped it open and took stock of the supplies. Enough gauze to wrap a mummy, with enough alcohol wipes to embalm one. And under that... Jean gave a low whistle. "Shit. Morphine."

"Captain thinks we'll be under way in a couple of hours. Can you wait that long, Pennant?"

Jean peeled open a syringe and plunged the needle into the morphine bottle, carefully drawing out a dose that matched the instructions. He swabbed his arm and took a deep breath. Just a scratch, he told himself.

Fuck, he hated needles. But this one...would be worth it. He gritted his teeth as he depressed the plunger, unleashing icy oblivion into his veins.

"Pennant?"

"Yeah, man. I found the meds. Good shit, man. Good shit."

Jean gritted his teeth and shucked off the rest of his clothes. Oh, his legs were seriously fucked up. He tucked a couple more blankets around himself, hiding his legs from sight. But they didn't hurt any more, and that's what mattered.

No. What mattered was Dairine. Getting home to

Dairine.

Jean lay down, drifting off on a morphine cloud. No wonder they locked this shit up.

FOUR

"Hi, I'm Doug. Are you the nurse?" a harried-looking crewman asked.

Audra hesitated. "No. I'm a meteorologist, but I've trained as a surgical assistant in case there's a medical emergency."

"That's better than the rest of us. We've got first aid and that's it. I'll take you to your patient." Doug reached for her bag and Audra let him take it. "This way."

She followed him to a part of the ship she hadn't seen before, but then, she'd only been aboard it for two weeks on her voyage south. Not long enough to injure herself so badly she'd needed medical assistance, anyway. Admittedly, she'd worked at Romance Island Resort for months before one of the other maids had attacked her. Audra rubbed the back of her head in memory of where Penny had hit her hard enough to knock her out. It was nice to have a job where violence or guys who pressured girls into sex weren't part of a normal day's work. Antarctica was so…civilised.

Or maybe it was because she was officially a meteorologist here, not a maid.

"We talked to the doc at Casey Station as soon as we picked this guy up. She said to give him some intravenous medication as soon as he wakes up. I wrote down the dosage for you and everything." Doug ushered her into sickbay and grabbed the patient chart at the end of the curtained-off bed. "Here."

Audra scanned the sheet. "He's on morphine? What's wrong with him?"

"Some pretty nasty fractures. Want to see?" Doug reached for the blanket.

Audra shook her head. "No! I'm good, thanks. I just need to put an IV in, right?"

"That's what the doc said. There's a phone there, and we have a videoconferencing hookup here, if you want to call her to check." Doug hefted her bag onto his shoulder. "Do you need anything out of this, or do you want me to take it to your bunkroom?"

"That'd be great, thanks," Audra said, still puzzled by the patient's notes. "When did you give him his last dose of medication?"

Doug paused in the doorway. "Oh, we didn't. He did."

"He did?" Audra turned her gaze on the patient. "What is he, SAS? Who breaks bones and then administers their own first aid?"

Doug shrugged. "Nah, not SAS. He's American. They have Special Forces or something like that. He dosed himself, but he smashed the bottle, so we don't know how much he took. That's why the doc said to wait until he wakes up, so you can ask him. Good luck." He left.

Wonderful. Her first real patient was a war hero, and she got to stab him with a needle. No wonder they wanted him awake first. God only knew what the American military trained their soldiers to do to someone stupid enough to stab them in their sleep. Nothing good, that's for sure.

She sighed, picked up the phone and called Casey.

Ten minutes later, she ended the call, none the wiser. Yes, the man had radioed for help. When the ship arrived, he was unconscious in his hut, lying beside a patch of damp carpet and a smashed morphine bottle. No one knew how much he'd taken, or when, or whether he'd taken more than one dose. So she had to sit and wait.

Audra wished she'd brought a book.

Sighing, she settled in a chair beside the mystery man's bed.

Unlike most of the men at Davis Station, he hadn't grown a beard. The dark stubble across his face said he'd been cleanshaven before his accident. His hair was shaved short, too, like a military regulation haircut.

Audra pulled back the sheet that covered his torso, baring his chest and his upper arms. Very well-muscled arms, like he might have quit the military, but he still trained daily. Now she understood why no one could say how many doses he'd taken — the man's statuesque body was covered in bruises, hiding the injection site.

"That'll teach you to wrestle with elephant seals," Audra remarked, trying to work out which arm was less bruised, and easier to find a vein in. She patted his hand gently. "You won't do it again, though, I bet."

He didn't even twitch under her touch. Maybe he was too deeply under with the morphine he'd taken. In that case, perhaps she should try to slide a cannula into a vein while he was unconscious and wouldn't feel it. Especially as this was her first.

Audra took a deep, shaky breath. She had to do this. But first, she'd just check the IV stand, to make sure everything was hooked up properly ready to go, with the correct dosage programmed in. Yes, of course it was. She just had to stick a needle through his skin, tape it in place, and connect the IV line. Simple.

She marched over to the sink and washed her hands with particular care. He wasn't going to get an infection from her.

"Please don't try to kill me for this," she said in a tone she hoped sounded calm, "but I'm going to place a cannula in your arm so we can give you medication to help with the pain. It might hurt a bit at first, and if it does, you just tell me, okay?"

No answer. Did a snore count? Audra didn't think so.

She slipped a tourniquet around his arm, tightening it until it cut off circulation and made his veins stand out. She continued to tell him what she was doing, though she knew he couldn't possibly hear her. If anything, it kept her from throwing the needle down and saying she couldn't do this. She'd trained to look at weather and wind and storms, not bodies.

Yes, she had trained for this, Audra reminded herself. An emergency surgical assistant, that's what she was, qualified to stab people in an emergency. And it was.

"You might feel a sharp scratch," she murmured, biting

her lip as she angled the needle.

Just like she'd practised. Just like she'd practised. Just like…

The needle pierced the skin and the clear reservoir at the top of the cannula filled with blood. Was that supposed to happen? She racked her brain and couldn't remember.

That tiny bit of blood didn't matter, she decided, swallowing. She finished inserting the cannula, removed the needle bit and taped it all off.

"There. When you wake up, I'll be able to give you your medicine right away," Audra said, lifting her head to smile at the unconscious man.

Blue eyes regarded her. Not unconscious any more. Had he been watching her all this time?

"I…um…didn't realise you were awake. I hope I didn't hurt you," she said. "Look, you were my first, but it's better than waiting until we reach a proper doctor at Casey. At least now you'll be all right for pain relief and stuff. If it knocks you out like the last dose did, you'll be home before you know it."

"Home," he said indistinctly, like he was drunk. Or drugged, which of course he was. "Darling, I'm home." At least, that's what she thought he'd said.

Audra didn't have time to think before he grabbed her, wrapping both arms around her so she couldn't escape. He sure was strong for a man lying in a hospital bed. He pulled her closer, forcing her head down. Her lips met his, and while she pressed hers firmly together, his tongue darted out of his open mouth to pry a way in.

"Darling, it's baby-making time," he said, more clearly, dragging her forward so she nearly fell on top of him on the bed. It took her a moment to realise that was what he intended.

Audra reached behind her, groping for the IV stand. If she could attach the IV line to his arm, maybe it would knock him out again. Soon. It had to be soon, because he was holding her so tightly it was getting hard to breathe.

"No. Let me go!" she insisted.

"Baby-making time, darling," he insisted, moving in for another kiss.

There! Her hand found the table where she'd left the medical supplies, and her fingers closed around something cold and hard. Audra jabbed the needle into his arm and the madman released his grip just enough for her to squirm free.

"Darling!" he protested.

"I'm not your darling," Audra snapped, brandishing the needle.

The man struggled to get up, but when he did, his legs bent…wrong. Broken, Audra realised. Both of them. No wonder he'd taken so much morphine.

He made a sound that strangled in his throat before he passed out, presumably from the pain.

"Now, do you want pain relief, or don't you?" Audra asked.

No response. He could be pretending, though.

"You try that again and I'm going to let you go without any drugs until we get to Casey," she told him, reaching for the IV line. She edged closer to him, ready to drop the line and run if she had to, but he didn't move. She forced herself to take her eyes off his face to connect the line to the cannula, then felt her breath hiss out as it was done without him waking. Maybe he truly was unconscious.

Still, she wasn't taking any chances. Audra scooted back out of his reach to turn on the pump.

The man might be worse than Jay Felix when it came to demanding sex, but he hadn't grabbed her again, so she owed him his medicine.

"Is he awake?" Doug appeared in the doorway.

"Not any more," Audra replied. She considered telling Doug about what the man had done, but decided it didn't matter. Besides, what if Doug didn't believe her? She hardly believed it herself. Talking about it wouldn't help her forget, like she wanted to. "He roused for a bit, but he's out again. The doc at Casey said to keep him medicated until we reach the station. Probably a good idea." Then he couldn't grab anyone else. She peeled off her gloves and threw them in the bin.

"Aren't you going to do that?" Doug blurted out.

And risk rape? Not bloody likely. "Anyone with first aid training can do it. Just hook up the next bag when the pump beeps. Easy." Audra started scrubbing her hands in the sink. She wanted to wash her whole body.

"Thanks, then. I'm sure Sean here would thank you, too, if he could," Doug said. "Or his next of kin will, when we get hold of her. We haven't been able to reach his wife."

Audra felt bile rise up in her throat. Lovely. Not only had Sean tried force her into bed with him, but he wanted to cheat on his wife. The arsehole deserved both broken legs.

"Where's my room?" Audra asked, not wanting to discuss the patient any more.

"Oh, I stuck you in Bunkroom Three. Figured you're

here first, so you get the porthole. The staff at Casey can fight over the rest." Doug grinned.

Audra shut off the tap and wiped her hands dry. Shit, they were shaking. "Thanks. Hey, do you have anything to drink on this ship? I could really do with one."

"Sure do. What's your poison?"

Audra wet her lips. "What've you got?"

She followed Doug out to the dining hall. In two days, she could hand Sean over to the doctor at Casey, happy in the hope of never seeing him again.

FIVE

When Jean awoke, the first thing he became aware of was the whistling wind outside. He prayed that the ship would make it through the storm to retrieve him before the morphine ran out. There hadn't been much in the bottle and he'd surely need another dose soon. Death wasn't an option. He had to get home to Dairine.

Jean pried his eyes open. Instead of the foam-insulated domed ceiling of the hut, he saw the cable-covered curve inside a cargo plane. Home. He was going home.

The next time he opened his eyes, the ceiling was flat, white and much closer. Disinfectant seared his nostrils and something behind him beeped. Hospital, his fuzzy mind told him.

As the days passed, the fog faded a bit, but never enough. Doctors talked of compound fractures and possible infection and all the metal things they'd inserted into his body to help the bones heal straight. Maybe they'd mistaken him for Wolverine. Surely these New Zealanders could tell the difference between a Canadian and the Australian actor who played the character in the movies. Not that he'd mind being Wolverine right now, so he could heal instantly and hop on a plane home.

Instead, days turned into weeks as they pumped antibiotics into his body and wheeled him in and out of the operating theatre. If he hadn't dragged his damaged legs into the water and along the beach, he wouldn't have to endure all this treatment, the doctors told him.

Jean agreed with them. If he hadn't done those things, he'd be a frozen corpse in a lava tube.

Then they told him there was a chance he wouldn't walk again.

Screw that for a joke.

When a woman walked into his hospital room and introduced herself as his physiotherapist, he nearly kissed her. Dairine wouldn't like that, though, so he controlled himself. Not that he'd have kissed the woman like he kissed his wife, of course. If Jean was one thing, it was faithful. He'd never love another woman the way he loved his wife. He'd do anything for her. Including doing everything in his power to walk again, so he could pass the medical assessments to go back to Antarctica to finish his research. Once he had his PhD, he could settle down in Vancouver with her like she wanted, take a teaching position somewhere, and be the best father he knew how to be.

Jean threw himself into his physical therapy like he was training for the Olympics. When they finally released him from hospital, he headed for the Antarctic Research Centre near the airport in Christchurch, where the US expeditioners had their staging area. His status as a PhD candidate at an American university earned him a desk and some temporary accommodation, where he spent hours working on his thesis in between daily sessions of physiotherapy. He would walk again. Without a wheelchair, without crutches, without leaning on anyone. When he returned home to Dairine, he'd be a whole man again, not half of one, he swore.

Daily, he fought the urge to call her, but he'd promised he wouldn't, because she'd said the waiting between calls while he was in Seattle had killed her a little each time, and it would be worse this time, with him on the other side of the world. He understood. He missed her just as much, of course, but while he was out in the field, discovering new things every day, she kept to her routine. She'd work and spend the evenings at home or with her family in Vancouver, while catching up with her friends on the weekends. He'd slot back into that life as soon as he could, he swore. Shit, what he'd give for a family dinner, with her family or his.

He took a break from thesis writing for another painful trip to hospital to remove all the pins and rods that had held his smashed bones straight enough to heal, followed by more physical therapy, until the day when Jean was allowed to walk without crutches. He was glad Dairine couldn't see him now, taking his first steps like the baby he hadn't given her yet, but he could count the days now. Soon they'd let him go home to her.

Finally, the doctors declared him fit to fly. He had to swear to do daily exercises and attend a clinic in Vancouver, but he felt whole again. Whole enough to be Dairine's husband.

Winter gripped Christchurch when he flew out of the city, headed for summer at home for the first time in two years. He couldn't wait to see Dairine again, six months earlier than expected.

Maybe he'd give her that baby she wanted before the week was over. He'd damn well try.

SIX

Audra clutched at the lectern with both hands. "So, all I have left to say is: let's go out there, fellow graduates, and take the country by storm!"

Polite laughter rose over the applause as Audra headed for her seat and finally allowed herself to relax. All through the Diploma of Meteorology course, she'd strived to get the best possible results. What she hadn't realised was that the student with top marks automatically became the valedictorian of the class, complete with speech responsibilities at graduation. Well, she'd discharged those responsibilities now, so all she had to do was collect her degree before she could head home to celebrate.

She waited for her name to be called. A quick walk across the stage with a handshake from the Director in the middle, before she was handed her piece of paper and allowed to return to her seat in the audience.

At the end, the Director stood up to give his speech, which was surprisingly short. When he was done, he waited for the applause to die down before he said, "I also have an announcement to make. As part of the Bureau's commitment to ongoing education, next year we're holding a contest. The prize will be a training voucher that you can use for courses, conferences or research, as long as it's relevant to your job. And you'll be paid for your training time, too, for the duration of your course."

Murmuring broke out among the audience. The Director waved his hands for silence.

"In order to win, we're looking for staff who can raise the Bureau's online profile, so we can continue to attract the best graduates for our diploma program. We're looking for blogs or social media accounts where our staff tell the world about a day in the life of a meteorologist, or photos of weather phenomena, or whatever it is about your job that you feel best represents the Bureau's mission and values. We feel that..."

Audra tuned out at that point. Most of her fellow students had already stopped listening, holding whispered conversations with those around them, or trying to catch the eyes of their family members in the other rows.

She didn't have any family members here – they hadn't been able to afford the flights, let alone the hotel accommodation. She couldn't deny that she was disappointed, but she'd never really expected them to come. Now, when the ceremony ended, it meant she could take advantage of her lonely state and corner the Director for a few questions about the contest.

But first, she could have one drink before driving home,

so she snagged a glass of sparkling wine from a passing waiter. It was definitely a champagne occasion.

"I liked your speech, Audra."

Audra nearly choked on her drink as the Director appeared beside her. He held beer.

"Thank you," she managed to say.

"I hope you're considering entering the contest. With a record like yours, you could use it to fund a Masters degree, or even your PhD," he continued.

That answered one of her questions. "But how would it pay for a PhD? I mean, there aren't any course fees. Is the money enough for a scholarship for the three or four years it'll take?"

The Director shrugged. "It's not enough to live off for three years, no. But you'd still have a full time job with the Bureau for that time, so you shouldn't need to. What it will pay for is equipment and expenses, conferences and travel. And you'd have the full support of the Bureau to complete your degree, so you'd have a study leave allocation."

"So, basically, the Bureau would pay me to get my PhD?" Audra asked. It sounded too good to be true.

"Ah, but first you'd have to win the contest. That's not going to be easy. We'll officially open it next week, and it'll run for six months, until the end of March. You'll have six months to create content that can…ah, go viral, I think it's called. Our PR manager is one of the judges, and she assures me there are several criteria you'll be assessed against. The quality of your message, the number of followers you have, how well you align with the Bureau's mission…like I said, it won't be easy."

Nothing was easy, especially not for Audra. Why should

this be any different? She waved away his concerns. "When you say social media, could it be an online video channel?"

Another shrug. "I imagine so."

"Then I think I'll be entering," Audra said, sipping her bubbly.

The Director beamed. "Good to hear! I look forward to your videos of…where are they posting you?"

"Officially, we don't find out until Monday," Audra said carefully. "But the Chief Meteorologist at Davis Station in Antarctica told me she'd requested a graduate this year, if a member of our class with the right training applied for a regional posting. I have it on good authority that I'll be on the next icebreaker south to Davis." Perfect for photos or video. After all, everyone loved penguins.

"But won't it be cold in Antarctica? You're from Perth, right? It doesn't snow there!"

At least the Director of Meteorology knew a bit about weather. Audra replied, "Yes. The coldest place on Earth, actually. And I helped install new equipment at Dome Argus last year, which isn't far from Vostok Station, where the coldest temperature ever was recorded. I'm dying to go back to the South Pole, Director. And this posting would be a full year, including winter. I'm told the winter storms are nothing short of spectacular."

The Director looked stunned. "I didn't think we sent graduates to Antarctica, let alone ones we hadn't fully trained yet. I'll be following your blog with interest."

Video channel, not blog. No one read web pages when they could watch a video. She didn't correct him, though. "Thank you, Director."

The Director moved off to speak to some of the other

executive staff who'd turned out for the graduation – or, more accurately, for the free food and drink – and Audra drained her drink, setting the empty glass on a table. She made her way out of the building to her car, sober enough to easily manage the drive home.

Not that it would be home for long. Eight months she'd lived in Melbourne, sharing a house with some other students, but that would change soon enough. Who'd have thought she'd one day call Antarctica home?

SEVEN

Jean climbed stiffly out of the taxi. Long flights had taken their toll on his body. He took care not to favour either leg as he shouldered his backpack and wheeled his duffle up the driveway to his house. The lawn looked like it was overdue for a mow – he'd take care of that tomorrow, once Dairine let him out of bed.

He dug his keys out and unlocked the door, grateful that the landlord hadn't changed the locks while he was away. He'd done that once while Jean was meeting with his research supervisor in Seattle, and he'd had to sit on the porch all day, waiting for Dairine's shift to finish so she could come home and let him in.

The smell of cooking hit him like a punch to the gut. He'd forgotten how good Dairine was in the kitchen. That smell meant she was home. A grin lit his face as he headed for the kitchen.

"You're home early," Dairine said over her shoulder as she stirred something on the stove.

"I thought I'd surprise you," he replied, closing the distance between them so he could kiss her.

Dairine spun on the spot, looking horrified. "J-Jean? What are you doing here?"

Jean stopped short, trying to tell if she was joking or not. "I'm your husband. I live here."

"No, you bloody don't! We're divorced!" she hissed.

Divorced? Jean couldn't seem to make his tongue say the word, and his mouth wouldn't close, either. "Since when?" he said hoarsely.

"Since more than a year ago! I told you if you go to the South Pole, I didn't want to see or hear from you again. You left, so I filed for divorce. I told them to send your copy to the university, seeing as I didn't know where you were."

"But I thought you wanted…children. You and me, we were going to start a family. Every day I was in Antarctica, I was counting down the days until I could come home to you." Jean stared at her in anguish. "I promised to give you a baby."

His gaze dropped to her belly, always so flat in his memory. It was anything but flat now. She looked like she'd swallowed a weather balloon.

"Is that…are you…whose is…when's it due?" He couldn't seem to form a coherent sentence while his heart crunched into fragments inside his chest.

"Ed and I are having twins, and they're due next month, if my obstetrician doesn't insist on delivering them early," Dairine said reluctantly.

Edward. That pasty-faced IT guy in her office who looked like he'd never spent five minutes outside in the sun in his life. Jean had seen Ed eyeing Dairine off at work parties, but Dairine had never taken any notice of him.

"Did he get you drunk at the work party, and that's when you slept with him? Is he going to be around to help you when they're born, or are you going to be a single mother with twins?" Jean bit out.

Dairine's hand delivered a stinging slap to his cheek. "Don't you talk about my husband like that! We celebrated out first anniversary a few weeks ago, Ed and me. He's everything a husband should be. He comes home at night. Takes care of me. And he's giving me a family, something you never managed to do."

Guilty as charged, but there were extenuating circumstances. "I was away so we could build a future together, once I got back. I'm here now, Dairine. Please don't do this."

"I already have," she said tartly. "Get out, Jean. You shouldn't be here. If you're looking for your stuff, I sent it back east to your folks' place. There's nothing for you here." Her expression told him what her words couldn't: there truly was nothing for him here.

Without another word, Jean turned on his heel and strode out of the house. It wasn't home any more.

EIGHT

Audra had almost decided on her graduation gift. She'd been ninety percent certain before the Director's announcement that she wanted an action camera for her second trip to Antarctica, as the lovely DSLR camera that Jay Felix had given her didn't always work well in polar conditions. Well, it worked for a little while, until the cold got to the batteries and fogged up the lenses. But these cameras were designed to work when it was cold and wet. Even better, they were easy to operate while wearing thick gloves. The only question now was…which model to buy? She could afford the top of the range one, and it would take awesome video to share on her yet-to-be-created channel, but…

Her laptop chimed, alerting her to an incoming video call.

Audra didn't even have to look at the name to answer,

"Evening, Jay."

"Congratulations," he replied. "I did get the date right, didn't I? It's your graduation?"

He wore a shirt tonight. It must be cold at the resort where he lived.

"It is," she said. "I'm now officially a qualified meteorologist."

"Why aren't you out celebrating, then?"

"Who says I'm not?"

Jay grinned. "Your webcam, for a start. I recognise your room."

A room he'd never been in, but it didn't matter. She'd started taking his video calls after a few weeks in Melbourne, and somehow they'd fallen into a strange friendship.

"Still celebrating, though."

Jay leaned forward so all Audra could see was his forehead. "I don't see any alcohol."

"I drank it already," she admitted. "But I'm picking out a graduation gift. I've decided I need a video camera for my first graduate posting."

"What's wrong with the camera I gave you?"

She knew he'd whine. That was Jay – everything was about him.

"It's a beautiful camera for a tropical island resort, but it's not so good in the snow."

His eyes widened. "You're going back to Antarctica?"

Audra beamed. "Yep. I can't wait."

"When do you leave?"

"Not sure yet. The first supply run leaves Hobart in October, so I have a few weeks, at least."

"Come up and visit me, then," he said.

Tropical Romance Island Resort would be a dream compared to wintry Melbourne weather. So tempting, especially as she'd be in Antarctica for close to eighteen months, depending on the shipping schedules.

"What about your latest girlfriend? That billionaire? Won't she object?"

Jay had shared every detail of his failed relationships with her since she'd left. Sometimes she'd had to fight to maintain a straight face, and leave the laughter until later. The black widow mail order bride was the funniest, but only Jay Felix could have done what he did with that virginity auction girl. As for the billionaire…she'd dismissed it as something the tabloids had made up, until Jay admitted he'd met the woman.

"Haven't you watched TV lately? I'm sure the first episode of *Rock Star Wants A Wife* aired this week."

"You didn't." Even as the words left her lips, Audra knew he most certainly had. A rock star who'd learned about love from reading romance books – though not enough romance books, if he was turning to reality TV to find a wife – would be a prime candidate for one of those shows that matched eligible bachelors with suitable girls, and filmed every awkward moment.

Quickly, she pulled up a search window and found the show. She flicked through the news reports until she found one about the contestants. A dozen girls from all over the country, all dolled up for the camera as they announced their desires for true love and other fairy tales. One face looked familiar, so she took a second, longer look.

Yep, that was Penny, all right. The lazy maid who'd

spent more time banging the men at the resort than doing her job. When Penny had been fired, she'd taken it out on Audra, almost braining her with some gym equipment. That psycho made the mail order bride look damn near harmless.

"Who won the show? Did you propose to her?" Audra asked.

Jay laughed. "I can't tell you who won. But I can tell you I proposed."

"Was it Penelope?" Audra demanded.

"What? I can't...how did you...I can't..."

Yes, in other words. He probably couldn't talk because she was there.

"I'll come up to the resort for a few days. I'll tell you the dates when I've booked my flights," Audra said.

"Don't bother booking the hotel, or the helicopter. You'll be staying as my guest."

She nearly refused, but she knew Jay wasn't offering it to make her feel obligated to him for the gift. It was just what he did for people. Besides, if she didn't like being there, she could leave. Shou, the helicopter pilot, knew her from when she'd worked there, and she could afford a hotel in town. Perhaps she should book one of those, just in case.

"All right," Audra conceded. "I'll bring my new video camera, so I can test it out."

"It'll be great to see you again."

That lost look in his eyes...damn. It was everything Audra had to steel herself against. She would NOT fall for it again.

"I've got to go. Things to sort out before tomorrow, and it's late. G'night," she said, ending the call midway through his goodbye.

It wasn't a lie. She had to watch that reality TV episode, and find out just how deeply Penny had gotten her claws into Jay. Audra might not want the rock star for herself, but friends looked out for each other, and Penny was bad news in anyone's book.

NINE

Jean wasn't sure how he made it to Seattle. The haze of pain that clouded his every step barely let him think, let alone notice his surroundings. Who knew a broken heart could hurt so much?

He'd tried calling Dairine, but the number had been disconnected. He'd considered calling her family to get her new number, but he knew they were very protective of their only daughter. Not only would he be wasting his time, but he'd probably get a lecture from her parents or one of her brothers about how unhappy he'd made her.

The one thing that saved him was a call from his research supervisor. Louis had received the thesis draft he'd sent from Christchurch, and he wanted to meet to discuss it.

Jean grasped at the only thing he had left – his half completed PhD, that Dairine had hated and finally divorced him for.

So as he walked through the university campus in Seattle, heedless of the rain, he ran through his original project plan in his head. He'd been surveying the king penguin populations at all the Antarctic and sub-Antarctic islands, chasing the one species that was reputed to be thriving because of climate change.

The numbers were clear: the king penguin population was on the rise. That finding alone was enough to earn him his PhD, and possibly some papers in the right journals.

His research had two significant gaps, though – Heard Island, and evidence of new penguin colonies. His trip to Heard Island had been cut short because of his accident, so he didn't have the final count for the colonies there. But he knew what he'd seen out there – a big colony of penguins in a site where they'd never been recorded before. If he'd been able to determine if the colony was breeding, then his career was assured. He could write papers about the development of the new colony, and maybe instead of a teaching position in Vancouver, he'd be offered a research position someplace more exotic. It didn't even need to be exotic, as long as it was the other end of the world from Dairine and Vancouver.

Jean trudged up the stairs to Louis' office, then forced himself to wait patiently outside while some undergrad student asked questions about the most basic principles of penguin biology. Jean smothered a yawn as he leaned against the doorjamb, counting the minutes until the student finally said, "Thank you, Professor," and hurried off to his next class.

He'd forgotten Louis was a professor. The man had

more letters after his name than in it, but he still liked everyone to call him Louis.

"The man of the moment!" Louis greeted him, clasping Jean's forearm as he leaned forward to pat him on the back. "How's it feel to complete your PhD in less than three years? And with your accident, too – you're a goddamn trooper, man!"

Jean's jaw dropped. "Finished? But I only just sent you my draft."

Louis grinned. "More than enough to get your degree, plus a couple of papers. Your sponsors will be thrilled. Maybe even enough to fund your postdoctorate research, too, hmm?"

Jean had never planned on doing a postdoc, but now…"I need to get back to Heard Island," he blurted out. "One more season in Antarctica, to make my numbers complete. That new colony we decided was theoretically possible? Well, I know where it is. I was on my way there when I got injured. I have to get back, Louis. Those are my penguins. My discovery. I can't let someone else find them first."

Louis' brow furrowed. "Another season out there? I know you were supposed to spend another year out there, but your results speak for themselves. You don't need to, you know. What will your wife say to you staying away longer?"

His ex-wife wouldn't care. Jean swallowed, not wanting to talk about her. "I do need to. I really do. I mean, we've got the funding for it still, right? My sponsors still want positive stories about their activities in Antarctica, don't they? Or has that changed?"

Louis chuckled. "Until they get permission to drill in Antarctic waters for oil and gas, of course they do. And a new colony…that'll mean plenty of pictures they can put out in the media, too. Everyone loves penguins, especially the babies."

"So I'll ship out to McMurdo in October, for my final year out there?" Jean suggested. "Maybe I can check some of the other islands on the way, and see the difference from year to year."

"We'd have to find another expedition headed out to Heard Island," Louis said thoughtfully. "Maybe even partially fund it, seeing as that's Australian territory out there, but they don't keep a permanent base on the island. Maybe if it's geology again, or deep ocean surveys, I might be able to get your sponsors interested." He clapped his hands. "Leave it with me. I'm sure I can work something out. In the meantime, let's discuss this thesis of yours. Between now and when you leave, you should have enough time to lick it into shape, ready to submit, if you don't find anything new out there. Maybe even draft a paper or two…"

Jean sank into a chair, grateful to be off his aching legs for a moment, and listened to Louis dissect the document as thoroughly as one of his biological specimens. The professor was a biologist to the bone.

TEN

Shou greeted Audra with a smile and a wave when she stepped out of Broome Airport terminal. The tropical heat embraced her like an old friend, making her regret her decision not to take a posting in the tropics instead of the frozen wasteland that was Davis Station.

Next time, she promised the tropical weather. If the cold got too much for her, she could always request a transfer to somewhere warm for her next posting. Maybe even do her PhD on cyclones, so she'd have to work in the tropics.

Ever the tour guide, Shou pointed out all the features of the landscape below as they flew north to the Buccaneer Archipelago and Romance Island Resort. Not much had changed, unless you counted the new campground and holiday villas at the pearl farm.

"What's it been like, with the resort's new owner?"

Audra asked as Shou paused for breath.

"Interesting," he bit out, clamping his mouth shut. Then he glanced at her, and decided to elaborate. "If I tell you, will you keep it confidential?"

Audra nodded. "I worked here long enough to know what happens at the resort stays at the resort. Penny walked free without even an assault charge, when she tried to kill me. If I managed to keep that quiet, nothing you tell me can be worse than that."

"Rape, but it got covered up." Shou looked angry. "He crashed my helicopter, too."

"Jay Felix did that? I don't believe it."

Shou nodded. "Believe it. It was on the Easter weekend."

The weekend Jay spent with Flavia, Audra remembered. He'd sent her a hamper of Haigh's Easter eggs, and when she'd called to thank him, he'd spilled the whole story about the girl's virginity auction and the weekend they'd enjoyed together.

"I thought he was busy with Flavia then. It must have been someone else."

Shou's expression turned grimmer still. "It was him, all right. The hotel manager caught them together. Him and the girl who sold her virginity."

Audra shook her head firmly. "That's not what he told me. Jay wouldn't do that." She'd experienced firsthand how persuasive Jay could be, but at no point had she been scared of him. He was the first man she'd ever met who actually listened to the word "no", even when he didn't like it and every bit of her body except her mouth screamed "yes". Her memory itched and her gaze darted to the seat beneath her. "I know it's not true, because their first time was here in your helicopter. Jay said he made a mess, and something about you trying to kidnap him." She didn't mention Jay's weakness for blood, and the trouble that had caused. That was Jay's secret, and not hers to tell.

"He left used condoms on my seat," Shou growled.

Audra laughed. "It could have been worse. Believe me."

Shou glanced at her. "You used to clean his villa when you worked here, didn't you? What could be worse than cleaning that up?"

Ketchup on the ceiling. Chocolate on the walls and the rug. Frogs and broken glass in the bathtub. Patching up Jay's fragile ego when something bad happened, as it inevitably did. "You wouldn't believe me if I told you," Audra said finally.

"Try me on the way back," Shou suggested, landing his helicopter with the gentlest bump on the resort helipad. "Welcome back to the resort."

Audra thanked him and climbed out, trotting across the tarmac to the gate. She caught a glimpse of a well-dressed woman waiting by the fence, before the woman crossed to the helicopter, taking a seat behind Shou. A guest, Audra guessed, on her way to do touristy things in town, as she wasn't burdened by any luggage.

Audra shouldered her own small bag of clothes and essentials, waved at Shou, and headed for the Pearl Villas. Jay had moved from the luxurious Villa Maxima to the slightly less opulent and definitely smaller Villa Penguin, which, if she'd guessed right, he now shared with Penny the psycho.

She breathed in the scent of frangipani and salt that was

uniquely Broome, but untainted by the earthy pindan dust that pervaded the mainland. The resort had a freshness all its own.

"You came!" Jay rose from the veranda, beaming. He enveloped her in a hug, holding her for a few seconds longer than necessary, until he added, "How could I have forgotten about those perfect tits of yours?"

Audra shoved him away. "Given how many you've seen since the last time you saw mine, I'm surprised you remember them at all. If you're just going to ogle me, then I'll turn around and leave. I'll block your video messages, too."

He swallowed with what looked like considerable effort. "All right, I'll try. It's just...I hugged you, and they were right there, and...fuck, it's good to see you."

"Not getting enough action from Penny, in other words?" Audra asked, unable to keep the sharp edge from her tone.

"I..." Jay darted a glance at the villa, then at the path to the main hotel. "Walk with me?"

Audra followed him down a familiar path to the private beach he'd taken her to when she'd been forced to act as his nurse and minder for a few days. Only a year had passed since then, but it felt like much longer. So much had happened in the intervening time.

This time, she didn't hesitate when she came to the crevasse between two rocks, where the ocean fed the lagoon at high tide. She'd jumped wider cracks in the ice in Antarctica. This was nothing. She sailed across and continued along without breaking stride, doing her best to ignore Jay's admiring stare as she overtook him. Gratifying as it was to hold a rock star's full attention, she knew how fleeting it could be. If another woman walked past, his eyes would follow her.

But the hidden beach was empty, so Audra turned to face him. "So? Did you invite me up here as a favour to Penny, so she could finish me off?"

Confusion creased Jay's face. "What? Penelope isn't on the island. She's gone home to her family."

"But you were stupid enough to propose to her, weren't you?" Audra persisted.

The Jay she'd originally met would have bristled at the insult. The man in front of her hung his head. "Yes."

"If you value your life, you won't go through with it," she said.

Jay snorted. "Are you seriously threatening me?"

Audra laughed. "I don't have to. She's the threat, not me. Remember when I took a blow to the head here, and you acted like you'd gotten one, too, writing Shakespeare on the bloody ceiling? She's the one who hit me, and she would have killed me if one of the personal trainers hadn't pulled her off me. She was mad because she got fired for bonking you in the lagoon, but she didn't attack you. The crazy bitch went for me, because she thought I'd dobbed her in. Like I needed to. Everyone saw you that day."

"That's who she was?" Jay exclaimed. "Fuck, I knew I remembered her from somewhere! I just couldn't work out where."

Silly rock star. Audra shook her head. "After I talked to you last week, I watched the first couple of episodes. It's so obvious she was gunning for you from the beginning. You know she slept with half the guys on the island while she was here? She was worse than you. And she used to do it during work time, too, so the rest of the housekeeping staff had to pick up the slack because she didn't do her job at all."

Jay wet his lips. "So, if we'd maybe had a disagreement and she'd decided not to speak to me, I should probably keep it that way?"

Too late. He'd already pissed Penny off. "Oh, Jay. You didn't."

"She left me a note." He kicked the sand, sending a spray of it into the lagoon. "They all leave me. I've read every fucking romance book in the library. The guys in those all get happily ever afters. All of them. Even the arseholes who should be locked up because of the way they abuse their women. It doesn't matter how fucked up those heroes are. They always get to be happy. Me, I get the girl and just when I think I'm happy…she buggers off, with barely a word. What am I doing wrong?"

Anguished rock star now. No, give him his due: he was an anguished, frustrated, clueless man who deserved her pity. Money couldn't buy love, or sense.

"Have you ever wondered if maybe you're not a typical romance hero?" Audra ventured. "I mean, how many of them actually have to try? Or read romance to learn what they should be doing?"

"Not many."

"It could also be the women you're choosing. Maybe they're just not right for you, which is why it never works out. Most people have to date a lot of people before they find someone worth sticking with."

"Hundreds?" Jay ventured.

Try thousands, Audra thought but didn't say. "Not usually, no. But I'm not sure a post-concert orgy where you don't even remember the girls' names counts as a date."

"I can't date like normal people do. I can't even meet people normally any more without being recognised. No one sees me as a person. Just a rock star."

Bloody hypocrite. The last time she was on the island, he'd moaned about how much he hated the band breaking up, so he wouldn't be a rock star any more. "I thought you liked being a rock star," Audra said carefully.

"When I'm on stage and shit, yeah. When I'm signing autographs and everyone looks at me like they think I'm awesome, shit yeah. But when I want someone to share my life with…I want someone who can see through all the bullshit to me." He eyed Audra. "Like you do."

"Yes, but…" That's because I've seen you when you're not being an arsehat, Audra thought, fighting to find a more diplomatic way of putting it. "That's because I've seen you drop the rock star façade, when you're vulnerable, and I helped you. It's hard to see you as an idol when I've seen you scared. I guess if I believed in such things, I'd say I've seen your soul. Raw and unpolished and real."

"But you still helped me." Jay grabbed her hands. "You helped me. You stayed. And even when you said you didn't want to talk to me while you were in Antarctica, you still took my calls and listened. You even gave good advice, which I sometimes followed."

Sometimes. Audra smothered a laugh. Sometimes was better than never, which was what she'd expected of him. "It was my job here, Jay. I was the maid assigned to the villas. It was my job to help you."

His grip tightened as she tried to pull away. "Maybe at first, but not after you left the island. I'd never have gotten over Phuong's betrayal if it weren't for you. Well, you and Xan." He cleared his throat. "And you're here now. Do you want to stay? I'm sure I can pull some strings to get you posted to a weather station up here instead of a place where there's nothing but penguins."

"No, Jay. I want to go to Antarctica again. It's amazing there. And there's…there's an opportunity to do further study there, too. Maybe even a PhD." She laughed. "Listen to me. I never thought I'd be able to afford to do it, but the thought of being the one to discover something, to add to the store of human knowledge because of something I've done, however small…it means I'm not just someone's maid, destined to clean up other people's messes for the rest of my life. I have the opportunity to make a difference for once in my life, and I'm going to take it, if I can."

"What do you have to do to get it? Apply to some university or other and convince the professors to take you? Those guys don't get paid much. Maybe I could – "

"NO!" She glared at him. "You are not going to pay off any professor, anywhere, to buy me entrance into a PhD program. Besides, it wouldn't work. It's a program they're offering through the Bureau. We have six months to build an online following, promoting how great it is to work for the Bureau. I'm going to do a video channel with regular vlogs about my life in Antarctica."

Jay nodded. "And wait for the right video to go viral. That's what happened for Chaya. Just…boom. One interview went viral and suddenly *Necessary Evil* was the most downloaded song on iTunes that day. It was mental."

"Are you offering to write me a song?"

It was Jay's turn to laugh. "Fuck, no. You wouldn't want me to. I never wrote any of our songs. I just performed them. But if I posted something, saying how I thought it'd be cool if all my fans followed you…you'd win for sure."

"Don't you dare." Audra ripped her hands out of his grip. "If I get this, it'll be through my own effort, not because I know someone famous. I earn things through merit, not through favours."

"But that's not how the world works," Jay argued. "It's who you know, not what you know. Chaya was one of a thousand bands, until we scored that TV interview because…because of who we knew. Sure, we're good, but there were plenty of other bands better than us. It was luck and circumstance and other people who made the band what they became. You don't get a couple million followers from just putting up a few videos and being good. You need more than that. Something that'll make the world want to watch every minute."

He wasn't wrong, but Audra knew all this. "I'll have penguins."

"Penguins won't make you go viral," Jay said. "You need to do more than that."

"What, then?" Audra challenged. The man might have millions of followers, but he wouldn't have the first idea on how to get them in the first place.

"Marry me."

"What?"

Jay swallowed. "Marry me. It's one thing you could do that would definitely get you the worldwide attention you want. The minute the media learn your name, they'll all go wild for you."

"Like they did for Flavia, you mean?"

"No. They buzzed around her because of the auction, not because of me. I still don't think the media know about my involvement. That's completely different," he insisted. "Marry me, Audra."

The man was insane. "You mean marry you and stay here? Instead of going to the South Pole?"

"That's what I'd like, yes, but if you really feel you need to go, I guess you could – "

"Stop. Just stop. The answer is no, Jay. No matter what you might think, or what I might have thought the last time I was here, I am NOT made to live my life as arm candy to a rock star, or as a maid in someone's hotel. I'm capable for more than that. I'm made for adventure, for discovery, for – "

"For the icy wasteland that's the South Pole?" he asked bitterly.

"Yes!" Audra exploded. "I'm made for the South Pole. Not for you."

He got that kicked puppy look. "Why not?"

Audra bit her lip. When he looked at her like that, it was hard to remember all her objections to him as a person. He was unbelievably good in bed, but he was as troubled as her brothers for all that, and she didn't want to spend the rest of her life propping up his ego while her own life went on hold. She'd done that for her family for as long as she could remember. Now, it was time for her to live her own life. And win that contest on merit, without cheating by asking for favours from Jay.

Cheating. The perfect excuse.

"Because you cheated on me. Not just once, but with hundreds of girls," she said.

"It wasn't cheating!" Jay protested. "We weren't together!"

"So if I go to Antarctica, and you stay here, and either of us sleep with anyone else, you don't think it's cheating because of geography?"

"No?" he ventured.

"Guess again."

"But we weren't together. It's not like we were married or anything," he insisted.

"I didn't cheat on you," Audra said softly. "All the time I was in Antarctica, I didn't sleep with anyone. While you…you probably slept with half the country."

"Who would you sleep with in Antarctica?" Jay scoffed. "There's no one there! Just penguins and seals and whales and shit!"

"In summer, there are plenty of people there. Researchers. People who keep the bases operational. More people than you have on this island in peak season. If I went to Antarctica looking for love, I bet I'd find it."

"You wouldn't find better than me." The arsehat had returned.

Audra stared at him steadily, measuring her words carefully. "Jay, even the penguins there are better than you, because they mate for life. They're faithful. Unlike you."

"Not as big as me. Penguins have tiny dicks."

She didn't want to know when he'd seen a penguin's genitals.

"An elephant seal, then," Audra retorted, trying hard not to laugh. Just the thought of getting close to an elephant seal, let alone…ugh. "But you know what? It doesn't matter. Here's something you missed in all your romance reading: cheaters never win. A man who cheats on his beloved never gets a happily ever after. It's one of the cardinal rules of romance."

"Never?" he whispered.

She met his pleading gaze. "Never."

Oh shit, if she stayed another moment, she'd give in to him. Again. And she couldn't. "Goodbye, Jay," she said, striding off before he could follow her. The moment she was out of sight, she broke into a run, hoping to reach the main building, where she could hide until the helicopter returned for her. No way was she spending any more time on the island with Jay Felix. She didn't want to do something else stupid. It was time for adventure again, at the bottom of the world. And she didn't need a man to help her succeed – this time, she'd do it all on her own.

ELEVEN

It seemed like no time at all before Jean was back at Sea-Tac Airport, waiting in the departure lounge for the boarding call for his flight to New Zealand. The first of several flights, really, but that didn't matter. The first time he'd done this, his heart had been filled with eager excitement at the adventure awaiting him at the bottom of the world.

Now, all he felt was grim determination.

Sure, there'd be adventure and excitement and all, but underlying that was his true goal. A simple one, really: to discover, so his name would be remembered. Some distant relation centuries ago had first described king penguins for science. Now it was his turn to make his mark, unfettered by family or a whining wife who wanted to hold him back from greatness. He was adding to the vast body of human knowledge through science – a noble cause, certainly.

Anyone could breed and work a boring day job. Only a handful of people got to make a difference, to discover things. He wouldn't screw it up this time.

Dragging himself home to a wife who didn't want him. Instead, he should have been taking the next flight back to Antarctica, to finish his research. Most people wouldn't have gotten a second chance when they'd messed up so badly, and no one got a third. This time, he wouldn't let any woman stand in his way.

His goal was as clear in his mind as it was when he started studying, without being clouded by thoughts of Dairine. She'd seduced him, he knew now, tempting him away from his true calling so that he could satisfy her dreams, while his shrivelled and died.

Sure, the sex had been okay, in that there'd been plenty of it, but he'd always thought a marriage ought to have a bit more to it than bonking like rabbits and the inevitable result: kids. Shared feelings, maybe. Love. Or similar goals. It was obvious to him now that the feelings and love had all been on his side, while Dairine had felt nothing for him. As for goals…well, he had his own now. But he wasn't sharing them with anyone, no matter how good she looked naked. No, shared goals meant shared glory, and he was having none of it.

Let Dairine see what she'd lost when she'd discarded him to get with that nerdy computer guy.

When Jean finally decided he'd had enough adventure for a bit and settled down for a little while to have kids, they'd know their dad was a great man who'd helped discover things. A scientist. A scholar. Someone to be proud of, with a reputation to live up to.

But all that was years away. He was young. He had all the time in the world to find a wife and have kids and all that. Right now, he had a PhD to complete, and a postdoc to plan.

And any woman who tried to seduce him away from his work would be in for a rude shock. No one would distract him from his goals this time. Not even if she owned a perfect pair of tits.

TWELVE

Audra planted her feet on the deck and took a deep breath. She hadn't counted on feeling nervous before her first vlog. Best to get started, then. She pressed the RECORD button.

"Hi, I'm Audra, a graduate meteorologist on my way to my first posting, and this is my ride."

She lifted the camera and panned across the deck, turning slowly on the spot until she'd shown them the full circle of her view.

"The *Aurora Australis*, a ninety-five-metre-long icebreaker that can cruise through sea ice more than a metre thick. It might be spring in Australia, but there's ice in Antarctica year round, so I've got my gloves, my hat and my polar thickness coat to keep warm. Most of the other hundred or so passengers are inside, grabbing something to eat in the mess hall, working out in the gym, chilling in the rec room or catching up on sleep in their bunks.

"The sea out here can get pretty rough, with the sort of ten-metre swell I'd expect to see in cyclones further north, but today it's relatively calm, so I'm out here in the hope of seeing whales. Humpback and southern right whales are headed south with me, to spend their summer in Antarctica."

She leaned on the railing, holding the camera steady as the ship cut through the waves. There wasn't a whale in sight, but she figured she might use the ocean footage for something else later when she cut the video. If she did catch a whale, it would be an added bonus.

A gust of wind tugged at her hat, so she shoved it further down on her head, stroking the faux fur like the cat it reminded her of. She'd splashed out in the stocktake sales while she was in Melbourne, buying a new hat and coat and gloves to supplement the standard expedition gear. Now she was glad of it – she'd stand out in the videos.

Audra waited until her fingers started to go numb, then turned the camera off and headed inside.

She took several videos over the next week, trying her best to make shipboard life look fun. She uploaded them over the ship's slow internet connection and watched the number of views slowly creep up. Maybe these viral video things were harder to create than she'd thought.

Three days out of Davis, they ran into a storm. Audra wasn't sure how big the swell was, but it tilted the ship to some crazy angles as it made most people seasick. Suddenly, inside the ship was the last place she wanted to be, with the stench of bile combined with bleach and disinfectant everywhere she went. Everyone else took to their bunks except the crew and a few unaffected passengers, Audra included.

While she was sitting in the near-empty mess hall, tinkering with the zoom on her ocean video to see if she'd captured any whales or not, she encountered Doug, who remembered her from her last voyage. They got to talking about her videos and her project, so he invited her up to the bridge to film the storm from the best vantage point.

Audra eagerly accepted, hurrying back to her shared cabin to retrieve her camera and stow her laptop. She left her fellow groaning passengers in their curtained-off bunks, and made her way carefully up the ladders to the control centre of the ship. With every step, she had to remind herself to keep three points of contact. It didn't stop her from being bumped against the wall whenever the ship lurched, but it kept her from losing her footing.

Audra exchanged nods with the captain, as his eyes darted from one display to another, before he peered out of the spray-spattered glass to the tempest outside.

"Wow," she breathed, her own eyes fixed over the seething sea as the waves laid siege to the deck. She'd seen the waves licking at the mess hall windows like they'd wanted to taste her lunch, but here they were enormous, from one rain-fogged horizon to the other. She lifted her camera. "Can I?"

She gripped the nearest railing and held her camera to the glass, her own eyes glued to the storm outside. A normal person would have been frightened. She should have been frightened. As a meteorologist, she knew what sort of power she was seeing, but she didn't care. Or, maybe more accurately, she did care, but she found it more awe-inspiring than frightening. No one could control this sort of power – raw, untamed, glorious. She didn't have enough words to describe it. Nevertheless, she tried, murmuring a description of the storm into the camera's microphone that couldn't do the phenomenon justice.

She hadn't thought anyone heard her until the captain remarked, "This is nothing. You should see the storms we get in Drake's Passage."

"Really?" Audra asked. In her head, she added an item to her bucket list: travel through a storm in Drake's Passage.

"Yeah. Worst patch of water in the world, but the only way to travel between South America and Antarctica. I wouldn't want to take this old bucket through there any more," he said.

Audra laughed. If the *Aurora Australis* was a bucket, it was the biggest, reddest bucket in the world. "She doesn't look that bad to me."

"That's because you're not an expert on ships."

She bristled for a moment, before conceding that he had a point.

"Most icebreakers are only good for twenty years or so before they need a massive rebuild. They take a lot of punishment between the storms and the ice they constantly have to shove their way through. This bucket has so many dents in her, it's no wonder someone's ordered her replacement. None too soon, either – she's twenty-six, and overdue for retirement."

For the first time, Audra didn't feel so secure. "Is she safe?"

"Safe enough, or she wouldn't be sailing this season."

Audra nodded, satisfied. Before she'd left Hobart, the Australian Antarctic Division staff had insisted she do an updated safety training course before she left, on her supervisor's instructions. Now, she wasn't just an emergency surgical assistant, but a safety officer tasked with preventing injuries, too.

"Don't be scared," the captain said. "We're not the *Titanic*. Plenty of lifeboats and supplies aboard for everyone if the worst were to happen and this ship sinks."

"Oh, I'm not scared," she replied, lifting her gaze to the window again. Was it strange for a meteorologist to sympathise with the storm? Maybe.

THIRTEEN

Jean deliberately turned his back on the storm outside. He preferred to be in the relative safety of McMurdo Station instead of the whiteout that had engulfed the rest of Ross Island. He wasn't the only one trapped in the station because of the bad weather – a bunch of scientists and technicians were due to replace the winter staff at the South Pole astrophysics station, which they all referred to as the Ice Cube. Jean wasn't sure if that was its actual name or some sort of nickname for whatever its official title was. Either way, they weren't happy to be stuck here instead of heading inland to start their research.

He'd joined them in drinking away their communal sorrows to the point where he was down to his last two bottles of whisky. If he didn't stop soon, he'd have nothing to celebrate with when he finally found that penguin colony.

Sighing, he reluctantly switched to water. He'd stick to beer until the storm blew over.

He couldn't really complain. He'd managed to get a lift out to New Zealand's sub-Antarctic islands with a cruise ship, so he'd already started his research for the season. Numbers were up at all the king penguin colonies, as he'd predicted, but the forced idleness meant he'd already had time to include his findings in his thesis and fire off a copy to Louis. So Jean was left to cool his heels, waiting for a ship to take him to Australian Davis Station, before meeting up with the oceanography survey ship that would take him out to Heard Island.

He didn't need to see the South Pole to be satisfied. Just one more island to conquer and he'd be a happy man.

FOURTEEN

"Welcome back to Davis!" Shelley enveloped Audra in a hug the moment she stepped off the icy helipad.

Audra returned the hug, still dazed at having to be flown to the station over a substantial slab of sea ice, too thick for even the icebreaker ship to negotiate. "Thanks, boss," she said awkwardly. "I don't remember that much ice when I left at the beginning of the year."

Shelley waved her hand. "That's because it all melted over the summer, of course. This is winter reminding us it's not done with us yet. And I'm not really your boss. Just on paper, because they had to put someone in charge. We both answer to Lord High Whatever-His-Name-Is in Kingston."

Audra laughed. "You don't know your own boss's name?"

Shelley shrugged. "There's a new one. I haven't met him yet. Hopefully I won't until the summer's over and I head back to the mainland. In the meantime, I hope you brought all the equipment with you, because we got the go ahead for another expedition to the South Pole to upgrade that weather station. We're both going this time."

Audra wanted to cheer. How many people got to visit the South Pole in their lifetime, let alone twice? This was why she'd taken the Antarctic posting.

"It gets better," Shelley continued. "There's a team of oceanographers doing a seabed survey off Heard Island. We got approval to set up a permanent weather station on the island last summer, but the crates are still in storage, because shipping schedules wouldn't allow for an expedition last season, what with that medevac and all."

Audra nodded. How could she forget? "Let's hope we don't have another one of them this year."

Shelley's eyes x-rayed her. "That's right, you had to help out with that one. Was it bad?"

Conscious of the other people around, Audra nodded again quickly, saying, "I'll tell you about it some time. Any chance we can go inside? I'd like to dump my stuff somewhere."

"Sure." Shelley led the way into the summer accommodation block. After they'd passed a number of rooms, she pointed at a door with Audra's name sticky-labelled to it. "This is you."

Audra squinted at the second label. "This one says Jean Pennant. Never heard of her. I don't think she was on the ship with me. So I'm not rooming with you any more?"

Shelley shook her head. "All the winter staff got assigned their own rooms, but this building's for summer researchers while they're not in the field. Jean's part of the

Heard Island expedition, which is why I asked to have her bunk with you."

Between Shelley's manic grin and the way she rubbed her hands together, Audra knew she had a secret she was dying to tell. "Go on, spill it," Audra said.

"Well, that remote weather station's only gathering dust, so I pushed for a spot on that expedition for a meteorologist. They said they didn't need a meteorologist, but they will need a safety officer for island operations." Shelley's eyes danced.

"So you volunteered me?" Audra guessed.

"Actually, that's how I managed to persuade the guys in Head Office in Kingston that we needed an extra meteorologist. Specifically for that project."

Already, Audra wondered what she could film while she was in the field. "What's out there?" she asked.

"Lots of animals. Your roommate's a biologist."

Everyone loved penguins. Seals could be cute, too. Audra exhaled slowly. "So it'll be a busy summer. A South Pole expedition and one to Heard Island, too? I hope I brought enough spare batteries."

"For what?"

Audra explained about her video channel, which Shelley demanded to see. Audra unpacked her laptop and pulled up the latest video she'd posted – the view from the bridge during the storm. Unlike the first few videos, this one had over two hundred views. Maybe not viral, but still a definite improvement, she decided.

Before Shelley had finished watching it, the computer pinged with an incoming video call.

Audra debated whether she wanted to answer it, but in

the end, she gave in and let Jay's call connect.

"Are you all right?" he demanded.

"Ye-es. I just arrived at Davis Station. Why wouldn't I be?" Audra replied.

"Your video! The ship in the storm!"

Audra burst out laughing. "You're watching my video channel?"

"Of course I am! It's been three days since you posted it, and you haven't been online at all. If I didn't reach you today, I was going to send a search party out to find you!"

Shelley laughed softly. "That's the bloke who isn't your boyfriend, right?"

Audra pressed her lips together. "That's right. And who never will be. Now you know I'm alive and not floating somewhere in the Southern Ocean, what do you want, Jay?"

Shelley left, closing the door behind her.

"I need your advice for a date."

Audra fought down her laughter. "A date. Jay, I think you've tried every romance trope in the book. Who have you set your heart on this time?" Before he could answer, she continued, "It's that new hotel manager, isn't it?"

"Maybe."

Audra chose her words carefully. "Jay, you really have to watch out when it comes to people you work with. I mean, I was just a maid, and I wasn't going to work there forever, but she's the hotel manager, and a lot harder to replace if you offend her enough to make her leave. Not to mention the trouble you'll be in if she accuses you of sexual harassment. And…you're not really all that subtle."

"I know. That's why I need your help."

Audra mentally added dating adviser to her list of roles

at Davis Station, then took a deep breath. "All right. Tell me all about it."

FIFTEEN

When Jean landed at Wilkins Aerodrome, he expected to see more than just a few boxy buildings and shipping containers with a Hagglund parked outside. He helped unload his gear – enough supplies for the Heard Island expedition – and watched the ski plane take off again without seeing any signs of another human being at the base.

Sighing, he started to load the gear into the back of the Hagglund, figuring he'd best get it stowed before he went searching for people. If there were any. Wasn't Wilkins the name of the base in that book he'd read at McMurdo, a tattered paperback with half the cover missing about some sort of spy mission at an Antarctic base where most of the characters were trying to kill each other?

If some femme fatale walked out of one of the sea containers right now, he wouldn't look twice at her. Not even if she stripped off her clothes and rolled around in the snow.

Okay, maybe a glance. She'd have to be pretty crazy to go naked in this weather.

"You the American?"

Jean turned to face a man who might've been his twin, given they were both shrouded in expedition-issue red coats over black everything else. "I'm the Canadian who just flew in from McMurdo. I guess that makes you Australian?"

"Nah, I'm a kiwi, bro, from New Zealand. That's a different country, south-east of Australia, in case you don't know."

Jean laughed. "I've been there. Spent six months living in Christchurch on the South Island. I still miss the Whittaker's chocolate. Chocolate tastes way different in the States, or even in Canada." Not that he'd had any chocolate during his brief stay in Vancouver. Everything tasted sour there.

"So, you ready to go, bro, or d'you need to use the little girls' room first?"

The slightest mention of kids turned Jean's heart to ice in his chest. "I'm fine. Let's go."

Jean had driven Hagglunds before, so he was more than capable of driving this one, but today he climbed into the passenger seat and passed the time by staring out the window at the endless ice, broken only by the regularly spaced markers and flags guiding them to their destination.

By the time they reached Casey Station, Jean wished he'd taken the other man's offer to use the airport bathroom. As the Hagglund bumped to a halt, Jean opened his mouth to ask for directions.

Before Jean could get a word out, the grinning driver pointed and said, "Bathroom's through that door and on the right."

Jean climbed out of the cabin and bolted across the snow for the building in question. When he returned to their parking spot, feeling considerably relieved, he found his gear piled on top of an empty pallet, while the vehicle and its driver were already on their way back to the airstrip. With chagrin, he realised he didn't even know the man's name.

He resolved to have better manners for the rest of the expedition. There was no point moping over what might have been – he had to move on, burying himself in research and discovery and all the things that were so much bigger than petty people who wanted you home every night for dinner.

After spending two nights at Casey Station, swapping stories with the Aussies who lived there, and drinking far too much of their beer, Jean found himself summoned to the helipad with his gear.

"The *Aurora Australis* is waiting offshore, on the other side of the ice shelf," the pilot told him. "Normally, they'd head in closer, but there's a nasty storm on the radar and they want to clear Davis before it hits. Get in."

More storms. This continent threw more tantrums than a toddler. Jean didn't need telling twice. He appreciated the shelter of a station over being caught out in a storm. He helped the pilot – Eric – load the aircraft and the helicopter's thumping blades were soon carrying them over the ice to the bright red icebreaker.

The first crewman he met introduced himself as Doug.

"You're looking much better than you did back in March," Doug remarked as he shook Jean's hand.

Jean found himself at a loss. "I'm sorry, I don't remember meeting you."

Doug chortled. "I bet you don't. You were completely off your face on drugs the whole time. Doctor's orders, of course. You were a real mess." His gaze raked Jean's legs. "Doc wasn't sure you would walk again after that. Guess you proved her wrong, hey?"

Jean nodded. "I wouldn't have passed the medicals to come back here if I couldn't. I need to finish my research."

"At Heard Island, yeah?"

Jean stared. Did the whole world know about his penguin discovery? It took a moment for realisation to dawn. "You collected me from the research vessel so they could finish their survey. So that's how I got on a cargo plane. From passing out in the Apple to waking up on a plane to New Zealand, I can't remember a thing."

"Ah, you've got Audra to thank for that. If it weren't for her, we'd've had no one to give you any pain meds until you reached Casey. Then you'd have remembered us real good – and the ship where we tortured you. You'll be seeing her at Davis, too."

"Who?"

"Audra. Pretty girl. Fair hair. Good sea legs and a passion for storms. She'd be great on an icebreaker crew, but she's smarter than that. Some sort of scientist researcher type. Curious about everything, so she really listens." Doug's smile died. "If I had a daughter, I'd want one like her. Don't forget to thank her when you see her. Say hi from me, too."

Jean nodded, hoping that would satisfy the man. Thank a strange woman for drugging him and doing things to him he'd rather not remember? That would go down well. She probably wouldn't remember him, anyway.

At Doug's invitation, he joined the crew in the mess hall for a few beers. He'd had time to try a few of the Aussie varieties, seeing as they didn't have any Canadian beer or even Budweiser, and no one had heard of Molson. Jean already knew the one with all the Xs on the label wasn't his favourite, but the VB ones weren't bad and the Crown ones were the best he'd had so far. So much for the famous Fosters beer — he hadn't seen a single Aussie drink it.

After only a few days aboard, the ship slowed to a halt by the edge of a large patch of sea ice. There was nothing for miles, except more ice. "Why are we stopping?" Jean asked.

"This is your stop, mate," Doug said. "We've got a pilot ready to take you to Davis, along with your gear. There's another bad storm front coming in, and we're hoping to make it far enough north to miss it. That means this is as close as we get to Davis. Either you hop in the helicopter, or you can come with us for a round trip via Hobart."

Jean didn't even need to think before he answered, "Give me five minutes."

At four and a half, he stood by the helipad with one bag slung over his shoulder and the other on the deck by his feet. The pilot was nowhere to be seen, but two crewmen had already loaded the rest of Jean's supplies into the helicopter.

By the time Eric appeared, Jean could barely feel his face. He'd have to grow a beard if this kept up. It might be nearly summer down here, but no one had explained that to the weather.

Eric grinned as Jean climbed stiffly into the copilot's seat. "You'll need to get used to Aussie time while you're working with us, especially out here. Time's just a guideline at best."

Jean rubbed his aching leg. The bones might have healed, but they'd hurt until the day he died. Especially in the cold. "Yeah, I'm learning that," he said, trying not to grit his teeth. Lateness was one of his pet hates. Dairine had never been on time for anything, and it had driven him crazy. He wouldn't miss that about her, that's for sure.

Ice, ice and more ice unfolded below, until the blocky buildings of Davis Station came into view, sitting on the only patch of rock in a sea of white. Eric brought the helicopter down behind the buildings, beside what he said was a lake and the station's water supply.

Jean began to help Eric unload his gear, but Eric waved him away.

"They heard us arrive, and I radioed ahead to tell them I have their special Christmas supplies. Give it five minutes and I'll have more volunteers than I know what to do with, helping me unload. Go report to the station leader for your accommodation assignment before he knocks off for the day."

Armed with Eric's directions to the station leader's office, Jean headed inside, out of the cold. He found the office occupied by a woman – definitely not a he. Cautiously, Jean knocked on the open door. "Hey, I'm looking for the station leader?"

She gave a tired wave. "That's me, for my sins. Who'd

have believed we could have a water shortage while we're surrounded by ice? Even with shorter showers, it only stretches so far. I'm Ali, by the way." She extended her hand across the desk.

Jean shook it. "Jean Pennant, climate change biologist from the University of Washington. Here to finish my PhD research out at Heard Island."

Ali stared. "Jean? Spelled J-E-A-N? We all thought you were a woman."

Jean made a show of patting down his chest, then his groin. "No, definitely not a woman." He grinned. "If it makes you feel better, I was told the station leader here was a man. I guess it's hard to tell when we're all dressed alike outside."

"True." Ali reached for a folder on her desk and cast her eyes down on the contents. "You're here for your accommodation assignment, yes? It looks like you're in luck. You're housed with the summer Met team in SAM, the Summer Accommodation Module." She pulled a page out of the back of the folder and marked it with two crosses. "You're here. Your sleeping quarters are here." She tapped the paper with her pen. "That's Living Quarters, where we do pretty much everything else except work and sleep."

"Sounds pretty simple," Jean said, craning his neck to look at the map.

"Here." Ali handed it to him. "I'll let you get settled in today. Tomorrow, one of the training officers will take you through all our station procedures, so you know what's what. They'll schedule you in for the next round of survival training, too, before you go on your expedition. Have fun."

That sounded like a dismissal to Jean, so he thanked her and headed out.

His boots crunched on the grey gravel road as he trudged up to his temporary home, a big, red barn of a place. As long as it was warm inside, he didn't care what it looked like. The sleeping quarters were easy to identify because they had people's names on the doors. Two to a room. He hoped his new roommate didn't snore, like the geologists he'd shared with on Heard Island last year. If he did, Jean would requisition some earplugs from Stores tomorrow.

Just like on the map, his room was right at the end of a corridor. Jean knocked cautiously, but he received no response from inside, so he cracked the door open. Light flooded through the window, revealing an empty room. Empty of people, at least, seeing as his roommate had already claimed the top bunk and half of the available storage space. A closed laptop sat on the desk, beside a box of tampons.

Jean's bag thumped to the floor. He knew a few marine biologists who used tampons in their waterproof camera housings to absorb moisture, but Ali had said he was rooming with a meteorologist, not a marine biologist or a photographer. An amateur photographer, maybe?

Jean checked the door. His name was definitely on it, below one that looked vaguely familiar: Audra Zujute. Where had he heard that before?

An image of Doug came to mind. That was right. Doug had talked about someone called Audra. It wasn't exactly a common name, so it was probably the same woman Doug said had nursed him aboard the icebreaker last year.

Probably best to take the crewman's advice and thank her, then, in case she remembered him later and thought he was an ungrateful asshole. Maybe if he saw her, it might jog his memory of the days aboard the ship. Hey, it was worth a shot.

In the meantime, he decided to check his email, seeing as Ali had given him the station's wi-fi password. Perhaps Louis had sent through some new corrections on the chapters Jean had emailed him from McMurdo. Sure enough, he had – enough to keep Jean busy for the rest of the afternoon and evening.

He lost track of time, reading comment after comment and making the required changes. The light coming through the window faded to darkness without Jean taking his eyes off his tablet.

It wasn't until the door handle rattled that Jean's thoughts strayed from anything that involved penguins. He leaped to his feet, smoothing down his shirt. The last time she'd seen him, he'd been badly injured and probably incoherent. He wanted to make a better impression this time.

As the door swung open, Jean marched forward, sticking his hand out. "Hi, I'm Jean-Pierre, your new roommate. You must be Audra. I believe I owe you for what you did on the *Aurora Australis* last year."

Her already large eyes widened as her face paled. "Shit," she said, before she turned on her heel and strode off.

SIXTEEN

Shelley found Audra hiding in the ladies' bathroom. "You weren't at dinner," Shelley said, "so I thought maybe you'd gone to bed early. But when I knocked on your door, you weren't the one who answered." Shelley settled on the bench opposite Audra. "So, what's the deal with Mr Muscles?"

Audra smothered a snort. Trust Shelley to have noticed. "He's Mr Pennant. Mr Jean-Pierre Pennant," Audra said, emphasising the French pronunciation. "The roommate you assigned me."

"No!"

"That's what he said." Right before he threatened her with payback for what had happened on the ship. Audra shuddered. If anything, those biceps of his looked bigger than ever, and he wasn't hampered by broken legs any more, if he'd passed his medical to work on a research team out here. "I can't share a room with him, Shelley."

"Why not? Afraid you'll see him undressing and be tempted to cheat on your rock star boyfriend?"

"Jay is not my boyfriend." Audra took a deep breath. "I just don't want to share a room with some strange man I don't know, who could break me in half without breaking a sweat."

Shelley gave her a funny look. "You've shared an expedition tent with strange men before. It never bothered you then."

Audra bit her lip. She was going to sound crazy, she knew it. "He was the guy on the ship last year. The one who was injured and had to be medevaced out."

"I thought you said that guy had two busted legs. We don't just ship a guy to the mainland for breaking bones. It's usually life-threatening emergencies they evacuate for, nothing less. It can't be the same guy."

"It's him, all right. He even said he remembered me from the ship."

Shelley smiled. "Wait, that's a good thing, right? You nursed him. Sounds like a good start to a romance story to me. And you could do worse. I mean, if you're not interested in the rock star any more, just think: you could have Mr Muscles wrapped around you, warming you up at night, instead."

Audra shuddered. "God, no. He's married, Shelley. I remember the ship's crew trying to contact his wife, to tell her he'd been injured."

"Just nice eye candy, then."

Audra took a deep breath. Now or never. "I was left alone with him for a bit. The doctor at Casey wanted me to wait until he woke up before I gave him any more pain medication so he wouldn't get an overdose. So I sat, and I waited. When he woke up, he grabbed me. Tried to pull me into bed with him. He kept insisting we had to have sex."

Shelley stared at her. "What did you do?"

"I stabbed him with a needle and managed to get out of reach. He tried to get up on his broken legs and he passed out." Audra closed her eyes. "Then I hooked him up to an IV and avoided him for the rest of the trip."

"Didn't you tell someone?"

Audra shrugged. "He was unconscious. Who would believe me? I barely believed it myself. I figured I'd never see him again, so it wouldn't matter. But now he's here. In my room!"

Shelley nodded slowly. "Okay. Do you think it might have been something in his medication that made him do that?"

"I don't know of any legal drug that makes men with broken legs so horny they feel the need to have sex with the nearest woman, willing or not. And he remembers me from the ship. He said so."

Shelley blew out a breath. "I'll speak to Ali and see what we can do. Maybe there's a spare bed in the temporary accommodation he can have."

"I'd appreciate it," Audra said, over the loud gurgle of her stomach. "Sorry, I shouldn't have missed dinner."

"Go scrounge something in the kitchen," Shelley suggested. "Carl's on tonight, and he's still talking about what a good kitchenhand you are, even though that shift you filled was weeks ago. I'm sure he'll be able to rustle up something for you."

Audra thanked her and headed off in search of dinner. Dealing with Jean-Pierre Pennant would definitely be easier with a full stomach.

SEVENTEEN

"You the new guy who flew in today?" demanded a middle-aged man with a bushy beard.

"Sure did," Jean replied, easing himself down on a chair. His leg was aching something fierce today. Good thing he had the bottom bunk – he'd never manage the climb to the top one. Now all he needed was a drink to take the edge off the pain. "Do you guys do welcome drinks here, or is that just the custom at Casey?"

The bearded man bristled. "We're just as hospitable as Casey. What's your poison?"

"Got any Fosters?" Jean asked.

Everyone laughed.

"Nah mate, all out of Fosters. Must've drunk it all. A XXXX, maybe?"

Another test. Jean knew the answer to this one, too. "Only if you're out of Crowns and VB."

"Not bad for a Yank," the bearded man said grudgingly. "Bruce. I keep the water running here at Davis."

"I'm Jean, and I'm not American. I'm Canadian. A biologist."

"I better get you that beer, then," Bruce said.

By the time he returned, they'd all traded names and professions, and Jean was in the middle of a comfortable conversation with the supply officers about field camp conditions.

"Pity you weren't here a few weeks back when the supply ship came in. Could've done with a seal charmer then!" Jen exclaimed. "You see, this huge elephant seal took a liking to one of our sleds. We weren't sure if he wanted to fight it or hump it. We'd loaded it up completely, but it couldn't take the weight of the cargo and the seal, and he was so determined to have his way with the equipment for the new hydroponics lab…" She continued with her story about luring the seal away with some fish, only to have him try to follow the trailer when the Hagg started towing it.

Of course, that was the perfect opening for Jean to tell the story about the pair of elephant seals that had humped his hut at the Falkland Islands on his first year out. It hadn't been funny at the time – it'd been damn scary – but he soon had the Aussies crying tears of laughter at his retelling now.

Jen wiped her eyes and gestured to someone behind Jean. "Come over here. You have to meet the new guy. He was just telling us about how he had a threesome with some seals!" She doubled over with laughter again.

"I wasn't aware that bestiality was legal out here," a calm, female voice said.

"Good one, Audra!" Bruce howled.

Audra. His strange roommate. Jean turned to see her properly before she ran away again. Just like Doug had said, she was young and pretty, with her fair hair twisted into a loose braid that hung down her back. She held a plate on one hand like a waitress about to serve the sandwich to someone.

Her eyes fixed on him, as dark and chilly as an Antarctic winter.

"Have you met Jean, Audra?" Jen asked. "He's a Canadian penguin biologist. I didn't even know they had penguins in Canada!"

"We don't," Jean corrected gently. "Not wild ones, anyway. But climate change is a global problem, and penguins are an important indicator species – "

"Sorry, I'm going to get an early night," Audra interrupted. With a wave, she was gone.

Jean swallowed the rest of his spiel. Probably not the right moment to wax lyrical about his PhD.

Jen patted his arm. "Sorry about Audra. She must be tired. All the planning for the South Pole expedition on top of her normal job. I don't know how she does it."

She hadn't looked tired. She'd looked like she wanted him dead and buried deep under the ice.

Jean shivered inwardly, but he hitched his smile back up and rejoined the conversation. He wouldn't let one woman distract him from his purpose here. He'd let Dairine do it last time, but never again.

They swapped stories until late, when as if by some unspoken agreement they all decided to call it a night.

He padded into the room he shared with Audra, wondering whether she was awake or asleep. Her even breathing persuaded him to let her sleep. Maybe she'd be less murderous in the morning.

EIGHTEEN

Audra knocked on the station leader's office door.

"Come in," Ali said, glancing up. "Ah, Audra. Is this about the weather report?"

Audra nodded. "I've been trying to plot a window between the storms, but I just can't find one big enough before Christmas. Just when we get the all clear for one, I get a new storm warning for Dome Argus. This has to be one of the worst summers on record."

"So the South Pole expedition gets postponed until after Christmas. I don't want anyone taking unnecessary risks." Ali peered at her computer. When Audra didn't leave, Ali asked, "Is there anything else?"

She shouldn't, but Audra had to ask. "My roommate, Jean Pennant. Shelley said she'd asked whether you can switch me to another room so I don't have to share with him."

"Well, we don't normally make women share with men, but this time there's an odd number of both, and we're full, what with three expeditions stuck here, waiting for the weather to clear. The only beds left are in the Medical Quarters. So unless you'd rather sleep in a hospital bed, I can't help you."

"It's just...I worked with him for a little while last season, and we didn't get along," Audra said carefully.

"Here?"

"No, on the ship."

Ali coughed irritably. "I didn't hear anything about trouble on the *Aurora Australis* last year."

Audra lowered her gaze. "I managed to avoid him for most of the trip, so nothing particularly bad happened. But things are different here at Davis. I think if we share a room for too long, there will be...an incident."

Ali eyed Audra as if she were a particularly interesting plant specimen. "An incident. You mean an argument? We get those here all the time. Especially in winter, when everyone's cooped up for months. You'd better get used to it now, because it'll be even harder when you're all living on top of each other in the SMQ."

Audra swallowed. She'd spent nearly a year at Romance Island Resort learning to keep her temper despite lazy colleagues, sleazy guests and the biggest challenge of all, Jay Felix. Antarctic expeditioners were so much more civilised than the people she'd worked with at the resort. "I'll do my best," Audra said.

"Good. Now, can you ask Shelley about her estimates for when that bloody lake will thaw? If it's still iced up by Christmas, we might have to ban showers altogether."

Both Ali and Audra winced at the thought.

"I'll run the projections myself," Audra said. "If I'm not headed inland for a while yet, and I'm still using up precious water, I want to know."

"Thanks." Ali returned to her work, and Audra took that as her cue to leave.

As she left the office, Audra sighed. So much for sleeping soundly at night. Every time Jean made a sound, she jerked awake, and couldn't get back to sleep until she was certain he was asleep, too.

Maybe by some miracle the weather would clear and she'd be on her way inland well before Christmas. A girl could hope.

NINETEEN

Jean reached Ali's office, only to discover she already had someone with her, so he found a chair around the corner and sat down to wait. No one had bothered to close the open door, so he heard the conversation clearly.

"My roommate, Jean Pennant," he heard a woman say.

Audra – and she was talking about him! Requesting a room transfer. That might not be a bad idea. Then he'd actually get some sleep instead of worrying that tonight she'd decide he wasn't allowed to live a minute longer. He wasn't sure he could bring himself to fight a woman. It just wouldn't be right. Even just the thought of it left a sour taste in his mouth.

She mentioned the ship, the icebreaker, where Doug said she'd nursed him. Except, by the sound of things, something had happened aboard the ship that made her hate him. Whatever it was, he didn't remember.

Maybe she'd just been traumatised by seeing his injuries. The idea lasted for a moment before Jean's reasonable side shot it down: she couldn't hate him that much for having two broken legs. It had to be something else. He wouldn't have made a pass at her, he knew that for certain. He'd still thought he was happily married then. What on Earth had he done to make her hate him so much?

He didn't dare ask. He'd learned that early on with Dairine. If he asked what he'd done wrong, she'd been ready to hand him a list. All women were the same, and he wasn't going to let another one complicate his life.

Audra strode up the passage, ignoring him. That meant it was his turn to talk to Ali.

He knocked softly.

Ali looked up. "If you're looking to swap rooms, I already told Audra no."

Jean shrugged. "I don't have a problem with her. She doesn't snore, doesn't leave her things lying around, and she doesn't smell bad."

"So what is the issue?" Ali asked.

"No idea. Look, I didn't come to discuss my roommate. I wanted to ask if you had any update on the *Investigator*, when it'll arrive so I can head out to Heard Island." He flashed a perfunctory smile. "It'll get me out of my roommate's hair, too." Hair that looked like it would be very soft to stroke, his traitorous brain added.

"At the moment, nothing's scheduled to arrive before January, so you'll be spending Christmas with us, and New Year, too."

Jean's shoulders slumped. "It's just that I have nothing to do. I've finished writing as much of my thesis as I can, and I've even put together a couple of papers for my supervisor this week, but I'm at a loose end. Is there anything you need me to do around the station?" He prayed he wasn't volunteering for kitchen shifts or worse, poo patrol – dealing with the sewage tanks.

"You're a biologist, right? Are you any good with plants, specifically hydroponics?"

Jean's grin was genuine this time. "Are you kidding? I worked as a lab tech in a hydroponics lab through my whole undergrad degree at the University of British Columbia. Would you believe that there's a particular type of chives that grow best when the only sound they hear is Justin Bieber's music? True story."

Ali laughed. "Good. I've got a couple of our construction guys drafting up a design for the new hydroponics building, but they could do with some help from someone who's actually run a facility like that. I'll send you over to the workshop this afternoon."

"I can go now," Jean said eagerly.

"You could, but they'll all be at lunch, so you may as well go eat." Ali's forehead wrinkled. "Look, I probably shouldn't say this, but…can you go out of your way to be nice to Audra? Normally, I'd say she's one of the calmest, most well-balanced members of the team at Davis. Nothing ruffles that girl. She used to work as a hotel maid for some celebrity resort, and that must have taken the patience of a saint. But today…" Ali sighed. "With looming water shortages, it'd be really great if we could avoid an incident, as she put it."

Jean fired off a salute. "Yes, ma'am. Us Canucks have a reputation for being nice. I'll get right on it."

He headed off.

Loud laughter dominated the dining room, spilling out into the corridor.

"That's the problem with you mets. One day you're predicting showers that never come, and when you say it's going to be fine we get another bloody blizzard! You need to train your weather better!"

A female voice piped up, "Yeah, it'd be nice if a meteorology degree came with mutant superpowers that let us summon storms or sunshine at will, right, Shell?" Audra's face lit up as she laughed. "I'll mention it to the Bureau. Maybe even put it in my next video."

"What are you doing next? I don't know how many times I've watched that one with the elephant seal who fell in love with Jen's sled."

"I had planned to do a sort of send-off video for the South Pole expedition, but because I don't have stormy superpowers," Audra flashed a cheeky grin, "I figured I might hang around outside the men's bathrooms and see who's willing to flash some skin so everyone back home knows how sexy the Davis crew are."

"I'll do it!" a man dressed in chef's whites said, lifting his leg into the air and pulling his pants hem up to the knee.

"Put that hairy thing away," Audra declared. "Wait until I have my camera ready."

More laughter, and Audra joined in, her eyes sparkling with mischief.

Jean stood in the dimly-lit corridor, evidently invisible to the occupants of the bright dining room, seeing his roommate in a positive light for the first time. Now he was certain she was the same girl Doug had praised. And she was more than pretty. Something about her just grabbed his gaze and wouldn't let go.

"Now, let's get this pool organised," Bruce said. "You both say Christmas, but it could be three days either way. So which is it – before Christmas, or after?"

"Before," said Shelley.

"After," insisted Audra.

The chef slapped his hand on the table. "I'm with Audra. Summer's so slow to start this year, the thaw's bound to be late, too."

Bruce shook his head. "Nah, Shelley's way more experienced. Audra's just a graduate. When she's spent the number of years down here that Shelley has, maybe her predictions will be as good. Climate change says everything's melting earlier than it should. So I'll stick with Shelley and say before Christmas."

Paul rose from his seat. "I'm so sure Audra's right that if the lake thaws before Christmas, I will personally lead a synchronised swimming team through the lake at New Year's." He grinned through the catcalls and cheers. "Audra can coach me. You're a swim coach, right?"

She finally stopped laughing long enough to say, "Yes, I used to coach. Not synchronised swimming. Mostly people who were just learning to swim, but yeah, I'll do it. If I'm wrong, and we have water by Christmas, I'll coach the Davis New Year synchronised swimming team."

"I'm in!"

"I'm in!"

"Me, too!"

"What about Bruce and the other conservatives? If they're wrong, are they going to go swimming, too?" Carl challenged.

Rumbles of agreement came from the others on the swim team. Jean's belly rumbled, too, but that was more in response to the delicious scents wafting up from the buffet, reminding him he still needed to eat lunch.

Audra held up her hands. "They can't go swimming in a frozen lake. I say they should perform a dance routine on New Year's Eve. And Shelley, being the accomplished dancer that she is, is the best qualified instructor."

"You're on," Shelley replied.

As the others argued over whose team they were on, Jean slipped into the room. He couldn't resist lunch any longer.

They were too busy discussing dance moves to notice him as he loaded up a plate. It wasn't until Jean had to decide where to sit that Bruce called, "Oi, Pennant! Which side are you on? Team Shelley or Team Audra?"

The others waved him over to a seat at their table, which he reluctantly took. It wasn't until he glanced up that Jean realised they'd sat him directly across from Audra.

For once, she didn't look like she wanted to kill him. She looked…curious. To Jean's surprise, he found that her eyes were an unusual shade of greenish gold, much like the cushion plants at Heard Island. Azorella eyes. And, just like the cushion plants, those eyes lured him in.

"Team Audra, definitely," Jean heard his voice say, in the slow, deep tone he used in presentations, or when he really wanted to win someone over. Dairine had called it his devil's voice, demanding that he not use it around her because it steamed up her panties.

Audra didn't look the slightest bit steamed up. In fact,

she looked as cool and crisp as the lettuce on his plate, which he recognised as one grown in the temporary hydroponics lab.

Still green, though, like her eyes.

Deceptively dangerous eyes, just like the cushion plant that had nearly killed him.

He breathed an inward sigh of relief as she rose and left, saying something about how she needed to put her findings into a report to give to Ali before she did the evening forecast.

The *Investigator* couldn't arrive soon enough to take him away from the temptation that was his roommate.

TWENTY

Audra ran the numbers again, but the results hadn't changed. She could have a proper shower come Christmas, and not before. Shelley was much too optimistic, suggesting the lake would melt earlier than that. Pity. She wouldn't mind seeing the guys do synchronised swimming in the lake. Even if she did have to coach them. She'd have to video that for sure. It might prove more popular than Jen's seal, which had almost a thousand views already. A thousand! Though, if Bruce had watched it over and over, maybe other people had, too.

It didn't matter, anyway. She was building a following, and it was more than the blogs the other graduates had. If she could just keep their interest until the contest closed in March, she'd have that training scholarship in the bag. A PhD might not be such an impossible dream after all.

Speaking of dreams...why was she so tired? Audra

rubbed her eyes, trying to stay awake. It wasn't time for bed yet. The sun still blazed outside, so it couldn't be later than mid-afternoon. It was only an hour or so ago that she'd been laughing with the guys in the dining room over lunch as they argued about dance routines in or out of the water. In the few days since they'd separated into their respective teams, the amateur forecasters had grown quite competitive. If she did end up coaching a synchronised swimming team, she'd have to video it, if only to prove that she was the first swimming instructor to work in Antarctica. She wouldn't have believed it herself, but Antarctica had a way of showing her just how impossible things weren't if you really put your mind to it. It was just a matter of money, time and a couple of crazy ideas.

Still, she'd done all she needed to for today, so she could relax. Maybe even read a little more of that sexy little romance about a stewardess she'd downloaded onto her ereader app last week. Mobile phone access was patchy at best down here, but her phone's size made it the perfect portable library, especially with the unlimited supply of ebooks she could get via the station's wi-fi network. The internet was an awesome thing.

Audra glanced at her watch. Her mouth dropped open. Midnight? How was that even possible? It was daylight outside, damn it!

It took a moment for her tired brain to respond to her outrage. Summer in Antarctica meant a few weeks of midnight sun, and a few weeks of total darkness come winter. She couldn't believe she'd forgotten. No wonder she felt tired. In six hours, she'd be up and formulating the morning forecast.

Audra smothered a yawn as she shuffled out of the Met office and up to the SAM where she slept.

At least her roommate would be asleep by now. She could sneak in, snatch a little sleep, and sneak right out again without him even registering her presence.

He would sleep well tonight, too. Ali had scheduled safety training for the new arrivals yesterday, so he'd have spent the whole day out hiking with a pack loaded full of supplies, building an emergency bivouac to sleep in for the night, before hiking all the way back again today.

Audra didn't envy him. Safety training was hell, but it was better than dying of exposure if you were caught out in the unpredictable weather.

Of course, tonight the weather was lovely. Clear and calm like a perfect summer's day, if it weren't midnight with snow on the ground. Audra's boots crunched on the road as she headed for bed. She paused by the LQ building, wondering if she should grab something to eat after having missed dinner again, but sleep's call was far more seductive than anything her stomach had to say.

Finally, she reached the sanctuary of the SAM. Audra pulled off her boots and stalked the corridors in her socks, not wanting to wake anyone. She pushed open the door to her sleeping quarters, gratified to see that Jean had had the good sense to draw the blockout blinds properly so it was dark enough to sleep.

She knew the room well enough not to need any light to make it to her bunk, either. Four steps to the ladder, a short climb up the rungs and she could fall into oblivion for a few hours.

One step. Two…and it all went to shit. She tripped over

something bulky in the middle of the floor and cracked her head on the ladder so hard she saw stars.

TWENTY-ONE

Halfway through the hike, Jean was tempted to quit. The combination of bone-numbing cold and his slightly out of practice legs made walking nothing short of agony. When he got back to the station, Jean swore to hit the gym. He'd been lax lately and it showed. He'd hurt worse during those months of physiotherapy sessions, though, so he just gritted his teeth and got on with it. The crazy Aussies wouldn't let him return to their island unless he showed them he could hike through the snow, dig himself a burrow and survive the night without proper shelter.

He could do all that, or he had been able to before the accident. Now, he just needed a little help, in the shape of some pain pills. Just as soon as he could sneak some out of his pack without anyone seeing. The last thing he wanted was to be declared unfit for duty and sent home before he found his penguins. If anyone did see him, he could just say he had a headache, but he hoped it wouldn't come to that.

Jean found his opportunity when they stopped for a drinks break. Sure, the medication took a while to kick in, but just knowing that the pain would ease as the hike continued instead of getting worse was enough to give him the boost he needed to go on.

Digging his snow shelter wasn't so bad – until he tried to stand up again. Then he realised his knee had frozen while he'd been kneeling in the snow. He crawled into his little snow cave, trying to massage feeling back into his leg before anyone noticed. This was the only time he'd ever have to do something like this, so he just had to suck it up and endure it. Heard Island was warmer, with barely any snow on the ground near the camp areas, or at least that's what he remembered. Big Ben, the mountain in the middle, was covered in snow year-round, but as the penguins ignored it, he could, too.

Later that night, as he tried to fight the claustrophobia of his temporary bivouac, which was nothing more than a snow cave lined with a plastic bag, he wished he had a roommate. Sure, it would be a lot more cramped than the room he normally shared, but he wouldn't be alone like he'd been in that lava tube on Heard Island, and Audra would be warm.

Warm and soft and…oh, no. He slammed the door on that thought before it could sneak inside properly. Audra was not someone he wanted to share a bed with, or anything else. They shared a room out of necessity and the fact that she was a pretty, curvy woman was irrelevant. She didn't like him, and that's how things should stay.

His traitorous mind filled his dreams with her, both

good and bad, so by morning he was even more wrecked than when he'd gone to bed. At least he had plenty of snow to cool his ardour before he had to face his fellow trainees. And a long hike before he had to look Audra in the eye again.

Yes, he'd gone too long since he last had sex. Years, actually. Jean knew he could have hooked up with someone in any of the cities he'd visited on his way to McMurdo, or even some of the friendly expeditioners he'd met along the way, but casual hook-ups weren't his thing, and they never had been. He'd married Dairine so young because he'd wanted more. So had she. More than he could give her, as it turned out.

There. Mission accomplished. After thinking about his ex-wife, his libido had officially retired for the day.

Jean crawled out of his cave and shared breakfast with the other trainees, before they packed up and headed back down to the station.

By the time they reached Davis, both of Jean's legs were screaming at him. He knew what that meant – he needed the stronger painkillers, the ones that knocked him out for hours which he kept in the bottom of his bag so he could avoid them like the plague. Thank goodness he had tomorrow off – he was going to need it.

He shared dinner with the other guys, forcing himself to smile and pretend nothing was wrong as he ate food he barely tasted. Once his plate was empty, he was free.

Jean grabbed his gear from outside the dining room and hobbled as fast as he could to his sleeping quarters. He dropped the pack the moment he crossed the threshold, kicking the door shut behind him. He pulled off his outer gear and left them where they lay, too tired to bend and pick them up. He staggered to his bed and knelt beside it so he could extract his pills from the hidden pocket in his bag. Jean washed down the tablets with the last of his bottle of water before he clambered onto his bed and lay still. After a moment, he decided the sunlight glaring through the windows was more than he could take, so he heaved himself out of bed and yanked down the blind.

Blessed darkness, and hopefully a reprieve from pain.

Jean sank into his mattress. When the drugs tugged at his pain, trying to take it away, he let them take his consciousness with them. Bliss.

Or at least it was until a screeching harpy smashed his peace into shards.

"What the fuck are you trying to do? Break my legs?"

Jean tried to explain that he was the one who'd broken his legs, but they were fine now, not hurting at all, but he wasn't sure the words came out right.

"So you just thought you'd leave your stuff lying around, not caring if I tripped over it? You expected me to be your personal maid, is that it?" Audra's eyes blazed. Green fire. Could you get green fire? She could. She had blood on her forehead, too, like she'd hit her head.

Jean scanned the room. He'd left his bag and clothes right in front of the door where they'd trip anyone coming in. He should have put them away before knocking himself out. She didn't deserve to be hurt because of him.

Mumbling an apology, Jean got out of bed, gritting his teeth as he limped around the room, putting it to rights. His field pack went out into the corridor, and he hung his outer clothing on the hooks where they belonged. He lined his boots up underneath his coat, like he usually did, but he'd forgotten in his haste to stop hurting tonight. Lastly, he shoved his bag back under his bunk, so she wouldn't see the pills he'd taken. They were perfectly legal – he had a prescription for them and everything – but if anyone here knew he was taking them, they'd ship him out for sure. Not going to happen.

Once again, he apologised to Audra. He mumbled an excuse about being tired after the safety training, which seemed to work.

She softened the tiniest bit, and nodded.

"You're bleeding. You should go to sickbay and get someone to look at that," he ventured, pointing at her forehead.

Audra's hand went to her hairline and came away red. "Yeah. Thanks," she said, sounding as out of it as he felt.

Jean swallowed. "I'm really sorry." And please don't report me for drug use, he thought but didn't say.

She didn't respond. Instead, she left.

TWENTY-TWO

Christmas morning dawned and Audra wasn't sure whether she was more disappointed at not getting to coach the synchronised swimming boys, or not being allowed a proper shower. She didn't want to be right when it meant that the lake was still frozen over.

She sighed and hopped out of bed. Jean was still fast asleep, so she dressed and headed for the LQ, where she knew they'd need every pair of hands to help with decorations and gifts.

Bruce would be playing Santa this year, just as he had last year, but now he sat on the floor amid a pile of gifts that still needed to be wrapped.

Audra grabbed two coffees from the kitchen and joined him. "Want me to be Mrs Claus again this year?" she asked.

"You're a godsend, Audra. I can't gift-wrap to save my life." Bruce took the offered coffee and drank deeply.

"Luckily I've had plenty of practice. Just like last year. Bring me the gifts and write out the label while I wrap." She surveyed the pile. "There's a lot more than last year."

"More researchers this year. I hope we haven't forgotten anyone in the Secret Santa."

"Me, too. It's a long trip to the shops for an extra box of chocolates."

Audra set to work, wrapping gifts that had come by ship from relatives and friends on the mainland, as well as those that expeditioners had bought each other as part of the Secret Santa program. Audra had been told she'd be buying a Secret Santa gift for Bruce, which had been easy. She could see the bottle of flavoured Russian vodka she'd bought for him before she left Melbourne, hiding behind an enormous stuffed seal.

"Oh, wow, someone loves you," Bruce said.

Audra looked up. "What do you mean?"

"Your family sent you a carton of mango beer."

The moment Audra saw the carton, she shook her head. "No, that wasn't my family. It's from a friend who lives in Broome." Jay, she was certain.

"A friend who'd like to be a lot more. That stuff's expensive."

Price wouldn't matter to Jay, but Audra was still surprised that he'd bothered to buy her anything. It was really sweet, even for him.

"More! Gah, your Secret Santa gift's mango liqueur!" Bruce set the bottle on top of the case. "And…a box of shampoo?"

Audra laughed. "That's from my family. With the water shortages, I've been using a dry shampoo, but I'm running low, so I emailed my sister and asked her to send a lot more. If I'm lucky, this will do me the whole winter, even if I wash my hair every day."

She wrapped her own presents, stuck on the gift tags, and moved on to the next item on Bruce's list. She had to pause for a moment to load more tape into the dispenser before she could finish wrestling the seal into its wrapping for Jen.

The stack under the Christmas tree was looking particularly impressive when Bruce suddenly swore. "Jean's not on the list. There's nothing for him." He eyed Audra. "You're his roommate. You must know him. What does he like?"

Avoiding her as much as she avoided him, Audra thought but didn't say. She barely knew the man, and if she'd ever felt the need to get to know him, it had evaporated in the heat of her embarrassment at shouting at him after his safety training.

As she'd watched him limp around the room, putting his things away and apologising, she'd been too tired and too angry to realise why he'd left his gear on the floor. It wasn't until she'd been sitting in sickbay for a while that her brain registered what she'd seen — a man recovering from what she knew had been horrific injuries, having just undergone a gruelling hike and survival training. She'd needed the day off after her first survival training, and she hadn't been injured. It must have been twice as hard for him. Then she'd spotted the empty pill packet in the bin under the desk and wondered just how much pain he was hiding from everyone. He'd passed his medical assessment, but at what cost?

Now she was torn between her desire to apologise and the need to keep his secret. He evidently hadn't wanted her to know, but now she did, and she wasn't sure she could apologise without blurting out the rest. So, she'd gone back to avoiding him.

Her gaze landed on the box of beer she'd wrapped for herself. She didn't need them, and she had plenty of gifts, even if she had sent Sam the money for the shampoo. "He likes beer, doesn't he? Give him mine."

"You can't do that! You already bought your Secret Santa gift. You shouldn't have to get two. Plus, that carton cost way more than you're supposed to spend."

Audra shrugged. "A six pack, then. You'll have to hide the rest of the carton somewhere until he leaves with the rest of the summer researchers, so he doesn't see it. We'll save it for the dead of winter."

"If you're sure…"

She nodded once. "Absolutely." Plus, it would be a sort of oblique apology for her behaviour the other night, without ever having to say the words to his face. Giving him the whole carton was worth that. Besides, it was Christmas.

"You're a better person than me," Bruce said fervently. "I wouldn't share that with anyone."

Audra wasn't sure what to say to that, so she just got back to work on her gift-wrapping.

TWENTY-THREE

Withdrawal symptoms from his pain meds wouldn't kill him, Jean told himself for what felt like the millionth time. He should never have taken them. Instead, he should have just put up with the pain until it went away on its own. He wouldn't be waking up on Christmas morning with the mother of all hangovers that he'd drunk nothing to deserve.

Speaking of mothers, he should call his. It was still Christmas Eve there – perfect timing.

Jean made himself look presentable, then dragged the desk chair into the best light beside the window before he turned on his tablet and tried to video call home.

His mother must have been sitting at the computer, she answered so quickly.

"Jean-Pierre? It's so good to see you. See? I told you he'd call," she said, dragging his dad into range of her webcam.

"Hi Mom, Dad," Jean said. "Yeah, it's really good to see you, too. Last Christmas I was stuck on some rock with no internet access, but this year I'm at one of the Australian research stations, Davis, so it almost feels like civilisation again. Or it would, if it weren't for all the seals and penguins outside." He peered out the window. Yes, he could still see the elephant seals who'd beached themselves at the haul-out area Davis used as a loading dock when the sea ice had melted, like now.

"I'm so sorry about Dairine, and the baby," Mom said. "I remember her calling me when she first filed for divorce, telling me she'd had to stick your things in boxes in her garage because it hurt her to look at them. She threatened to throw everything in the garbage, but I made her send them here so she wouldn't have to look at them any more. I put them…"

Jean was still stuck on the first thing she'd said. Baby? "Did she lose the baby?" Jean interrupted. No matter what he felt about Dairine, he wouldn't have wished that on her.

"You mean you don't know?"

Jean shook his head. "We're not exactly on talking terms any more. That's one of the reasons she divorced me, and married some other guy who could give her kids when I couldn't."

"But you did, baby. She was so proud you got her pregnant right before you left for your research trip that she called me every week until she had a miscarriage. She said she told you, but you never replied."

Jean felt like he'd been punched in the gut. "I never got her message. I should have been there for her. Instead, I was on some guano-encrusted rock, counting penguins."

Jean knew the divorce had been his fault, but to lose their baby as well? That cut deep. "Mom, if I'd known…"

"I thought so. That's what I told her, but Dairine wouldn't listen. She got her divorce and married some other man, who gave her twins. They're really cute — she posts pictures of them on her social media almost every day."

Twins. Jean suppressed a snort. Dairine would just love having an instant family in one hit like that. He'd bet her husband was proud.

"I hope she's happy," Jean said. It came out more bitterly than he'd intended.

"I think she mostly is, but sometimes the baby blues hit her really bad and then she calls me. Her family aren't happy with her about the divorce, so she gets lonely sometimes." Mom coughed. "I really think you should give her a call."

No. Not even if the Earth's poles flipped and he found himself at the North Pole instead of the south one. "Mom, I really don't think — "

"Come on, it's Christmas. It would really cheer her up," Mom coaxed.

"I'll think about it," Jean lied. Okay, it wasn't really a lie, because no matter how hard he tried to block the thought of Dairine out of his head, she'd still come creeping back to taunt him for not being a good enough husband. A good husband would have been by her side when their baby died. "Has it snowed yet?"

"Not yet, but the weather forecast said it should overnight. I can't imagine Christmas in summertime. It just seems so wrong. Are you swimming and drinking plenty to stay cool?"

Jean laughed. "Mom, I'm in Antarctica. On the actual southern continent, not far from the South Pole. The lake behind us is frozen solid, the beach has icebergs and there's still snow on the ground leftover from winter. The water's below freezing. Way too cold for swimming."

"How's your research on those…what are they? Emperor penguins?" she asked.

"King penguins," Dad corrected. "I told you, he's out there counting king penguins. That's why he has to go to so many islands. Emperor penguins live on the mainland, on the ice." He grinned. "Right, son?"

"That's right. They look really similar, though, or at least the adults do. The juveniles are the easiest way to tell what you've got. Juvenile emperors are grey, but kings are brown. And both parents look after king penguin babies, but it's just the dads for emperors."

Jean talked about his research and life in Antarctica, while his parents told him about their friends and family back in Canada, half a world away. Everyone else seemed to be living such ordinary lives, while he was here, having an adventure. Jean wouldn't trade places for the world.

After nearly an hour of chatting, his parents ended the call, but not before his mother had given him Dairine's number and made him promise to call her.

One day, maybe he would. One day far into the future, when he still didn't feel so raw about the divorce. Or the baby he'd never known about until now.

Today it was Christmas, and he was allowed to celebrate. After all, last Christmas had very nearly been his last, and he was lucky to have survived until this one. That deserved a beer and some good cheer.

Pulling on his coat, Jean headed out to the LQ for Christmas lunch with the whole of Davis.

TWENTY-FOUR

"I think I've eaten too much," Audra groaned, letting her fork clatter to her plate. "But it was so good!"

"Best Christmas lunch I've had in a long time," Shelley agreed. "Of course, last year I had to cook, which was a disaster from the beginning."

"What happened?" Audra asked.

Shelley laughed. "I got into the kitchen. Some people are amazing cooks, and I take my hat off to them. Some of us…are better kept out of the kitchen. Right, Lesley?" she shouted at a woman in chef's whites.

Lesley wagged a finger at Shelley. "You're not volunteering to be a kitchenhand again, are you? You'll have Carl chasing you out with a frying pan, if you so much as set foot inside my kitchen." Lesley nodded to Audra. "You're fine, though. You don't burn the broccoli, pour a week's worth of mashed potato down the sink or flood the place."

Audra stared at Shelley. "You're seriously that bad in the kitchen? You sound like my sister, Sam. She burned one of those noodle cups once. Oh, and instant soup."

Shelley lifted her nose into the air. "I'll have you know I'm a domestic goddess. The sort with minions and acolytes and things who do all the work. Why do you think I'm here while my stay-at-home husband gets the house and kids?" Her tone turned wistful. "I wish I'd been there this morning, though. Video calls just aren't enough."

It had been enough for Audra, though she didn't say so. Her family had clustered around Sam's second-hand laptop – Audra's old computer – and exchanged Christmas wishes with her this morning. The boys hadn't stayed long to talk, because they'd been tasked with cooking Christmas lunch on the barbeque, and her father had followed them to supervise. Sam and Mum had laughed, explaining that last year, they'd burned the sausages, so they'd been warned not to be so careless this year. When Mum had left to prepare the salads, Sam had stayed on just long enough to bemoan how much she missed Audra, because Christmas dinner just wasn't the same without her.

Of course it wasn't. Audra had spent the better part of a week preparing everything for Christmas dinner, and at least two of them cooking, every year until last year, when she'd finally had a break. She wondered who cooked now she didn't live at home any more, but she wasn't game to ask. Taking care of her family had been a fulltime job before she left, and she didn't want to admit how nice it was not to have that responsibility any more. Because that made her a bad daughter and a bad sister, didn't it?

Bells chimed outside the LQ, reminding Audra to whip her camera out.

"Santa's here!" someone cried, pointing out the window. "Look! He has his elves and reindeer and everything!"

The reindeer – expeditioners kitted out in the station's white hazmat suits, with felt antlers clipped to their hoods – and similarly green-suited "elves" pranced around outside the window for a bit, before heading inside. The sound of bells grew louder as Bruce…whoops, Santa's entourage appeared and took their places around his tinsel-covered throne.

Audra's name was one of the first he called, so she dutifully kissed Santa's blushing cheek and took her gifts back to the table to show Shelley. Shelley's turn came soon after, so she handed the camera back to Audra, who set it on the table in front of her so it could record the event without her help. She'd edit it later. For now, the two women sat back, sipping their drinks, as the other expeditioners collected and unwrapped their Christmas gifts.

Jen shrieked with delight at her seal, to the room's amusement, and Bruce carefully tucked his vodka away under his throne as he called the next name: "Jean!"

Jean squeezed through the crowd to reach Bruce. Audra's sharp eyes noticed he favoured one leg more than the other, but she didn't think anyone else had spotted his limp. He hid it well.

He took his gift from Bruce, then tore open the wrapping in front of everyone and held the beer up like a trophy.

The construction guys in the corner, all recruited from

the same mining project in Hedland that had been permanently mothballed, whooped and cheered. They recognised the beer, all right.

Jean didn't seem to realise what he'd received. He peered at the label, shrugged, and returned to his seat at the table with the construction team.

Shelley leaned toward Audra and said in a low voice, "Funny. I don't remember his name on the Secret Santa list when I paired everyone up. Isn't that your favourite beer?"

"A lot of people like it up in Broome," Audra defended herself. "Maybe someone decided to educate the Canadian with some of Australia's best beers."

"Or maybe someone gave it to him in the hope that he'd share it with you."

Audra shook her head. No way was someone at the station trying to matchmake her with her roommate. "They'd have to be the only person on the station who doesn't know about how I shouted at him the other night." Davis was like a village – once one person heard something, everyone knew it.

"Or they figured he'd need a sizeable bribe to get back into your good graces?"

That made Audra laugh. "It'll take more than beer to get on my good side."

Shelley looked uncomfortable. "I know that, but still. He hasn't behaved anywhere near as badly here as he did on the boat. Everyone talks about how friendly and helpful he is. The same sort of things they say about you." She hesitated, then ploughed on. "I imagine if he'd caused any trouble for you, you'd have raised the whole SAM, just like you did the other night."

Audra was still embarrassed at the memory, but that wouldn't stop her if Jean tried to get her to share a bed with him. "If he had, you wouldn't have had to wait to hear the gossip. You'd have heard me ripping him a new one all the way across the compound at SMQ."

"True."

A loud crack, like a gunshot, sounded outside, followed by several more.

Audra's eyes met Shelley's. "The lake," they both said together, sprinting for the door. They paused only long enough to grab coats and boots before they headed outside.

Sure enough, the solid surface had fractured in several places, and water sloshed between the gaps. Audra pointed her camera at it for a few minutes, before it became apparent that nothing else was going to happen. She switched it off and tucked the camera into her coat pocket.

"We can shower tonight," Audra said. She'd never craved the feeling of hot water cascading over her body quite this much.

"I think there'll be quite the queue," Shelley said, nodding toward the crowd who'd joined them outside.

"You know what this means, though? It means the new computer model I made works. An error margin of minutes, not days or weeks, like it was before." Audra's heart soared. "If I could test the model on some of the inland lakes, maybe we could turn it into a tool for predicting climate change effects. Maybe even turn it into a big enough project for me to do a PhD."

"You're as crazy as I was, looking for excuses to stay," Shelley grumbled. She eyed the crowd. "What about the bet they had going? Between the dance troupe and the synchronised swim team? My guys said before Christmas and yours said after, so for it to happen exactly today…"

"We could call the whole thing off," Audra said slowly, "or we could say it's a draw and they both have to perform at New Year's Eve. Let the other staff at Davis vote on the winner." She couldn't help grinning.

Shelley shrieked with laughter. "Oh, that's brilliant! A draw it is. We'll do it. Just wait until you see their faces when I tell them."

"Actually, I'd better start researching synchronised swimming. I may have coached, but it was all in swimming strokes for races or rescues. Not exactly pretty."

"Bite your tongue! Once you get their shirts off, those boys will be all kinds of pretty. I have to make mine dance." Shelley frowned. "And decide on a song."

"Good luck!" Audra called as she headed for the SAM and her laptop. Game on.

TWENTY-FIVE

"Don't forget your six-pack of sunshine!" Paul called after Jean, pointing at the beers Jean had left on the table.

Jean snatched up the box and tucked it under his arm. Fruit beer. What a strange gift. At first, he'd thought they were taking the piss, or at least that's what they called it when they were trying to feed him a crazy idea like it was some sort of scientific law. But the more they waxed lyrical about beer made from mangoes, of all things, the more he figured they must be telling the truth. Especially when they told him to ask his roommate, because she'd worked near the brewery that made it.

He wasn't about to ask Audra anything. After shouting at him the other night, she'd gone back to avoiding him. Which meant she was probably still out celebrating, so he could lie down on his bed and nurse his medication-induced hangover for a bit without anyone knowing. Maybe even take some Tylenol to take the edge off. If anyone asked, he'd say he'd overindulged at Christmas dinner. He wouldn't be lying, either. The last time he'd had a Christmas dinner that good, his mom had made it.

Jean stretched out on his bed, planning to stay there just long enough for his legs to stop aching.

He woke what felt like hours later, stiff from lying in one position for so long. Jean blinked the sleep from his eyes, wondering what had woken him.

"Merry Christmas to you, too, Jay," he heard Audra say.

"Did you get my present?" asked an eager male voice with a strong Aussie accent.

"Yes, thank you," she said. "I'll have to fish out some ice from the lake to celebrate the thaw with it."

"How's your Christmas been so far?"

"Lovely. Actually, it's my first white Christmas. There's still snow on the ground, even though it's summer."

"Mine sucks," he said.

Audra made a sympathetic sound. "What happened?"

"Nothing happened. I'm just home with my family, because that's what you do at Christmas. And they're taking turns, telling me off for signing up for that reality TV show, because that's what they do at Christmas."

Jean wanted to ask which reality TV show Audra's friend had been on, but he held his tongue. She might not have noticed him and he didn't want her to bite his head off for eavesdropping.

"I've already told you what I think about it. You can't expect me to suddenly change my mind and tell you they're wrong. It wasn't one of your brightest ideas." Audra sounded like she was trying not to laugh.

"Yeah, and I agree with you now, but that doesn't make it any easier. They're treating me like a teenager again. Irresponsible and incapable of making my own decisions. If you'd agreed to marry me, they wouldn't be doing this. They'd be too busy making wedding plans with you. I wish you were here."

Jean's mouth hung open. She'd turned down a marriage proposal? It didn't sound like he was some stranger she hated — she took his calls and he sent her Christmas presents when the postage to here must've been astronomical.

"Jay, even if I was there, I wouldn't be at your parents' place. I'd be at home, making Christmas dinner for my own family. To be honest, I'm happier here."

"I don't want to be here, either. Can I come visit you?" Jay asked.

"There's not enough water for showers, it's bloody freezing, and the recent storms have confined all the researchers to the station, so we're packed to the rafters with people. Even if you did find a way down here, you'd be lucky to get a couch to sleep on."

"I could share with you."

Audra snorted. "No, you couldn't. Besides, I already have a roommate."

Audra glanced at Jean's bunk and met his eyes.

Uhoh. Sprung.

Jean made the best of it. He sat up and shifted so he was visible in the angle of Audra's webcam. "Hi!" He got his first look at Audra's boyfriend, as that's what he had to be. The man looked familiar, somehow, but Jean couldn't place him.

Jay's eyes widened. "You're sleeping with another man?"

"Yes, Jay, and it's none of your business. You know what my advice is? Go home. Go back to the island and forget about your family. Family's great, but they can be a bit much sometimes. You've made your obligatory visit, and you don't have to stay any longer than you want to. Go home!"

"You really think so?" Jay had forgotten Jean already, it seemed, in light of his own problem. Some boyfriend.

"Yes! Now you go and enjoy your Christmas and your new year, too. I'm going to make like a Disney movie and go build a snowman." Audra ended the video call.

Now what was Jean supposed to say? He wanted to apologise for eavesdropping, but he'd been here first. She'd woken him up with her call.

He decided on a different tack. "So, is that your boyfriend?" Jean asked.

Audra scowled. "No. We used to work together at the resort. He still lives there."

"What reality show was he talking about?"

"*Rock Star Wants A Wife*. It only ran for one season and hopefully won't run again."

Nope. That didn't compute. Jean ventured, "Was he one of the wives, or…?"

Audra blew out an angry breath. "He was the bachelor. It didn't work out, because she was a homicidal bitch. Are we done with twenty questions, or are you going to ask me my bra size, too?"

With a huge effort, Jean managed to keep his eyes from straying to her breasts. He'd probably pushed his luck too far already, but he'd never been one to quit while he was ahead. "Why do you hate me so much?"

Hurt flared in her eyes. She opened her mouth, closed it, then opened it again. Still no words came out. Finally, she said, "I don't hate you. I don't hate anybody. Not even Jay and he…never mind. You probably wouldn't think he did anything wrong, either."

It wasn't an answer, but it was an improvement.

"Can we start over?" Jean asked cautiously. "Pretend I didn't have that accident last year, that you didn't have to nurse me, and that we're meeting for the first time as colleagues?" She looked too young to be a PhD candidate, but he'd been wrong before. He extended his hand. "Hi, I'm Jean-Pierre Pennant. I'm doing my PhD on king penguins with the University of Washington and this will be my third summer in Antarctica."

Audra took a deep breath. "I'm Audra Zujute. I'm a graduate meteorologist with the Australian Bureau of Meteorology and this is my second summer here, but I'm about to join an expedition to the South Pole as soon as this bad weather clears. My second trip there."

Jean whistled. "I haven't seen the pole yet."

Audra shrugged. "I haven't seen Heard Island yet, so we're even."

It was on the tip of his tongue to invite her to come with him, but Jean clamped his mouth shut. He wasn't on some holiday where he could bring a pretty girl along after he'd known her for all of five minutes. They were both here to work, before heading off in different directions to pursue vastly different research interests.

Audra closed the lid of her laptop. "By the way, I'm going to post a flyer on the noticeboard. First synchronised swimming training session will be tomorrow at three, by the lake. Just in case you hadn't heard we're on for New Year's Eve."

She left without waiting for a reply.

It wasn't until she was out of sight that he realised he hadn't gotten an answer to his question about her friend. Jean still couldn't remember where he'd seen the man before. If the man had been on reality TV, he couldn't be hard to find, so Jean grabbed his tablet and searched for the guy.

Pictures of Audra's friend filled the screen. Jay Felix, the lead singer of Chaya. Fuck. Jean had watched the band play live once. They'd driven all the way down to Seattle when he was still at college. Good concert, too.

So how did a young meteorologist come to be friends with one of the biggest rock stars in the world? No...not just friends. The man had asked her to marry him. She'd refused, but she hadn't left him alone like a normal person would. No, she still taunted him with the possibility that she might one day change her mind. She was leading the poor guy on.

Dangerous, just like he'd thought. He'd started to warm up to her, but that stopped now. Jean didn't have time to be distracted by some seductress who played with men's hearts like she did with Jay's.

She'd soon learn she was wasting her time with Jean. He'd show her he was a heartless bastard, immune to her charms, and then he'd escape to Heard Island. Like the Aussies said, no worries.

TWENTY-SIX

Audra took a deep breath. Now was not the time to tell them she'd never coached adults before — only children. And she'd never watched synchronised swimming at all until yesterday. Only the knowledge that Shelley hadn't danced competitively since high school and had never coached anyone kept her from backing out.

They couldn't stay in the water for more than five minutes, so the routine had to be very short. These guys could learn something short in a week, if they practised every day. If they messed up, at least they'd have a good laugh about it. She'd promised to feature the Davis Dolphins, as they'd styled themselves, on her video channel.

Audra surveyed the men lined up in front of her. All men. She cleared her throat. "Okay, because I've been told we're only allowed in the water for five minutes a day, we're going to have to practice this on land before taking it into the water. I've put together a really simple routine that we should all be able to do with only basic swimming skills. If you can float, submerge, and kick to the surface again, you should be fine. Is there anyone here who can't swim?"

Eight heads shook. They were all Aussies, except for Jean. Bloody hell. Now she was even more nervous.

"Good. Even more good news is that you can stay in your snow gear for the next few training sessions, as we'll be working in that snowfield." Audra pointed. "Okay, I want you to make a circle over there, and I'll show you the routine. Then I'll talk you through it so you can try it."

Snow crunched beneath their boots as the group walked with her to the practice field. She shouldn't be so nervous, but she was. "Spread out so I don't kick you," she said, waving her arms.

Audra took a deep breath and lay down in the snow. With all those men's faces peering down at her, she forced herself to describe the routine as she did it. When she got up, dusting snow off her clothes, she tried not to grin at the first snow angel she'd created. She had to look professional, not like a kid who wanted to build a snowman next.

"Okay, your turn, gentlemen," she called. "Lie down in the snow, make sure you can see me, don't worry about anyone else, and let's go!"

Who was she kidding? This was exactly like teaching swimming. Using half her body to demonstrate the moves while shouting the same thing over and over, interspersed with encouragement. With her arm in the air and one leg still waving around, Audra felt her body relax. This was easy.

One of the men scrambled to his feet. "I can't do this.

It's ridiculous." Jean stormed off.

Bewildered, Audra stared after him. What had happened to starting over?

Carl sat up. "He's right. This is ridiculous. So ridiculous it's going to be awesome. We could be the first synchronised swimming team in Antarctic history!"

The other guys sat up, too, smiles slowly warming their faces as they nodded. "He's a wanker, Audra," said one of the guys she didn't know. "Don't listen to him."

Audra blinked back tears. "I know. It's hard not to hear it, though, because he's my roommate. Wish he'd go to the bathroom and do it there instead."

A roar of laughter erupted, and she felt better still. Yes, she could do this. Jean could go bugger himself.

TWENTY-SEVEN

Staring down at the woman lying in the snow, with her white jacket and hat framing her smiling face making her look like some sort of snow angel, Jean almost forgot yesterday's resolution not to think about Audra. The seven other men standing around shared his thoughts, he was sure of it. Why couldn't she have stayed angry at him, like she was yesterday? Today she looked sweet and cheerful and waiting to be kissed…

"Your turn, gentlemen!" she sang out, springing to her feet.

Wincing, Jean lay down in the snow. He hadn't made snow angels like this in years. And the moves really were pretty simple. It was basically the same sequence repeated three times, then a couple of extra circles with his arms and it was done.

"Everyone got it?" Audra asked.

Someone said no, so they ran through the whole thing again. Jean was proud to say he didn't make a single mistake.

"Okay, now has everyone got it?" It seemed everyone had, so Audra continued: "I want you to close your eyes. I want you to imagine diving into the water at your favourite swimming spot. The beach, the pool – whatever you fancy – but don't make it too warm. The water's cool, so it'll be a little shock at first, but you'll quickly get used to it."

Jean visualised the college pool in Vancouver where he used to swim laps every morning. He could almost smell the chlorine, amplified by the humidity in the air. No, that water hadn't been cold. They'd heated it all year round so he could swim lap after lap without freezing.

A gust of wind blew across the station, bringing the smell of the icy sea to his nostrils. Ice. Salt. Cold water. He wasn't in a pool anymore. Instead, he was immersed in the Southern Ocean.

Audra continued, "You're going to push through the water and surface…"

Jean's head broke the surface and another gust of wind froze the water in his hair. He sucked in a desperate breath, then another, as he took stock of his surroundings. He was back in Atlas Cove, far from shore.

"Remember to kick your legs," Audra said.

Jean tried to kick, but his legs weren't responding, just as they hadn't at Heard Island. He was back in that nightmare again and this time he wouldn't survive. There was no Dairine to go home to. She didn't want him. He'd drown here and no one would care.

No!

Jean surged to his feet, breathing hard. "I can't do this. It's ridiculous." Before anyone could see the tears in his eyes, Jean hurried back to the station buildings. He knew he was limping, his legs stiffened by lying in the snow, but this time he didn't care. He headed for the men's bathroom in the SAM, which was empty at this time of day. He scrubbed at his face until all traces of tears were gone. He was ashamed of himself. What, was he afraid of water now? And swimming?

He dried his face and stared hard at his reflection. He wanted to head back outside and apologise to Audra for disrupting her class like that, but what was he supposed to tell her? He couldn't say he'd developed a fear of water. She and the others would laugh their heads off.

He was certain of one thing, though. He wouldn't be swimming with them in the lake, in case he freaked out like that again.

TWENTY-EIGHT

By the time New Year's Eve rolled around, Audra was exhausted. She was also worried about how her synchronised swimmers would actually manage their routine in the water when they'd only practised it in the snow, but she dismissed that thought as soon as it surfaced. Their performance wasn't a reflection on her. And it didn't matter how good they were. Not to them. They were intent on making history. It was almost enough to tempt her to join them.

"No, you can't," was Carl's response when she'd mentioned it. "We still need our coach, standing out of the water to remind us what to do, and you need to film it. My kids are waiting to watch this video. Besides, you've already made history all on your own. You're the first ever Antarctic swimming instructor, and synchronised swimming team coach. If anyone ever says it's impossible for a swimming teacher to work in Antarctica, we'll be able to point at your video and tell them that's bullshit, because you did it."

Mollified, Audra resolved to keep her clothes on. It was hardly a hardship – the air temperature wasn't much above freezing, and the water was colder still.

She and Shelley had agreed to let their groups perform as part of the evening's entertainment, before the bar opened and everyone could ring in the new year. Shelley's dancers went first, so everyone crowded into the LQ for what Shelley promised would be a fun performance.

Where was Shelley? Audra surveyed the room. Everyone was there – even Jean, who'd been avoiding her all week. But she couldn't see Shelley.

Laughter erupted by the entrance to the kitchen, and Audra raised her camera high to see over the crowd. When the dance troupe came into view, she couldn't help laughing, either. They were all clad in their thermal underwear and nothing else.

The group lined up on the impromptu stage with the diminutive Shelley standing front and centre, dressed in a particularly fetching set of rainbow striped long johns and a matching top.

Shelley struck a pose. "Hit it, DJ."

Music blared through the speakers: Beyoncé's *Single Ladies*.

Audra laughed so hard she was certain the camera footage would be too shaky to see when she checked it later, but how could a girl not laugh when a dozen well-built men pranced around onstage in their underwear? With her boss, no less.

She had to admit, they'd be a hard act to beat, but even as the swim team clapped hard for their colleagues, they muttered to each other how it took more guts to perform in icy water instead of just their underwear.

Once Shelley's dancers had finished, everyone trooped outside to find a good spot by the lake to watch. The swim team – who'd decided to call themselves the Davis Snowmen, because it was too bloody cold for dolphins down here – disappeared inside a sea container that now sat on their snowy practice field, acting as their temporary change room. Audra waited outside, camera in hand, worrying that Jean was right about this being a ridiculous idea. He wasn't in sight among the crowd. Audra squared her shoulders. If he wasn't here, he'd be the one missing out. Her boys were going to put on an awesome show, every bit as good as Shelley's dancers. Sure, they'd picked a Disney song and not a Beyoncé one, but where else but Antarctica could you have snowmen in summer? They'd even spent the morning building a row of snowmen along the lake shore between the sea container and the water.

"Hey, Audra, can you get someone to turn on the music?" a muffled voice said from inside the sea container.

Audra repeated the request and the PA system started playing the snowman's song about summer from the movie *Frozen*.

The container door slammed open and seven men skipped out, wearing white shower caps with carrots on their heads and tighty whities below. Audra's jaw dropped. She didn't remember them mentioning this part of the performance.

Carl winked at her. "Watch us win this for you, coach."

They marched into the lake until they were waist deep, when they formed up and kicked off the routine they'd practised in the snow. She had to admit they weren't bad at all. They'd added their own little flourishes to make the audience laugh, so they got a rousing cheer as they hit the ninety-second mark and made their way up the shore to their change room. They all paused to pose in the doorway before the door clanged shut behind them at the end of the song.

"Fuck, I'm freezing," Audra heard someone say from inside the container.

"Oi, watch where you're putting that carrot!"

She didn't think anyone else heard, as the watching crowd cheered and applauded before heading back inside for a drink.

Soon, only Audra and Shelley stood beside the lake, waiting for the swim team to emerge.

"They win, hands down," Shelley said. "Swimming in that frozen lake in their undies? That takes balls."

"Yeah, I think I left mine in the lake," someone shouted from inside the container.

"Do you think he meant…?" Shelley began.

Both Audra and Shelley laughed.

The men emerged, now dressed as heavily as the girls, and hotfooted it up to the LQ.

"Save me some champagne!" Audra called as she and Shelley brought up the rear.

Shelley watched them go. "I thought your roommate was supposed to be swimming with them."

Audra winced. "He, um, backed out in the first training session."

"Before or after they decided to dance in their undies to a Disney song?"

"Before, actually. I wasn't in on the undies decision."

Their boots crunched on the gravel for a few moments before Shelley said, "Did you hear the *Investigator*'s due to arrive within the week? It could be as early as tomorrow."

"Is that the survey vessel that's going to Heard Island?" Shelley nodded.

"What about the South Pole expedition?"

"We don't have a date for that one yet. The next two weeks really aren't favourable. At this rate, it might be February before we leave." Shelley kicked a stone off the path. "I have to send you to Heard. You know that, right? The Director wants you to install the weather station there. Even if it means you miss out on the South Pole."

Audra sighed. "I know. And Heard Island has all that wildlife, like you said, which is what the video channel viewers want to see most. My most popular video so far is that one of Jen's seal. Though that might change when I post today's one."

"Do you think you can handle it by yourself? I mean, you'll have a whole team out there with you, who you can ask for help if you need it, and once you get the satellite uplink working on the island, I'll only be a short call away. So will Kingston, if it comes down to it. But you'll be the only meteorologist, and their safety officer. Lives will depend on your daily forecasts, and the decisions you make."

Audra managed a smile as she waved in the direction of the lake. "They survived all right. It's not like I haven't been forecasting for expeditions before, and Heard Island isn't as cold as Dome Argus. I should be fine."

"Heard has its own dangers," Shelley insisted. "There's a reason we don't keep a permanent base there. The whole island is a volcano, too, though I don't know the last time it erupted. It might not be active any more. Have you asked your roommate about his accident there last time?"

"No," Audra admitted. She hadn't asked him much at all, and she didn't intend to, but the expedition's safety was far more important than her personal feelings toward the man. She'd put everyone in danger if she didn't find out how to avoid a similar incident to the one that had given him his limp. "But I will."

"Good." Shelley grinned. "Because I don't want to miss out on this South Pole expedition. It'll probably be my last, as I won't be returning after the summer's over. I miss my husband and my daughter, and I don't want to miss any more of her growing up. I might even want more children."

Children. The furthest thing from Audra's mind right now, especially in relation to her future.

"Then I'd better do a really good job at Heard, so they'll give me your job when I get back," Audra replied cheerfully, but the statement wasn't as flippant as she tried to make it sound. She would do an amazing job, she vowed, so she could win both the competition and a more permanent place out here.

The swim team was just the start. If she really wanted to make her mark on the world, she'd need to do more than just make a few videos. She needed to do something truly remarkable. Unique. Newsworthy. She only wished she knew what.

TWENTY-NINE

Jean typed furiously, determined to finish these papers before the Investigator dropped him off at Heard Island for what could be his last ever expedition. What had happened last time could happen again, and he might not survive. That meant leaving a research legacy behind to live on after him. He'd already sent the current version of his thesis to Louis, telling him that if he didn't get any new results from Heard Island, he wanted his supervisor to submit it for him. A posthumous PhD was better than none at all.

It wasn't that he wanted to die. No way. Jean wanted to live and discover and have a long, prosperous career after his PhD. He was just being practical, that's all. That stupid swimming class had brought back his nightmares with a vengeance, and now he was about to set foot on that cursed island again, the nightmares seemed all too real.

He didn't waste time socialising with the crew aboard

this ship. They were just his ride to Heard Island, where he'd be working alone for weeks until they returned to pick him up. He had enough supplies to last six weeks, though he only expected to be there four at most.

Someone pounded on the metal hatch to his cabin. "Hey, Pennant. We're approaching Heard now. ETA 1600."

Jean checked his computer. He had two hours, then. "Fine." He skimmed through what he'd written. It would have to do. He emailed the draft papers to Louis, telling him he'd be out of communication range for four to six weeks.

In a matter of hours, he'd be preparing to count penguins. Jean grinned. He packed his laptop and the few items that weren't already stowed, and carried his bags up on deck. Some of the crew had already started to bring his gear out of the hold, so he helped them, glad of the extra time he'd put in at the station gym at Davis. His mind might be weak enough to let the nightmares in, but his body was strong enough to fight off almost anything.

The mountain came into view first – cloud-topped Big Ben, white with snow and glaciers so that it looked like a mirage among the clouds. He knew better, though. Big Ben's old lava tubes had nearly been his undoing.

The captain declared the ocean too rough to send him out tonight, so Jean found he had to wait until morning, when the swell had died down a bit, or so he hoped.

Jean just nodded and returned to his cabin to get more work done.

Day dawned with smaller waves, so Jean wolfed down his breakfast and set to work with the other crew, loading the Zodiacs. He went ashore with the first boat, filled to the gunwales with supplies, and he soon found himself lugging boxes from the rocky beach to a safe spot above the waterline, where his camp would be for the next month. Once the boats were unloaded, they returned to the ship for more, but Jean plodded on, dragging box after box until he'd stacked far more than he remembered bringing from McMurdo. Had Davis sent him extra supplies? The boxes looked like the ones he'd seen at the Aussie stations. He hoped they hadn't sent him a crate of that foul black spread they liked so much. Beer wouldn't be so bad, though.

The Australian Antarctic Division had promised him a hut, and it looked like the boats were bringing it ashore now. It looked for all the world like a water tank, wallowing in the waves as two boats towed it across Spit Bay and into the shallows. It took six of them to wrestle it ashore until someone managed to push it over on its side. Then it only took three people to roll it up to the campsite.

"Where do you want us to set it up?" a crewman panted.

Jean pointed at the spot where they'd assembled the mess hall last year. "That'll do nicely." He paused. "Do you need a hand?"

"Nah, we got this."

Jean nodded. "Mind if I go take a look at the penguin colonies on the beaches on the other side of the spit? I'll need to do a bit of reconnaissance to work out how long it'll take to survey everything here before I'll need a lift west to Atlas Cove."

"Knock yourself out, mate. I'll come find you when we're done."

The American crew he'd worked with last time wouldn't have let him escape set up. Jean decided to get out of there before the Aussies changed their minds. Grabbing his field pack, he set off past the ruins of the old sealers' camp to where the penguin colonies were supposed to be. It was easy going for a while, as long as he avoided the cushion plants, but then he hit snow. Well, snow on one side and a freezing cold pond of water on the other side, which was no choice at all, really. Of course Jean picked snow.

His boots plunged into the soft powder nearly to the knee, but he ploughed on, determined to reach Doppler Hill or at least a high enough vantage point where he could see the hill. He yanked one foot out of its snowdrift and set it down again, only to hit ice. His foot shot forward, catapulting the rest of him backwards into the snow.

Swearing, Jean staggered to his feet, bruised and angry but not ready to give up yet. He pressed on.

Four more missteps later, the last one landing him quite painfully on a pile of rocks hidden under a light dusting of snow, Jean admitted defeat. The ice evidently extended much further than he'd realised – he'd probably found one of the glaciers named but not marked on his map.

He glanced in the direction of the camp to make sure he was out of sight, then dropped to his hands and knees to crawl over the snow so he wouldn't slip a sixth time. By the time he reached rock, he was more than ready to stand up again, if only to stop his knees from freezing up completely. He walked carefully back to camp, where he found the guys stacking empty pallets and preparing to leave.

"We're pretty much done here," the crewman in charge said. "Unless you need anything else, we're shipping out. See you in four weeks, and don't forget your radio check-ins."

Jean nodded. He eyed the Zodiacs. If he took one of those and kept close to the beach, he wouldn't have to hike across the glacier at all. "Can I keep one of your boats?" he asked.

The crewman shrugged. "That one's supposed to be yours, anyway. You should have enough fuel for that and the generator, as long as you don't try to head to Australia or the mainland in it."

"I'm staying right here, where my research is," Jean said firmly.

"See you in four weeks, then."

The guys piled into the remaining boat and cruised across Spit Bay to the *Investigator*.

Jean stood on the beach for a moment, watching them, but his knees threatened to seize up again, so he decided to warm them up a bit more with a walk along Elephant Spit to Spit Point, where the reports said there was a small colony of king penguins. At least there wouldn't be any snow to trip him up, or ice to pitch him on his ass.

THIRTY

"You sure you're going to be all right here with him?" Kevin asked, shielding his eyes as he stared at the sun, trying to angle the solar panels just right. "He pretty much hid in his cabin the whole trip and didn't talk to anyone. Completely up himself, too good to associate with lowly crew like us." He sniffed. "What is he, some big, important American academic?"

"Just a PhD candidate, same as most of the other researchers on your ship, except for the professor," Audra replied cheerfully, kneeling in the volcanic dust to check the connections to the satellite dish. Everything seemed sound to her. "I don't know what his problem is, except that he had an accident last year and had to cut his trip short, so this might be his last chance to finish his research."

"Still doesn't explain the attitude," Greg grumbled, testing the door on the toilet cubicle. "This is done. Sleep quarters and the bathroom. Have you got the power hooked up yet, Kev?"

A yell came from inside the tank hut, before the door flew open and a man stuck his head out. "Warn a man before you plug in the power. I didn't hear the generator start up." Darsh glared at the other two men.

Kevin held his hands up in surrender. "Hey, don't look at me, mate. I'm still setting up the solar panels and the genset's over there by the fuel drums. The only way you could've gotten shocked is if the batteries are charged. They weren't supposed to be. Lemme test them." He pulled out a multimeter and proceeded to check the storage batteries. "Looks like you have enough power for two days here, as long as you don't turn the hut into a sauna with the heating. The solar panels should charge up enough during the day to get you through the night, but you've got the generator as backup, just in case. Oh, and Carrie figured you might want something other than dehydrated field rations, so she packed you some of today's bake, last night's leftovers and what looks like a month's worth of chocolate. I hope she didn't give you all the Tim Tams!"

"Radio me if she has, and I'll make sure not to eat them all, so there's some left to tempt you guys back to pick us up," Audra said. "Right, so if everything's all set up, I should try the satellite connection to see if it's working." She pulled her laptop out of her pack and propped it open in her lap. "Okay, I think it's found the network. Logging on…and I'm in! Anyone want to know which song's number one in this year's Hottest 100?"

Kevin and Darsh exchanged a glance. "We were wondering if you could include us in your video of the camp. Maybe even say we helped you set up and all."

Audra laughed in delight. "You've been watching my video channel?"

All three men nodded. "It was cool to see Christmas at Davis. It kind of made us want to hurry to get there sooner. And that video with the seal…"

Everyone loved Jen and the seal. Audra needed to record more footage of the seals here, and hope they were just as popular as Jen's one.

She clambered to her feet. "Right, let's find a spot where I can film the camp and maybe get a good shot of the ship and the beach, too."

The guys lined up, and Audra started recording.

"Welcome to Heard Island, where we've just arrived. The valiant crew from the *RV Investigator* have set up our camp here at Spit Bay, for which I'm very grateful, because they're very busy men. After dropping us off, they still have to help out another expedition who are mapping the sea floor and ocean currents of the Antarctic convergence, which I believe has never been studied at this kind of depth before. So a special thanks to Kevin, Darsh and Greg, for taking the time to make sure I can still broadcast to you from this lonely island, and thanks to all their crewmates still aboard the *Investigator*. Here's to a good summer for research!" Audra panned the camera around the camp. "I'll take you on a tour of my luxury accommodation later, and maybe even let you join me for dinner. Wait 'til you see the gourmet cuisine we get out here. You'll wish you were here!" She switched the camera off. "I feel like such an idiot talking to myself like that," she admitted.

"You don't sound it," Kevin reassured her. "Everyone at

the bases wants to know what the Penguin Weather Girl's up to next, and it gives our families back home a bit of excitement. They'll think we're famous for getting a spot on your show."

That made Audra laugh. "Let me do one last check to make sure we've got everything, and you guys can head back to the ship, if you want. I should be able to handle unpacking. When Jean comes back, I'll put him to work, too."

To her surprise, Kevin folded her into a hug. "You tell us if he causes you any trouble, right? You're the ranking safety officer on the island, which puts you in charge. Don't forget that." He gestured toward the Zodiacs. "You did a great job towing today. I'd take you on as crew any day, if you get bored doing science stuff at the stations. Will one boat be enough? If you want a second one, we can probably spare it, but I'd need to get you another drum of fuel."

"One's fine, honestly. I doubt we'll even use it. After all, my job's to set up the weather station and he's counting birds, I think." Audra grinned.

"Good luck with bird boy, then. I think he's coming back now." Kevin jerked his chin in the direction of the Stephenson Glacier. "What kind of idiot climbs a glacier without snow chains on his boots?"

"I'll make sure he's wearing them tomorrow. I'm the safety officer, after all. If you could just tell him you're going, to make sure he doesn't need anything else that I've forgotten, I'll go check to see that the video's uploaded okay." Audra headed for the hut.

She'd just confirmed that the video was already live on her channel and a few people had watched it, when Darsh knocked on the door of the hut. "It's up," Audra said.

"Thank you," Darsh replied. "I checked the stove and the lights and the heating. Everything works. You know where the spare gas bottles are, yes?"

"Yes," Audra said, pointing out the window, where she could see Kevin and Greg boarding their boat. "It looks like they're going. You don't want them to leave without you. You'll be stuck here with us for a month."

"I guess not," Darsh said with a shy smile, and he left.

Audra watched through the window as they motored up to the ship, before the *Investigator* cast off her moorings and manoeuvred out of the bay. A little frisson of fear curled around her belly. Davis had been isolated, but this was an island in the middle of nowhere. An island she shared with only one other person: a man she barely knew, and what she did know of him was hardly encouraging.

Jean stood on the beach, looking out to sea. As if compelled by some desire to follow the only other people within miles, he set off along Elephant Spit, his eyes fixed on the ship steaming away.

Audra sagged. She was hot and sweaty from carrying all the gear into camp, and dirty from setting up the hut and the satellite dish. She'd give a lot of money for a hot shower right now, but showers were once again an impossible luxury. They had enough water for drinking and food preparation, but if they wanted wash water, she had two options: a bucket of seawater or melted snow.

Not wanting to bother with either of those icy options, Audra pulled out some of the supplies she'd packed for the South Pole expedition she'd never joined. A pack of wet wipes were more than enough to get her clean, even if they were nowhere near as satisfying as a shower. She switched on the heater, stripped off, and went to work.

THIRTY-ONE

Jean hadn't made it halfway along the rocky spit before he realised that the brown lumps lined up like sausages weren't rocks at all. Instead, he'd walked into the middle of an elephant seal haul-out area, and the huge creatures were waking up.

Not good. Especially as seals could move faster than a tired man with a limp. They wouldn't even have to do anything. If one of them landed on him, it'd crush him under tons of fat and muscle.

For the second time that day, Jean admitted defeat. Today just wasn't a good day for penguins. Maybe tomorrow he'd have better luck with the boat. He backed away from the seals as slowly as he dared, before they lost interest in him and flopped back down, dormant once more.

He trudged back to camp, resolving to unpack his

supplies so he had all the food safely in the hut, along with as many of the water casks as he could fit in there to keep it from freezing. A quick scan of the camp revealed no food or water – nothing but empty pallets that had once held his supplies. Had the ship's crew shifted everything inside for him? He should have thanked them. When he made his regular radio check-in tonight, he would. He'd tell the radio operator to thank…shit. He couldn't remember any of their names. He'd been so caught up in his own dread at being back here that he'd forgotten to ask. They must think he was a complete dick. Well, he had been.

Sighing, he grabbed the handle and opened the hut door.

"What the fuck are you doing here?" he cried…

…and stopped dead, like a deer caught in headlights.

The most divine pair of headlights evolution ever gave a woman. Two globes of creamy soft flesh, garnished by a pair of pink nipples that made him think of cotton candy, and wonder if they'd taste as sweet. His gaze travelled down more creamy curves, to thighs that looked as soft as silk, glistening with moisture. What would it feel like to glide between them, deep inside her as he buried his face between that perfect pair of tits?

His blood rushed south to salute her like the beautiful woman before him deserved.

Audra covered her breasts with her arm and twisted to turn her back on him. "Stop staring and get out. And if you're going to jerk off, do it where I don't have to see or hear it."

His mouth unable to close or even form words, Jean stumbled out of the hut and closed the door with shaking hands.

He couldn't get the picture out of his head. If he'd been a religious man, her body looked like the answer to a lifetime of prayers. Even now, he couldn't stop thinking about the things he wanted to do to her.

As if that would ever happen. The woman hated him. Probably even more now he'd walked in on her naked.

In all her naked glory…

Groaning, Jean strode for the bathroom and slammed the door behind him. Yanking down his pants, he let his imagination go wild. Just for a few minutes, he allowed himself to dream about what it would be like to make love to the girl he'd seen in the hut just now. Not quick and joyless, like sex with Dairine, but slow and sensual and pleasurable so when she reached her peak, Audra would moan and cry out his name.

His hand was a poor substitute, but he made do. Had to, so he wouldn't pitch a pop-up tent in his pants every time he saw her from now on. Because she was stuck on this island with him now, for the next month. And he couldn't afford to give in to distraction, or desire.

He let out a shuddering sigh and cleaned himself up, leaning against the bathroom wall to support his shaky legs and weak knees after such a powerful release. She didn't need to know that he'd jerked off, just like she'd told him to. He chided himself for his loss of control, staring at her like that instead of having the decency to avert his eyes. He hadn't expected to come face to face with a goddess who could have starred in his most erotic fantasies, is all. She would feature in those fantasies now he'd seen her, as he'd never get that picture out of his head. Fifty bucks said he'd be dreaming of cotton candy tonight.

So much for being alone on the island!

"Jean?" Audra said tentatively. "I'm finished, and I'm decent. It's safe to come back inside now."

He emerged from the bathroom, keeping his sheepish eyes on the ground so he wouldn't look at her. Couldn't look at her, now he knew what was under her boots and expedition gear.

The pinnacle of evolution. The most perfect pair of –

Jean arrested that thought before it went any further. He was here to find penguins, not fantasise about his roommate.

"What are you doing here?" he asked again, more politely this time.

"Setting up a permanent remote weather station, and keeping both of us safe until the ship returns for us in four weeks. Which just got a lot harder. When you walked in like that, I nearly pushed you back out the door on your arse." Audra's brow furrowed and she set her hands on her hips. "Next time, knock, all right?"

"Yes, ma'am," he said to her boots. "I'm sorry. I'm really, really sorry. I didn't know anyone else was here and to walk in and see..." He waved at her body, not trusting himself to say what he was thinking. All those superlatives wouldn't sound like the compliments he intended them to be. Instead, he'd sound like the sleaziest work colleague who ever crawled out from under a rock.

"Yes." Audra coughed. "Tell you what. Let's forget about it, and do our best to make sure it doesn't happen again. We're going to be working closely together for the next few weeks and – "

No, they wouldn't be working together. She'd be doing her weather stuff here and he'd be off hunting penguins. They'd be roommates, that's all. Ones who spent as little time together as possible, just like at Davis.

Nevertheless, he nodded and agreed to her suggestions, which should stop him from seeing her naked again. Good thing, too. If he came face to face with those incredible tits again, he wasn't sure he could resist the urge to drop to his knees and beg to touch. To taste. Two things he would never, ever do, he swore.

THIRTY-TWO

Audra couldn't get the image out of her head. The way he'd stared at her. Hungrily, desperately…yes, there'd been plenty of lust in his eyes, but something else, too. Longing? Like he really, really admired what he saw, and he wanted…

What a married man shouldn't want from a woman who wasn't his wife! Audra scolded herself.

To his credit, he hadn't acted on the urge, and he'd apologised for it. Plus, he was staring at her shoes and not her boobs. That put him a cut above Jay, in her opinion.

"I'll make dinner tonight, but tomorrow's your turn," she said. "Carrie packed some of last night's pasta into a supply crate, and it looks like there's enough for two."

"Who's Carrie?" he asked.

"The cook aboard the *Investigator*. Kevin told me she gave us some other treats from her stores, too — "

"Who's Kevin?"

Audra blew out a breath. "Did you avoid everyone on the *Investigator* like you avoided me at Davis? Don't you know the names of anyone you work with? Kevin just spent most of the day helping me put this camp together with Darsh and Greg."

He stared miserably at the floor. "I figured I'd set up camp when I got back. I wanted to get a feel for the island so I could plan out my research schedule. He just asked me where to put the hut. I didn't realise you were all here working while I was…"

Audra almost felt sorry for him, but she'd seen researchers like him before. Usually, it was their first trip south and they weren't familiar with the rules established to keep them safe. Jean hadn't been particularly safe last trip, though, so maybe he'd missed out on a proper briefing. That made it her job.

"Okay, here goes: Antarctic expedition 101. First, we establish base camp. No research until we know where we'll eat, drink, sleep and go to the loo. The bathroom, I mean. We don't skip meals. We don't skimp on sleep. And we definitely don't leave camp alone." She fixed her gaze on him. "D'you hear me?"

He lifted his eyes to her face in outrage. "What? You expect me to tag along with you while you do weather things, when I have more important research to do? No. That's bullshit. It's not going to happen."

For a moment, the mischievous part of her wanted to tell him, yes, that he'd be forced to follow her around, carrying her equipment for four weeks. She could do it, too, though she'd probably get into trouble for it much later, when his university found out what she'd done. They were paying for her to be out here, after all. Jean was a minor inconvenience. An inconvenience who came with the significant perk of being a penguin expert. If anyone could help her get good wildlife videos that would go viral, it was him.

Audra wet her lips. "Actually, it'll probably only take me a day or two to set up the weather station, once I work out where to put it. I figure if I tag along with you for the first few days, it'll help me get a feel for the best place to install it. Once it's in, I'm free to help you with your research." She grinned. "I've always wanted to learn more about penguins."

He shook his head. "I'm not sharing my findings with you. Not before I've had a chance to write and submit my thesis, or at least some papers."

Audra suppressed a snort. He was one of those researchers. "Keep your secrets. I don't care about them. Who would I tell, anyway? But you're going to have to learn to cooperate and share information, at least a little. Because the person who pisses off the meteorologist won't get the weather forecasts. And knowing when it'll rain, or snow, or the tide's going to be unusually high, or there's a bad storm coming in, will make a big difference to what you get done. Is your secret penguin business worth so much to you?"

She could see him thinking, sizing her up. Funnily enough, his eyes didn't once stray to her chest.

"So, for two days I help you with your weather station, and for the other twenty-six, you're my research assistant?" he asked.

Put like that, it didn't sound fair. But twenty-six days of penguin watching…

"Pretty much, yeah. Barring bad weather, of course. Which I'll warn you about, because we don't want a repeat of your accident from last year." She bit her lip. "For my own safety, and for yours, I need to know what happened, to stop it from happening again. Whether you love me or hate me or something in between, I really am here to help you accomplish what you didn't last year. So, what do you say? We work together until we have to leave this lovely place? Do we have a deal?"

His eyes were still searching. Maybe he didn't trust her yet. Good thing he didn't have to for this to work. "We do," Jean said finally.

"Good. Shake on it." She held out her hand.

A tingle ran through her fingers at his touch, before his hand engulfed hers. He was as gentle as warm water as he shook her hand, and the warmth spread all the way up her arm. Strange. It sure hadn't felt like this when he'd grabbed her on the ship.

As if to prove her point, he released her of his own accord, without needing to be stabbed.

Audra let out a breath she hadn't known she was holding. Things were off to a better start than she'd expected.

THIRTY-THREE

Why was she here? Oh, that's right. To stop him from falling in a hole again. Jean wanted to laugh. She was a far more dangerous distraction than any cushion plant, because if he fell into her hole, he'd never get out. He wouldn't even want to try.

Outside, where it was cold and she'd have to keep her clothes on, he'd be able to concentrate better. In here, in such close quarters, it was a lot harder.

While she heated up dinner at the tiny gas burner, he unrolled his sleeping bag on the bunk across from hers. The shelves above both beds that might have doubled as bunks if there'd been more people on the island now held the bulk of their supplies. Including the pack of wet wipes he'd found her stroking down her body when he'd walked in earlier…

He had to stop. This was doing his head in. Jean racked

his brain for something, anything, to take his mind off how much he wanted to take this woman to bed. To lie her down on his bunk and taste…

"Do you want me to tell you about what happened last time?" Jean asked loudly, hoping to drown out his own thoughts.

Audra glanced over her shoulder. "Yes, please."

So he did. He started with the cushion plant, the cave, then coming up in the middle of the cove and swimming ashore. Dragging himself into the Apple hut and calling for help. Help that finally came, in the form of herself.

He left out two things that she didn't really need to know. First was the penguin population he'd thought he'd seen. There was a reason he'd been out alone that day, and he barely knew the woman. He definitely didn't trust her. The other…he wasn't sure why he didn't mention Dairine. Maybe because it was more than a little embarrassing to admit that he'd used his ex-wife as the motivation he'd needed to live. Holding on to someone who didn't want him made him weak, and he didn't want Audra to think that. Or maybe it was because just thinking about his ex-wife or saying her name hurt so much. More weakness, right there. That's why women didn't want him. They wanted some guy who'd step in and save them from everything, not someone who risked everything for a dream.

"Okay, I think it's ready." Audra divided the food into two bowls and handed him one. "I hope it's not too hot."

The pasta sent up a cloud of steam, but it smelled delicious, so Jean took the risk, which paid off. It tasted as good as it smelled and the heat helped chase off some of the chill in his bones he hadn't even noticed until now.

Audra sat with her bowl in her lap. "If I understand your story correctly, there's probably only two things we need to do, in order to avoid a similar accident." She held up a finger. "One, we be careful around cushion plants. You'll have to point them out to me tomorrow, so I know what to watch out for. And two, neither of us leaves camp alone. Not even for a short walk."

Jean wanted to argue about the alone bit, but with his mouth full, he just nodded. She wouldn't understand why he'd gone out looking for those penguins alone. The weather wasn't much of a secret, like a new species or a remarkable recovery from extinction would be. Besides, she wasn't a researcher. She had a science degree, sure, but she wasn't driven by the same passion to discover like he was.

If he ever did settle down with a woman, he'd want her to share that passion. There had to be women researchers out there who were truly passionate about their work. Maybe one day, he'd wind up on an island with a seal researcher, or maybe even a marine biologist, and…

"What's your plan for tomorrow?" Audra asked.

Count penguins, like he intended to do every day for the next four weeks.

"Check out the king penguin population at Spit Point," he said. It wasn't as far, and he could sit in the boat, which would give his legs a rest after today. They'd already started aching and tomorrow, they'd be agony.

"Okay. How long will that take?"

He considered. "A day. Maybe two. I usually try to get each colony a few different times a day, over a couple of days, if I can. It makes the count more accurate."

Audra nodded. "All right. Does it have to be two days in a row, or any two days while we're here?"

"Any two days."

"And after that?"

"There's meant to be a huge colony near Doppler Hill. If it's as big as the old reports say, we're looking at a week, at least. Maybe more, depending on how long it takes to get out there. And then the same again for a second pass. We'll need to take the boat – "

Audra held up a hand. "Wait. I think I remember Doppler Hill from one of last year's expedition maps. The geologists were studying the Stephenson Glacier, which runs down Big Ben, between us and the hill, and into the little meltwater lagoon at the bottom. They said they did it on foot. Are you saying they took a boat instead?"

"I don't know," he admitted. "I never made it that far south. We were supposed to come here after I was finished at Atlas Cove, but then I had that accident and – "

"Everything went south," Audra finished for him with a smile.

"Yeah." Jean resumed eating his dinner.

"It looks like we should have enough time for all of it, even allowing for some days off for bad weather, which we're bound to get out here." Audra nodded, looking satisfied, then started eating.

"I thought you were supposed to control the weather. That's why you came along, right?" Jean ventured.

"I wish!" Then she laughed, and once again Jean couldn't take his eyes off her.

If he'd believed in magic, he'd call her a witch, because every time she smiled or laughed, she had him enchanted.

THIRTY-FOUR

Audra started the outboard motor and set off at a slow cruise, parallel to the shore. "So, are you going to teach me a bit about penguins so I know what to look for?"

"What do you want to know?" Jean shouted back.

Audra thought a moment. "Well, why aren't we stopping to count those penguins, or those ones? There's dozens of them all the way along here, at least two different kinds, but you're not even looking at them, let alone asking me to stop. I thought you needed these numbers for your research."

"They're not king penguins," Jean said, pointing. "The black and white ones over there are gentoo penguins. The ones with the bunches of yellow feathers on the sides of their heads are macaroni penguins. Not the right species. I'm only studying king penguins."

"Why?"

He looked surprised by the question. Slowly, he answered, "Because they're different to all the others." He lifted his chin. "Tell me what you know about penguins."

Audra had to think about that one. "They eat krill."

"Not king penguins. They like bigger fish and squid. Stuff that swims more than a hundred metres below the surface. They're one of the deepest divers."

"They mate for life."

Jean winced. "Actually, king penguins don't. Especially if the chick doesn't survive. They find a new mate right away, because they breed for most of the year."

"The dads look after the babies while the mums go fishing."

"King penguins share parenting. They have crèches for the juveniles, but the babies go from mom's feet to dad's and back again."

Audra racked her brain for something else. "They like sitting on icebergs." She knew he was going to refute this one – all the penguins she'd pointed out were sitting on rock, not ice.

"King penguins avoid ice. Their colonies are all on rocky beaches at sub-Antarctic islands. And the juveniles camouflage better with the rock. I'll show you when we find the colony."

"They're endangered, especially by climate change," she said triumphantly.

"You'd be right for most penguin species, but not with king penguins. King penguins are flourishing, mostly because they were nearly wiped out by whalers and sealers."

"But they're not whales or seals. Why would they kill penguins?" Audra demanded.

"Did you see those big, rusted cauldron things on the edge of camp, near the old wooden huts?" Jean asked. When Audra nodded, he continued, "Those are trypots. They'd cut up whale and seal blubber and boil it down in those to get the oil. And they needed fuel for the fires. Did you notice there aren't any trees on the island?"

Audra hadn't, but a quick scan now told her this place was almost as barren of plant life as the mainland. All she saw were the brown and green mounds Jean had called cushion plants, or azorella. "Did they burn all the trees?" Even as she said it, it didn't make sense. Unless the penguins had used the trees for something, but they didn't seem to miss them now. Especially if, like Jean said, they were recovering.

Jean laughed. "Everyone says that. No. Hydrocarbons are a much better fuel than wood. Penguins have a lot of fat on them, so they used to feed the fire with the biggest penguins they could find: king penguins."

"Oh, no! That's horrible. Tell me you're joking," Audra demanded.

Jean shook his head. "I wish I were. Like I said, they nearly died out. Now they're not being used as firewood, the populations are recovering. That's why I'm out here, counting birds and comparing it to the satellite photos. I've already submitted two papers. That's why I was too busy to socialise on the ship." He sounded bitter.

Now Audra felt even worse for criticising him about it earlier. Not to mention it was kind of cool how he was following one of the few species that weren't dying out. She opened her mouth to apologise.

"Stop the boat!" Jean shouted. "Those are king

penguins, and we need to count them, photograph them, and count them again. Especially the babies in the middle. Ready?"

Audra shut off the motor and dropped the anchor. The water was so clear she saw it clunk to the rocks below. She pulled out her camera. "I'm ready."

THIRTY-FIVE

Jean clambered stiffly out of the Zodiac, tired and hurting but happy. The last population estimates for the Spit Point colony were around a hundred and fifty pairs, but both he and Audra had counted over two hundred, on both trips. Judging by the number of juveniles, there were still a few adults out fishing, too, which could push the number higher still. He'd have to check his notes to make some estimates, but it was possible that this colony had doubled in size since the last survey. That kind of population growth was just unheard of. A finding like that was a paper all on its own, even before he'd made it out to Doppler Hill or Atlas Cove.

The walk up the beach to the hut was nothing short of torture. All of yesterday's bumps and bruises had grown into a bone-deep ache pretty much from the waist down. Probably a good thing the only action he'd get for a while would be in his dreams, if last night was any indication. He glanced at Audra. Penguins would fly before he told her how she'd sat astride him naked in last night's best dream.

He'd have to wait until she used the bathroom so he could take some pain pills to take the edge off again. He hadn't brought the strong ones he'd taken at Christmas, which were probably what he needed right now, but the hangover afterwards just wasn't worth it. Not when he had fieldwork to do.

As they reached camp, Audra said, "You get started with dinner. I'll be with you in a minute."

Jean hotfooted it into the hut, determined to get the pills down his throat before she was done in the bathroom. Then he could make dinner.

When Audra cracked open the door, he had a pot of water heating on the stove and his head down in a box of supplies from McMurdo. "We ate the last of the bread with lunch, so it's field rations all the way from here on in. Which do you want, the chicken pasta or some sort of lamb curry?"

"Curry," Audra said instantly. She craned her neck to read the package. "Does it come with rice, or do I need to find some?"

Jean flipped the package over. "No rice. But I think I saw some in the bottom, under the chocolate."

Audra perked up. "Chocolate?"

"It's the good stuff from New Zealand, too. I spent months recovering in Christchurch, and the one thing I remember most is the chocolate." He grabbed a bar for himself and tossed one to Audra. "Beats Hersheys."

"Beats what?" Audra mumbled with her mouth full.

"Don't you have Hersheys chocolate in Australia?"

Audra shrugged. "I think we might have it in the gourmet shops. The chocolate and the ice cream syrup and every kind of pop tart they don't make at home. Expensive, though. I don't think I've ever had it. Cadburys was good enough for us." She tapped the bar she'd nearly finished. "This is good."

Jean felt his pain start to ebb as the water boiled, so he could walk over to the stove with barely a hint of a limp. He added water to their dehydrated meals and sat down to wait. At least it beat cooking and doing dishes afterwards.

They ate in silence. Audra because she seemed to be savouring the spicy food, and him because he had to alternate between curry, rice and big gulps of water. Next time he'd pick dinner, and he'd make sure it was something that wouldn't set his tonsils on fire.

Audra finished first. "I'll just boil some water for tea before I turn the gas off for the night."

Jean nodded, struggling to finish his food when all he wanted was to record his results and make a start on that paper. The desire to work won out and he stretched out on his bunk, tapping away at his tablet.

He wasn't sure how much time passed before he heard someone calling his name. "Mm?" he said without looking up.

"I asked if you wanted some tea."

Jean shook his head and kept working.

He was interrupted by a cup shoved between his face and the screen, full of something that steamed and smelled of flowers. "What's this?"

"Tea."

"I said I didn't want any."

Audra didn't move the cup out of the way. "It's a sleep tea. Helps you relax, which might help with those nightmares you keep having."

Jean jerked his head up so he could meet her knowing eyes. "I don't have nightmares."

"If you say so, but you sure are restless at night."

Rather than tell her what had kept him up last night, Jean grabbed the tea and took a cautious sip. It tasted of flowers and not much else. "Thanks."

He didn't remember finishing the tea until Audra reached in front of him to take the empty cup away. He was too intent on getting his thoughts down about the paper before he forgot.

"Are we going out to Doppler Hill tomorrow?" she asked.

"Yeah," he replied.

"Then lights out in five minutes. We both need sleep, as we'll have to hike across the glacier."

Once again, he met her resolute gaze. "You're not my mother." Thank the universe for that.

Audra laughed. "Nope. I'm something worse. Your expedition leader, and the safety officer. Our safety tomorrow depends on both of us being well-rested and alert. I will confiscate whatever I have to in order to keep us both safe. You're not breaking your leg again on my watch, bird boy." She dropped something heavy onto the bunk beside him. "And this is for you."

Jean picked up the hot water bottle. "I don't need this," he lied as welcome warmth spread through his fingers. If anything could soothe the ache in his legs, it was this, but he didn't dare admit his weakness to her.

"Which pain meds are you taking, then?" Audra proceeded to list the name of every pill he'd brought with him.

Jean clamped his mouth shut and shook his head.

"We both know that's bullshit. You've been limping since yesterday, and now you're not. Tell me which ones you've taken or I'll go through your bags. I will drug test you, Jean, if I think you've taken something that compromises the safety of this expedition."

Glowering, he dug out the pill package and held it out to her. Audra read the box, nodded once, then handed it back to him.

"What about the ones you were taking at Christmas? Did you bring those?" she demanded.

Jean sagged. "No. I stopped taking them before New Year's." He had to ask. "Are you going to report me for them?"

"Your name was on the prescription label on the box, so I presume they were legally yours, just like the ones you took tonight."

Cautiously, Jean nodded.

Audra took a deep breath. "If I have to choose between working alongside a man who's exhausted and has slower response times because he's in constant pain, or one who's taking pain medication that I know about and can compensate for, I'll pick the second. It takes an incredible amount of guts to come back here after what happened to you last time. I mean, I saw what state you were in. Which is why I can't let it happen again, and why I'm willing to help you now. You're a bloody trooper, Jean." The way she said it sounded like a compliment.

"Thanks," he said awkwardly.

"Now accept the bloody hot water bottle, or I'll wait until you're asleep and shove it into your sleeping bag with you."

Audra inside his sleeping bag. Now that would be interesting. Jean grinned. "Yes, ma'am," he said.

THIRTY-SIX

Jean stretched out on his bunk, lifting his tablet in front of his face so he could reread the chapter he'd written on Heard Island. The only thing missing from his thesis now was the elusive Atlas Cove rookery.

"So what did you think of dinner?" Audra asked.

It had been her turn to make it, and Jean had dutifully eaten it, though his was all gone now. He couldn't even remember what it tasted like. He couldn't say that, though.

She laughed. "We're a pair, aren't we? The rest of the world is celebrating Valentine's Day with their nearest and dearest, or the people they'd like to be, yet here we are, on an island so isolated that it may as well be a secret known only to penguins and seals. Working!" She waved at her open laptop.

"Valentine's Day?" Jean checked the date on his tablet. That meant they'd only been on Heard Island for three weeks. It felt like longer. They'd surveyed both Spit Point and Doppler Hill colonies, set up Audra's weather station, and they still had a week to spare.

"Yes, Valentine's Day," Audra said. "You know, when couples get all romantic?"

Jean shrugged. "I've never really done much for Valentine's Day. It's just a big commercial stunt, to get people to spend more money on stuff they don't need. Flowers. Chocolates. Greeting cards. Fancy food. Pointless, really." That had always been Dairine's opinion, and Jean had agreed with her.

"Flowers and cards might be a bit over the top, but I draw the line at fancy food and chocolate. If you didn't enjoy the mango chicken as much as I did, I'll keep the rest for myself. And as for the Tim Tams…ha! Good luck getting any of those out of me." Audra brandished the cookie package.

"Now that's harsh. Those rations are for both of us." Jean had grown quite fond of the Australian cookies, which Audra usually shared.

"What'll you trade me for them, bird boy?"

Jean considered for a moment, before he said, "I have a bottle of whisky from home that I planned to drink once my work here was done. We're finished with our fieldwork here, earlier than scheduled. That's worth celebrating for sure, even if we still have the survey at Atlas Cove still to go. Worth a glass or two now, though."

Audra wet her lips. "You know, I've been thinking about Atlas Cove. I'm supposed to set up the second weather station there. I know we're meant to wait for the *Investigator* to return and transport all our equipment up there in a week or two, but it looks to me like there's already a camp up there we could use. If we loaded a Zodiac with all the bare essentials and picked a calm day, we could make it up there by ourselves. Even if it's too rough to head back, we could just radio the *Investigator* to pick us up there instead of here. By all accounts, it's a more sheltered anchorage out there. What do you think?"

Jean wanted to hug her. More than anything, he wanted to find those Wharf Point penguins. He knew he hadn't imagined them. "I think it's a great idea," he said. "There is a hut there, and we made sure everything was operational last year. We'd need food, water, fuel and our packs. That's it, really. As long as the weather's good, but I'll leave that in your capable hands." It was a standing joke between them that, despite her protestations to the contrary, Audra did actually control the weather, because they'd only lost one day to bad weather in the entire three weeks.

She looked surprised. "You're brave to go back there, after what happened last time. Are you sure?"

No. He wasn't brave. It wasn't courage driving him at all, but the desire for adventure. To discover. To be the first. "In one of the expeditions a few years back, there's an unconfirmed report about king penguins breeding at Wharf Point, where they've never been seen before. A new colony would show that they're not just recovering, but expanding. I was trying to get a good view of their beach last year when I…when I had the accident."

Audra nodded knowingly. "So that's why you came back. You want to discover something no one else has seen before, and share it with the world. They're your penguins, just like these are my weather stations. And here I thought you were just some ex-military survivor type, trained to survive, no matter what. Instead, you're a scientist, in the truest sense of the word. Like the early explorers who came out here, risking their lives to discover, or the most dedicated medical scientists, injecting themselves with diseases so they can prove their vaccine works. We'll get to Atlas Cove, and if your penguins are there, I'll help you find them."

Jean's eyes met hers. She did understand. Like few people ever could, and no woman he'd ever met. More than ever, now he understood why everyone she worked with seemed to sing her praises. He'd officially joined the choir. He didn't want to sing right now, though. Instead, he experienced the overpowering desire to kiss her.

"I better pour that whisky," he said. He found two cups and poured them each a measure.

Audra cautiously sniffed at her cup. "It doesn't smell like any whisky I've had before. And you drink it straight?"

"It's cinnamon whisky. It comes from Canada, but we managed to convince enough Americans to try it that now you can buy it pretty much everywhere in the States, too. Try it. You'll like it."

They both lifted their cups.

"To the Atlas Cove expedition," Audra said.

They both drank. Jean felt the familiar burn coat the back of his throat, but Audra erupted in a coughing fit.

"Oh God. I don't know how you can drink this straight. It's like setting fire to your whisky and drinking it while it's still ablaze," she rasped. "Give me a mango beer any day."

"That might mix quite well with this," Jean said. "I got a six pack for Christmas that I haven't opened. We can try it when we get back to Davis."

"Ugh." Audra ripped open the cookie package. "I'm going to need these to get the taste out of my mouth." She bit off the end off a cookie, then stared at it a moment before she turned it around and bit the other end off.

Jean had seen other Aussies do this with coffee, but this wasn't the same. "Wait, don't – "

Audra dunked the cookie in her cup and wrapped her lips around one end, like the cookie was a giant straw. She gave an enormous slurp before her eyes widened in surprise. "Well, it's better than drinking the stuff straight," she said, blinking. She leaned in to suck on the cookie again.

"I should try that," he found himself saying. Anything to get the image of her blissfully sucking, her lips wrapped around... Jean shook his head and bit down on his own cookie, then dropped it into his own drink. "Oh shit."

Audra laughed at him and reached over to help him fish it out at the same time as he did. Their fingers tangled in the cup and warmth spread through Jean's whole body at the contact. He stared at her.

"You have chocolate on your nose," he said, wanting to wipe it away. No, he wanted to lick it away.

A blush coloured her cheeks, like she could read his mind. Her fingers tightened around his. "Jean, I – "

He kissed her. Softly at first, as her lips melted against his, then with more passion as he tasted chocolate and whisky and her. The perfect woman for him. The one he wanted more than anything. The one whose lips parted as she kissed him just as desperately as he kissed her.

Jean reached out to pull her close. Now he had her, he never wanted to let go.

THIRTY-SEVEN

One moment she had her hand stuck with his inside a cup, the next she was kissing Jean like her life depended on it. Like it was the most natural thing in the world. Like she wanted to climb into his lap, tear his clothes off and have her way with him.

Strong arms closed around her, reminding her of the day they first met.

The day she'd found out he had a wife.

Oh God. She was kissing a married man. That made her almost as bad as him.

Audra wrenched herself away from Jean, backing up until her back hit the wall of the tiny hut. She was still breathing hard and her heart beat so fast it was thrumming in her chest.

Out of passion for a married man who was cheating on his wife.

"Don't you ever do that again," Audra said, her voice shaking with fury. She stormed out of the hut, or tried to, but her foot caught on something. She managed not to fall over, though, so she kicked the obstacle out of her way and continued out without another word.

For what felt like hours, she marched up and down the beach, mad at Jean and even more angry at herself. She was as bad as Jay. Worse than Jay. He might have cheated on her, but he'd never seduced someone he knew was married.

When she crept back inside the hut, the smell of whisky was almost overpowering. Audra's foot clinked against the empty bottle, which had fallen on its side. Had he drunk the whole thing while she was outside? Judging by the snoring coming from his bunk, he most certainly had.

Fine. He could nurse his hangover all the way to Atlas Cove tomorrow. She'd forgotten to tell him that the forecast was perfect for their boat trip tomorrow morning, but now it was a fitting revenge for the cheating bastard.

THIRTY-EIGHT

When Jean woke the next morning, Audra still wasn't there. A kettle steamed on the stove, though, and several casks of water were missing. Had she left without him?

Bitch.

He stumbled out of the hut and breathed a sigh of relief when he spotted the Zodiac still on the beach. She'd loaded it with boxes of supplies and the water casks, and was now wrestling a gas bottle over the side. A fuel drum sat on the beach, waiting its turn.

"We leave in twenty minutes, so hurry up," she shouted.

Jean didn't need telling twice. He hurried back inside to pack his things, wrinkling his nose at the whisky fumes inside. No wonder he had a headache, breathing that in all night. After she'd changed her mind about wanting to kiss him, she'd kicked over the bottle in her haste to get outside. By the time Jean had gotten to it, the bottle was empty. So much for celebrating when they found his penguins.

Now he hated Valentine's Day more than anything.

He shoved his sleeping bag on top of everything else in his pack, not bothering to check how many ration packs he had in there. He knew they'd have enough – he hadn't touched them since he'd arrived.

Next, he poured some hot water in one of the dehydrated breakfast pouches and made himself a coffee while his breakfast was doing its thing.

Audra slammed the door open and grabbed her pack. "Are you coming, or what?"

Jean shouldered his pack, seized his coffee in one hand and his breakfast in the other, and followed her to the beach.

He managed to burn his mouth on the coffee, trying to drink it all before he needed both hands to help Audra load the boat. It seemed she'd packed everything, though, including the fuel drum. Superwoman.

He should never have kissed her. Should have kept his distance and satisfied himself with just dreaming about her until his job here was done. Now, he might have put the last part of his fieldwork in jeopardy.

"We are still going to Atlas Cove, right?" he ventured.

"Of course," she shot back. "Did you drink so much last night that you forgot?"

That shut him up. She'd had more alcohol than he had, before she'd kicked over the bottle so he couldn't drink any more.

The waves were headed northwest, the same direction they were going, so the trip was a lot smoother than Jean expected. Audra's thunderous expression had turned into one of intense concentration, but he figured if he didn't want her to kill him, he was still better off not talking to her.

He tried to keep his eyes off the water below them, turning his gaze instead on the coastline as they zoomed past. Glaciers cascaded off Big Ben like frozen waterfalls down to the sea. The mountain's peak was shrouded in cloud again today, making it look like the volcano was actually erupting. It wasn't, of course. Jean had asked the geologists last trip, who'd laughed and told him he'd know from the earthquakes that the volcano was stirring, long before anything came out the top.

So, he was back to worrying about the water, which would be just as cold as the last time he'd been here in Atlas Cove.

His breath caught in his throat as they rounded Wharf Point. The memory was too strong, after going over it so many times in his nightmares. This was where he'd nearly died. Where it could all happen again. Jean didn't open his eyes until he felt the bottom of the boat scrape against the beach.

"Give me a hand, will you? I need to secure the boat so we can unload it," Audra snapped.

Jean nodded, turning his back on the water to do what was necessary. He could do this. He could, he told himself.

He carried their gear up to the Apple hut that was still a hazy part of his dreams, still repeating his mantra in his mind.

"I want to get the uplink set up today, so I can start data collection in the morning. Are we good to do penguin hunting tomorrow after we set up the weather station?"

Audra asked.

Once again, Jean nodded. He needed to get his head straight, on task, and right now he wasn't sure he could face the Azorella Peninsula. Maybe if he took the boat, he'd be able to get close enough to the penguins to get an idea of whether there really was a population here, and return with Audra on the land side of the bay.

Tomorrow, he told himself.

THIRTY-NINE

Jean had barely said a word to her for all of yesterday, and most of this morning, so Audra was surprised to hear the boat engine fire up. She stumbled out of the hut just in time to see Jean headed out into the cove.

"You better not be leaving without me!" she shouted.

He hollered back something about penguins, pointing across the cove.

Of course. That new penguin colony he'd been so eager to find until yesterday, when he'd agreed to help her with her weather station first. So much for that idea. Selfish prick. A quick peep inside the hut told her he'd left most of his gear behind, so at least he'd be coming back.

That left her alone to her own devices, but that wasn't such a bad thing. Her instructions were to find an elevated position near the western camp to install the second weather station, and she knew just the spot: on the little peninsula just north of camp. The Azorella Peninsula, her map said, named for the cushion plants all over it. It would be best to set up her station as close as possible to one of the spots where earlier expeditions had taken their observations, Shelley had told her, though Audra had already planned to do that. If she won the Bureau's contest, she could do her doctorate out here, collating all the new weather data and comparing it to past observations, to see if anything had changed.

But first, she had to win that contest, which meant kicking things up a notch. Her videos were getting more views — a few hundred each — but she wanted to try live streaming again. The satellite uplink was securely fixed to the roof of the hut. Her laptop was connected to the internet via the uplink, and her camera fed everything it filmed direct to her laptop. Now was the time to see if it worked.

She grabbed the weather station and strapped her camera to her wrist. Audra paused to zip her coat up properly as she stepped outside, then marched with her head held high to the hill above the camp. From her vantage point, she could see Jean's boat cruising just offshore, maybe a hundred metres up the bay. She hoped he found his penguins.

Audra set to work, assembling the weather station like the expert she now was. It only took her a few minutes, leaving plenty of time to do that video.

Audra summoned a smile and turned on the camera. "Hi. Welcome back to Heard Island. If you're watching this now, it means I've succeeded in doing a live video. If you're watching this later, I guess I need to work on that live bit. I have an excuse, though – just check out the view."

She panned the camera around slowly, pointing out Big Ben, the camp, the cove and even Jean. She lifted a hand to wave at him while the camera was pointed in his direction, and he pointed back at her and shouted something she couldn't hear. Ah well. If he'd wanted to tell her something, he shouldn't have given her the silent treatment this morning.

Or maybe he was so excited about finding his penguins that he wanted to share the excitement with her, as the only other person on the island.

"I think our biologist has found some very special penguins he's been searching for, so let's take a look and see if we can spot them, too."

Audra turned the camera to the shore below her, where there were plenty of penguins and seals sunning themselves between the tumbled rocks. All adult penguins, though, and she knew Jean had been looking for babies. Audra glimpsed movement out of the corner of her eye, but when she turned to face what she thought she'd seen, she found only more rocks. And then…one of the rocks moved, and opened its beak. Audra blinked. Not rocks at all, but brown penguins – the very same that Jean had been looking for. No wonder he was so excited.

She counted them out loud for the camera, telling what was probably one sole viewer about how juvenile king penguins were originally thought to be a completely different species to their parents, because they looked so different to the tiny grey babies or their majestic, black, white and gold parents.

A sudden shiver ran through her, as though a goose had

walked over her grave. It wasn't like she was cold or scared. It was followed by another shudder, as Audra realised the rock beneath her was moving, too.

She remembered Jean's warning about sinkholes, so she backed up toward the concrete pad with a row of squat support pillars along one side which was all that remained of an old research camp that had probably been abandoned before she was born. That bit had to be stable.

Audra reached the concrete safely, then turned the camera on herself. "Sorry about that. I'm standing on an active volcano and Big Ben behind me is grumbling a bit, making the earth move." The ground shook again, illustrating her point for her. "But it's all right, this volcano hardly ever erupts. See?" Audra turned to face the peak, lifting the camera higher. Even as she watched, a curl of smoke issued from the mountain. "Well, now don't I feel silly. A mountain making a liar out of me. It's only smoking, though…"

Above, a grey avalanche thundered down the side of the mountain, before it spent itself in the snow. An eruption. A real volcanic eruption. She hadn't just seen it, she'd caught the rare event on film. If she was lucky, one of the news channels would pick up her video because of this.

"Wow," Audra managed to say. "You just saw Big Ben erupt. I hope I'm safe down here."

The ground beneath her feet bucked, throwing Audra off balance. She tried to steady herself, but she might as well have been standing on jelly and not concrete. All she could do was put her arms out to break her fall.

She landed hard against one of the concrete pillars. Hard enough to feel the sickening snap as it broke her arm.

Audra couldn't help it. She let out an agonised scream.

194

FORTY

Jean scanned the far shore, searching for the penguins he knew he'd spotted last time. Even with his binoculars, he couldn't be sure if they were king penguins or not, and the chicks blended into the rock so well he'd need to be a lot closer to spot them.

He considered asking for Audra's help – two pairs of eyes were better than one – but she'd barely spoken to him since that misguided kiss. She'd been playing with him, for her own reasons, Jean decided. She didn't care about him or his research, and she wouldn't help him now. So he set off alone in the boat, trying not to think about how cold the sea was beneath him. If he did, he'd head right back to shore. What kind of man was afraid of a bit of cold water?

Audra would laugh at him if she knew.

Jean glanced back at the camp, where she stood on the beach, waving her arms and shouting something he couldn't hear.

"I'm going to find my penguins," he shouted back, stabbing a finger in the direction of what he hoped was the new colony. "And don't think you can stop me," he added to himself, turning his back on her. He pulled on his balaclava, not wanting to wear a scarf across this face that might come loose in the wind. He needed both hands free to hand the boat and his binoculars.

When he next looked, she wasn't standing on the beach any more. Instead, he saw a red-coated figure climbing the ridge above the camp that led to the Azorella Peninsula, where that plant had nearly killed him. He watched her with his heart in his throat, dreading the moment when she, too, took a wrong step. It was just like the woman to find the surest way to distract him from his search – by putting herself in danger of breaking both her legs like he had. If she expected him to follow her and drag her back to camp, she was sorely mistaken.

She knew the risks of venturing into the old lava field. Sinkholes, lava tubes and who knew what else lurked there, ready to trap the unwary. The whole island was an active volcano. It almost looked like it was smoking this morning, but it was probably just cloud.

Jean raised his binoculars to get a closer look at the cloud at the peak, and his blood ran cold. Through the lenses, he could see grey smoke billowing up…and what looked like ash or small pieces of rock landing on the snow.

He had to warn her, at least. But she'd disappeared from sight.

Jean waited for a long moment, hoping and praying that she'd reappear so he wouldn't have to go after her. After what seemed like an eternity, she appeared at the highest point of the ridge, waving cheerfully at him.

"Crazy woman," he muttered, then cupped his hands to his mouth to shout a warning about Big Ben.

She just smiled and waved, then peered down at the rocky beach, ignoring him and the volcano.

Swearing, Jean followed her line of sight to a cluster of penguins. King penguins.

He brought the boat in closer, hardly daring to hope that he'd found the colony at last. First he saw a dozen penguins, then he rounded a particularly large piece of volcanic rock and his breath caught in his throat. Not a dozen. Hundreds of them. Far too many to be just a group out fishing.

Jean raised his eyes to the ridge, wanting to shout his thanks to Audra, but she'd evidently grown some sense and headed for somewhere safer. Good. That left him free to count the penguins, take some pictures, and maybe even get close enough to see if they kept a crèche of babies sheltered behind them. Just a little further…

Audra screamed.

Jean gritted his teeth. She'd probably just seen a spider, he seethed. This was his last chance to find his penguin colony and finish his PhD research with the kind of results any biologist would die for.

A biologist who knew damn well there weren't any spiders in Antarctica.

What if she'd fallen into a sinkhole like he had?

That's what had ended his research trip last time, Jean reminded himself angrily. This was his last chance.

But what if she'd hit her head? Or lost consciousness,

which is why she'd only screamed once?

Jean's mouth went dry. Could he sentence a woman to die just so that he could satisfy his own ego, chasing a bunch of smelly birds? Worse, letting her die the same way he nearly did in his nightmares?

Jean swallowed.

Fuck the penguins. Audra's life mattered more than they did.

He threw the boat into a ninety degree turn, running it aground on a rock near the penguins. He leaped out, set on only one thing: saving Audra.

Penguins shuffled out of his way as he sprinted across the rocky beach, until he reached the end of their territory. He scrambled up the slope, nearly falling several times, doing his best to avoid the treacherous cushion plants. When he reached the ridge, he couldn't see her, confirming his worst fears.

"Audra?" he shouted. "Audra, can you hear me? Where are you?"

He caught a glimpse of movement as a red sleeve waved among the ruins of an earlier campsite halfway up the next rise. If she was anything less than critically injured, he was going to drag her down to the boat to finish the penguin survey with him.

He strode up the slope, keeping his breath to fuel his furious pace. He had to skirt around the concrete pad to see her properly, where she lay hidden behind the supports of some long-gone structure. When he reached her, he stopped dead.

The pain on her tear-streaked face was unmistakeable. She might not have fallen down a sinkhole, but she'd still managed to injure herself. From the fearful look in her eyes, she'd already gone into shock. He wouldn't get anything coherent out of her. He'd have to get her back to camp, where there was food, warmth and a first aid kit. There he'd assess her injuries and radio for help.

He leaned down and scooped her up. She was surprisingly light in his arms.

"Nnnno," she said, then swallowed. "Please. Please, you're hurting me."

FORTY-ONE

Her throat raw from screaming, Audra didn't trust her voice. And she definitely didn't want any more pain. The white-hot throbbing in her arm was bad enough.

Jean lifted her up, bumping her arm and sending a fresh bolt of agony all the way up to her brain.

"No, don't," Audra tried to say, but hardly any sound came out. "Please don't, you're hurting me." She reached for her useless right arm, pulling it across her body to support the broken limb. A red light blinked on her wrist. With her good arm, Audra switched off the camera, which had miraculously survived the fall unscathed. She ripped the Velcro strap off her wrist and cradled the camera to her chest beside her injured arm. "All right."

She closed her eyes, breathing slowly in an attempt to ignore the pain. How could anything hurt this much? Audra was grateful to Jean for carrying her, as she wasn't sure she could stay on her feet without falling to her knees and sobbing every few steps. How had Jean done it? Gotten himself from here to the hut with two broken legs? Her legs were fine, and she was worse than useless.

"Relax. I'm taking you back to camp so I can help you. I've had the same first aid training as you, so I'll be taking just as good care of you as you would of me," Jean said softly, in the sort of tone she'd use to a frightened puppy.

And it worked. She did relax, secure in his arms as he carried her back to the hut.

When they reached the beach, she saw the boat bobbing in the middle of the cove. He'd have to swim out to get it. She lifted her good arm to point it out to him, and the camera slipped from her hand. A sharp clack told her it had fallen on the rocks underfoot.

"Wait," she rasped. "Need to pick it up."

Jean dipped low, supporting her body on his knees as he crouched to retrieve it. "I'll put it in my pocket, to keep it safe," he said.

Audra nodded. She wanted to tell him about the footage she'd taken of his baby penguins, but as she opened her mouth to speak, Jean rose awkwardly to his feet and the movement made the pain in her arm stab her all over again. She cried out, unable to form words any more.

"I know it hurts. I'll get you back to camp so I can help you," Jean said, starting forward.

His every step jolted her, until the pain became a steady throb to the beat of his boots. It would only hurt worse if she had to walk, though. Tears flowed down her cheeks, but she didn't care any more. As long as they didn't freeze, nothing mattered but making the pain end.

After an eternity, they reached the hut. Jean took his time opening the door, but he didn't seem to want to put her down to use both hands, either. Finally, he got it open and carried her inside, then set her on the floor between their bunks.

"Okay, can you tell me where it hurts?" Jean asked, patting down her legs.

Audra felt the strangest desire to laugh at him for using this as an excuse to feel her up. "My arm's broken," she said, pointing.

"That's all?"

She glared at him. "It hurts like hell. Isn't that enough for you?"

He almost smiled. "You sure you're that badly hurt if you can make jokes like that?"

Audra struggled to sit up so she could unzip her coat and extract her injured arm to show him. "Do you think I'm bullshitting now?"

His eyes widened in shock. "No. I…when I broke my legs, and radioed for help, one of the guys asked me something and I replied with a joke. I was already half gone on morphine, I think. That's what he said. That I couldn't be badly hurt if…"

She didn't have the patience for his rambling. "Find me something I can use to splint this." She scanned the hut. "There. One of those things should do." She pointed at a box of foot-long plastic strips, the sort she'd seen the geologists use as markers. The plastic had a slight curve and was a bit longer than she needed, but should be rigid enough to give her arm some support.

"You'll need a bandage to secure that," Jean said,

handing the piece of plastic to her.

"So find me a first aid kit. There should be one in your field pack, or mine, if you forgot yours." It wouldn't surprise her if he had. Jean wasn't big on safety, and it showed. Her broken arm wasn't his fault, though.

"There's a bigger one under your bunk. Thirty years' worth of bandages." He reached into the storage cubby beneath her bed and pulled out the box, showing her the faded cross on top. "See?"

She saw. Grabbing a couple of rolls of wide bandage, she ripped open the first package and set to work, wrapping it around her arm and the makeshift splint.

"Shouldn't I be doing that? I'm qualified in first aid, you know," Jean said.

"I'm fine," Audra bit out through her gritted teeth. Bloody hell, but it hurt. More tears leaked down her cheeks, so she bowed her head to hide them from Jean. She was nearly done.

Jean didn't take his eyes off Audra. "You know, I think there might be something here to take the edge off the pain. I remember another bottle of morphine in among the bandages."

Audra breathed a sigh of relief as she tucked in the end of the bandage. Drained, she lay down while Jean rummaged through the first aid kit.

"Got it," he said. "Now, I need to know your weight for the correct dosage. And don't you even think about lying about it. I carried you halfway around the cove, so I'll know if you take a few pounds off the total. But I'll give you the dose for the lower weight, which means it won't be as strong as if you'd told the truth."

She'd probably lost weight out here, what with all the exercise she got trekking around the island, but Audra named the weight she'd been the last time she set foot on some scales.

Jean prepared the syringe with practiced ease. Of course. He'd practised on himself, probably in this very hut, when he'd been in a lot more pain than she was now. "Where do you want it?" he asked.

Audra eyed the needle. If it was anyone else administering the injection, she'd take it in the thigh, but this was Jean. The man who'd grabbed her and tried to force her into bed the day they met, but also the man she'd shared sleeping quarters with for months without him doing anything untoward. Unless she counted that misguided kiss the other night, but there had been extenuating circumstances. And alcohol.

She turned her gaze on Jean. Did she trust him?

He offered a watery smile. "Funny how the world works. I'm back here, holding a syringe of morphine, but this time it's you who needs it, not me. Who'd have thought I'd ever get the chance to pay you back properly for what you did on the ship?"

No way was she taking a sedative from Jean. "I'm fine," she said hoarsely. "It doesn't hurt. I'll be fine until the boat comes to pick us up. You should...call them."

"You can't be serious."

"Call them or I'll stab you again with this needle." She wouldn't, but she glared at him with all the fierceness she could muster so he believed she would.

"Yes, ma'am." Jean crossed the hut and flicked on the radio. "*Investigator*, this is Jean Pennant on Heard Island.

What is your ETA at Atlas Cove?"

The radio crackled. "Pennant? What are you doing at Atlas Cove? Aren't you supposed to be at the camp at Spit Bay?"

"I felt like taking the boat for a spin."

"You're crazy, you know that?"

"Yes," Jean replied blithely. "But what's your ETA?"

"A week."

Audra's eyes met Jean's. No way was she enduring this sort of agony for a week.

Jean wet his lips. "What if I told you we have an injury that requires urgent medical attention?"

A pause, where only hissing static filled the airwaves, followed by, "If you've broken your legs again, I think the research leader here will break your arms, too, for cutting his research short. But only if his PhD students don't get to you first. The volcano's erupting and they want to study it."

"We know. Audra fell during one of the earth tremors. She's the one who's injured."

"Audra? The met?"

"Yes."

More static.

"We're three days from your location. I'll give you a better estimate when you radio for your next check-in. Over and out."

Audra ripped open a sterile wipe, yanked down the shoulder of her shirt and swabbed her arm. It was broken anyway. A little needle wouldn't make it hurt any worse. She took a deep breath. As she exhaled, she eased the needle into her arm, emptying the syringe into her flesh. There. Now she couldn't change her mind, because the drug was already circulating in her bloodstream.

She dropped the syringe back into its packaging and pressed a gauze pad to her arm to stem the tiny trickle of blood. With difficulty, she struggled to her feet. She took two steps before she collapsed on her bunk, just as she'd intended. It was harder to get herself out of her outer gear and into her sleeping bag with only one arm, but she managed it.

Audra turned to fix Jean with her stare. "Promise me you won't hurt me."

"Once that stuff kicks in, I promise you won't feel a thing," he assured her.

Not good enough.

Audra shook her head. "Promise you won't hurt me. Promise you won't touch me."

Hurt filled his eyes. Because she'd guessed his intentions, or because she'd wounded him by suspecting he'd touch her without her permission?

"What if you have a bad reaction to the drugs, or you have some sort of infection or…need another dose?" he asked, swallowing.

"Promise you won't touch me unless there is a genuine medical emergency and I will die if you don't," Audra amended. She could feel the lassitude sweeping through her. She understood how people got addicted to this stuff. It made her feel…fluffy.

"I swear to you, I won't touch you unless your life depends on it." Jean settled on his bunk. "But I will watch over you until the ship arrives with a medic who can set that arm properly."

"Thank you."

The staring competition continued until Audra's eyelids weighed so heavily that they closed of their own accord.

FORTY-TWO

Never in his life had Jean had so much trouble keeping still, but he did it. Every second he stared at her, lying on the opposite bunk, he just wanted to take her in his arms and swear to her that everything would be okay. That he'd take care of her.

But he was a man of his word, and he'd promised not to touch her. So he sat on his own bunk while his brain buzzed with questions, and kept his hands to himself.

What did she think he'd do to her? He'd carried her for more than half a mile. His arms ached at the effort, but he wasn't complaining. He'd felt worse. He'd done worse, dragging his own body along the same beach.

That's why he'd done it, he told himself. Because of his own bad experience, he wasn't willing to let someone else endure the same pain. Even if she had tried to seduce him away from his work.

Jean shook his head. No, she hadn't. Her words just now confirmed it, while her fear-filled eyes demanded his answer. She didn't want him to touch her.

Was that why she'd jerked away from that kiss the other night? She hadn't been teasing him, playing hard to get, pretending to reject him when he knew damn well she'd wanted that kiss as much as he had. She'd responded with more passion than he'd expected, after all. And then…

She'd panicked. And told him not to touch her.

So who had touched her in such a way that made her terrified of men?

Jean wanted to pound the asshole into a crater. A crevasse. And then bury him so deep he was a corpse by the time anyone dug him out. Because it had to be a man. Some asshole had hurt her, and when he found out who…

Because it wouldn't be a stranger. Jean knew that much about rapists and cowards who hit women. Most of them knew their victims, which meant whoever he was, Audra knew him, or she thought she had.

He opened his mouth to ask her, but while he'd been lost in thought, she'd succumbed to the morphine. Good. That meant she wasn't in any pain, at least for a little while.

She might have told someone. A trusted friend, perhaps. The rock star she talked to online?

He crossed the hut to the shelf where her laptop sat, open. At a touch, it woke up. She'd been working on it before she went for her walk, and forgotten to switch it off. The internet icon at the bottom blinked from offline to on.

Internet access? Out here? How on Earth had she managed that? They were miles from the Spit Bay camp. He shot her an admiring glance. For a meteorologist, she sure knew about a lot more than just the weather.

The laptop chimed, telling him a video call was incoming. He swiped the screen, trying to reject the call before it could wake up Audra, but a picture of the rock star appeared instead. Fuck.

"Audra? Are you okay? Tell me you're okay!" the Aussie demanded.

"She's sleeping," Jean said. He took a deep breath and made a decision. "Look, it's just us at the camp and when I tried to do first aid, she wouldn't let me touch her. Has…do you know if someone's hurt her in the past?"

"Who the fuck are you? And what have you done to her?"

"I haven't done anything!" Jean protested. "She wouldn't let me! There was the volcano, and the earthquake, and she fell, and then…" The sound of her scream would echo in his next nightmare, he was sure of it.

"Put her on."

Jean picked up the laptop and tried to point the camera at Audra's sleeping form. "I can't. She's asleep. Look, she's injured and it's just us on the island until the ship returns. I need to know what happened to her, because she won't let me help her."

The Aussie's expression grew flinty. "If Audra says not to touch her, then you don't fucking touch her. I'll send help." He ended the call before Jean could respond.

Send help? Did the man even know where they were? Help was three days away, in the shape of the *Investigator*. Not some strange Australian, thousands of miles away. Until then, it was up to Jean to keep them both warm, hydrated and fed.

They had food and gas for the stove enough to last them a week, plus whatever emergency supplies remained in the hut. He had enough fuel to power the generator for that time, too, if he was careful. Water wasn't a problem, as long as it was above freezing outside and they had fuel to melt more if they needed it. There wasn't enough morphine for a week, but they might be able to stretch it out for another day or two if she took a lower dose. If they ran out before the ship arrived, though, the withdrawal would be brutal. He knew that from experience.

More than ever, he wished he'd never used the other bottle of morphine for himself. Maybe he would've been able to remember the day they met, so now they might have been friends, instead of awkward colleagues, and she'd have told him about her past.

Jean returned to the hut, which wasn't much warmer than outside. He could do something about that, at least. He switched on the ancient space heater left behind by some earlier expeditioner and set about heating water for dinner.

He pulled out the package of dehydrated food pouches. His mouth turned dry when he saw that the first one was Audra's favourite, mango chicken. He set that aside. She might want dinner later.

Jean poured water into a different pouch and ate the lot without tasting a single bite. It's not that the meal was tasteless – the package said it was some sort of curry – but that his thoughts were on anything but food.

First, he had an injured woman who was his first responsibility. Her even breathing told him she was still asleep and not suffering any ill-effects from the drugs. But a broken arm wasn't life-threatening, and their ship was on the way to pick them up. Plus, it would be light for hours – polar summer sure took some getting used to. He could just pop down the beach to that penguin colony and…

But what if he found another sinkhole? Or he fell and broke something when the volcano caused another earthquake? There'd be no one to help him, and what if Audra needed him?

He'd come so far, to be so close, and still not see them. This island had to be cursed.

Ah, screw it. He'd sleep on it, and make up his mind in the morning, when Audra might be awake.

Jean checked to make sure the stove and the heating was switched off before he climbed into his own sleeping bag, rolling so that he could see the sleeping woman on the other side of the hut.

Was it worth it? Missing out on the most important part of his PhD research, just to make sure she was okay?

Sure, he was disappointed, but it was nothing compared to the devastation he'd feel if something worse happened to her, and it was his fault. If even her broken arm was his fault, which it kind of was, seeing as he'd agreed to come to this end of the island instead of staying in the relative safety of Spit Bay. If he'd known this would happen, he'd have stayed there and not even considered a trip west to Atlas Cove.

So he had his answer, didn't he?

Yes. She was worth it.

FORTY-THREE

Thumping woke Jean from a dream he couldn't quite remember. He hoped it wasn't a pair of elephant seals again, humping against the side of the hut. They'd nearly knocked one of the huts over last time, and as no one else had seen the seals in action, everyone had just thought he'd done a poor job of assembling the hut. When the truth of the matter was that no hut, no matter how well put together, could withstand the pounding of an elephant seal really getting into the action with his lady friend.

He should tell Audra that story. Maybe it would make her laugh, or at least smile.

He stared up at the foam ceiling. The hut didn't feel like it was shaking, so the thumping must be coming from somewhere else.

Jean pulled on a coat and cracked open the door so he could stick his head through. Funny. Outside the insulation of the hut, it almost sounded like a helicopter.

He glanced at Audra, but she was still asleep, so he dressed and headed outside to investigate.

Jean almost didn't believe his eyes. A bright red helicopter sat in the clearing where last year's camp had stood. Eric emerged from the hallucination, carrying a stretcher Jean recognised. He'd woken up in one on the cargo plane to Christchurch.

"How did you get here so fast?" Jean stammered.

Eric looked grim. "The *Aurora Australis* is on its way to Fremantle for repairs. Once we got close enough to fly here and back to the ship on one tank of fuel, they dispatched me to collect her. Where is she?"

Audra. He'd come to take Audra away. Jean's heart constricted in his chest, but he managed to say, "She's in the emergency hut. She was asleep when I left, though."

Eric nodded and led the way. Between them, they strapped her sleeping body to the stretcher and carried her to the helicopter, where Eric secured the stretcher further for the flight.

When Eric looked satisfied, he climbed into the pilot's seat. "Is that your boat?" he asked.

"My boat?" Bewildered, Jean peered in the direction Eric pointed. The boat which had floated away yesterday while he'd been busy taking care of Audra was now beached on the rocks, between two seals. "Yeah."

"You should tie it up more securely than that. One good wave will sweep it right out into the cove, and I wouldn't want to swim after it. There were a pack of orcas around Wharf Point, trying to get to the penguins."

His penguins. Jean sighed. Not his penguins any more.

"Sure. I'll get right on it."

He headed for the boat. The vessel had taken on a bit of water while it had been off sailing on its own, but it had lost pretty much everything else, including the anchor and the ropes he'd tossed inside it yesterday. His notebook was gone, too, but then he hadn't had time to write any notes yesterday before he'd given up on research altogether so he could help Audra.

Who was now flying away from him, perhaps forever. He raised a hand to wave at the helicopter as Eric took off.

Not willing to waste time searching for the anchor that was probably at the bottom of the ocean by now, Jean grabbed the side of the boat and dragged it up the beach, beyond the high tide line, and tipped it upside-down. The engine had probably drowned overnight, so he'd best leave it for a bit before trying to start it. He didn't want the engine dying on him in the middle of the cove.

Besides, he had to radio the *Investigator* for check-in, and tell them he was still alive, like Audra usually did most mornings, right before she delivered her daily weather forecast. Shit, he was going to miss her.

FORTY-FOUR

Audra waited for the helicopter to stop rising before she let the pilot know she was awake, and had been for some time.

"I wondered," he said. "I'm not sure if you remember me, but I'm Eric. You're the girl who does the videos."

"You've watched them?"

"Yeah, we all have. It's cool to know what's going on at the bases, and the Antarctic Division's been sharing them on their website." He paused. "When we heard you needed help, the guys and me changed the route a bit so we'd be able to swing by and pick you up. I'm lucky I'm the only pilot this trip, so I got to fly you."

"Why is there only one pilot? I thought there were usually more."

"We're working with a skeleton crew this trip, because the ship's damaged and needs repairs."

"Which ship?" Audra demanded.

"The *Aurora Australis*, of course. After she broke her moorings in that storm off Mawson, she hit an iceberg. Didn't go all *Titanic*, though, so once the shipping company had sent out some seaworthiness assessors, they said we could sail her to the shipyard in Fremantle. All non-essential personnel got sent back to Mawson, and they'll fly everyone out who needs it. So you're our only passenger this trip."

"I didn't hear anything about it. Wow. That must have been really scary."

Eric shrugged. "We got off lightly. She's due for retirement anyway, and no one got hurt. It's not as bad as a volcano and a broken arm, like you."

Audra winced as her arm twinged. "I guess Antarctica's really throwing her worst at us this year. Ah, how long until we reach the ship? Just that the pain drugs I took at Heard are definitely starting to wear off and I'd really like some more."

"There's a first aid kit beside you. There should be something in that to help."

Audra checked the box. Paracetamol. Ibuprofen. Codeine. All pills that could probably take the edge off, though nothing as powerful as the morphine she'd taken yesterday. "Got any water to wash these down with?"

Eric passed a water bottle over his shoulder. It was a stretch, but Audra managed to grab it with her good hand. She swallowed whatever the recommended dose was of all of them, then debated whether she wanted to sit up to see out the windows or if she was better off lying down. If she could undo the straps on the stretcher one-handed, of course. Pain wasn't going to be her only problem. What if they wouldn't let her return to Antarctica because of her broken arm? She'd been looking forward to the long, dark winter. Hell, she'd even bought a new dress in Melbourne for the Midwinter dinner.

"Do you think they'll get the *Aurora Australis* fixed in time to finish the winter resupply run?" Audra asked.

Broken arm or not, if there wasn't any transport, she wouldn't be going back to Antarctica until spring.

"Doubt it," he replied. "I heard they're talking about getting one of the French or American icebreakers to do it instead. Otherwise, they'll have to fly stuff in to Wilkins. Some of the supplies are still aboard our vessel, though, so they can't make the trip until we've unloaded everything and shipped it over to Hobart."

So there was a way back to Davis. Audra breathed a sigh of relief. She only needed to convince the doctors that she was fit enough to be on that ship.

FORTY-FIVE

Back at McMurdo, Jean was surprised to find how alien all the American accents sounded to him after so many weeks among Aussies.

"So, how was Heard Island? Did you get to meet the Penguin Weather Girl?" Heidi, one of the astrophysicists he remembered from last year, asked.

Jean's head hurt. "The what?"

Heidi laughed. "The Penguin Weather Girl. She's a meteorologist working down here, but her video channel makes Antarctica sound like paradise, instead of hell frozen over. In her last video, she said she was on the same team as a penguin researcher on Heard Island, so I thought of you. Do you know what happened to her?"

His blood turned to ice. "What happened to her?"

"Well, that's it, isn't it? None of us know, and she hasn't uploaded a new video. Talk about a cliffhanger! She's got half the world wondering, and the other half are guessing who her mystery man is."

Audra had been taking videos all over the place, but Jean had thought she was doing it to send home, or to entertain her friend who kept pestering her with video calls. Could she really have a video channel? And what had she said about him?

"I don't know about any videos," he said. "Can you show me?"

Heidi shrugged. "Sure." She swiped and tapped her tablet a few times, then handed it to him. "Here. That's the one she released a week ago." She hit play.

A familiar Aussie voice came from the tablet: "Hi. Welcome back to Heard Island. If you're watching this – "

Just the sound of Audra's voice made Jean's heart melt. He watched her show off Heard Island, before she pointed the camera at him. The barely recognisable figure waved at her from the boat, but he couldn't hear his own shouted warning about the volcano.

What he saw next made his breath catch in his throat.

Penguins. Dozens of them, milling around just like he remembered, but behind the adults, in a depression hidden among the rocks, she'd found the crèche where they kept the juveniles. Audra was an angel.

"How many people have seen this?" Jean asked urgently. If the whole world knew about his penguins, then his paper wouldn't be as groundbreaking as he'd hoped.

Heidi angled the tablet so she could see the screen. "Oh, about eight million or so, which is why everyone's speculating about what happened to her."

Jean skipped back in the video, so he could watch the

baby penguins again. He had to thank her. Personally. Properly. Somehow.

"So do you know her? And do you know what happened?" Heidi pressed.

"She broke her arm. A passing ship airlifted her out and took her back to Australia," Jean said.

Heidi looked crestfallen. "Is that all? So why hasn't she posted another video, then?"

Realisation dawned. "Because when she broke her arm, she asked me to keep her camera safe. I've still got it." He'd found it in his coat pocket the day she left, so he'd carefully packed it with the rest of her things and they were all sitting in his quarters now, waiting for him to find a way to get it all back to her.

"Seriously? So you do know her! I'll have to watch the videos again and see if I can spot you in any of them." Heidi looked ready to burst with joy. "Ooh, I fly out tomorrow. I can take the camera with me and put it in the post when I reach New Zealand."

"No," Jean said immediately. "I…I wouldn't know what address for you to send it to." Plus, he intended to be on tomorrow's flight out, and the next flight to Australia after that. He might not know her address, but he could meet the icebreaker in port, and be there when she disembarked.

He needed to thank her, and return her things. But more than that, he needed to tell her…things. About feelings and how empty he was without her and how, if she'd let him, he wanted to keep her safe always.

But before he did that, he needed some answers. And he knew exactly who to ask.

FORTY-SIX

Once the ship's doctor had set her arm, Audra flatly refused to stay in sickbay.

Jodi, the doctor, protested, "But I'd really like to keep you under observation, just in case – "

"I'll sleep in the same bunkroom as you, but I'm not sleeping here," Audra interrupted. "Last time I was in this ship's sickbay, it was my first time as an emergency medic and the patient had two shattered legs. I don't want to remember that, thank you."

Reluctantly, Jodi agreed, but only if Audra wore a sling that kept her arm secure across her chest while she was aboard the ship. If the ship ran into a storm, she didn't want Audra to risk doing even worse damage if her injured arm hit one of the bulkheads.

When the ship ran into a storm, Audra amended in her head as she accepted the sling. Not staying in sickbay meant taking less potent pain medication, too, but that could only be a good thing. The withdrawal symptoms after only one dose of morphine were bad enough – anything worse would put her back in sickbay where she didn't want to be.

Jodi showed her to her sleeping quarters, then asked Audra to join her in the mess hall for lunch.

Audra almost drooled at the selection of food on offer. She hadn't eaten anything that didn't come out of a dehydrated food package in weeks. She eyed off a particularly mouth-watering chicken parmigiana until she realised she couldn't cut it with her right arm out of action. Reluctantly, she chose the stir-fry instead.

Jodi sat with her. "I didn't realise you were the first responder to that American last year."

"He's Canadian," Audra corrected. "And I wasn't really. They didn't have a medic aboard the ship at the time, so they picked me up from Davis to help out until he could see a real doctor at Casey."

"Me. I spent last summer at Casey, and this summer at Mawson." Jodi took a bite of her chicken. "I remember him. He was a mess. I haven't seen anything that bad since I was working the Emergency Department as a med student and a guy got run over by a truck. So, do you know what actually happened to him?"

Audra swallowed a well-crunched snowpea. "Well, it wasn't a truck. He fell down a sinkhole on Heard Island. The place is riddled with lava tubes and he went through the roof of one. He said he had to swim out, and drag himself up the beach to an emergency hut to call for help."

Jodi gave a low whistle. "Wow, no wonder he looked so bad. By the time he arrived at Casey, I couldn't get anything sensible out of him. He kept calling me darling, or at least that's what I thought until I tried to contact his next of kin. Turned out his wife's name was Dairine. He thought I was her, and he was muttering about a baby. He even tried to kiss me once." She laughed. "Morphine makes people loopy, all right."

Audra managed a smile in response, but beneath it, her mind churned. So, did that mean he hadn't been trying to cheat on his wife when he'd grabbed her? He'd honestly believed she was the faraway Dairine when he'd tried to get her into bed? It didn't excuse him, of course, but it matched better with his behaviour ever since. It made him less of a dirty, cheating bastard who tried to force women to sleep with him and more of a…well, normal bloke who'd been away from his wife too long.

If it weren't for his wife, Audra might have reconsidered her resistance to his kisses on Valentine's Day. She might even have welcomed more. As it was…Audra sighed. She'd probably forgive him for mistaking her for his wife, and in the unlikely event that she ever saw him again, she'd thank him for taking care of her when she broke her arm. After all, he had carried her quite a way.

Whoever she was, Dairine was one lucky woman. She'd married a real, live romance hero, and Audra hoped she appreciated what she had.

FORTY-SEVEN

"Hi, this is Jean Pennant from McMurdo. Can I speak to Shelley, your Chief Meteorologist, please?" Jean waited for the woman at the other end to send someone searching for Shelley, but instead his call was transferred almost immediately.

"Hello, this is Shelley," she answered on the second ring. "Hello?"

"Ah, this is Jean Pennant. I'm a biologist. I was at Davis at the beginning of the season before heading out to Heard Island." He felt silly being such a coward and not blurting out his questions straight away, but he couldn't risk pissing the woman off and not getting any answers.

Her tone turned wary. "I remember you. Audra's roommate." A dangerous pause stretched before she added, "So, how is she?"

Jean sucked in a breath and blew it out. "She broke her

arm."

"Yeah, I saw that. On the video. I also saw you were there."

He smiled mirthlessly. So someone had recognised him as the red blob in the boat. "Yes. It's about that, really. She wouldn't let me perform first aid. Do you know why that might be?" He'd bet his entire PhD scholarship that she did.

"Well, it's hardly surprising, is it?"

Jean froze. From the blasé way she spoke, it sounded like everyone knew about Audra's abusive past. Everyone but him, of course. "I guess not," he said slowly. "I mean, it's obvious someone's hurt her. She wouldn't say who, though."

It almost sounded like Shelley snorted. "She's too nice sometimes. But I'm not. I have no problems naming names, because no woman should have to go through what she has."

"So name them, then," Jean challenged, dying to know.

"I don't have to. It's all there in the video she took." Shelley sounded smug.

Jean only knew of one video. "The penguin one?" he guessed.

"Bingo."

She'd said something about her abuser in the video? He'd have to watch it the whole way through, instead of just the baby penguins.

"Ah, can you remind me?" he ventured.

That was definitely a snort. "Why, have you forgotten already? That's convenient."

"I wasn't there for all the video," he defended himself. "I was out in the boat for part of it, and I haven't watched it all."

"Not the video, you idiot. On the ship. The day you met her."

He'd hurt her? Was Shelley mad? There's no way he would've done anything to hurt Audra. He just didn't have it in him to hurt a woman, let alone do something that would leave her that scared that she'd refuse medical assistance.

"I don't remember anything of my time aboard the *Aurora Australis* that first time. Not Audra, not anyone. I was sedated on Heard Island and I woke up in a cargo plane," he said, desperate for her to believe him. "I couldn't have…I wouldn't…I…" He stopped. Protesting wouldn't get him answers. He'd done something, and he needed to know what so he could make it right. "Please tell me what happened."

So Shelley repeated the story Audra had told her, omitting no details to spare his feelings.

Jean had been a right asshole, he knew that now. It explained why she'd been so shocked to see him in her sleeping quarters at Davis, why she'd cringed away from their kiss, why she wouldn't let him touch her in that hut…It was a wonder Audra had deigned to speak to him at all, instead of having him arrested for what amounted to attempted rape the day they met.

Somehow, in his drug-addled brain, he'd mistaken the meteorologist for Dairine, and in his clumsy attempt to give his imagined ex-wife what she wanted, he'd ruined his chances with Audra. Now, more than ever, he had to see her, if only to apologise, and try to make amends for what he did.

He thanked Shelley, and ended the call as politely as he could. He had a plane to catch, and he had to find out where on Earth the port of Fremantle was, because Audra's icebreaker would dock in just over a week's time.

FORTY-EIGHT

Audra smoothed down the skirt of the dress she felt was way too formal for the deck of an icebreaker, or walking through the port city of Fremantle. She looked like she was dressed for a date, not for a doctor's appointment and a bunch of x-rays. She didn't have a choice, though – her only other clothes were more suited to Heard Island and not a hot March day in Western Australia.

"I'm almost jealous," Jodi said. "That dress looks so much better on you than it ever did on me."

"I'll wash it and give it back to you, as soon as I've picked up some of my own clothes from home," Audra replied quickly. She'd made one phone call as the ship arrived in port, telling her family she'd be in Perth so she'd be home for dinner.

"No, you keep it. It never fitted me anyway."

"I'll pay you for it, then. Transfer the money through

when I next get to a computer," Audra said.

"If you like." Jodi gestured for Audra to go first along the gangway to the wharf.

It felt strange to set foot on dry land again after weeks at sea, but Fremantle was as familiar as it had ever been. Fishermen lined up along the wharf, while a tourist in a souvenir cap topped with a garish kangaroo sat watching them from a bench in the shade of a crane. Audra breathed in the smells of home, and they were both strange and welcoming. She'd been away too long.

"C'mon, I called us a cab," Jodi said, pointing.

Audra followed her to the taxi, but her attention wasn't on the directions Jodi gave the driver. Instead, her eyes were fixed on the outside world, and everything she wanted to leave behind to return to Antarctica, if Jodi cleared her to go back to work.

Audra drifted through the x-rays and tests, answering some questions and letting Jodi handle the rest. They'd been through this already on the ship, so none of it was new until Jodi said, "This is healing nicely. Let's get this cast off and replace it with a brace."

That perked Audra up. "You mean I'll be able to shower properly again?"

Jodi laughed. "Sure. Oh, which colour would you like?"

Faced with a choice between camouflage and a bright polka-dot print, Audra picked the dots.

"That'll show up well against the ice," Jodi said.

Some time later, her arm feeling much lighter in her new brace and sling, they rode back to the wharf in another taxi.

"So, what's the verdict?" Audra asked finally.

"You'll probably be wearing that for three months, while

you're on restricted duty," Jodi began.

Audra's heart sank. "So they'll probably give me a desk job in Head Office?" So much for the Midwinter dinner.

"I don't see why. Being the station meteorologist is mostly a desk job, anyway. You'll be restricted from doing most of the chores, though, and the rock-climbing wall will be off limits." Jodi grinned. "Most people would be happy to get a Head Office posting instead of wintering at one of the stations. Are you feeling all right?"

Audra breathed again. "I am now. Thank you. It'll be my first winter out there, and I've been told what to expect, but I've been looking forward to it. Maybe next summer I'll change my mind."

Jodi paid the driver and helped Audra out of the taxi. "Now, let's go get our stuff, so we can abandon ship and head home."

"Yeah." Audra looked up at the icebreaker, saddened at the thought that she wouldn't be travelling back to base on it. A new ship and a new adventure awaited, or maybe even a cargo plane, if Eric's predictions were true.

Then someone called her name.

Audra scanned the wharf, looking for the source.

Jean rose from the bench where he'd been sitting, pulling off his kangaroo cap. "I wasn't sure if it was you before, out of your expedition gear."

Jodi asked softly whether Audra wanted her to stay. Audra shook her head, so Jodi headed up the gangway and out of sight.

"What do you want?" Audra addressed Jean. Then, "What are you doing here?"

"I need to talk to you."

Audra didn't respond.

"About what happened on the ship." He paused, then added, "The day we met. What happened on the ship the day we met."

"I don't want to talk about it. In fact, I'd like to forget it ever happened," Audra replied, taking a step toward the gangway.

"Wait! Please. I need to apologise."

That got her attention.

"Why? After all this time, why do you suddenly need to do it now?" Audra asked.

Jean cleared his throat. "Because I only just found out last week." At her snort of disbelief, he continued, "I honestly don't remember anything about that ship." He jerked a thumb at the icebreaker. "I passed out in an Apple hut on Heard Island and I woke up in a cargo plane. I know it's no excuse, but I was so out of my mind with pain and drugs that I don't remember anything in between."

Audra wasn't sure whether to believe him or not.

"You've lived and worked with me for months. Have I ever not apologised when I've done something wrong? Straight away?" he asked.

One example stood clear in her mind. "You didn't apologise for that kiss."

He managed a sad smile. "That's because I'm not sorry I did that. It was an awesome kiss. Best Valentine's kiss I've ever had, bar none."

Audra blew out an angry breath. Men. They were all alike. Cheating, horny bastards who only wanted to get into her pants. She turned away.

"Please, Audra, wait! I'm sorry. I'm sorry for trying to

force you to sleep with me on the ship. I'm sorry I didn't apologise the moment we met at Davis. I'm sorry I didn't remember the day I met you. And I'm sorry for any pain or trauma I caused you. I've never done anything like that before, and I never want to again. I'm sorry. You see, I must have thought you were – "

"Your wife, Dairine. I know," Audra interrupted. She stared into his anguished eyes for a moment before she nodded. "Don't worry about it."

"But…I hurt you. I swear, I never wanted to do anything to hurt you."

"Shelley told you, didn't she?" Audra read the confirmation in his expression, so she went on, "I didn't tell her everything."

Jean's eyes implored her. "Tell me. Tell me exactly what happened, and then tell me what I can do to make it up to you. I'll even buy you lunch while you do it."

Audra nodded and led the way to one of the nearby cafés. Though she wasn't really hungry, she ordered something off the menu and sat down with Jean at one of the indoor tables, where there was air conditioning.

She took a sip from her drink, and told him everything. From finding out she was needed on the ship to leaving him in Jodi's care at Casey. His eyes widened in surprise when she told him how she'd stabbed him, and that's when she believed him. Believed that he really didn't remember any of it, and that his apology was sincere.

A sudden thought occurred to her. "Did I do anything while I was on morphine? Anything that I don't remember?"

Jean drained his drink and gestured for the waiter to get

him another one. "You snored."

Audra smacked his wrist. "I do not snore!"

He seized her hand. Her good hand. "All right, if you say so."

Sea ice eyes met hers, and Audra was momentarily lost. Mesmerised. How could such icy depths seem so warm?

"What are you doing this afternoon?" Jean asked.

"I'd planned to see if I could find any fresh mangoes, and eat as many of those as I can without being sick, then pick up some clothes to wear, before going to dinner at my parents' house."

Jean stared. "You mean this is your home town?"

"Yes."

"Can I come with you?"

Audra hesitated. "Why?" she said finally.

Jean lifted her hand to his lips and kissed it. "Because I enjoy your company, and I've missed it. And because if this is your home town, you know it way better than I do. Without you, I'll be lost."

He's married! Audra screamed at herself in her head. He's married and it doesn't matter if he looks at you like that, he's not yours!

She yanked her hand back. "Maybe. First, I need to figure out what I'm going to do about money, seeing as I left Heard Island without my wallet or phone or even a spare pair of socks."

"I can help with that. I've got all your gear in my hotel room," Jean said.

Like that didn't sound dodgy at all.

He continued, "I've got your camera, too. I really think you should – "

"Can you get them for me?" Audra interrupted.

"What, you mean go through your stuff to find your wallet and phone?" He looked stunned at the idea.

At least he hadn't pawed through her underwear. "They're in a pocket just inside the main section, sort of zipped to the back of the backpack. You'd just have to open it and you'll see it," Audra said.

"Or you could just come up and get whatever you need." He eyed her curiously, until realisation dawned in his eyes. "You don't trust me. After what I did when we met. I guess that's fair. I'm still willing to do anything you say to make it up to you for what I did."

"Just get me my things."

He gave her a mock salute. "Yes, ma'am. You want to come sit outside the hotel while you wait, or do you want me to meet you back here?"

Audra wasn't sure what she wanted any more. "Where's your hotel?" she asked.

Jean pointed. "Over by the fishing boat harbour with all the seafood restaurants."

A short walk from the wharf. "Okay, then," Audra said, gesturing for him to lead the way. But instead of heading for the sprawling, heritage building near the café strip, he turned toward the fishing boat harbour. Audra held her tongue until after they'd crossed the railway line and were approaching some of the seafood restaurants before she asked, "Are you sure you know where you're going?"

"Yeah," he responded cheerfully. "It's over there by the water."

Audra didn't remember any accommodation past the fishing companies. Surely it was just the seawall protecting the harbour. Was Jean sleeping aboard a boat?

Right near the end of Mews Road, where Audra could see nothing between her and the open ocean, Jean turned left. "This one's mine," he said.

To her surprise, he pointed at a row of two-storey apartments that Audra had never seen before. They didn't look new, either. "I didn't even know these were here," she marvelled.

"Want to come up after all? The view's great from the balcony."

Still she hesitated. She'd shared a room with him for months and he'd never laid a finger on her. They'd shared a hut on isolated Heard Island, and he'd had plenty of opportunities to cause all kinds of trouble. Even on the coldest nights, he'd never suggested sharing a sleeping bag, though she'd seriously considered it. It had been cold at night without her hot water bottle.

Damn it, it was the middle of the day in her home town, with plenty of people about. And she wanted to see the view. "Yeah, I'll come up," Audra said, following Jean up the stairs.

FORTY-NINE

This was a mistake. She didn't even like him, Jean told himself as he strode up the steps. She hadn't looked happy to see him, though it was a relief that she looked healthier than the woman who'd flown out of Heard in a helicopter. But she had accepted his apology, which was a start. Maybe she just needed time to warm up to him, after believing him to be an asshole for so long.

Or maybe this was a huge mistake and he should leave before he caused her any more trouble.

He pointed to her bag, then headed out to the balcony. That way, he wouldn't have to watch her leave, and walk out of his life forever. He'd just hear the door shut, and...

"I found my wallet and phone." Audra stepped out onto the balcony beside him. "Everything in that bag smells awful, though. It's been weeks since I did any washing, and it shows."

"There's a washing machine here and a dryer," Jean replied. "I have a big box of laundry powder, too. I used a lot to wash my stuff when I first got here, but there's still plenty left, if you want it." He'd wash it for her if it meant spending more time with her, and he usually hated laundry.

She looked thoughtful for a moment, then said, "If you let me do my washing here, I'll do my best to be your tour guide for the afternoon."

He didn't hesitate. "Deal."

Water soon cascaded into the washing machine full of Audra's clothes, so it was her turn to hold up her end of the bargain. True to her word, Audra walked him through the century-old prison, then took him to see the remnants of a four-hundred-year-old shipwreck in the maritime museum. When they walked out of the museum, Audra suddenly stopped. She closed her eyes, inhaled deeply and threw her arms wide as if to embrace the breeze.

"Ohhh, the Fremantle Doctor," she said in what Jean thought sounded like a moan of longing.

A mental image of her moaning in pleasure flashed through Jean's head, distracting him. Yes, he wanted that. So much. Baby steps, though. First, he had to persuade her to like him.

It took a moment for her words to register. "You need to see a doctor?" Jean asked.

Audra laughed. "No, I've seen enough doctors this week. The Freo Doctor is what we call the afternoon sea breeze. It blows away the summer heat and makes everything wonderful."

The smile on her face was definitely wonderful, Jean thought but didn't say. Instead, he said, "Where to next?"

"The markets. I need those mangoes."

Jean followed her into the markets, through the crowded stalls of souvenirs and all sorts of goods. Soon, he had a collection of odd items to send home to his parents, while Audra blissfully swung a bag of fruit by her side.

"Now all I need is a knife," Audra said.

"Plenty in my kitchen, if you want. Use whatever you need, while I shift your clothes into the dryer," Jean suggested.

To his shock, she accepted his offer.

Swearing under his breath, he dragged the tangle of wet clothes out of the washer and battled to get it all into the dryer. A couple of socks made a bid for freedom, but he added them to the drum before he switched the dryer on.

When he returned to the kitchen, he found Audra had sliced up several of the mangoes, and was partway through dissecting a chunk of watermelon.

"You'd have made a good biologist," he commented, eyeing her precision with the chef's knife.

Audra laughed. "No, I wouldn't. I don't have the patience for it. And the dissections…ugh, no thanks. Not to mention collecting dung samples, or baiting traps with all sorts of disgusting things. I like the weather much more." She blushed. "And the weather has a power to it that I just can't resist. Plants and animals just don't leave me with the same awe."

Jean nodded. He understood. The only time he'd ever felt awe around any animal was when they'd encountered a pod of whales last summer. "What about whales?"

"Okay, I'll give you that, but there aren't many jobs for whale biologists, unless you work on one of Japan's scientific whaling vessels." Audra scooped up the watermelon slices and set them on a plate. "I think I bought too much. I hope you're hungry."

He helped her carry the food out to the table on the balcony, waiting for her to choose a chair before he sat in the other one.

"I know they're not exactly awe-inspiring, but penguins are still important," he began. "They're an essential indicator species – "

"Of climate change. I know," Audra interjected with a grin, popping a piece of mango into her mouth. She swallowed, then said, "You've told me a few times. You're passionate about your penguins, and your research, which is why I'm still wondering why you're here." Green eyes gazed at him over a slice of watermelon.

He swallowed. "I told you already. I came to apologise. And…to thank you. That last video you took on Heard Island helped my research more than you know. Right now, you're at the top of my list of acknowledgements for my thesis."

"Uh, thanks. But you could've just sent me a copy. It'll make interesting reading while I'm waiting for the computers to come up with the next weather forecast."

"I will." This was where he was supposed to talk about feelings, wasn't it? "I wanted to see you. I missed you, and it might be a long time before I see you again. And I wanted to thank you in person." He sounded so stupid he would've walked out.

Audra didn't, though. Her lips turned up in a tiny, enigmatic smile. "Yeah, you said that, too. And now you've done both, so mission accomplished. Whereas I have to be at my parents' house in just over an hour for dinner, so I should probably get going."

No! Don't go! He wanted to grab her and say the words out loud, but then he'd just look like a bigger idiot than he already was. "Can I come?" he blurted out instead.

FIFTY

Audra's jaw dropped. Jean wanted to meet her family? Why? This could only end badly. Then again, that might be a good thing. The way he'd mumbled and repeated himself made him sound like a shy teenager trying to work up the courage to ask her out. Instead of a married man who should know better than to do any such thing.

Audra wet her lips. "My family isn't particularly wealthy, and my father lost his job when the mining boom ended. You're probably better off having dinner at one of the seafood restaurants here."

Jean shrugged. "My family's not rich. I'd rather have dinner with you than eat lobster alone." His eyes widened. "Or do you mean they won't have enough food for all of us? I could buy something and bring it along."

He was so close to the mark, but Audra didn't want to admit it. "Actually, I'll be picking dinner up on the way.

There's a pizza place near their house." If she didn't, there was no guarantee she'd get dinner at all.

"So how are you getting there?" he pressed.

She hadn't thought of that. It wasn't like she had a car any more. "Taxi?"

"I have a rental car. I can drive you," Jean offered. "I'll put your bag in the trunk, and I can drop whatever's in the dryer off tomorrow. Unless you want to take it now, and dry it at home. I mean – "

"It's not home." The moment Audra said the words, she knew they were true. She hadn't been here in almost two years. Broome, Melbourne, Davis, even Heard Island – all those places felt more like home than her family's crowded state housing handout. She might not have a permanent place of her own right now, but Davis was home for as long as she was posted there. "And yes, you can drop things off tomorrow. My parents don't have a dryer, and the neighbours nick things off the line if you don't watch it."

"So you want me to come?" he asked eagerly.

Yes. The answer surprised her, but it wasn't about Jean. Not really. Her family would be on their best behaviour with a stranger there, and her brothers would be less likely to ask her for money. Of course, he'd leave after dinner, to go back to his hotel room, while she stayed in the tiny room she'd shared with her sister since Sam was born, but it would only be for a few nights until she flew out to Hobart to meet the ship taking her home. It wasn't such a hardship. After all, she hadn't seen her family in ages.

"Sure. But I'll have to order you an extra pizza," Audra said. "What would you like?"

Jean shrugged. "I don't mind. Whatever you

recommend. Do you know how long it's been since I had fresh pizza?"

Audra tried not to laugh. "About as long as me, I imagine." She made the call, placed her order, and zipped up her bag, ready to go. Then she reached for it with her right hand and realised her mistake. She was going to have to pretend to be a frail female and ask Jean for help.

"Hey, I'll get that," Jean said before she could ask, slinging her backpack over his shoulder like it weighed nothing.

"Thank you." She tried to make the words sound as grateful as she felt.

As she climbed into the passenger seat of Jean's hired hatchback, Audra realised she couldn't have driven it even if she wanted to – one arm wasn't enough.

She directed Jean south, feeling a strange tightening in her tummy as the stacks of the refinery came into view. "Not far now," she said, hoping the pizzas would be ready by the time they reached the place. Anything was better than cold, though.

Jean looked stunned when he saw the stack of boxes waiting for them. "How many people are in your family?" he asked.

"I have three brothers and a sister, plus my parents. All of the boys will eat a pizza each. Maybe more. Besides, it's always been the rules in my parents' house that whoever's up first the morning after pizza night, they get to eat the leftovers for breakfast."

"Cold pizza for breakfast?" Jean looked ill.

Audra laughed. "Of course not. Heated up in the microwave. It was usually me and Sam up first, because I'd have to work."

"Sam's one of your brothers?" Jean guessed.

"No. Samantha is my little sister. She's in Year 12 this year, and she wants to go to university, like I did, but she hasn't decided what she wants to study yet." Audra expected him to be bored, but Jean waved for her to continue, so she did. "Tadas – we call him Tad – he lost his job about the same time Dad did, and he's been depressed about it for as long as I can remember. Occasionally he gets a new job, or an interview for one, but it never lasts long. He has the worst luck. Benediktas is an apprentice electrician. He's actually not too bad, but he's had his tools stolen a few times, which means he can't work until he buys new ones, which he really can't afford on an apprentice's salary, so it's taking him longer than normal to finish his apprenticeship. Leonas is my youngest brother. He was born after me, but before Sam. Leon had a nasty car accident a few years ago. He had head injuries and nearly died, but he hasn't really recovered from it. So if he says anything strange, it's because of his brain trauma."

"It sounds like your family's had a run of bad luck," Jean said, his eyes on the road.

"Not all of us. Not Sam, and not me," Audra said.

He glanced at her. "A broken arm isn't bad luck?"

"Getting accepted into the graduate program, being selected to go to Antarctica twice, being part of a South Pole expedition and a trip to Heard Island, where I got to see a volcano erupt…all those are incredibly good luck," Audra said. She waved at her polka-dot brace. "This doesn't even start to even it out. I'd have to break both my legs, too, to – " She stopped when she saw his white-knuckled grip on the steering wheel. "I'm sorry. I shouldn't have said that."

He barked out a harsh laugh. "Maybe you're right. Maybe I've been so lucky with my scholarship and all that my accident was just the universe trying to keep things balanced, but it tipped things too far the other way. I guess that means I'm due some really good luck soon, then."

Audra had never heard him sound so bitter. "You'll get your PhD. That's a good thing, right?"

"I guess after three long years, it's sort of lost its shine. Yeah, I'll get it, but after all the hard work it doesn't feel so important any more. My plan was always to finish my PhD, then take a postdoctorate or teaching post at a university. Settle down and have a family."

Audra's blood ran cold. A family, with his wife. That's what he meant. She had to remember that even after spending a lovely afternoon with him, he was nothing more than a work colleague. One who was married to someone else.

FIFTY-ONE

Jean expected a lot worse than the house Audra identified as her parents' one. Sure, the garden was mostly dead weeds, but so was the rest of the street. The beaten-up car in the front yard made him wince, though.

"Was that the car your brother crashed?" Jean asked.

"One of them," Audra answered through gritted teeth. "The first one he left at the crash site. That one used to be mine. He borrowed it without my permission while I was working in Broome and did that to it."

Jean swore. "What did your parents do?"

Audra swallowed. "Nothing. It's Leon."

What kind of parents let a boy wreck his sister's car without some sort of punishment? Jean fumed. She was a graduate, barely out of college, with probably a huge debt to pay off and not exactly a high-paying job to do it on. If she hadn't needed the car, she could have sold it to help pay off her loan. If her brother didn't have the money, then her parents should have done something.

"C'mon, let's get these pizzas inside before they get cold." Audra's tone had turned dull and lifeless, much like the dried weeds crunching underfoot.

Jean grabbed the boxes and followed her to the front door.

She knocked several times before someone finally came to the door.

"I thought I heard something, but then I thought, nah, it's too early. So good to see you!" a female voice exclaimed.

The screen door clanged open and a girl with bright green hair threw herself at Audra.

Jean strode forward to intercede even before Audra let out a pained yelp. "Careful. She has a broken arm," he boomed, bringing his own arm up to shield Audra's from her overzealous sister.

To her credit, the girl backed off. "How did you do that?"

"It was a volcano," Audra began shakily.

The girl didn't let her finish. "A volcano? There are volcanoes in Antarctica?"

Audra described Heard Island to her sister as they followed her inside. Jean tried to keep his expression neutral as he surveyed the interior, which had definitely seen better days. Better decades, too, seeing as the décor looked like they'd picked the colour scheme before Audra was born and not done anything to it since.

"Where do you want me to put these?" Jean asked, lifting the stack of boxes.

"On the dining table," Audra and her sister said

together.

They both laughed, then the sister said, "I'll get some plates." As she leaned over to extract them from the kitchen cabinet, she hollered. "Oi! Audra's here and she brought dinner!"

Three men marched into the room, and made a beeline for the table. They each picked up a pizza box, ignored the plates, and headed for the front room. Not one of them said a word to him or their sisters.

Jean felt his anger build. She'd been away for months, and even bought them dinner. What kind of family didn't say hello or thank you? They hadn't offered to pay her back for the pizzas, either, and those hadn't come cheap. Someone should have picked her up from the port, instead of letting her find her own way here. Did they just take her for granted so much that they'd stopped caring for her? It just wasn't right. Audra deserved better. So much better than this.

Audra didn't seem surprised. "Where are Mum and Dad?"

The girl rolled her eyes. "At the state housing office again. They sent a nasty letter, saying they didn't have as many kids any more, so they didn't need a four bedroom house. Because I'm the only one who's still a kid, they're only entitled to a two-bedroom unit. So they took all the doctors' reports for Leon and Tad, and all the paperwork from welfare and Ben's apprenticeship, and they're trying to convince them that we do need this house, otherwise they'll need to find a new place for Leon and Ben and Tad, and a new place for us, and they're saying the waiting list is a couple of years."

Audra nodded. "Bloody bureaucrats." There was no venom in her tone – just tired resignation. She gestured toward the table. "Have something to eat, Jean."

He was as bad as they were, taking her for granted. First out on Heard Island and now here. He should've paid for dinner, not her. Too late now.

Feeling both girls' eyes on him, he took a plate and lifted two slices from the nearest box. Then he was lost. "Are we sitting at the table or joining them?" One glance at Audra's polka-dotted arm gave him his answer. He might not have done enough to repay her kindness before, but he could start now. "I'd prefer to sit at the table, if that's all right."

The girls nodded, then made their own selection. Audra slid into the seat on one side of him, while her sister took the other.

"Who's he, then?" the sister asked through a mouthful of pizza.

Audra swallowed. "This is Jean, a biologist who was working with me at Heard Island. Jean, this is my sister, Sam."

Sam's eyes were more golden than the green of her sister's. "What are you doing here?"

"Audra said she'd show me around for a bit while I'm in Fremantle, so she invited me along to dinner to meet her family," Jean said.

"How long are you staying?"

"I fly out in a few days."

At this, Audra slumped slightly in her seat. Did that mean she was relieved, or disappointed? Or just tired?

"I'll be right back," Sam said, jumping to her feet. She hurried out of the room.

Jean looked askance at Audra, who just shrugged.

One of her brothers sidled into the room. He jutted his chin at Audra. "So, when are you going to pay to get the car fixed?"

She slumped down further in her seat. "I already told you, I'm not, Leon."

"But I need it for Leteesha!" he whined.

"Then save up your dole cheques and buy your own car." Audra sounded bone weary.

"But that's not soon enough. If you give me the money, I'll pay you back. I just need five grand. Davo down the road has this sick Skyline that needs a new engine, and he only wants a couple grand for it. Couple grand for the car, couple for the engine and a new paintjob, and I'll be able to get Leteesha back." His eyes glowed. "C'mon, sis."

"Don't you already owe her for the damage you caused to the car out front?" Jean asked, annoyed.

"Wasn't me," Leon whined. "And who the fuck are you? Stupid Yank."

Audra clamped a restraining hand over Jean's arm. "Jean's my friend from work. And he's Canadian, not American."

"Same difference," the boy sneered. "Go on, sis, give me the money. I know you got it."

"She's still not giving it to you," Jean snapped.

The boy backed down a little. "You her boyfriend, then, telling her what she can do with her money?"

Jean had had enough of this little punk. "Yes. And we're saving for a house, so we need every cent we earn for the deposit. Including the money you owe her." Under the table, he crossed his fingers. He'd be gone in a matter of days and she could tell them whatever she wanted then.

Leon turned his belligerent eyes on Audra. "That true?"

Audra swallowed. "Yes," she said softly, then more loudly, "Yes. It is."

"Where you buying, then? If Mum and Dad lose this place, we can all come and stay with you. There's a new housing estate being built just south of here, near the beach. That'd be good."

Jean barely managed to suppress a shudder. "Christchurch, in New Zealand. It's a lot colder then here, but it's closer to Antarctica." He slipped an arm around Audra's shoulders and felt her stiffen. "It's what we both want."

The front door clanged open and an older couple walked in, looking just as tired as Audra.

"Oh good, dinner," her father said, helping himself to some pizza, while Audra's mother rounded the table to give Audra a hug.

Her mother held out a hand to Jean. "You must be Audra's boyfriend. I'm Jolanta."

Too late Jean realised he still had his arm around Audra. "I'm Jean-Pierre." He shook hands with the woman. "I headed up the Heard Island expedition with Audra for my PhD research."

She nodded with what Jean hoped was approval. "Not bad."

Audra's dad stuck out his hand. "I'm Lukas. I hope you have better luck getting Audra to settle down than we have. She spends far too much time and money travelling around, when she should be saving it. Jobs can vanish like that." He snapped his fingers.

Audra shrugged off Jean's arm. "Dad, I've only been travelling for work. They pay me for it. Which reminds me, I should get some of my summer clothes while I'm here. I only brought winter ones with me, and they're too hot for March." She rose and disappeared in the same direction her sister had gone.

Jolanta settled into Audra's seat. "So, Jean-Pierre. What sort of research do you do?"

FIFTY-TWO

Audra stepped into the bedroom she and Sam had shared for more than fifteen years and didn't recognise it. "Where is everything?"

Sam glanced up from her computer – Audra's old laptop. "When you moved out, I bought a desk at the local op shop and the boys helped me move your bed out so I could fit the desk in here."

"What about my clothes?" Audra asked, opening the wardrobe door. Nothing inside was hers.

"The boys moved your stuff to the garage."

"Even the boxes I sent from Melbourne?" Audra persisted.

Sam nodded. "Everything. You know how cramped it used to be in here. If I'd moved out first, you'd have spread out, too."

Audra's mouth was dry. She'd counted on staying here

tonight, but there was nowhere for her to sleep. It wasn't home any more. Her words from earlier, come back to haunt her. "The garage. Right."

She strode through the house, managing a smile for Jean and her parents as she headed for the back door. The garage was full of spiders and junk they didn't want any more. Her books, her clothes, her…everything she owned that wasn't at Davis was now in the garage, if one of their dodgy neighbours hadn't stolen it.

Audra flicked on the light, holding her breath as she worried about what she'd find. She exhaled in relief as she spotted the two boxes of clothes she'd mailed from Melbourne last spring, looking a little dusty but still sealed. Underneath those, it was a different story. A collection of water-stained boxes and garbage bags that hadn't been there before filled her with dread.

Waiting would only make matters worse, she told herself as she reached for the nearest bag. She laughed when she realised it held nothing but tinsel. Not her things at all.

None of the bags held her stuff, she discovered, which made her turn her attention to the boxes. A little water probably wouldn't have damaged her clothes, but her books were a different matter. Cautiously, she opened the first one. It was mostly full of books, except for a couple of items of clothing on top. Smiling, Audra pulled out the ball gown she'd worn to her Year 12 formal. She'd been the only girl in white, and while she hadn't won Belle of the Ball, she knew she'd looked good. She hadn't gained much weight since then, either, so it should still fit…

Audra held the dress up against her and looked down. A deep purple blotch spread across the fabric, like someone had spilled wine or ink down the front. A quick glance at the box told her the culprit – the dark cover of a book that had evidently been soaked through at some point in the past, bleeding through her dress until it had killed that, too.

Letting the ruined dress slip from her fingers, Audra dropped to her knees, desperate to check her books, but the further down she got, the worse they became. Covers had run and bled; pages pulped together until the books resembled papier mâché bricks. Textbooks. Fiction books. Her high school yearbook…

Her family had left her most precious possessions out here in the rain to rot.

A tear trickled down Audra's cheek, followed by another. She swiped them away. It was just stuff. It didn't matter. Not really. Except that…it did. It really, really did.

"Hey, are you all right?" Jean's voice cut through her self-pity.

Audra rose, praying that it was too dim in the garage for him to see her tears. She nodded. "I'm fine. I was just looking for a few things, and I think the roof might have sprung a leak, because some of them…" More tears filled her eyes and she had to stop talking to focus on blinking them back.

Jean's eyes landed on the open box. "Hey, is that your high school yearbook?"

That did it. Audra burst into tears.

Jean's strong arms encircled her, pulling her against his chest. Safe. She felt safe. For the first time in how long? Too long.

Since he'd carried her in his arms on Heard Island, her memory piped up. Carried her and protected her and cared for her like no one else had.

Gradually, Audra became aware of Jean's voice, murmuring, "It'll be all right. If there's anything I can do, just tell me. I'll help. I swear I'll help. Anything. Just tell me."

Audra choked back a sob. "I can't stay here. I need to go. And I need to take anything that isn't already damaged, before it gets wrecked, too."

"What do you need me to carry?"

She pointed at the Melbourne boxes. "Just those two."

"Consider it done." He hefted one in his arms and carried it through the gate to his car, followed by the other one. "Anything else?"

She wished there were, but Audra shook her head. "That's all."

"Do you want to head back to Fremantle, to the hotel?" Jean asked.

She could sleep in a hotel. It wouldn't be cheap, but it was only for a couple of nights. She could afford it. Audra nodded.

Jean offered her his arm. "Let's go say goodbye to your family, then, and I'll drive you back. You've had a rough day, and I bet your arm hurts."

He was right. Perfectly, wonderfully right. If only he wasn't already married to someone else. Audra smothered a sigh and headed inside with him. It was time to say goodbye.

FIFTY-THREE

Jean parked the car outside the hotel and they both got out.

Audra began, "Thank you for – "

"Want to come up for a drink?" he asked. "I know what it's like to have your past stuffed into a garage for storage. Forgotten. Only one step away from going into the garbage, like you don't matter any more, when you do."

Audra sighed, dropping her gaze to the pavement. "I want to, more than you know, but I really shouldn't."

"We're both adults, capable of making our own decisions. What your family thinks about it doesn't matter," Jean said.

She bit her lip. "But what about your family?" She raised her eyes, which were full of hurt. "What would your wife say if she knew you were asking strange girls up to your hotel room for a drink?"

Jean barked out a laugh. "My ex-wife lost the right to say

anything about what I do with my life the day she filed for divorce. When she shoved what remained of my possessions into boxes that she hid in a garage. That'd be about two years ago, now. So if she did have anything to say, it'd be along the lines of how it's about time I moved on, seeing as she's remarried and all. They've got kids, too. Twins."

Audra gaped. "You're divorced?"

He managed a smile. "You know, I think this is the first time I've ever been happy about it. Yes. I'm divorced. I was already divorced the day I fell through a sinkhole on Heard Island and broke both my legs; I was divorced as I swam through a lava tube and across Atlas Cove back to camp, chanting my ex-wife's name like a mantra, because, like the fool I was, I believed she loved me as much as I loved her, and that she wanted me home. I was divorced the day I first met you on the *Aurora Australis*, though I don't remember it, and I was divorced for the months I spent recovering in New Zealand while the doctors and medical staff did their damnedest to get me to walk again. But I didn't know until I arrived home in Vancouver, and walked into my ex-wife's house, to find her married to another man and carrying his child. Children, even."

Tears sparkled in Audra's eyes. "But why?"

"I never did ask her that. I figured it was too late to do anything about it, by the time I found out." As he stared into Audra's eyes, Jean realised he'd made a mistake in not asking. "Maybe I should. I don't want to mess up that badly again. Especially not with you." He pulled out his phone, thanking whatever powers of the universe had made sure he had Dairine's phone number for this moment, and made the call.

The phone rang four times before she picked up. "Hello?"

"It's Jean. Please, Dairine, don't hang up. I know you don't want anything to do with me anymore, and that's fine, but I have the right to know why."

Dairine sounded uncertain. "Why?"

"Because I've met another woman who means the world to me, and I don't want to make the same mistake twice." Jean saw Audra's eyes widen, but he ploughed on. "You don't even have to talk to me. Tell her. I'll hand the phone to her so you can say whatever you like. Dairine, my ex-wife, this is Audra." He thrust the phone at Audra.

Audra gingerly took it and placed it by her ear. "Ah, hello? I'm Audra."

FIFTY-FOUR

"You're Jean-Pierre's new girlfriend?" an Irish voice demanded.

Audra was momentarily tongue-tied. She'd expected a Canadian accent like Jean's, not an Irish one. "Ah, not yet. I thought he was married until about five minutes ago. I just asked him what happened to make you divorce him, and…he called you."

Dairine laughed. "So he's still a coward, is he? Doesn't like a direct confrontation. Still walking away from his responsibilities. All right, I'll tell you, and it'll serve him right when you break it off, too."

Audra stiffened, not liking Dairine at all. Perhaps divorce had been a lucky thing for Jean. Audra wet her lips. "Thank you," she said, forcing herself to be polite. After a moment's thought, she hit the speakerphone button so Jean could hear her, too.

"Jean-Pierre Pennant walked out on me to follow a dream. I told him not to call me and not to come back if he meant to go to the ass-end of the world and leave me alone. He left, so I filed for divorce."

Jean nodded, his eyes downcast.

"But was that all?" Audra persisted. Was it such a crime for a man to follow his dream? To go out and do what it took to get his PhD in one of the most hostile environments on Earth?

"What do you mean, was that all? He promised to take care of me. To get a job where we could live near my family. To give me children!" Dairine insisted.

But while he was following that dream, he was bettering his education, so he could get the sort of job where he could take care of a family, Audra wanted to scream at the woman.

"I would have given her all those things, if she'd let me," Jean said softly. "It was only one more year to wait, until my doctorate was done."

"Selfish, that's what he is. He'll do the same to you," Dairine continued, as if she hadn't heard Jean.

"Did he cheat on you?" Audra persisted.

"I'll say he did! He may have married me, but he gave his heart to those birds. Those bloody birds at the bottom of the world!"

Bestiality with a penguin? Didn't the woman know how bad they smelled?

A burst of laughter threatened to escape, but Audra managed to smother it in time. "I mean…with a woman? Or a man?"

"Are you trying to tell me he cheated on me with you?"

Dairine demanded.

Audra drew a deep breath. "No, I'm not. I didn't meet Jean until after you were divorced, or so he tells me." Their first meeting loomed in her mind, pushing her to ask the question worrying her the most. "Did he…was he ever violent toward you?"

Dairine laughed again. "That coward? He wouldn't hurt a single, living thing. Not even bugs in the house. Instead of killing spiders like any normal person would, he'd catch them and carry them outside so he could release them. Besides, if he'd dared raise a hand against me, my brothers would have killed him."

Audra's breath hissed out in relief. "Thank you."

"You're welcome. And I'll tell you something else for free, so you don't make the same mistake I did. Jean-Pierre Pennant isn't worth your time. One day he'll be telling you he loves you and wants to give you the world, but the next day, he'll be gone, chasing a bird or some more letters after his name. If you make him choose between the birds and you, the birds will win. So save yourself some heartache and run while you can, before you start believing his lies. He loves himself and his precious research first, and you'll be lucky to come a distant second. If you turn your back for just a moment, he'll run off to the ends of the Earth to chase some new discovery, leaving you high and dry. Don't let him do it to you."

The faint sound of a baby's wail came through the phone.

"That'll be Thomas. I have to go. Run, you hear me, girl? Run while you can." Dairine ended the call.

Audra handed Jean back his phone.

"She's right," he said sadly. "I'm just a PhD candidate now. And then there's my postdoc, which could be anywhere. Biological research involves fieldwork, and I chose a field where – "

Audra pressed a finger to his lips to silence him. "I have one more question for you. How many girls have you invited to share your room for the night since you married her?"

Jean swallowed. "One. Just you, tonight." He paused. "And no men, ever."

Audra laughed softly. "I think I will come up for that drink. And maybe whatever else you implied in your invitation."

Jean held up his hands. "I'm only offering you drinks, I swear."

Audra met his gaze squarely. "Well, after tonight, I think we both need a drink. A big one."

FIFTY-FIVE

Jean keyed open the apartment door, gesturing for Audra to enter first.

Without waiting for an invitation, she seated herself on the couch. "We both know she's wrong, right?"

The door slipped out of Jean's fingers and slammed harder than he'd intended. "What?"

"When you had to decide between me and your research out on Heard Island, you chose to help me instead of continuing to count your penguins. Even when you knew it might be your last chance to finish your research. The selfish arsehole your ex-wife described wouldn't have bothered to help me. At least, he wouldn't have until he was finished with his task. And you're not a coward, either." Audra took the shot glass Jean handed her and gulped the contents.

And choked.

Jean leaned forward to pound her on the back. "You okay?"

"Fine," Audra said, coughing. "It's that god-awful whisky again, isn't it?"

Jean nodded. "Cost me a damn fortune, but I'm not going back to Antarctica without it."

Audra nearly choked again at his words. "You're going back?"

"Just like she said. We had to make a few concessions to get me a spot on this year's Heard Island expedition. One of them involved me spending the winter at Davis as its botanist, taking care of the hydroponics. My research supervisor said it would give me plenty of time to finish my thesis without distractions." He met her eyes. "I fly out in two days. That's why all I can offer tonight is drinks, because you deserve so much more than a one night stand. I know I can't ask you to wait for me, but – "

"Enough of the self-sacrifice shit, bird-boy. Women can spend the winter in Antarctica, too, you know. And I'm willing to bet you a whole bottle of that horrible whisky that we'll be on the same flight south."

"But…but…your arm…" Jean floundered.

Audra held up her brace. "Broken. Yep. But fixable. And it's not enough to get me out of the work roster back at base. The boys on the icebreaker told me the only reason they brought me here to Fremantle is because they were due here for repairs and didn't have time to detour to one of the mainland bases to drop me off. They're shipping me back on the next flight south, so Shelley can go home. I'm the winter meteorologist at Davis Station this year." She smiled. "I get a nice payrise for it, too."

"Would you like a roommate?" he ventured.

Audra's smile widened. "That depends entirely on how good you are in bed."

Jean swallowed. "Rusty," he admitted.

"Me, too."

They stared at each other for a long moment before Jean broke the silence. "If we're spending the whole winter together, we should take things slow. I mean, you're injured, and I never, ever want to hurt you. Plus, it's been so long that I've probably forgotten how to pleasure a woman properly, if I ever knew."

Audra scrunched up her face. "So maybe we should start with something simple? Like kissing?"

"Kissing is never simple," Jean said, shifting to the seat beside her. "The moment has to be just right, and so much depends on doing the right thing at the right time. First, your lips touch, then they move together until you're sharing each other's very breath. And then – "

Audra laughed. "You talk too much."

"Only when I'm scared or nervous."

"I don't believe a man who could swim across Atlas Cove with two broken legs, among seals and killer whales and all sorts of things, radio for help and then do first aid on himself, is afraid of anything. Let alone some graduate meteorologist with a broken arm."

"The beautiful, talented meteorologist I'm deeply in love with," Jean corrected.

Audra blushed. "You missed intelligent. And besides, how can you know you love me when we've barely even kissed?"

He reached out and pulled her against him, careful not

to touch her injured arm. "Oh, I know. When I heard you scream, those penguins could go screw themselves for all I cared. I couldn't lose you."

She lifted her good hand to caress his face before she kissed him. Azorella-coloured eyes regarded him as her tongue invited his out to play. It felt as natural as breathing to kiss her back with as much passion as he could muster. Breathless. Lost. Found. He'd swim the Southern Ocean for this woman. Or just kiss her forever, if that's what she wanted.

"I love you, Audra," he gasped out.

She smiled. "I'm fast falling for you, too, if I haven't already. You're one up on me. I've never fallen in love before and you have."

"What I had with her was nothing…NOTHING…compared to this." Jean waved at them both.

"One kiss."

"More," he insisted, drawing her closer.

Faint music came from beside Audra.

"Damn, that's my phone."

Jean drew back. "Go on, answer it."

"Hello?"

Audra listened for a moment, before she hit the speakerphone button. "Jay, how did you know I'd even answer my phone?"

"Because you're not online, and I saw from your ship's webcam that you're in Fremantle now, so you have phone access again. Good. Because I need your advice."

"Stalker?" Jean mouthed.

Audra shook her head. "Did it occur to you that I might

not be online because I'm busy?"

"Of course not," Jay scoffed. "You got injured and needed to be evacuated. Isn't that enough to get you sick leave?"

Audra bit her lip and met Jean's eyes, trying not to laugh. "There are other kinds of busy, Jay."

"Fine. Whatever. Just tell me what to do and you can get back to whatever you were doing."

Audra's breathing became deliberately even. "Be quick, then."

Jay took a noisy breath. "I'm certain of it now. I'm in love with her. And I can't lose her, but I don't know what to do. I helped her with stuff, like you said, but I don't think she even noticed. I invited her to the wedding and she's promised she'll dance with me. But if I tell her how I feel, I might lose her anyway, because she'll tell me to fuck off if she's not interested. What do I do?"

Audra didn't look like she had a ready response for him, so Jean leaned over and said, "Dude, if you really love her and don't want to lose her, do whatever you have to do. If it means carrying her across a beach and fighting off about fifty rogue elephant seals, that's what you got to do."

A long silence, followed by, "Who the fuck are you?"

"Sorry," Audra whispered, then in a normal tone she continued, "You remember my roommate, Jean-Pierre? I'm sure I told you about him. And he's right, you know."

"Your roommate fought off elephant seals for you?" Jay demanded. "He's the guy who picked you up in the video, isn't he?"

"What video?" Audra asked.

Jean cleared his throat. "The one you were taking when

you fell."

"Oh." Audra's brow creased. "How did you see it?"

"You streamed it live," Jay said. "It was like a TV show, ending on a cliffhanger, when that guy picked you up and then the feed went dark." He coughed. "I might've panicked a bit there."

Jean snorted. Her rock star friend would have been lost out there. That's why he thanked his lucky stars he'd been the one on Heard Island with Audra. Who knew that cursed island better than a man who'd nearly died there?

"That's how I knew what ship you were on," Jay continued. "I…um. I did what you told me not to. I linked the video on my social media accounts and asked people to find you and tell me you were okay."

One of the biggest rock stars in the world, the uncrowned king of social media, had told the world about Audra. That explained how her video had gone viral.

"You diverted an icebreaker to pick me up?" Audra squeaked. "Jay, I only have a broken arm! Sickbay at any of our bases could handle something so simple."

"I was worried!" Jay protested. "And you're only angry at me about the ship, right? Not the video?"

"What video?"

She didn't know half of the world had seen it, Jean realised, a few seconds before Jay did.

"I should go," Jay said. "Have fun with your roommate." He hung up.

Audra turned to Jean. "Do you know what he did?"

"I do now," he replied, reaching for her phone. He pulled up her video channel and showed the latest one to her. "Everyone at McMurdo had seen it, and Davis.

Because your friend shared it, the video went viral."

Audra peered at the screen. "Nine million views?" she whispered. Not even Flavia's videos had been that popular.

"You're famous."

She didn't look happy. "Can I hole up here until we fly out?"

"Absolutely. I'll sleep on the couch, so you can have the bed."

"We could share the bed, you know," Audra said. "I wouldn't mind."

So tempting. He'd been right to call her a seductress, but she did it effortlessly. Almost like she wasn't aware of her appeal. "I screwed up when we first met. Just because I was off my face on morphine isn't an excuse. I owe you better than that," he said. He nodded at her brace. "What if I accidentally bumped you in the middle of the night? I don't want to hurt you."

Her shoulders slumped. "Fair enough. It'll be a while before I'm ready for a goodnight kiss, though. My body still seems to be on Heard Island time."

"I crossed so many time zones to get here, my body doesn't know what time it is. Want to watch a movie or something?"

Audra nodded.

Jean flipped through the hotel's selection of on-demand movies. Two chick flicks, a horror movie from a franchise that had grown tired two movies ago, and an X-Men movie that must have come out while he was in Antarctica. "What about this one?" he asked, hoping against hope that she wouldn't pick one of the chick flicks that Dairine would have insisted on.

"Sure. I haven't seen that one."

Had she even glanced at it? "You like superhero movies?" Jean asked.

"Of course," Audra answered. "They're like romance novels – the bad guy never wins, and there's a happy ending."

Jean shook his head. "Comic books and superhero movies are the complete opposite of romance books."

"Have you ever read one?"

"Of course not!"

Audra smiled. "Well, I like both. Unless you do your research, you don't have enough data to draw conclusions. The chances of you being good in bed are getting slimmer and slimmer if you've never read romance."

Her tone might be teasing, but her words could be all too true. That hurt. "Maybe I'm terrible in bed, and that's why she left me," Jean said, stabbing the button on the remote control so the movie would start.

They watched in silence, sitting side by side on the sofa, but they may as well have been in different worlds. Jean wasn't sure what to say to bridge the abyss between them, either. Things had been going so well until he'd suggested the movie. Had he picked the wrong one?

"Want to watch another one?" he asked when it finished. "I think I saw – "

Audra covered a yawn with her hand. "I think I'm going to go to bed. Can you help me undress?"

"Ah..." He couldn't say no, could he? It's not like he didn't want to undress her. He'd dreamed about it.

"The medic on the ship helped me dress this morning. She was really helpful. If I was at home, I'd ask my sister, but seeing as I'm here with you..." Audra's eyes begged him. "I figure you've seen me naked before. It's not that big a deal, right?"

No. Yes. Fuck. Those dream tits would be his undoing, and he knew it. "Yeah, I'll help you." Jean followed her into the bedroom, watching her edge her dress up one-handed until the hem revealed a pair of pink cotton panties. He'd have expected something sexier from Audra.

As if she could read his mind, she said, "I didn't have a change of clothes aboard the ship. Only what I was wearing and what they could dig out of the lost property box. All my underwear is back at Davis."

"There should be some in the dryer here," Jean replied, trying to distract himself as he helped her pull the dress over her head. The bra she wore wasn't something out of lost property, he was certain. Her breasts filled out the cups like it was tailor-made for her. He itched to take it off, so he could cup her in his hands and...

Audra turned her back. "Can you unclip my bra, please?"

Jean swallowed. "Sure." He did as he was bid, and held his breath as she slid the straps down her arms. Now she wore nothing but those childish pink panties.

Audra turned to face him again, and Jean forced his gaze to stay on her face. No lower. No matter how much he wanted to...

"I just want to say that those are the most perfect pair of breasts DNA ever gave a woman," Jean blurted out. "I should have said that the first time I saw them."

Audra gave a sad smile. "I've heard that line before. Well, except the DNA bit. That's new."

"Probably because it's true. And any man who's lucky enough to see them who didn't tell you that is an idiot." Still he held her gaze, because to look down was to be utterly, utterly lost.

"I'd like that goodnight kiss now," she said.

FIFTY-SIX

Audra took a deep breath. "And I'd like it with your shirt off, please."

What was she thinking? She'd never taken the lead with a man before. But his admission that he cared about her, even loved her, had made her brave. That and the compliment about her breasts.

Jean nodded, and pulled his shirt off.

Audra feasted her eyes on the muscles that hadn't diminished since the first time she saw them, more than a year ago now. Strong enough to carry her to safety. Caring enough to comfort her when she cried. Gentle enough to pull her close, like now and…

Passion ignited as his lips touched hers, as if their Valentine's kiss had lit a fire that still smouldered under her skin. Her nipples snapped to attention as they made contact with his chest, just as eager as the rest of her for his touch.

She wanted. No, she needed…

Audra barely noticed as her back hit the bed, with Jean half on top of her. Warm fingers stroked her breasts, giving her nipples the attention they so desperately craved, as her tongue tickled his, begging for more. His mouth moved south, bestowing a dozen kisses along her throat as he descended on her breasts, to kiss her a hundred times more.

"Oh yes," she moaned, wrapping her arms around him to hold him tighter. "Oh…ow!"

Jean jumped off the bed, his arms raised in surrender. "What did I do wrong?"

"Nothing," she breathed, cradling her injured arm. "It was me. I got so caught up in the moment that I tried to pull you close with both arms, forgetting this one's out of action."

"Well, I'm sorry. Sorry I distracted you so much you forgot you were hurt. You need to take care of that arm so it heals properly." Jean jerked his head toward the living area. "I'll make up a bed on the couch for myself, so I won't be far away if you need me."

"We could still share the bed," Audra said. When Jean opened his mouth to protest, she held up her right hand. "I always sleep on the right side of the bed, with my arm on the edge. The only way you'll bump it while we're sleeping is if you manage to roll over the top of me and hit it just before you fall on the floor."

"We should take it slow," Jean insisted. "This morning, you barely wanted to speak to me. I don't want you to do something you'll regret. Especially when you're under the influence of pain medication. That kind of consent's questionable at best, and – "

"This morning, I had to remind myself every few minutes that you were a married man who wanted to cheat on his wife," Audra interrupted. "And my pain meds wore off while we were at my parents' place. I need to take some more before I go to bed, because this is starting to seriously hurt."

Jean fetched her a glass of water and her box of pills, then sat on the corner of the bed. "I don't want you to think I'm the sort of man who tries to drag a girl into bed with him on the first date."

Audra almost choked. "Too late for that. Besides, we've never actually been on a date. We've lived and worked together for three months, and shared sleeping quarters for most of that time. Normal relationship rules don't apply here, because nothing between us will ever be normal, and I don't want it to be. Sleep with me while we're sharing this hotel room, and tomorrow, I'll take you on a date. I'll take you to an island breeding colony of penguins, the like of which you've never seen before."

Finally, Jean laughed. "You want our first date to include penguins? I think if I wasn't already in love with you, I would've fallen hard the moment you said that. You're the perfect woman. And if you want, I'll sleep with you. But there won't be any sex between us until your arm's completely healed. That I promise you."

That's what you think, Audra thought but didn't say, as Jean snuggled up behind her. He wouldn't last three days before he caved.

FIFTY-SEVEN

Audra sat back and stretched her arms above her head. It had been three months and she'd officially decided Jean was the stubbornest man alive. She'd told him so, too. Not that it changed anything.

Her nightly weather forecasts were as predictable as her evenings:

Dark, well below freezing, with a high chance of a storm, but zero chance of sex.

Slowly but surely, she was getting to him, though. For the last three months since they'd arrived back at Davis, they'd made out like teenagers, exploring and experimenting until he learned to read her body's signals so well she swore he worked magic with his hands and his mouth whenever he touched her. Audra hadn't been shy, either: now she knew his body nearly as well as her own. Well, most of it, anyway. She'd never seen him without his blindingly white boxer briefs. The only exception had been that day at Penguin Island, when he'd traded his briefs for board shorts and ventured into the water with her. It wasn't until they'd waded in waist deep that he'd confessed to his fear of the ocean after swimming across Atlas Cove last year.

A fear he'd sworn to conquer today, and she intended to be there to cheer him on.

As if on cue, her phone rang.

"Are you ready? It's taken the guys half the morning to cut through what turned out to be more than a metre of ice, but the Midwinter Pool is about to open."

"Sure, Bruce. I've got my camera charged and ready to capture every moment," Audra replied. "Heading over from the Met Station now."

She left the computers compiling their data, hoping that when she returned they'd have done most of her work for her on the evening forecast.

The Midwinter Pool was just the beginning of the dark day's celebrations, and she'd agreed to be a part of it. She found Ali and John standing poolside in their heaviest outdoor gear, with Bruce carefully stirring up the pool surface so it didn't ice over until everyone had taken a dip. Everyone brave or crazy enough to, anyway.

Audra lifted her camera and pointed it at the pool ladder. "It's the Winter Solstice here at Davis Station, so some of our bravest expeditioners have decided to celebrate with a swim. All right, who's first?"

To her surprise, Jean emerged first, wearing the same red board shorts she remembered from Penguin Island, a pair of sneakers and nothing else. At thirty below zero, he had to be cold, but he grinned and winked at her before he slipped the safety rope around himself and climbed down the ladder into the icy pool.

Audra saw him hesitate, but she didn't think anyone else noticed. It might be a dark day, but it was ideal for conquering the demons that had plagued him for so long. Jean met her eyes and nodded once. He knew what she was thinking.

He pushed off into the middle of the pool and ducked under the surface of the freezing water before he emerged again, still grinning.

"It's lovely!" Jean shouted. "You should all take a dip!"

He was shaking as he ascended the ladder, but he could blame that on the air temperature. He staggered off to defrost and Audra found herself filming the next crazy expeditioner.

One by one, her colleagues took the icy plunge until Bruce shouted, "Last call!"

Audra glanced at John. The doctor bit his lip, but he nodded.

Audra passed the camera to Ali, explaining how it worked. Ali held it between her gloves like a piece of precious china.

Audra shucked off her outer gear until she stood in nothing but her bikini and the safety rope. Fuck, but it was cold. She fixed a smile on her face and wrapped her hands around the ladder. How was it possible for the metal to be colder than the air? The water was the warmest part, she told herself, ignoring the ice floating in the pool. Jean had done it, no matter how terrified he was. She was just cold.

Just like a day teaching swimming at the beach, when she'd had to show her class how warm the water was so they'd join her. Audra crouched on the ladder, then pushed off into a starfish float on top of the water.

"Two minutes," John said, reminding her of the time limit. The human body could only withstand these sorts of temperatures unprotected for five minutes before things started to shut down.

It felt so good to be in the water again, no matter how cold. She stroked across the pool toward the ladder, reluctant to leave the water.

But there was more water waiting – warmer water, too, and Jean.

Her teeth clacked together as violent shivering wracked her, but Audra still managed to get the words out. "Now for a dip in the hot tub!"

The midwinter spa – an inflatable pool the guys had rigged up with hot water just outside the station entrance in a sheltered spot out of the wind – held only two men and a woman, and none of them was Jean.

Before she could ask, Lesley said, "He's gone inside. He said he had something special to prepare for the Midwinter dinner tonight. Is it true you're going to stream it live on your video channel?"

The competition might be over, but Audra still posted at least once a week. "The beginning, at least," Audra said. "I wanted to film the swim live, too, but Ali said there'd be too much swearing for that. She was right – I'll have to edit a lot of it out before I post the video."

Everyone laughed, which was perfect timing for Ali's appearance with Audra's camera. She filmed them in the hot tub for a minute, then switched the camera off. "Where do you want me to put it?" Ali asked.

Audra waved at the SMQ building, where all the winter expeditioners now slept. "Leave it on my desk. I'll download it when I get in."

Lesley stared at Audra's arm. "Hey, you're not wearing your polka-dots any more. Is that just for the swim, or...?"

Audra smiled. "I got the all clear from the doctor this morning. No more polka-dots. My arm is officially healed. Which probably puts me back on the kitchen roster."

Lesley wrinkled her nose. "Which reminds me I have work to do. Time to go back inside."

Audra rose, too. "I should join you. I have a video to edit and upload before dinner."

She needed to get her body back to normal temperature, too, before she sought out Jean.

FIFTY-EIGHT

"I don't know about you guys, but I'm going inside for some antifreeze," Paul said, hefting himself out of the hot tub.

Jean was the first to follow him. He'd had his swim and now he deserved a drink as much as the next man. Besides, once Audra had finished filming, she wouldn't hang around outside. Idly, he wondered whether she'd have gone for a swim if the doctor hadn't insisted that anyone with an injury wasn't allowed in the water. A video of her in the water would definitely go viral, he thought as he traded his soaked shorts for warm, dry clothes.

Probably best that she hadn't, then, Jean decided. He didn't want to share her beautiful body with the rest of the world. Especially not tonight. Midwinter was…special, and he wanted it to be a memorable one. That meant only one drink at the bar, because he'd need his wits about him.

Everything had to be perfect.

He drained his beer and excused himself, telling the other guys that he needed to get things ready for tonight. They raised their drinks in salute and wished him luck. Jean knew he needed it.

Part of him wanted to go hide out in hydroponics with the plants for a bit, but he knew he needed to find Audra and thank her for her help in persuading him to face his fears today.

She wasn't in any of the living areas, so he headed for her sleeping quarters. Sure enough, she sat at her desk, frowning at something on her laptop.

Jean knocked on the open door. "Was I good enough to make the cut for your video?" he asked.

Her frown vanished as her whole face lit up. "Hell yes! That was amazing. So brave of you." She threw her arms around his neck and kissed him.

Instant antifreeze, that's what she was, as his body blazed with desire at her touch. He wasn't sure how he'd managed to resist her this long. Even now, he could feel his pants growing uncomfortably tight. Every fibre in his body wanted him to tear off their clothes and thrust himself deep inside her. But he couldn't. Not yet. Not until her arm had healed.

He kissed her with just as much passion as the first time, if not more. God, he loved this woman. More than anyone or anything else in this world. He slid his hand under her shirt, questing upward until he found what he wanted: one of her perfect breasts, quivering under his fingers as her heartbeat raced just beneath her soft skin.

"You're cold," he murmured between kisses.

Audra grinned up at him. "Well, it was cold outside, and I did stay out there for a while. The Midwinter Pool is only open for one day of the year. I wouldn't have missed it for the world."

"Let me warm you up." Jean kicked the door shut as he advanced into her room. He'd planned to do this much later in the day, but adrenaline still buzzed in his blood, egging him on to thank her properly now. Not later.

She let him pull her to the bed, helping him divest her of her shirt and that bothersome bra. Those breasts. He could worship them for hours, and Audra would probably let him, too, but he had other things in mind now.

Jean dropped to his knees before her. "I know it's too soon," he began, feeling his voice crack with nervousness. How could this be scarier than jumping into icy water? He didn't know; just that it was. "But…Audra, I love you so much. Will you…?"

FIFTY-NINE

"Will you…will you…" Jean stammered.

Oh hell, he was kneeling at her feet. He could only be asking her for one thing. Audra's mind went blank. Would she?

Jean swallowed and tried again. "Will you…let me go down on you? It's something I've never done before, but I think I understand the theory well enough to do a decent job."

Audra nearly burst out laughing. "Yes!" she cried instead, half out of relief and half in panic at not having an answer to the other question she thought he'd ask.

With his help, she shimmied out of her jeans. Before she could add her knickers to the pile of fabric on the floor, he lifted her up and set her on the bed. He joined her, kneeling between her feet as he pushed her bent knees apart. The way he stared at her sent hot shivers deep inside her, where she wanted him to be. Soon. Tonight, if she had any say in it. She'd hook her fingers into those boxer briefs and drag them right down to his ankles, just like he was doing with her knickers now.

For the first time, she lay completely naked before him, and the blue fire in his eyes told her he liked what he saw. She glanced down. The tent in his pants confirmed it.

He leaned forward, his face so close to her that she could feel his breath warm inside her when he exhaled. He traced her folds lightly with his finger, so light that it tickled. She shivered, and he ducked his head between her thighs. Next, she felt what could only be his tongue, rougher and more sure, following the same path as his finger. Slow and delicate, always exploring, always tasting. Using just that wicked mouth of his, he'd worked out that he could push her over the brink of an orgasm by working his magic on her nipples alone. If…no, when he tried the same technique lower down, she'd be utterly, utterly lost. The whole station would hear her scream.

Jean must have felt her stiffen, because he raised his head to meet her eyes, no longer teasing her. "Did I do something wrong?"

Audra shook her head. "The more you touch me, the more I want to feel you inside me. And the spot you're looking for, that you probably heard about in your theory? It's right here." She sucked in a breath as she touched his thumb to her clitoris.

"You are nothing like any other woman I've ever met before." Jean's thumb circled around the spot he knew drove her wild, as Audra held her breath. "And inside you…" He pushed a finger slowly into her, watching her as she took quick, shallow breaths.

He could make her come using just his fingers. Audra knew it, but she still wanted more. "Please," she said.

"How can I refuse?" With two fingers this time, he pulled in and out of her, his eyes never leaving hers as he maintained a slow, steady pace. "How am I doing so far?"

Oh, it felt good. To finally feel any part of him inside her was better than good. But she wanted… "More," Audra moaned.

Then his mouth was on her and Audra could think of nothing else. There wasn't room for anything else in the universe except his body and hers and the pleasure he gave her filled every inch of it. Of her body and her mind. Any more and she'd explode into a million tiny shards, flying in all directions like the blizzard she'd forecast for tonight.

"Oh, Jean, Jean, Jean…" How long had she been sobbing his name? Long enough for him to be wearing his biggest grin.

Jean eased his fingers out of her and licked them clean, before he took one last, languorous lick of her lady bits, making her gasp.

"Did I do all right?" he asked. "I meant it to be a thank you for helping me find the courage to go back into the water today, but I enjoyed myself so much I got a bit carried away." His eyes widened in alarm. "You're not…crying, are you? Shit, did I hurt you? I knew I should have waited. I knew it!"

Audra seemed to have lost the ability to talk. Or to think, really. "I'm fine," she started to say, but Jean cut her off.

"I'll see you at the dinner tonight," he said, hurrying out

of the room.

Audra sighed. To the ceiling, she said, "Like I said, I'm fine. So's my arm. My tear ducts do this weird thing where I cry when I'm happy. Or if I have mindblowing sex. Which was both until you left."

She glanced at the arm brace sitting on the desk. Evidently she'd have to tell him the good news after dinner.

SIXTY

If he'd stayed a moment longer, he'd have completely lost control. Jean crouched in the corner of the hydroponics lab, hidden by the green things he grew to help sustain the station, and buried his face in his hands. She deserved more than the out of control asshat he'd been the day they met. He couldn't live with himself if he hurt her again. And he couldn't go through with his plans for tonight, even if that's where he'd pinned all his hopes and dreams for the future.

He needed to get himself under control, and do things right, or this wouldn't work.

What if he'd used up all his courage on this morning's swim, so he chickened out of the most important part of the celebration? What he needed now was someone to tell him he was being an idiot, and he could conquer two fears in one day.

If only the best person for the job wasn't Audra.

Jean almost laughed at himself. If he had to ask her for help, he'd screw this up for sure.

A light on his tablet flashed, so he reached up to the counter to grab it. Probably just a routine email.

He was surprised to find it was an incoming video call from none other than Jay Felix. He still didn't know how Jay had managed to track him down, but Jean imagined a man with his wealth could do things ordinary men like himself could only dream of.

Which made Jean only feel more inadequate for what lay ahead.

"Are all Canadians as crazy as you?" Jay demanded before Jean could even say hello.

"Probably not," Jean admitted. "You Aussies are corrupting me."

"If everything goes well tonight, you'll have to come up for a round of golf on the roof with me. I already told Audra she can have a villa on the island for a month any time she wants, as thanks for what she did to help me win my wife. We could all go jetboating through the whirlpools. And whatever else we can think up that my lovely wife says is okay." Jay frowned. "She might veto the roof golf, come to think of it."

The rock star was married now, Jean remembered – Audra had showed him pictures in the news.

"Congratulations, by the way," Jean said. "I think you broke the hearts of half the women in the world with that wedding."

"I know one that didn't break," Jay said.

So did Jean, which gave him hope. "She's really happy for you. For you both, I think. She said she met your wife once, and she liked her. She's British, right?"

"Yeah, but she's Aussie now, too. Been here long enough." Jay's eyes narrowed. "Don't distract me. I want to make sure you're not backing out."

From thousands of miles away, this man Jean barely knew was reading his mind. Jean forced out a laugh. "She turned you down. More than once, you said. What makes you think she'll say yes to me?"

"Have you cheated on her?"

The question caught Jean by surprise. "Of course not. What kind of man cheats on the woman he loves?"

Jay coughed. "Yeah. Uh, she's still going to do that live video of the dinner tonight, right?"

"I think so," Jean said.

"I'll be watching," Jay said. "Me and probably a million other people who want to watch you propose to the Penguin Weather Girl. No pressure, of course." He grinned and ended the call.

Jean snorted. No pressure at all. The rock star and his million other people could watch and think what they liked – they didn't matter. The only person in the world who mattered was Audra. And Jay's talk of penguins had given him an idea.

SIXTY-ONE

"Are we ready?" Ali asked.

Audra checked one last time to make sure her camera captured the whole table. It did. Satisfied, she took her seat, laying the remote control beside her plate so she could start recording on Ali's command. She absently smoothed the skirt of her dress, wondering once again if she'd dressed too formally for the occasion.

A glance at the blokes, all clad in suits and ties, reassured her. Lesley and Ali wore dresses, too, but still she worried that she'd been silly to buy silk when a simple cocktail dress would have done. But the pattern on the fabric, which reminded her of one of Monet's garden paintings, had caught her eye every time she'd walked past the shop until one day, she hadn't been able to resist buying it. Jean hadn't said anything to her yet. In fact, he wasn't even here.

"Where's Jean?" she asked.

Everyone glanced around the table, as if expecting him to magically pop up beside them.

All except Ali, who said, "He's been in the hydro lab for most of the afternoon, but when I last saw him, he was on his way to his quarters to get dressed. Chris, Bruce…does someone want to go see where Jean is?"

"I'm here," came the deep Canadian voice that made Audra's core clench. Especially after this afternoon.

Her breath caught in her throat as he came into view. Dressed in a suit, Jean could have graced the cover of a romance novel about kinky billionaires. One look at him and she understood the appeal. She wanted to leap into his lap and go to town on him like the sexiest secretary ever.

"Take a seat here, then." Ali pointed to the chair beside her, and opposite Audra.

Jean barely glanced at Audra. He turned his attention to Ali, who had risen.

Audra hastened to switch the camera on. She was sure only Jay and the other expeditioners would be watching live, but she kept her promises. The Midwinter dinner would be broadcast live, even if she was distracted by dirty thoughts about Jean.

Ali launched into her speech, welcoming them all to the dinner and reminding them about the explorers who'd first come to Antarctica, and all the hardships they'd faced. She raised a toast to the darkest day, for it truly was the darkest day of the year. The sun wouldn't rise at all at Davis in June – it wouldn't even peek over the horizon until July. They all drank in thoughtful silence.

"It might be the darkest day of the year," Ali continued, "but it's been a particularly bright year for us. So much light in the darkness." She made Jean stand up. "The first we heard about Jean-Pierre was when we got a request for an emergency medic. Audra volunteered and took good care of him all the way to Casey. No one thought he'd manage to pass a medical and return, but he surprised us all by turning up here at Davis on his way to Heard Island. Of course, this time he took Audra with him." She waited for the laughter to die down before she went on: "He not only finished his PhD, but he submitted his thesis in record time, and it's been accepted, he found out this week. So first, I'd like you all to congratulate Dr Jean-Pierre Pennant."

Enthusiastic applause erupted around the table. It wasn't just polite, either – people looked genuinely happy for Jean.

Ali proceeded to go around the table, listing each person's achievements, from academic and research milestones and projects completed, through to Lesley saving Bruce from an angry penguin that had popped up in the pool this morning. Lesley couldn't stop laughing, but Bruce just looked embarrassed.

"And last, but not least, even if she is the youngest here at Davis, there's Audra." Ali gestured for her to stand up, which Audra did. "It's her first winter here, which she almost missed, after she ran afoul of a volcano and then took a cruise back to Fremantle with the *Aurora Australis*. She graduated at the top of her class for her meteorology degree, which is why we welcomed her back here for her second tour of Antarctica. Her innovative new video project has been shared all over the world since she first called Davis home, and it's earned her both the coveted, inaugural Bureau of Meteorology graduate research scholarship, and a research grant from the University of

Washington, where she's just been accepted as a PhD candidate studying the evidence of climate change at Heard Island."

Audra blushed at such a paean of praise. Sure, it was all true and her PhD candidacy had only been confirmed this week, but it still sounded far too ambitious for a girl who'd been nothing but a hotel maid two years ago.

"Normally, this is the point where I'd officially open the dinner, but Dr Pennant asked to say a few words, so I'll let him have the floor." Ali sat down.

Audra tried to do the same, but Ali signalled to her to stay where she was. As Jean started to speak, Audra began to realise why.

"I came here six months ago, chasing the only two things in the world that mattered to me: penguins, and my PhD," Jean said. "I already knew Antarctica was dangerous. It had nearly killed me once, on my first expedition to Heard Island, but like many of the old explorers, I refused to be beaten. Some people called me dedicated. They were the polite ones." He pointed at Audra. "She called me stubborn, and she was right, though I didn't see it at the time. It took a volcano, and another accident, to make me realise that there might be more to life than my PhD. Something more important than penguins."

A few people laughed.

"She showed me things I'd never noticed before. Things I took for granted, but I shouldn't have. I even learned a few things, from her and from penguins. And she made me see that penguins alone will never be enough."

More laughter.

"So here I am, in my penguin suit, about to do

something no penguin in history ever has." Jean stepped forward, then sank onto one knee before Audra. Icy blue eyes regarded her, warm with love. "When most penguins find a partner, they mate for life. For a long time, I've been jealous of that, but it turned out I hadn't yet met my mate. I'm pretty sure I have now, and I want to be the first to ask her before some other penguin tries to muscle me out of the way. She's looking so beautiful tonight, I bet they're queuing up outside in the blizzard just to get to her."

Even Audra laughed at that one. She tried to keep her breathing even, both hoping and dreading what he'd say next. At least now she had an answer for him.

Jean cleared his throat. "Audra, I love you, and I always will. I promise to bring you fish whenever you ask, and mind any eggs we might one day have while you go off to pursue your own career. I'll always help you take care of yourself, even if you never have another broken wing. I want to spend the rest of my life with you, whether it's here in Antarctica or anywhere else in the world you want to call home. Audra, will you marry me?"

Everyone – Audra included – was laughing too hard for anyone to hear her reply, so she had a moment to consider her words. Then silence descended over the party and it was her cue to speak.

Audra wet her lips. "I'm not really ready to think about eggs just yet, and now my broken wing has healed, I hope I never break anything else again. Choosing a mate for life is a very big decision, and six months ago, I would have said it wasn't something I was ready to consider." As Jean's eyes widened in panic, Audra winked at him, and he relaxed again. "But fish on command…what more could a girl ask for?" She raised her voice to be heard above the laughter. "Yes, Dr Pennant. I'd love to marry you."

If anyone hadn't heard her, the way Jean joyfully jumped to his feet and kissed her probably gave them a clue. But while he kept one arm around her, his other hand reached for the camera to switch it off.

Audra glanced at the grinning faces around the table. "You all knew, didn't you? Was I the only one who didn't?"

Jean ducked his head. "Actually, I wanted to do this in private, the moment I got confirmation about my PhD, but I'd promised your friend Jay that I'd ask you in front of the camera. After what happened earlier today, I hid out in the hydroponics lab, telling the plants and myself that I could do this. I was so sure I'd screwed up.."

Now wasn't the time to talk about tears, or sex. "One bit of good news Ali didn't mention is that I got the doctor's all clear this morning. That means I'm officially not injured any more."

Jean nodded, loading his plate up with food. It took a moment for her words to register, and when they did, he dropped the serving spoon with a clang. "Your arm's completely healed? No more light duties or…taking it easy?"

It was Audra's turn to nod. "So you might not want to drink too much with dinner tonight. I'm thinking of turning in early, and I'd like the good night kiss you promised me."

"Not fish?" Jean held up a platter of smoked salmon.

"Oh, I want my fish, too," Audra replied, helping herself. So far, the darkest day of the year had proven to be the best day of her life. And it wasn't over yet — if this afternoon was anything to go by, the best was yet to come.

SIXTY-TWO

When dinner was finished and people were picking at the remains of dessert, Ali announced that she was off to bed. Everyone took that as the signal to disperse, heading off alone or in twos and threes for the bar, the pool table and the movie theatre.

"Shall we go?" Jean asked Audra, hoping she hadn't changed her mind. She seemed unusually interested in the proposed movie marathon.

"Please," she replied with a roguish wink that hit Jean right in the groin.

It truly was the best night of his life. Audra had agreed to marry him, and if he'd guessed right, the moment they got some privacy, the clothes were going to come off and what happened this afternoon would be nothing but mild foreplay. They'd make love for the first time with his ring on her finger. Jean glanced down and realised he hadn't given it to her yet. He'd been so caught up in getting his proposal right, that he'd left he box in his pocket the whole time.

In the corridor outside their sleeping quarters, he stopped. "Wait. I forgot to give you this." He pulled out the box and flipped it open, preparing to drop to his knees again, but Audra seized the box before he could.

"That's beautiful," she said.

"I saw it in Fremantle, while I was waiting for your ship to arrive. The emerald reminded me of the colour of your eyes. I know engagement rings are supposed to be diamonds, but this – "

"This is perfect," Audra said firmly, holding out her hand. "You should put it on me."

Jean slid the ring onto her finger. To his relief, it fit. And looked like it belonged there.

"Thank you," she said, wrapping her arms around him for a lingering kiss.

Jean was this close to pinning her against the wall and having her right there in the corridor, but Audra deserved better than that. The whole station might know what they were doing tonight, but that didn't mean they needed to see it.

"Your room or mine?" Jean managed to say.

"Mine. Further from everyone else because it's on the end, and if we're lucky, no one will hear the noise we make over the blizzard."

Jean liked the sound of that. The memory of her crying out his name this afternoon was still fresh in his memory, and he intended to make her do that a lot more before tonight was over.

Good thing it was the longest night of the year.

SIXTY-THREE

Audra threw her camera on the desk, not caring where it landed, and gave Jean her full attention. To hell with decorum and professionalism and all that shit. She wanted him. Now. And there was nothing to stop them.

Their next kiss made her knees weak, so she wrapped her leg around him to hold herself steady. His hands cupped her arse, pressing her groin against his, and she went wild, climbing him like a koala. Her legs circled his hips as her arms twined around his neck, their lips fused together like she wanted the rest of their bodies to be.

He'd loosened his tie and the top couple of buttons of his shirt, making him look even more sexy in the suit, if such a thing were possible.

God, he was hard as a rock between her thighs, and she rubbed against him like a cat in heat. She needed to feel him inside her. Now.

"Condom," she panted, reaching for the box on the shelf. Pinching a foil packet between her fingers, she reached down to free him from his suit pants. She unzipped his fly just fine, but the belt needed two hands, so she gave up on it, delving inside his pants for what she wanted. Hot and hard and in her hand. Finally. She stroked the condom down his length, licking her lips in anticipation. Not that she'd taste him tonight, or at least not yet.

Audra hitched up her skirt and tightened her legs around him, feeling the rough scratch of his wool pants against her thighs when all she wanted was that sleek shaft. So much.

"Fuck me. Now," she said, pressing against him so that his tip entered her.

Jean's eyes were on fire with lust as he pinned her against the wall. Or the door. She didn't know, and she didn't care.

"I'm not going to fuck you," he said, sliding a finger inside her. "I make love to my fiancée, the same way I will every night when you're my wife."

His finger was gone, and she ached for him. Any part of him. "Please," she whispered.

With one smooth thrust, he filled her completely. Perfectly.

"Oh, yes. Just like that, Jean," she moaned. It was like he'd been made for her.

He picked up the pace as she urged him on, eager to feel her first climax with him inside her. Almost too soon, she crested that wave, crying out his name as she flew over the other side into bliss. It took her a moment to realise what he'd been repeating the whole time. As he drove deep inside her with one final, earth-shaking thrust, he said it again. "I love you."

She loosened her legs from around his waist, moaning a little at the feel of him still inside her. She was shaking, but so was he. "I love you, too, Jean. So much."

"I made you cry. I never want to make you cry," Jean said, easing out of her.

Suddenly empty, Audra found herself struggling to stand on her jelly-like legs.

"Like I tried to tell you earlier, I cry when I'm happy. Really, really happy. Like when my fiancé fulfils my fantasy of having a quickie with a sexy man in a suit up against the wall." She grinned up at him as she tried to blink away her tears. "See?"

"Actually, we did it against the door."

His eyes met hers and they both laughed.

Audra wet her lips. "Maybe…we should try it again, and see if it's any better with the wall?"

He glanced down. "Another time, maybe. I didn't expect to be spent so quickly for our first time. I'd planned something slower, more romantic, where I'd last longer…" Frowning, he started to clean up.

Of course he'd planned this. Audra was willing to bet his plans would be even more incredible than what they'd already done. She couldn't wait. "Then you're in charge for round two," she said.

Jean nodded. "So tomorrow, maybe, if you're feeling up to it?"

Audra stared. "Tomorrow's hours away. If you haven't recharged by then, I'll deep-throat you myself until you're ready, and I never do blow jobs." She eyed him. Jean definitely wasn't small, but he wasn't enormous like Jay.

Maybe she'd make an exception for Jean.

Ah, who was she kidding? If Jean so much as breathed a hint that he'd reciprocate with stellar oral sex like he'd demonstrated this afternoon, she'd be on her knees in a moment.

His smile seemed sad. "I've never done it twice in a night. Lower sperm counts the second time, you see, so there wasn't really any point."

Audra's heart melted for him. Jean's first marriage really had been a miserable one. "Your first wife was an idiot. The point to sex is to enjoy it, and procreation's just a possibility afterwards, if you don't take precautions. How could any woman not enjoy sex with an incredible lover like you?"

"She never let me…never wanted…she wanted me to be quick, and she wanted kids. That was all." Jean looked uncomfortable.

No wonder Jean hadn't been in a hurry to sleep with her. Being nothing but a breeder was no fun. And what a waste! Crazy woman.

Audra took a deep breath. "Well, I'm not her. And I don't want to talk about her ever again. Especially not tonight. Tonight's just for us. As for kids…I'm in no hurry to have them, if ever. I have an implant that's good for another four years, so maybe we can talk about kids then. Not tonight. I had plans for tonight, too, you know."

Jean perked up a little. "Yeah?"

"Yeah. I'd planned to dress up, maybe dance with you a little after dinner, and then seduce your socks off."

He cocked his head to one side. "How were you going to seduce me?"

Audra grinned wickedly. "When I got you onto the

dance floor, with your body pressed against mine, I was going to whisper in your ear that I'm not wearing any underwear."

Jean paled. "You weren't? You mean that whole formal dinner, with the video and everything, when I proposed to you…you weren't wearing underwear?"

"Nope."

Jean swallowed. "I think…I might be ready for round two now. Except this time I want to take some clothes off first."

Oh, yes! Audra wanted to squeal with delight. "You're in charge."

SIXTY-FOUR

Jean didn't want to be in charge. That was one of the things he loved most about Audra – the way she made sure they did things together, as equals. Putting him in charge meant she was less than him, when she was so much more.

"What if I lose control like I did this afternoon?"

Audra grinned and pushed him onto the bed, straddling his lap. "Then the whole building's going to hear me scream for joy." Green eyes challenged him to do his worst as she ground against his groin. "Bring it on, bird boy."

He kissed her, claiming her mouth for all the wonderful things she said and the wicked things she could do with her lips and her tongue. Tonight, she tasted of mango, like the beer she'd finally admitted to giving him for Christmas.

He shrugged out of his jacket, lost the tie and belt and started working his pants down over his hips, while Audra took care of his shirt buttons. When she peeled off his shirt, leaving just his pants, Jean rose, lifting her up with him, so his pants slid to the floor. He kicked them away, once again mesmerised by Audra's eyes as she stared into his.

She slid a hand into the waistband of his boxer briefs. "These better be coming off," she said, snaking her fingers around his shaft.

Jean didn't need telling twice. He set Audra on the bed so she could watch.

Down went the briefs, so he stood naked before her. "This is what you get," he said softly. "I hope it's good enough for you. If it isn't, I'll be hitting the gym in the morning so I can do better."

Her eyes danced. "What if I want you to do a different kind of workout in the morning? Here with me instead?" Audra patted the bunk beside her.

He sat beside her, pulling her back into his lap like she'd been earlier, only this was much better than before. Now all that lay between them was the silky fabric of her dress, and she was already hitching up handfuls of the skirt to help remove that.

The way she sat astride him now reminded Jean of his fantasies of her, back on Heard Island. "You need to be naked," he said, lifting the dress over her head so that her breasts popped free.

All clothing cast aside, she was a dream come true, from her loving green eyes to the perfect breasts pressed against his chest, right down to her toes, already curling with pleasure as she ground her hips against him.

"Shall I sheath you?" she murmured.

Condoms meant no worrying about kids, or sperm counts, or being quick. This would be sex for the sheer joy of it – his pleasure, and hers.

He dropped his voice to the devilish tone that hadn't worked on Audra before. "Sheath me."

It worked now. Her hand unrolled the condom along his length, but her eyes begged him for what he wanted most.

He cupped her face in his hands and kissed her, at the same time as he surged into her from below.

Audra gasped, then returned his kiss, giving his cock a squeeze as she clamped down on him.

She met his second thrust halfway, dipping her hips to take him deeper. She rode him, all right, with a fierce determination that took his breath away. She took as much pleasure as she gave, this incredible woman who was way better than any fantasy.

He could feel his peak building, but he wanted…no, he needed to see her come first. To hear her moan his name like there was no one else in the world, and no one else she wanted more. He felt her shudder as her muscles clenched around him, before she sucked in a breath so she could cry, "I love you, Jean. Oh Jean!"

Only then did he allow himself his own release, lost in the blissful high of the woman who still clung to him, wrapped around him like she was made for him alone, when the truth was that he was made for her. To love her, to take care of her, and to bring her joy like this every moment they were together. Forever and always, through all life's adventures.

The next book in the Romance Island
Resort series will be out in 2017

ABOUT THE AUTHOR

Demelza Carlton has always loved the ocean, but on her first snorkelling trip she found she was afraid of fish.

She has since swum with sea lions, sharks and sea cucumbers and stood on spray drenched cliffs over a seething sea as a seven-metre cyclonic swell surged in, shattering a shipwreck below.

Demelza now lives in Perth, Western Australia, the shark attack capital of the world.

The *Ocean's Gift* series was her first foray into fiction, followed by her suspense thriller *Nightmares* trilogy. She swears the *Mel Goes to Hell* series ambushed her on a crowded train and wouldn't leave her alone.

Want to know more? You can follow Demelza on Facebook, Twitter, YouTube or her website, Demelza Carlton's Place at:

www.demelzacarlton.com

Books by Demelza Carlton

Ocean's Gift series
Ocean's Gift (#1)
Ocean's Infiltrator (#2)
Ocean's Depths (#3)
Water and Fire

Turbulence and Triumph series
Ocean's Justice (#1)
Ocean's Trial (#2)
Ocean's Triumph (#3)
Ocean's Ride (#4)
Ocean's Cage (#5)
Ocean's Birth (#6)
How To Catch Crabs

Nightmares Trilogy
Nightmares of Caitlin Lockyer (#1)
Necessary Evil of Nathan Miller (#2)
Afterlife of Alana Miller (#3)

Mel Goes to Hell series
Welcome to Hell (#1)
See You in Hell (#2)
Mel Goes to Hell (#3)
To Hell and Back (#4)
The Holiday From Hell (#5)
All Hell Breaks Loose (#6)

The Rock Star's Wedding

DEMELZA CARLTON

Book 6 in the Romance Island Resort series

ISBN-13: 978-1-925799-10-1

ISBN-10: 1-925799-10-7.

DEDICATION

This one is for the January Girls.
For keeping me (marginally) sane, no matter what Jay Felix
chose to do.
Without you, he might not have lived to find his happy
ending.

ONE

Funeral bells sounded far more cheerful than the trill of Xan's phone. At least, Xan thought they would. Not that she really wanted Jerome to die. She wanted him to live a long, lonely and hopefully painful life. No, she wasn't that cruel. She had loved him once. Before he'd slept with a girl almost ten years younger than him and broken off his engagement with Xan to marry the pregnant girl. Now…

Now, she had to answer the damn phone.

"This is Xan," she bit out.

"Ms Lane, I have a doctor on the line, asking for our events coordinator. Specifically, weddings. Do we even have one of those?" Philly giggled. "Getting married in paradise would be so romantic!"

Xan made a mental note to hire someone for the role. Once Jay's wedding was broadcast on TV, everyone would want to book a wedding at the resort, and she'd have to handle them all. It would definitely make her job easier if she could hand them over to someone else. In the meantime, though… "Put him through to me."

"Yes, Ms Lane."

The phone beeped and Philly was gone.

"Xan Lane, manager of Romance Island Resort. How can I help?" Xan intoned, wondering why Jay wanted a doctor at his and Penelope's televised wedding.

The woman's voice surprised her. "Hello, Xan. I need to book a wedding. When's your earliest available date?"

Xan recovered quickly. "Ah, we haven't really started taking bookings yet. You see – "

The woman laughed. "That's not what I heard. If you're planning to host an event for Jason Felix, you can handle pretty much anything."

Jason, not Jay, Xan noted. "Where did you hear that?" Xan asked.

"My sources don't matter. I trust them, so I know my information is correct. I had booked a venue for a wedding in a few weeks' time, but that venue is no longer sufficient for my needs. Your resort should meet my requirements. So what's the earliest date I can book?"

This woman sounded like Gaia's sister, if the billionaire had such a thing. Xan knew how to deal with her sort. To start with, she had to up the stakes, then double the price. "For weddings, if you intend to have a photographer, you'll need to book the entire resort for the two nights on either side of the day of your event. You are welcome to use this to accommodate your guests, of course. And the wet season's just started, so with the weather as wild and unpredictable as it usually is, we couldn't host a big event until the start of the dry season, in May next year, or more likely June. In rough weather, the island is completely isolated, as the swell is too high for jet boats to reach us, and if the wind's too strong, a helicopter can't land, either." Xan grinned and sat back, waiting to hear the woman's response.

The woman's voice was calm. "The first Saturday in May, then?"

Xan choked. "But that's when Jay's booked – "

The woman laughed again. "You seriously think Jason will marry one of those reality TV show girls? You're dreaming, Xan. I suggest you speak to Jason about it during the week. I'll fly up to the resort in a week or so to inspect the place, to make sure it'll meet my needs, and we can confirm a date then. Oh, and so we're clear, I'll want the entire island for a week before the wedding, and a week afterwards."

Who had the kind of money to book an entire island for a fortnight? Gaia, or one of her billionaire friends. Jay was going to be pissed off. Xan's grin widened. Oh, she was definitely going to talk to Jay about this one. Hopefully he could handle her, so Xan wouldn't have to. "All right," Xan said. "Let me just get your name and details."

"Sure." The woman rattled off answers to Xan's rapid-fire questions, then said a curt goodbye and ended the call.

Xan glanced at the hotel registry entry on her screen. Doctor Alana Miller wanted a wedding at the island. Well, she'd have to get through Jay Felix first. And if there was one thing Xan knew about Jay, it was that he hated spoiled, rich bitches.

TWO

Jay visibly paled. "She's coming here? She wants to have her wedding here?"

Not the reaction Xan had expected. This was the first time she'd seen Jay scared of anyone or anything. "So she says. I said I'd have to talk to you first. I'll ring her back and say we're booked out for the next decade, if you like."

Jay grasped Xan's arm. "NO! Don't do that! Give her…give her whatever she wants. Did she say when?"

Xan shook him off. "I told her she'd have to wait until the dry season. May or June."

Jay relaxed a little. "That gives me six months."

"Six months? It's only September." Xan frowned. "Who on earth is Doctor Alana Miller? I've never heard of her."

Jay smiled wanly. "You might know her as Angel Black. The lead guitarist and songwriter of Chaya, my band. Or she was, before she up and quit and forced me into retirement."

This was news to Xan. "So you know her pretty well, I take it?"

"Sure."

"Why didn't she ask for you, then?" Xan pressed.

Jay swallowed. "Oh, I haven't talked to her in a while." The decking beneath his feet suddenly seemed mesmerising. At least, it was to Jay.

"What did you do?"

"I…it doesn't matter, okay?" When Jay raised his head, his eyes looked haunted. "Let's just say the last time I spoke to her, she told me to leave the country or she'd cut bits off me without any anaesthetic. Bits I'm attached to."

"Some doctor," Xan remarked. "Are you sure she's not a serial killer instead? Maybe a reincarnation of Jack the Ripper, out to kill blokes who sleep around instead of hookers?"

Jay's lips smiled, but his eyes didn't. "She is a doctor. But she might be a killer, too, so don't do anything to get on her bad side, Xan. Don't even touch her. If you don't believe me, ask Jo. She'll tell you the same. Fuck, she's probably her maid of honour. Even if I said no, Jo would insist on having the wedding here. Take the booking and do what she says."

Xan pressed her lips together. "Even if she wants to turn the lagoon pink to match her bridesmaids?"

Jay laughed. A little hysterically, but it was definitely laughter. "Angel Black won't want pink. If she even wears white, I'll be surprised." He sobered. "Cost it up and give her a quote. Whatever she asks."

"And double the price so she decides it's not worth it?"

Jay shook his head. "Fuck, no. It's not that she can't afford whatever she wants. It's…if she wanted to, she could buy both Jo and I out and own this resort without having to borrow a cent. I spent money on a lot of rock star shit over the years, but she invested every dollar and…she has money from her family, too, I think. Some sort of inheritance. Just…get used to the idea of hosting a rock star's wedding. Because you will be."

Xan raised her eyebrows. "Two of them. Yours first, remember?"

"Yeah." Jay's eyes returned to the deck. "Yeah, mine first." He didn't sound particularly eager about it.

Perhaps Penelope was turning into a regular bridezilla, Xan thought. She chose not to push the issue.

"Right. Two rock star weddings next May. Good thing I have nine months to prepare!" she said, heading back to her office.

Just nine months. She'd need it. One televised celebrity wedding would be trouble enough, but two? Shit, having twins would be easier.

THREE

Xan stood by the helipad, biting her nails. She'd lost count of the number of times she'd considered calling Philly and telling her to cancel the meeting she'd asked the girl to set up. But every time, she hadn't cancelled, because she needed to get this mess sorted. She was the manager of a multi-million-dollar resort. She shouldn't want to hide under the desk every time the phone rang. What was she afraid of, after all?

Not Jerome. Not that lying, cheating, smarmy schoolteacher-in-training who'd broken off their engagement because he couldn't keep it in his pants while she was away. He should be afraid of her. After all, she kept rock star Jay Felix in check on a daily basis.

Well, mostly in check. She hadn't managed to stop him from swimming nude in the lagoon this morning, like every other morning. She'd pretty much given up on that. This morning, she'd just raised her coffee in salute to the daft bugger, watching to make sure the sharks didn't get him until he swam out of sight. Just another morning at Romance Island Resort.

And today would be just another lunch at the brewery. There'd be plenty of people she knew. The food would be wonderful, as always, and the beer would be brewed to perfection. She could only have one and still be able to drive, but she didn't want to be drunk for this meeting. Sober would be best, or nearly so. She could get drunk afterwards, if she had to. Hours afterward, when she returned to the resort, in the privacy of her unit. Or on the Penguin jetty. She'd gotten accustomed to walking out there of an evening while Jay was filming that reality TV show, and he hadn't asked her to stop when he'd returned. If anything, he seemed to welcome her company. He needed to spend more time with Penelope, his bride-to-be, or a gaggle of fans in town, like the first time she saw him. She'd still been the manager of the backpackers then, driving a vanload of guests into town for the day. How things had changed, she mused, waving to Shou as he circled his helicopter in to land.

It wasn't until he touched down on the helipad that Xan realised he had a co-pilot today. A co-pilot who jumped down from the helicopter and marched past Xan without a word, though she did wave to Shou before she disappeared through the gate.

For a moment, Xan considered chasing the girl down so she could introduce herself and demand to know her business at the resort, but she didn't have time. If she didn't fly off now, she'd miss the meeting…and she'd have to reschedule. No. She couldn't endure another day of this dread. This ends now, she told herself as she climbed into the seat behind Shou.

FOUR

Jerome's first mistake was to try and hug Xan the moment he saw her. His second was to attempt to kiss her.

Xan tried to feel bad about accidentally elbowing him in the gut and headbutting him in the face, but his nose had made such a satisfying crunch that she knew she'd be lying to herself.

His third mistake was for the first words out of his mouth to be, "She said she was going to get rid of the baby."

She should have walked out of the brewery right there and then. Gods knew she wanted to. But all the weeks of frustration had built up too much not to burst under this pressure.

"Oh, so cheating on your fiancée and getting some kid pregnant isn't a problem if the girl gets an abortion?" Xan hissed, keeping her voice low so the whole room wouldn't know her business. Gossip travelled fast in a small town, after all.

"But the baby wasn't mine!" Jerome said.

Xan failed to see how that improved matters. "You mean while you were cheating on me, she was cheating on you?"

"No, I never cheated on you. I wouldn't, Xan, you know that."

She'd dealt with enough dodgy backpackers to know a liar when she met one. "Oh yeah? She was all over you in those pictures on your social media account. Even my mum said you two were together."

"That was for her parents' benefit," Jerome said. "See, Kelly had too much to drink at one of the school dances. Smuggled alcohol in, just like we used to. I was a student teacher at her school, helping supervise the kids at the dance, so I spotted her and took her aside before her teachers caught her drinking. I called her parents and said she was sick, so I'd drive her home. We weren't in the car more'n five minutes before she was spilling her guts about some boy she went to school with getting her pregnant. She begged me to help her by saying I was the baby's dad, not the boy from school, until she got the money together to have an abortion.

"She was your friend, and she said you'd want me to help her. Said you'd understand. So we took a bunch of pictures and put them on her social media accounts and mine. Told everybody we were in love and going to have a kid."

Xan forced herself to stay calm. "And no one minded that you'd slept with a girl ten years younger than you? A student at the school where you worked?"

Jerome scratched his head. "Well, her parents were a bit surprised at first. So I hung out at her place a lot with her, making them believe we were in love."

"What did you have to do to make them believe that?" Xan asked, keeping her voice level even while she wanted to scream at him.

"Well, just a bit of a kiss and a cuddle at first, but when they still didn't believe it, we sort of arranged for them to catch us in bed together. Once or twice. Or maybe a few more times." Jerome raised his hands in surrender. "Just to sell the story, honest! There wasn't any other way."

"You slept with one of your sixteen-year-old students while you were engaged to marry me. Not just once, but a few times. In my world, no, in most people's worlds, that's cheating, Jerome." Xan wet her lips. "Not to mention it makes you a paedophile, too. She's barely legal – and still at school!"

"Barely legal's still legal, and it wasn't cheating. I didn't love her – I only love you! I'm sorry if you see it differently. Maybe I made a mistake, but I'm sorry. We belong together and you know it. I'm sorry. You weren't around to ask, but I figured you'd want me to help your friend. You were never supposed to know!"

If the man dug his hole any deeper, he'd bury himself in it. If he hadn't already.

"Jerome, like I said before on the phone, it's over. I won't marry a man who can't stay faithful." She rose and headed for the bar. She could have one drink, and she intended to have it. The hard bit would be not pouring it over Jerome's stupid head.

"Hey, Xan. Nice to see you in town again. They keep you busy out on that island, don't they?"

Xan smiled at Steve, the manager of the Mangrove Hotel. They'd been nodding acquaintances when she ran the backpackers, but they'd become colleagues when she started working at Romance Island Resort. In fact, she'd negotiated a range of tour and day trip packages with him, where tourists could stay at his hotel in town and spend a day or three sampling the island's delights while they were in Broome. Together with the day trippers from the construction camp at Lorikeet, all the new tourist traffic had meant that the Resort had experienced its best earning season since it opened.

"Yeah, it's the platypires. There were so many new ones born this year, their mothers couldn't keep up, so we've had to bottle feed them." Xan tried to keep a straight face.

"Platypires? I haven't heard of those," Steve said, sipping his beer. Mango, by the smell of it.

"Oh, you don't get them on the mainland. They've been hunted almost to extinction over here. Kind of like drop bears on the east coast, or Nannup tigers down south. But on the islands, they're really flourishing." Xan's ginger beer arrived and she took a deep gulp to hide her laugh.

"What do they look like?"

"Oh, like a cross between a platypus and a vampire bat. You know, a duck bill with the tail, but sort of leathery wings with a furry body. They use their echolocation to find their prey in the dark."

"Oh yeah?" Steve raised his eyebrows. "What do they eat?"

"They don't. They're blood drinkers, like giant

mosquitoes. See, on either side of their beak, they have fangs, and – "

A heavy hand landed on Xan's shoulder. "Who's your friend, babe?" Jerome asked, bristling at Steve.

Steve wiped his hand on his shorts, then held it out for a shake. "Steve. I manage the Mangrove Hotel. Not as luxurious as Xan's resort, but we've been refurbishing it. Got a new restaurant opening soon. Oh, that reminds me. We're planning a big party to celebrate when it opens. Next Staircase, it'll be. I'd love you to come."

"We'll be there, won't we, Xan?" Jerome said.

Steve looked surprised. "Of course, if you're Xan's partner, you're very welcome to join us."

"Wouldn't miss it," Jerome said sweetly. He kissed Xan's cheek. "Gotta go, babe. You have a think about everything I said, and when you're ready to admit you were wrong, I'll forgive you with open arms. I'll see you at the party."

Xan wanted to scream, or at least wash his slimy kiss off her face. Instead, she forced herself to remain calm and finish her beer before she headed back to the resort.

FIVE

The whole flight back to Romance Island, Xan debated whether she'd done the right thing or not. Sure, her head and every reasonable thought pointed toward a damn good decision to tell Jerome to bugger off, but if it was so right, why was her tummy clenching so tightly she thought she'd be sick? If she'd had sex at all in the last year, she'd wonder if she might be pregnant, but she was hardly a candidate for an immaculate conception. No religion to speak of, unless you counted her fascination with the deities of Ancient Greece, but that wasn't worship. More…rabid curiosity, fuelled by her father's stories from when she was little.

Shou wisely left her to her thoughts, for which Xan was thankful, until he broke his silence to tell her they were approaching the resort.

Such a relief to be home, Xan thought, before she caught herself. She was lucky to be able to call a luxury resort home, even if her unit was hardly in the same class as Jay's villa or even the standard hotel rooms.

She wanted to burn off some of the energy her body still seemed to buzzing with – one of those fight or flight reflex things, she guessed – and eyed the lagoon as they flew over. It was low tide, and a bit rough. At high tide she wouldn't have minded, but some of that coral was pretty brutal if the currents pushed you into it, and it broke the surface when the tide was as low as it was now. A walk around the island would have to do, she decided. A brisk walk involving several laps around the island.

Shou touched down on the helipad in one of the gentlest landings Xan had ever experienced. She glimpsed her own thunderous expression reflected in the window and almost laughed. Shou evidently didn't want to antagonise her further, or maybe he thought he was the source of her bad mood. As if he'd ever caused anywhere near as much trouble as Jerome did. Even Jay couldn't do that. Sure, Jay was a daily nuisance and the bane of her job, but he was a minor irritant compared to Jerome's ability to turn her life upside down. After all, she'd loved Jerome. Probably still did, at least a tiny bit, which might explain that sick twisted guts feeling. Either that or she'd eaten something off at the brewery, which just wasn't possible.

So she was still in love with Jerome. The two-faced, cheating bastard who possibly had unprotected sex with children. Who didn't deserve her. But who had also flown halfway round the world to apologise for being a wanker, and beg her to take him back. Sort of.

Or so he'd said. He could be a lying bastard as well as a cheating one. Who knew how much he'd changed in the time she'd been away? She'd been so starry-eyed when she last saw him. So eager to travel the world with him so he could teach wherever they wound up. Third world countries where teachers were scarce. The ends of the earth. Wherever.

People changed, she knew. After all, she had. Time and experience and circumstance and growing up and…

Xan almost ran into the same girl she'd seen this morning. The helipad gate wasn't big enough for the two of them, so they both backed up and offered to let the other go first.

The girl let out a breathy snort. "I should take that offer, or Shou might fly off without me and leave me stuck on this rock with the dickhead who still fancies himself a rock god."

"You're here to visit Jay?" Xan blurted out.

"He begged me to come before I head south again. I should've known better. He didn't understand the word NO then, and still doesn't. Men never change. Least of all him." She glared in the direction of the Pearls, as if Jay could feel the heat of her gaze through the jungle.

That didn't sound like the Jay Xan knew. He had changed in the short time she'd known him. Well, he'd changed a bit. She couldn't remember the last time she'd had to call Maintenance to help load him onto a wheelbarrow because he'd drunk himself into a stupor. Oh, that day on the beach with the auction girl, Flavia, but he hadn't been drunk. Maybe he just hadn't had a reason to get that drunk. It's not like his wife had left him…again. Not that she'd seen Penelope around the island much lately.

"Did you see Penelope while you were at Jay's villa?"

Xan asked.

The girl laughed bitterly. "The last time I saw Penny, she tried to kill me. If I saw her again, I'd break her other arm myself. Meier wasn't desperate enough to hire her again, was he? She spent more time shagging the chefs than doing her job last time, and I bet that hasn't changed."

"Meier's gone. I manage the resort now," Xan said coolly. She stuck out a hand. "Xan Lane. And you are?"

"Audra. I used to work here, and pick up the pieces when Penny didn't do her job. Now, I'm happier than ever that I left."

Xan recognised her name. "You're the first girl who lost her job for sleeping with him, aren't you?"

Audra bristled. "No, that was Penny. I resigned to take up a graduate position before I did anything with Jay, not that it's any of your business." She sniffed. "I notice a lot of staff missing from when I worked here. I take it he didn't just restrict himself to fangirls – he slept his way through the staff, too? Is that how you got your job?"

Xan figured she deserved that. "No," she said. "Meier hired me. If I'd known who the owner was, I wouldn't have bothered applying. I've seen better behaved toddlers."

Audra grinned. "He painted Shakespeare on the wall in ketchup and chocolate for you, too, did he? I wonder how many girls he's won over that way."

Xan shrugged. "I'd have to ask Jackie. She cleans his villa. But she hasn't mentioned anything about wall art. Maybe he's run out of chocolate. Or lost his copy of Shakespeare."

"He still spends plenty of time in the library, though," Audra said cryptically. "Not that it's done him much good. I still said no. Good luck. If you're the last woman left standing, he'll target you next. Don't bet against him, is my advice." She headed through the gate and climbed into the helicopter beside Shou. She gave Xan a nod as they rose from the helipad.

More confused than ever, Xan wanted to head to her house and dig out that last bottle of rum. She deserved it after a day like today. Instead, her feet headed for the Penguin jetty.

With each step, she debated her choices. Forgive Jerome. Stomp. Ditch the cheating bastard. Stomp. Give him another chance. Stomp. Knee him in the groin so hard he'd never get it up again. Stomp. Accept that he'd made a mistake that he was now heartily sorry for, and –

"Cheaters never get the girl," Jay seethed, hurling something out over the ocean. He bent down and picked up a rock from the pile at his feet, before pitching that, too. "Did you know that? In all the romance books you've ever read, can you name one where a bloke who cheats, wins?"

Xan didn't need to think hard. "No," she answered.

"So I'm doomed, then. Doomed to never find love because I fucked up without even knowing." Jay dropped the next stone over the side of the jetty where it sank like…well, a stone.

"You didn't know cheating on a girl is bad?" Xan found it hard to believe even Jay could be that stupid.

"Of course I knew that. That's why I don't do it. Have you ever seen me doing anything even remotely unfaithful to any of the girls I've been with at the resort?"

Xan combed her memories. The problem was, he never seemed to be with a girl long enough to be unfaithful. Well, there was the reality TV show, where he'd had to date multiple girls at the same time in order to meet the show's tight production schedule, but cheating would imply that he'd had a clear favourite among the contestants, and nothing she'd seen of Jay with the girls had led her to believe that was the case. She'd watched the first episode when it aired last week, and only because she'd known he'd choose Penelope in the end had she noticed that the girl got a few seconds more screen time than the others.

Speaking of Penelope…had Jay told her about Audra's visit?

"No," Xan said slowly. "But what did Penelope say when you invited Audra to visit?"

Jay's hand swooped down, seized a stone, then sent it flying out to sea. "Nothing. Penelope hasn't said a word to me since she left the island. She just left me a fucking note. No proper goodbye, nothing." Another rock soared away, narrowly missing a seagull.

"Planning a wedding can be stressful, or so I've heard," Xan murmured.

"She's not planning a fucking wedding. She left me, I said. Said she doesn't want to marry me. After what she saw on the show and how I said similar things to the other girls to what I said to her. Says I can't really love her, and I betrayed her by letting her fall for me with my rehearsed lines. When I was fucking honest with all of those girls!" A rock splashed into the sea beneath the jetty. "So what if I said the same thing a few times? I'm a rock star who's awesome in bed. I'm not supposed to spout spur-of-the-moment sonnets for every fucking girl I meet! I'm not fucking Shakespeare!"

Funny. Audra had mentioned Shakespeare, too. "So you got lonely and invited another girl over who you knew Penelope wouldn't like to make her jealous?" Xan guessed. That sounded like a Shakespearean plot, for sure. She should know – her father might have made a Classical scholar of her, but her mother had introduced her to Shakespeare almost as soon as she could read, or learn to keep quiet in the university theatre.

"Fuck, no!" Jay shouted, then dropped his voice to a more normal volume. "No. Audra is…my friend. A friend I thought might help me, but she said she prefers the elephant seals at the South Pole to being with me, after she says I cheated on her." Jay sighed heavily. "But it's not cheating if you're apart!"

Yes it is, Xan thought. It didn't matter that Jerome was in the UK while she was here in Australia. The moment her fiancé climbed into bed with another girl, he'd cheated on her. "It doesn't matter how many miles apart you are," Xan said slowly. "If you're in a committed relationship with someone, you don't fool around with someone else, or it's cheating."

"Yeah, but when there's no commitment or relationship or any fucking thing like that, it's not the same. I went on tour. I'm supposed to…what'd she call it? Make myself accessible to my fans or some shit. Make the dreams of as many fangirls come true as I can. It's not easy, you know, having to make sure you're better than their best daydream. Takes skill, you know? And a shitload of stamina. So when I'm finally finished with the farewell tour, and I get to just be me for a bit here at the resort, I find she's fucked off to Antarctica without telling me. Like I don't matter!"

Xan didn't blame Audra at all. In fact, she wanted to cheer the girl on, and wished she'd known a bit more so she could say so in the brief conversation they'd shared on the helipad. "Sounds like you showed her she didn't matter first, sleeping around while you expected her to wait for you. That's a double standard right there, Jay."

He fell to his knees, spilling rocks over the side of the jetty. "I didn't expect her to wait. I figured she'd do whatever she was doing before we met, like I was doing, but when we met again, there'd be fireworks all over again. Good ones, not that she'd blow up in my face and say she'd rather sleep with a seal. A fucking seal!" He lifted his shirt. "Do seals have six-packs? Do you know a single seal who has abs like this?"

Though Xan admired Jay's toned tummy as much as the next girl, she definitely sided with the absent Audra. "You're hardly the most subtle bloke. What do you expect, asking a girl you haven't seen in months to sleep with you the moment you meet again?"

"I didn't ask her to sleep with me!" Jay protested. "I asked her to fucking marry me!"

SIX

Xan took a moment to stop herself from laughing. How much had Jay had to drink this time? "Why are you so set on getting married?" she asked carefully. "The mail order bride, the virginity auction, the reality TV show…and now an old friend who worked here before Meier hired me. If you ask me, it smacks of desperation. Which is pretty strange, considering how easily you seem to charm the women you want. What am I missing, Jay?"

"Angel's wedding," he mumbled, so quietly she barely caught the words.

"Your bandmate, right? But if it's her wedding, she's the one getting married, not you."

"The invitation said to bring a partner."

Xan waved her hand. "But you know that's just a courtesy, right? If you don't know the name of your guest's partner when you write the invitation, which can be printed a year in advance, that's what you put on it, so they can still bring a partner along if they want, and she or he still has an invitation."

"Not this time. Not when it's from Angel. It's her telling me to bring a partner because she thinks I need one." He eyed the jetty boards, avoiding her gaze.

"And you always do what she says?" Xan asked.

He looked up. "Fuck yes! I like living, with all my bits attached, thanks."

"But it didn't say wife, did it? Your invitation? It just said partner, right?" Xan pressed.

"Yeah. The wife bit…that bit…that was me." He kicked a rock off the jetty. "I said I'd come with my wife, and we'd be so in love we'd put the other couple in the shade."

Tempting fate, of course. The beginning of a true Greek tragedy. Or a Roman farce, seeing as this involved Jay Felix.

"You could just bring a partner for the night. You don't seem to have a problem keeping a girl interested that long. I'm sure there are hundreds of girls who'd kill for the chance to attend a wedding with you."

"Bring a fangirl to Angel's wedding?" Jay's eyes widened in horror. "She'd crucify me. Once Jo was done with me, because she'd never forgive me, either. This won't be a public wedding. You'll see. Angel won't allow any media on the island. Shit, she'll probably have armed security guards stationed along the beaches, ready to shoot down any aircraft within range, drone or manned."

Xan still didn't understand what passed for logic in Jay's mind. "But she'd be happy have a reality TV show starlet or some girl whose virginity you bought in an online auction at her wedding." She almost added something about his black widow mail order bride, but stopped herself in time. Phuong's betrayal was a low blow that still had the power to upset him. Xan might not like Jay, but she wasn't that cruel.

"She wouldn't have known," Jay said.

Xan snorted. "That reality TV show aired its first episode last week. The whole country knows about your very public search for a wife. Paige told me the studio is in talks to sell the rights to this season to one of the big networks in the US. Everyone wants to watch the music world's hottest bachelor find a wife, live in their living room. Your Angel would have to be living under a rock in a bunker with no access to the outside world not to know about THAT."

Jay sighed heavily. "She's not my angel. Never was, never will be." His shoulders slumped and all the fight went out of him.

Finally, Xan understood. "How long have you been in love with her?"

"What's it matter?" Angrily, Jay swept the remaining rocks off the jetty with his foot. "She's marrying that psycho, not me. And Audra says cheaters never get a happily ever after, so I'm fucked on all sides now. Doesn't matter who I go to her wedding with, because whoever she is, we won't be happy." He laughed bitterly. "Because if I cheated on Audra by getting with fangirls on just that one farewell tour, I've cheated on Angel hundreds, maybe thousands of times. Doesn't matter that there was no love or relationship involved with any of them. She'll never want me."

"Sometimes the one person we want is the one we can't have," Xan said. That was the whole bit about the hero's quest in all the ancient stories, right? A hero haring off after some impossible goal?

"Would you get back with a guy who cheated on you?" Jay challenged.

Xan hesitated. Would she get back with Jerome? "No," she answered finally. "It's too big a betrayal. I hope his dick shrivels up and no one ever loves him again."

Jay plucked at his shorts. "You want my dick to do what? Hey, there's nothing about that in any of the books. Never being loved is enough, don't you think?"

Yes. Maybe it was. Xan would settle for never seeing Jerome again, to be honest, let alone any shrivelling. Except….there was the problem of the reopening of the Mangrove Hotel. Maybe she and Jay could help each other out.

"You know what?" Xan said. "If you come with me to an official function in town next month, I'll make a deal with you. If you still can't find an acceptable partner to attend your bandmate's wedding with, I'll go with you."

"And marry me, too?" Jay realised his mistake as soon as the words left his lips. "Okay, sorry. I shouldn't have said that. Forget I said it. She'll already know you're the hotel manager here, and she won't believe…"

"That's right," Xan interrupted. "What do you say? Is it a deal?"

"Yeah." Jay eyed her with what Xan might have called relief. "Thanks, Xan. I guess that makes us friends, doesn't it?"

Xan nodded, biting her tongue before she blurted out the bit about her friendship coming with an absolute lack of benefits. Instead, she wished him a nice evening, and headed back to her house, vowing to help him find a better date for the wedding than her. Whatever it took.

And she had to meet this Angel, who had the power to both terrify and enthral a man like Jay Felix.

SEVEN

Xan didn't have long to wait before, once again, she stood by the helipad, watching Shou guide his aircraft unerringly to the X marking his spot. The hatch cracked open and Xan met the eyes of…a man who jumped out of the helicopter like someone accustomed to it. Between his buzz-cut and a bulked-up body that would put Jay Felix to shame, she marked him as military – or ex-military, perhaps.

He surveyed his surroundings, pausing briefly to offer Xan a nod of acknowledgement before he completed his circuit. Only then did he step forward to take Xan's extended hand. "Trevor Sullivan, security consultant," he said with a strong American accent. Northern, not Southern, but that's all she knew about American accents.

Xan tried not to wince at his firm handshake. "Xan Lane, manager of Romance Island Resort," she said, extracting her pulverised fingers from his grip.

Fortunately, he didn't seem to notice, as he exchanged nods with Jay, who stood silently beside Xan. "Felix," Trevor said.

Behind Trevor, a child hopped out of the helicopter, and Xan's jaw dropped. The dark-haired girl looked perhaps twelve years old, moving with a dancer's grace as she landed on the pavement and crossed to stand behind Trevor.

Was it school holidays? Xan wondered. Bring your daughter to work day? Because she'd expected to meet the enigmatic Angel, not some security consultant and his daughter.

"And this is…" Trevor began, waving in the direction of the girl.

Xan turned on a child-friendly smile and extended her hand.

"Don't," Jay hissed.

The girl shook her hair out of her eyes, before directing a glare at the helicopter blades responsible for mussing her hair. "Doctor Alanna Miller. We spoke on the phone." Huge, dark eyes sucked at Xan's soul as the girl – no child, that was certain – made no move to shake hands. The eyes flicked mercifully to Jay for a moment, before returning to Xan. "Is there anything you don't know about this island?"

Xan wet her lips. "I'd like to think there isn't, but some of my staff might have more detailed knowledge than me about their specialty. That's why I pay them, after all."

Alanna nodded. "Fair enough." She jerked her head at Jay. "Does he count as staff?"

Xan tried and failed to hide her smile. "I don't pay him, so probably not."

Alanna made shooing motions with her hands. "You're

still not my favourite person, Jason. Go back to safely sunning yourself on your private beach. I'll send for you if I need you."

Without a word, Jay left.

The dark eyes settled on Xan again. "Shall we start, Xan? I've seen the helipad, so let's begin with transport. Jo mentioned ferry services and a dock. I'd like to know the frequency and travel times before you show me your function facilities."

Xan nodded and led the way toward the main jetty, hoping to catch sight of Jay's retreating back as he headed back to his villa, but he'd evidently fled in such a hurry that he was nowhere to be seen. After less than five minutes with the woman, Xan began to understand why Jay was so afraid of her.

EIGHT

"So where are we going again?" Jay grumbled as he fastened his seatbelt. To give him credit, he actually looked decent, dressed up. He wasn't wearing a tux or even a suit, but in a shirt and chinos he seemed…almost civilised. Maybe it was the shoes. After seeing him barefoot or wearing thongs, she'd wondered if he actually owned any other shoes, but he'd managed to surprise her again. If all her efforts failed and she did have to attend the doctor's wedding as his date, at least he'd look good.

"We're going to a private party to celebrate the reopening of the Mangrove Hotel, after all its renovations," Xan explained patiently. "We have an arrangement with them where they send their guests to us for a day trip or weekend package, and we send ours here on the nights when there's Staircase to the Moon. Like there is tonight, for example. It's likely to be the last one this dry season, which is why Steve wanted to have his party tonight. He said the public will get one part of the lawn, but we'll get a cordoned off area for VIPs, because it's a private, invitation-only party." One she hoped Jerome wouldn't manage to get into.

"So why d'you need a date? Don't you want to socialise a bit, maybe find a friend for the night?" Jay asked, too damn perceptively.

"Not everyone hooks up with random strangers for one night stands," Xan snapped. "Some of us have standards. Want to be sure of our feelings before we get into bed with someone, though sometimes even that's a huge bloody mistake." She clamped her lips shut before she said any more.

"What's his name?"

"What?"

"What's his name?" Jay repeated. "Mr Bloody Huge Mistake?"

Damn him to the underworld and back. With harpies, just like in his namesake's legends. "It doesn't matter."

Jay peered out the window at the islands below. "It does if he'll be at the party tonight, and you want a pretend date to scare him off, and maybe make him feel inadequate. What'd he do? Make the mistake of thinking you wanted more than one night, when you just wanted a quick fuck?"

Xan clenched her fists. "Gods help me, Jay, if you weren't my boss, I'd punch you for saying that. Is there no filter on your mouth at all?"

"Nope," he replied cheerfully. "Look, sorry if it's offensive. But I know how these things go. I've watched movies and read books. Things go wrong when the fake date doesn't know shit. I figure I know you, but I don't know him. So, help me not fuck this up for you. Do you want me to help you get him back, or to leave you alone? Is he a stalker?"

"No, he's not a stalker. He's not a one-night stand, either. He's the wanker I was engaged to marry, before he cheated on me. I found out just before I got the job at the resort. He's…he says he wants me back, but like you said, cheaters never get the girl. Definitely not this girl. But he was there when Steve told me about the party, and he sort of invited himself along as my partner before I could stop him. If I arrive with you, I figure that'll mean he can't get in."

Jay frowned. "So you don't need me to make him jealous."

"No." Though it couldn't hurt if Jerome thought she had moved on to someone better.

"So no normal date-like behaviour? You don't need me to kiss you breathless, or invent pet names for you, or know what your favourite position is?"

Only in books did people have favourite positions. Honestly, most men only knew two or three — on top, on the bottom, or from behind. The rest were invented for the porn industry, Xan was sure of it. "No," she repeated. "We are what we are. Colleagues from Romance Island Resort, helping another hotel manager celebrate a special occasion."

"Fine," Jay sighed, pouting. "If you change your mind, let me know. I figured it was the only chance I'd ever get to kiss you. Maybe not, then."

Xan clenched her fists again, but then she caught his grin before he turned his face away. "You're baiting me, aren't you?"

"Yeah," he admitted. "You're funny when you're pissed off. Bit scary, too, but where's the fun if there isn't any danger?"

"Bloody rock star," she muttered under her breath. It was too late to back out now, but she heartily wished she'd never asked him to the party. She crossed her fingers, hoping he could behave himself enough not to get chucked out of Steve's party. Maybe she'd have been better off alone.

NINE

"Do I get to hold your hand?" Jay asked, nodding toward the couple in front of them.

"No, because we're not a couple," Xan said, pasting a smile on her face as she gave her name to the hostess. The woman found Xan's name easily and ticked her off, but Jay presented a bit of a problem.

"I'm sorry, Mr Felix, but you're not on the list," the wide-eyed woman stammered. "I'll see if I can find the manager."

Xan leaned forward and said something she never thought she'd say: "It's all right, he's with me."

"Your…partner?"

Jay glowered. He really didn't like that word.

Xan laughed. "After a fashion. Jay owns Romance Island Resort, but I'm the manager. Seeing as he was in town, I invited him along as my date, so he could meet

35

some of the other hotel owners and managers here."

"Oh, in that case…" She waved them through, turning her attention to the next group of guests.

"Do you kiss on a first date?" Jay persisted.

"This isn't a date."

"You told her it was."

It was like bringing along her brother, if she'd had one. Xan's respect for Jo jumped up a notch.

Xan scanned the guests who'd already arrived, searching for Jerome. She didn't want to see him, but she wanted some warning before he came near her again. After a few minutes, she was satisfied that he hadn't managed to gain entry to the party.

"What do you want to drink?" Jay asked, gesturing at a waiter with a loaded tray. He'd already claimed a condensation-coated beer.

"Juice," Xan decided, reaching for the glass. She wanted her wits about her for a bit longer before she started drinking anything stronger.

She expected Jay to wander off in search of fangirls, but he stuck to her side much like the devoted date he wasn't. Not that he needed to – a white picket fence separated the crowd in the beer garden next door from the thirty or so guests in the private party area. The public stood six deep at the railing overlooking the mangroves, while there was seating for all the guests at their stretch of railing.

When Jay was halfway through his second drink, he asked, "So, where's the mistake?"

"I don't know," she admitted. "I haven't seen him yet."

As if someone in the hotel had heard her, all the outside lights went out.

"Well, that helps," Xan muttered.

She knew what was coming, though. The buzz humming through the crowd spilled over into the party area as the first sliver of reddish moon appeared on the horizon. Gasps and whispered superlatives followed as the moon rose higher, as if too much noise might make the celestial body sink out of sight.

Minutes passed and the blood orange staircase emerged across the tidal flats, forming a path up to the moon the water reflected.

"Beautiful," Xan sighed. She'd seen Staircase to the Moon so many times from this very beer garden, as well as from Romance Island, but it never ceased to enchant her.

"Yep. Nature's bloody awesome up here," Jay said. "It's more of a real staircase here, too. At the island, it's more like one of the resort paths, with maybe a couple of steps when there's waves."

Maybe bringing Jay along wasn't such a bad idea after all.

As the moon climbed the sky, it paled from red to white, the staircase all but vanishing. The lights came back on and a small army of waiters appeared, bearing trays of food and drink. In front of the railing, chairs were shifted to make space for a stage.

Xan had forgotten about the live band that played here on Staircase nights. Her night improved another notch, so she reached for a cider instead of juice this time.

Jay clinked his drink against hers, then pointed at the band setting up. "Do you know them? Are they any good?"

Xan shook her head. "I don't know. I guess we'll have to wait and see."

Jay dragged a table and two chairs over to a spot beside

the picket fence with a good view of the band. He claimed one seat for himself, gesturing for her to take the other. Xan gratefully accepted.

They sat in companionable silence for a few minutes, until Jay finished his drink. "Want me to get you another one?"

Xan had plenty left, so she shook her head.

Jay took off in search of his next drink. Over on the stage, the band launched into their first number. They weren't bad, even if they were covering another band's familiar song. But that's the way the world worked, wasn't it? As an unknown band, they'd have to play what was popular, instead of their own, original songs, until they'd built up enough of an audience who appreciated their unique style and wanted nothing else.

She heard Jay sink into his chair. "How long did you have to play other people's songs before you had enough fans to play your own?" she asked, not taking her eyes off the band.

"One fan's enough for me, if it's you," Jerome replied. "Have you thought about what I said?"

Xan swore. "What are you doing here?"

"I said I'd be here. And I'm here for you, Xan. Here to win you back. Here to make you see the truth about how I helped your friend Kelly and I'm the only man for you."

Xan turned away. "Go away, Jerome. I told you I'm not interested. If the only man for me is a cheating paedophile, then I don't want any man at all."

"You don't mean that. Tell me you don't mean that."

"She usually says what she means. Xan doesn't mince words," Jay jumped in. "And that's my seat, mate." He set his beer on the table, placing a bottle of cider pointedly in front of Xan.

"I don't see your name on it," Jerome snapped, jutting out his chin.

Xan rose. "Take mine, Jay. I'm not staying."

Both men protested, but Xan didn't want to listen. She couldn't be bothered with pissing contests. She found another table near the railing and claimed that for herself and her cider.

Less than a minute later, Jay joined her. "Was that the big mistake?"

"Yes," she admitted.

"He's a fucking idiot."

Xan silently agreed. That also made her one for falling in love with the bastard, but everyone made mistakes. At least she hadn't married hers.

The band struck up another tune. Xan liked this one.

Evidently, so did Jay. He dumped his beer on the table. "Excuse me, I believe they're playing my song."

Xan watched in fascination as Jay strode right up to the stage, so the lights showed his face, and gestured for the microphone. After a brief discussion with the singer, Jay jumped onto the stage, mike in hand.

"Let's try that again, shall we? Just like in the Arena — with energy!"

The grinning band members turned up the volume, produced a second microphone, and proceeded to back Jay up as he belted out the lyrics with his eyes closed.

At the end, Jay looked right at Xan, who clapped her approval for the performance. He gave an exaggerated bow, then held a quick, whispered conference with the band before they launched into another number, with Jay as their frontman.

Some of the guests recognised him. Both in the beer garden and the private party, people lifted their phones to photograph Jay's impromptu live performance.

Xan's phone stayed in her handbag, where it belonged. Though she'd never tell him, Chaya had always been one of her favourite bands, so she sat back, sipping her cider, content to just enjoy the show.

TEN

"Ah, Ms Lane?" a soft voice asked.

"Nngh?" Xan had lost count of her drinks hours ago, but she was fairly sure she'd drunk less than Jay, who now sat with the band beside the darkened stage, sharing laughter, stories and enough alcohol to drown a whale.

She wasn't about to join them, though, and she was quite happy drinking alone, as long as Jerome didn't join her. Luckily, he'd vanished.

"Ms Lane, when you're ready, see Hotel Reception about your room key. All tonight's guests are staying in the deluxe apartments by the pool, as it's quieter than the rooms overlooking..." The waitress waved at the beer garden on the other side of the temporary picket fence, where the public staircase party had turned into a proper drunken revel.

Xan nodded and thanked the girl, without taking her

eyes off the revellers. The last time she watched Staircase to the Moon from this lawn, she'd been among the public patrons, as the designated driver for a bunch of backpackers who'd been staying at the place she managed back then. It felt strange to be on the other side of the fence, as one of the upper-class VIPs. She half expected someone to tap her on the shoulder and tell her she didn't belong, but of course no one did. This was Australia; moreover, this was Broome. The laid-back lifestyle here was nothing like the prim and proper sort of thing that went on back in the UK. If the Queen herself held a garden party in Broome, it would either be on this very lawn, or at Romance Island Resort, and she's get an invitation just as easily as she'd scored one to this event.

The waitress carried her full tray of drinks over to the band. They raised their glasses in one raucous, clinking toast to cheers of "Yeah!" and "Right on!" before draining the drinks dry. As if this was their final cue, they rose as one to ascend the stage, not for an encore, but to pack away their gear.

Jay, never one to clear up after himself, or do a day's work at all, sauntered over to Xan. "Top blokes," he slurred, grinning. He nodded at the empty bottles on the table beside Xan. "I hope you're not planning on driving after those. The police in town get real narky about drink driving."

Xan rose and half a dozen…whatever-they-weres swam woozily up to her head. Shouldn't have drunk so much. "No. We're staying the night here. We'll head back in the morning. I'll be fine by then."

Jay snorted. "If you drank all those, you'll have a

hangover by then."

Xan shrugged. "So will you." She bent her surprisingly unsteady steps toward Reception.

Jay held the door for her, which was probably a good thing, as her feet seemed to want to trip over themselves right now. Shouldn't have had that cider. Or the other ones. Maybe the cocktail had been a mistake, too. Too sweet. She was pretty sure she hadn't finished that one, at least.

"Your key, Ms Lane," the receptionist said, though Xan couldn't remember her name. Everyone knew her, that's all. It was a small town thing.

"What about him?" Xan demanded, jerking her head at Jay, then wishing she hadn't. Woozy as buggery. "He needs a key, too. He's not sharing mine." She closed her fist around it.

The receptionist blinked, then produced another key, which she handed to Jay. "For you, Mr Felix."

With a wink and a whistle, Jay led the way back outside, helping Xan out the doors and up the stairs. For once, Xan didn't protest about him touching her. Mostly because if he let go, she was certain her knees would buckle and she'd hit the floor. This was why she didn't drink. Now, why wouldn't the bloody key go into the lock? And which lock was it, when there were three of them?

"Here, lemme help," Jay said, taking the key. The lock behaved for him, clicking after barely a moment, letting him swing the door wide open. "C'mon, Xan, let's get you to bed."

She felt her body tilt dizzily, and opened her mouth to protest, then closed it again when she felt something soft under her back. Bed. Just what she needed right now, to sleep off that hellish cider.

"Now I get why you invited me. You needed someone to carry you to your room. You don't drink much, do you?"

Xan peered blearily at Jay. What was he doing in her bedroom? "Bugger off," she mumbled. "I'm not sleeping with you."

"You don't have to. There's another bed," Jay said.

No. She was not sharing a bed or a room with Jay Felix. "Out. Getcherownroom."

"My key's to the same room number as yours. Looks like we're sharing. At least your ex won't be likely to try and sneak in with me in here." Springs creaked as Jay threw himself on the other bed. His bed.

Bloody hell. Xan peered blearily at him. If she had to share a room, better Jay than Jerome. "I'm not sleeping with you," she repeated.

"Yeah, yeah. So you keep saying. Bet you're out before I am, though. I hope you don't snore."

Xan struggled to get under the sheets so she could pull one over her head. "You better not, either."

She vaguely heard Jay say something in response, but she wasn't listening any more. The cider pulled her under into welcome sleep. It'd serve him right if she snored, too.

ELEVEN

Xan awoke in an unfamiliar bed, shrouded in crisp white sheets that screamed hotel room. Definitely not her unit, where she only used the blue sheets she'd bought in town. She lifted her head to look around, and that's when the tides turned – from drowsy calm to pounding surf, beating at the inside of her head. Nope. Just…nope. She subsided onto the pillow.

Something on the bedside table caught her eye – a scrap of paper. Xan groped for it and held the note in front of her eyes.

Jay Felix's Fuck That Hangover Cure, she read.

1. Take the pills and drink the water. All of it.
2. When the pills kick in, take a shower or if you're feeling up to it, join me for a swim.
3. Room service said they're working on Step 3.

What pills, she wondered, risking a glance at the

nightstand. He'd left her two tablets, still in their plastic and foil blisters, and a bottle of water. They turned out to be pain relief, the sort sold over the counter in the supermarket, which was safe enough, Xan decided, downing them with a gulp of water.

She sipped the rest of the bottle slowly, feeling distinctly seedy, but not like she was going to be sick. And as for joining Jay for his morning swim…no bloody way was she swimming naked with him in the hotel pool. She'd shut herself in the shower and lock the door so he couldn't walk in. He might like wandering around with everything hanging out, but she had higher standards.

Her headache ebbed away slowly, until the weak sunlight filtering through the blinds no longer seared her eyes. When Xan felt halfway human again, she heaved herself out of bed, grabbed her overnight bag from the dresser, and headed for the bathroom.

She stood under the spray for ages, luxuriating in the unlimited, high-pressure, hot water, so unlike the eco-friendly facilities back at the resort. Well, those in the staff accommodation, at least – she knew the villas had much better bathrooms than this one, though the main hotel rooms were probably on a par with this. No surprises there, seeing as Steve had refurbished these rooms with the same contractors that Meier had used for the island. Yet another small town thing.

Reluctantly, she shut off the water and towelled herself dry. Just as she hung up the towel, she heard a door slam. Jay returning, she guessed, hurrying to dress in case he burst into the bathroom. She had locked the door, but it wasn't exactly a super-secure deadlock.

Sure enough, Jay knocked on the door. "You decent in there? Or getting into your bathers so you can join me for a swim? I'm done, but I'll go down again if you want the company. The pool's colder than the lagoon, by the way."

"I'm always decent," Xan called back, pulling her t-shirt over her head. She reached for the door handle and hesitated. "What about you?" The last thing she needed was to get an eyeful of Jay's nude body first thing in the morning. Watching him swim naked in the lagoon was one thing, but in this hotel room, it'd be much more intimate.

"Nope!" he replied. "Rock stars are born to be indecent. Goes with the territory."

Xan took a deep breath, opened the door and strode out, fixing her gaze on the ceiling. "Can you put a towel on or something and let me know when it's safe to look?"

Jay laughed. "You're not this squeamish most mornings. And yes, I've got a towel round me. Happy now?"

Xan risked a glance. "You're wearing board shorts! I thought you said you weren't decent?"

"I'm not. But their pool is colder than the lagoon, like I said, and there's a difference between swimming naked in the lagoon on your own private island and skinnydipping in someone else's hotel pool."

Maybe Jay did have a little common decency, after all. Not that Xan intended to tell him. "I'd have thought you'd like having a new audience to show off to."

"Not the audience I had in mind. It's not as much fun unless the audience appreciates your performance." Jay's grin turned wicked.

"I'm sure all the other hotel guests wouldn't have minded waking up to a naked rock star outside their window," Xan said.

Jay shrugged. "Probably not. You don't."

Xan saw red. "How many times have I told you to put something on in the mornings? Maybe I just got sick of wasting my breath."

"Maybe. Doesn't explain why you still watch me swim, every morning."

Xan turned away, hoping to hide her flushed face. He could see her through her kitchen window as clearly as she saw him?

"I'll go see about that room service, then I'd like to take a shower. You'll be done in the bathroom by then, yeah?" Jay tossed over his shoulder before he closed the door behind him.

Xan sank onto the bed, her head in her hands as her headache returned with a vengeful stab. She knew she shouldn't watch her boss swim his perfectly sculpted body past her window every morning, but it's not like she was peeping through his bedroom window to see him naked. He put everything on very public display in the island's lagoon, where anyone walking past could see him!

When she got home, she resolved, she'd have her morning coffee at the kitchen table in future, with her back turned firmly to the window.

She noticed her phone blinking, meaning it had received a message. Sure enough it had – a text message from Jerome, apologising for last night and asking to meet her for breakfast this morning. Not bloody likely. Xan stabbed her finger at the delete button, feeling a peculiar satisfaction as Jerome's words vanished. Good riddance.

Jay burst back into the room, grinning. "Room service

has arrived!" He carried a tray loaded with more food and drink than two people could eat. Definitely more than Xan could eat.

"I don't want anything," she said. If Jerome's message hadn't made her feel sick, her hangover definitely did.

Jay set the tray down on the table by the window. Overlooking the pool, damn it, as if to continue mocking her. "You want the rest of my hangover cure, don't you?" he coaxed. "I mean, after dancing on the tables, accepting my marriage proposal and then having wild sex with me all night, you've got to have a hangover."

"I didn't drink that much, and I've never danced on a table in my life." Xan said. "Cut the bullshit, Jay."

He sighed. "Well, I tried. Another time, maybe. But my hangover cure's gold, and it only works if you follow all the steps. That means breakfast."

Her head throbbed. "If I eat anything, I'll only bring it back up," Xan said. "I might manage a black coffee. But that's it."

"I'll make a bet with you. You try my rock star hangover cure, and if it works, I win."

"You win what?" Xan asked.

"If you lose your hangover by the time we check out, you'll dance with me at Angel's wedding."

"And if I throw up?"

Jay frowned. "Dunno. What do you want from me, Xan?"

"If I win, you stop swimming naked past my kitchen window," Xan said. If he removed temptation altogether, she'd never have to look at it.

He shrugged. "If that's what you want. You won't win,

anyway." He lifted a frosty glass jug and poured two tall glasses of something pink and icy, before handing one glass to her. "Deal. Drink up."

Gingerly, Xan accepted the glass. "What is it?"

"Iced watermelon juice. The secret cure to all hangovers," Jay said smugly. "Ask the chefs at the resort. It was my standing breakfast order, when I first arrived, and after Phuong…yeah. Then. They're talking about adding it as a permanent item to the room service menu next season. Calling it the rock star detox or something." He chugged down half his glass, looking expectantly at her over the rim.

Xan sighed. Oh well, if she was going to be sick anyway, at least she'd get something out of the deal. She took a cautious sip, then a second one. It wasn't half bad.

Jay wasn't even watching. He threw himself on his bed, remote control in hand, and clicked on the TV to the morning news.

With his attention elsewhere, Xan poured herself a second glass of juice, feeling her headache finally retreating.

"See? It works," Jay said softly.

So he hadn't been ignoring her after all. So much for the end of temptation. "I'm not dancing on a table," she said.

"The dance floor's fine by me," Jay replied, uncovering the rest of their breakfast tray. "Now, how do you feel about pancakes?"

Xan eyed the fluffy stack, topped with berries and what looked like maple syrup. To her surprise, her stomach rumbled with hunger. "Optimistic."

"Good. Because I wanted the eggs." Jay grabbed the other plate, piled high with protein, and proceeded to dig in.

TWELVE

Xan drove for ten minutes before Jay piped up from the passenger seat, "This isn't the way to the airport."

"No," she admitted, watching the speedometer to make sure she didn't go over the limit. "Shou got called to help out with mustering on one of the inland stations. It's that time of year. Pretty much any pilot or aircraft that can fly is out mustering or on fire patrol, because the volunteer fire brigade wants to burn off as much fuel as they can before a bushfire starts by accident. There's already been one firenado. Took out two helicopters, which is why he's been roped into mustering this year. He treats that helicopter the way most men behave around their cars — no one drives but him."

"Not me," Jay said cheerfully. "I'm happy to let you drive."

"I thought you'd lost your licence, so you can't drive,

even if you wanted to," Xan said.

"Oh, I can still drive, but I'm not allowed to until March. So until then, I can drink as much as I like and never have to worry about being the designated driver. So drive on, and I think I'll have a beer." Jay reached into the back seat.

"It's barely ten in the morning!" Xan hissed.

"Then it's afternoon in Sydney, what with daylight savings and all." Jay popped the cap off the edge of the dashboard. "Still cold, too."

"Where did you get that?" Xan asked, glancing at the back seat, which held a case of beer that she definitely hadn't loaded in there.

"A gift from the band last night," Jay said smugly. "One of their mates videoed us jamming together last night and stuck it up on social media. I shared it on my account, and the fangirls all went crazy for it. The guys sold more music overnight than they've sold in the last five years. So they bought a carton of beer to thank me. It's the one you like, the ginger. I figured it's because of you I was there last night, so it's only fair you get the beer. Except this one. And anything else I drink on the drive back, because it's so fucking boring."

The Cape Leveque Road wasn't boring, especially not if you were the one driving that treacherous ninety-kilometre stretch of red dirt, but the mention of her favourite beer had even Xan tempted to drink in the morning. But she couldn't – this was definitely a road you needed all your wits about you to tackle. Even her low alcohol beer was off limits until they reached the pearl farm. She promised herself a cold one from the restaurant tap, once they reached it.

But first…the task at hand. Xan turned onto the road marked by a thicket of signs, warning motorists of everything from the speed limits, the fire danger (which seemed permanently stuck on EXTREME of late) and the waste disposal site to dangerous wildlife like cows and crocodiles. She scanned the placards for the most important one: the big one proclaiming which roads were open, and to which vehicles. The resort's fleet of four-wheel-drives could withstand most conditions, but she'd seen this road closed to even her sturdy cars, sometimes for weeks at a time. If anything really brought it home to her how remote the resort was, it was this bloodstained road.

"It's open," she breathed, relieved. There had been talk of resurfacing this road before the wet season started, but until the council road crews set a definite date, nothing would be done. They usually gave everyone on the Dampier Peninsula plenty of warning, too, so they could get supplies in before the road closure. Admittedly, the last couple of times, she'd been notified only a day or two in advance, but she'd assured the blokes at the council that she didn't mind being the last to know. Not everyone could afford to fly or boat in whatever they wanted, like Romance Island Resort. A message about upcoming roadworks could be sitting in her inbox, unopened, right now.

After fifteen minutes of bumping along a road so rutted it made her teeth rattle, Xan swore that if there wasn't an email in her inbox, telling her they were grading the road tomorrow, she'd call every person in the council offices until there was. Driving on this was like crossing the world's widest cattle grid, designed to keep elephants out. If she knew the road would be this bad, she'd have waited another day in town until a pilot was available. Anything to get her to the pearl farm and the short jet boat ride to the resort.

"Oi! You're making my beer froth over!" Jay complained, wiping his hand across a damp patch on his pants.

Xan ignored him and kept driving. The view in her rear vision mirror was a cloud of red dust, and before her stretched what could easily be mistaken for the road to hell. No, the road through hell, seeing as most of the Dampier Peninsula, the pearl farm included, were as much a part of paradise as Romance Island itself, if a little less luxurious.

Idly, she wondered if she could drop Jay off at the devil's place along the way, seeing as the beer-drinking rock star at her side was about as far from angelic as a man could get.

He had cured her hangover this morning, though, she reasoned, and he had behaved like a gentleman, despite having to share a room last night. Hell, he'd even behaved himself at the party last night, which had probably proved quite a challenge for him with his bad-boy reputation.

Maybe Jay Felix wasn't all bad, then.

Of course, that's the moment an explosion came from Jay's side of the car, tilting them dangerously sideways.

"What did you do?" Xan shouted over the ringing in her ears. She was wrong. Jay was the devil's spawn.

"I finished my beer," Jay replied with dignity. "You blew a tyre. That's why all resort cars carry two spares on the back."

He was right, Xan realised as her heart sank. She slowed to a stop and turned off the engine.

This will be easy, she told herself. It's just changing a tyre, and like he said, there are two spares on the back. It couldn't be simpler.

"So who's changing the tyre? You or me?" Jay asked. "Want to flip a coin for it?"

Xan stared at him. Somehow, he'd managed to crack open another beer. "No," she decided. "I'm doing it. You stay here and…don't drink any more of the beer, okay?" She climbed out of the car before he had a chance to reply.

First, she rounded to car to check which tyre it was. She'd never had a flat tyre before, let alone changed one. Sure enough, it was the front one on the passenger side – the one under Jay. Okay, next, she needed a tyre that wasn't busted. That meant one of the ones on the back of the car.

She surveyed the two round, tyre-shaped boxes bolted to the back door of the four-wheel-drive. Each bore the heart-shaped logo, proclaiming it the property of Romance Island Resort. And each one was secured by a lock on one side. Xan pulled the keys out of her pocket and breathed a sigh of relief as the first little silver key she tried fitted snugly into the passenger side lock. Turning it was another matter, though – the key barely budged. She tried the other key, but it wouldn't go in at all. Okay, she had the right key, but maybe there was some grit or something in the lock. Leaning over, she blew hard into the lock, then took a deep breath and did it again. If this didn't work, she might have to wash it out with some of Jay's beer, she thought, stifling a laugh. Fortunately, no beer was necessary, as she managed to force the key around in the lock until something clicked.

Nothing else popped free, though – least of all the tyre compartment. Try as she might, Xan couldn't seem to tug or pry it open. She considered asking Jay to try his muscles on it, but she dismissed the idea almost as soon as she'd thought of it. She didn't need a man for anything. Especially not to do something as simple as opening a box. But she'd like to kick a man in the car for opening a box.

Figuring it couldn't hurt, Xan kicked the underside of the box. Tentatively at first, then with more viciousness the second time, and she felt it budge. She dug her fingers into the dusty seam she'd persuaded to appear and it widened, then widened again. By dragging on it with all her weight, Xan managed to pull the cover off the tyre, releasing a shower of crusted, dried mud that had glued the compartment shut, only to find it still stuck fast to the car by several hefty bolts. Honestly. You'd think people stole spare tyres off the back of cars, this was so securely fastened.

Swearing, Xan opened the boot of the car, hoping there'd be a collection of tools to help her, but the back of the car was empty except for some dusty water casks under a stained, threadbare towel. You'd have to be desperate to drink the contents, which might have been sitting in the Kimberley heat for months, if not years, but it was perfectly fine to use in the radiator if you were caught out in the middle of nowhere. And if you had to drink something…you could probably boil this sterile by just leaving it in the sun for a couple of hours. But dodgy water didn't do much to help her with a wheel.

She tried undoing the bolts with her hands, but they were stuck fast. Gritting her teeth, she looped the towel around one, twisting the flannel until it tightened around the bolt, before she tried again. She felt the tiniest bit of movement, so she twisted the towel tighter still and hung onto the end, adding as much of her weight as she could without falling over. She definitely felt something move that time. Little by little, she loosened that bolt until she could remove it with her fingers. One down, two to go.

After what seemed like an eternity of panting, pulling and swearing, she finally managed to free the wheel, which was so heavy she almost dropped it. Okay, she did drop it, but controlled the fall by keeping it between her and the car, so Jay didn't see.

Once it was on the ground she rolled it like the world's heaviest hula hoop around the side of the car to the wheel it had to replace. There she leaned it against the gravel rampart edging the road and found herself staring at the flat tyre with still no idea of how to switch one wheel for the other. Sure, she knew she had to lift the car up and loosen the bolts so the wheel would come off, then fasten the new one in its place, but all she had was a towel. No way did she want to drive down this road without four tyres firmly fastened to the car, stuck tighter than barnacles on a whale's bottom. This was impossible. Not even Jay could change this tyre. She'd be better off heading back to the main road or the nearest community to ask someone for help, or at least a jack to lift the car. May as well ask to borrow a spanner, too, while she was at it.

The electric window whined down, setting Xan's teeth on edge even before Jay's head appeared.

"How much longer will you be with that tyre?" Jay asked. "Just that the beer's too warm to drink now, so I don't have much else to do. I could help, you know, if it'll speed things up a bit. I swear I won't tell anyone at the resort. It'd totally ruin my rock star reputation if they knew I actually did a bit of work occasionally. Though I suppose there's worse things to be caught doing than knowing how to change a tyre."

Xan wanted to tell him where to stick his offer, but she was hot and tired and more than a little fed up. "Sure you can help," she snapped. "Find me a jack and a spanner, and this'll go a hell of a lot faster."

Jay stared. "How'd you get the wheel off the back without tools?"

Xan held her towel aloft.

"Fuck me. Little Miss Know-It-All is Little Miss MacGyver, too. If I find the tools for you, will you tell me how you did it? A towel. Fuck!"

Xan didn't have the energy to respond in kind. Instead, she just nodded.

Jay cracked open his door and headed straight for the back of the car.

"Nothing in there but water and my magic towel. I already checked," she said, not moving from her rampart perch.

Jay wasn't listening, as usual. He leaned into the boot and Xan heard him shifting the water casks over the crackly plastic boot liner. Fine. Let him find out for himself.

After a few minutes, Jay gave up, closing the back of the car. Xan waited for him to reach her before she started to say, "See? I told you – "

Something clinked on the gravel beside her. A roll of black canvas, strapped together like a lumpy swag. Jay unrolled it along the top of the rampart, revealing a selection of tools including a jack and…a whole selection of wrenches. She could have kissed him.

Instead, unable to stop herself, Xan burst into tears.

"How about I make a start on that tyre while you…um…do whatever you need to do,' Jay said awkwardly, dropping to his knees at her feet. No, beside the tyre, Xan corrected herself, sniffling.

"I don't know how to change a tyre. Or the thing about hangovers and watermelon. I don't know everything," she whispered.

Jay looked up at her, his expression rueful. "Angel taught me about the watermelon. It's all about alcohol and dehydration and electrolytes and shit. Tyres…well, the first time I changed one, Jo did most of the work. We were between towns on a family road trip Dad made us take. I think we were fourteen or fifteen. The tyre blew on this patch of two-lane highway. Not a house in sight for miles, and one of us complained about stopping and how boring the trip was. Not sure if it was her or me. Not that it mattered. He made us both get out and fix that fucking tyre. Jo broke half her nails and I ended up scraping my hands raw on something. Couldn't play guitar for a week when we got home. But we got that fucking tyre changed, and I'll never forget it. Want me to show you, so you'll know what to do next time?"

Xan wanted to nod, but she forced herself to ask, "What will I have to do to repay you? I've already agreed to dance with you at your friend's wedding."

Jay coughed out a laugh that sounded more human than his usual brash chuckle. "Fuck, if you stop crying, that's more than enough for me. I never know what to do with crying women. Jo's fault. The only time she cried was when she was hormonal, but if you tried to comfort her, you were just as likely to get a kick to the groin or a punch in the face. So I wanna help, but I also don't want to get kicked or punched, if you know what I mean. If you don't try to kill me, that'd be awesome."

Xan laughed through her tears. "You're so full of shit, Jay. Is any of that true?"

He shrugged. "Don't believe me, then. But ask Jo. She'll tell you. She gave me a black eye once. Angel laughed herself sick when she found out."

Xan wiped her face with her hands. "Where did you find the tools?"

"Under the boot liner. There's this bit where the carpet's cut so you can pull it up, and there's a cavity underneath. On a normal car, that's where the spare tyre is, too, but on a four-wheel-drive, there isn't enough space for the tyre and the tools, so just the tool kit goes in there. We didn't find them, either, until Dad told us where to look."

Xan met Jay's gaze, looking for some sign of the arsehole she was so used to. He looked like a normal bloke, maybe even a good man, who was telling the truth. "All right. Show me," she said finally.

Jay tipped his imaginary hat. "Yes, ma'am."

THIRTEEN

Jay made surprisingly short work of the tyre change, even as he explained to Xan what he was doing. She insisted on helping him stow the tools back in their hidey-hole, so she'd know where to look next time. Back home, she'd never owned a car new or expensive enough to have an onboard tool kit. She wasn't even sure if her ancient hatchback had had a spare tyre.

When they climbed back into the car, Xan wasn't sure what to say. Just thanking him didn't seem enough, but she also couldn't shake the feeling that he had an ulterior motive in helping her. In her experience, Jay was never nice. So why now?

They drove in silence for some time, until Xan caught a flicker of movement in the corner of her eye. It looked like…flames. No, it couldn't be. Then she saw more, licking at a clump of grass as tall as the car. "Is that a bushfire?"

she asked, her stomach starting to churn once more. She'd heard stories of the swathe of destruction Australian bushfires left in their wake, but she's never seen one. She never wanted to, either.

Jay barely glanced at it. "Not yet. Only the grass is burning, so it's just a grassfire. You said the volunteer firies were burning off today, so that's probably all it is. They know what they're doing. They won't let it get out of hand."

This didn't soothe Xan's tummy at all. If anything, it awoke a flock of butterflies that made her feel even worse. Still, onward she drove, knowing that the sooner they left this road, the safer they'd be from fires of all kinds.

A dark shape darted across the road with a flash of orange, barely clearing the roof of the car.

"What the fuck?" Jay shouted, staring after it.

"What?" Xan asked, forcing herself to keep her eyes on the road. "What was it?"

"A bird. A big, black bird carrying a branch that was on fire." Jay rumpled his hair with one hand. "Fucking creepy is what it was."

Too many beers, too early in the morning, Xan thought, concentrating on the road instead of Jay's drunken hallucinations. Birds didn't carry flaming branches.

"Another one!"

Xan saw the flicker of orange move as the bird flew low across the road.

"That one dropped the branch," Jay remarked.

Smart bird, Xan thought, fighting the steering wheel as the rutted gravel tried to force her onto the wrong side of the road.

Jay stayed mercifully silent for a while, as Xan negotiated

a series of blind bends. There was smoke in the air, blending with the dust, reducing visibility even more than usual. Not for the first time this morning, she wished she was flying over this instead of driving through it.

"I wonder if that's a third bird, or it's just one flying arsonist," Jay remarked.

This time, Xan slowed down to watch the bird. This one dropped its branch onto a clump of grass, which smoked for a moment before it flared up into glowing flame.

The dry grass here grew as high as the car, in what looked like a hedge all along the road. It went up like paper. One moment, everything was flaxen yellow; the next, a wall of roaring, searing orange.

Fire. Fire was all Xan could see, on both sides of the road. Red and orange above and below, so she couldn't see anything else. Could feel the flames crisping her skin…

She slammed the car to a stop. She couldn't drive in this. Couldn't go anywhere when she couldn't see, and the heat…

"What are you doing?" Jay asked. "Xan?"

"Fire. Can't drive through the fire," she said. And she couldn't. Just…couldn't.

"You have to. You have to keep driving," Jay insisted.

"Can't," she repeated. Orange. The whole world was orange. And she was a duck, about to become crispy…

"Xan. Either you drive or I do. I'm not dying in a fucking fire in the middle of nowhere."

"Can't. I can't and you can't."

"Fuck that. Move over."

Jay grabbed her round the middle and hefted her into his lap. Before she could protest, he squirmed out from under her, climbing over the park brake into the driver seat.

"Seat belt on, Xan." She felt him reach across her, then something clicked before a band tightened across her chest. Seatbelt. Yes.

Jay gunned the engine, sending the car skidding a little in the gravel. "You don't wait out a bushfire. You outrun it or you die. Angel survived a bushfire with that psycho. I'll never hear the end of it if I can't do what he did."

What? None of that made sense. Jay never made sense.

The car bumped over the ruts, faster than Xan would have driven. Good thing she had a seatbelt on, she thought muzzily.

"Like a fucking tunnel of fire!" Jay whooped, sending the car down the middle of the road like he owned it. For the moment, he did.

Xan clung to her seat, wanting to close her eyes, but not able to tear her gaze away from, yes, the tunnel of fire that thrilled Jay but terrified her. Jay was right. She could actually die on this road. And of all the people to die with…Hades would probably take her along with Jay, damning her by association. She'd let an unlicensed driver drive her car. A work car. Through an inferno. If she made it out of this, she'd buy a lottery ticket. Who was she kidding? She was going to die. Dead girls didn't buy lottery tickets.

But the road wore on, with Jay swerving, revving the engine and cheering every k of the way. And then…orange gave way to green. Scrubby green, but green, nonetheless. Somehow, Jay had carried her through the fire. A miracle, for sure.

The car bumped from gravel to tarmac and Xan almost cheered as loud as Jay, or she would have, if any sound had come out of her mouth.

The smooth northern end of the Cape Leveque Road rolled beneath them, and Jay accelerated to match the speed limit. He wasn't that bad a driver, she had to admit. Naomi must have caught him on a really bad day.

Xan didn't relax until she saw the sign warning them about the turnoff to the pearl farm. It wasn't home, but it was near enough. Just a short boat ride back to the island. Where there wouldn't be any fires, Xan swore.

Just before the turnoff, they met a barricade blocking off the road, manned by…

"I thought you'd learned not to do stupid things on the roads, but this makes drink-driving through a school zone look harmless. Did you even see the road closure signs?" Constable Naomi Nelson demanded.

"Nope!" Jay said cheerfully. "Unless you mean the ones about cows and crocodiles. We didn't see any this time."

"We?" She peered into the car. "Xan? You let this idiot drive?"

"She's feeling a bit under the weather. I told her she shouldn't have tried that delayed shipment of sashimi, but she wouldn't hear of it. Had to make sure the quality was good enough for the guests," Jay jumped in before Xan could speak. "We had to stop a few times along the way 'cause she was feeling sick. She really wasn't up to driving, and the fire got pretty hot out there. Close to the road, too."

"That's why the road's closed," Naomi snapped. "If you've moved the barricades, you'll lose more than your licence. Putting people at risk by opening a closed road…"

"I said I never saw a barrier. There wasn't one. We…had

to stop. A lot. We've been on the road a while."

"Xan?"

Xan managed a weak smile. "The road was open when I drove onto it. No barricades. We just…got delayed."

Naomi frowned. "You do look pretty green. Are you feeling okay?"

No. She'd nearly died in a fire and been saved by a madman who was now lying to cover for her. Whatever pills Jay had given her had worn off some time during the drive, so her headache was coming back with a vengeance, probably fuelled by all the smoke she'd inhaled during that hellish drive.

The police officer's frown deepened. "I should arrest him and extend the time until he can get his licence back, but it's barely a hundred metres to the driveway, and that's private property, so he doesn't need a licence…" She turned to Jay. "Have you been drinking?"

"No," he lied.

"Do you think you can drive this vehicle to the farm office, without crashing into anything?"

"Sure," Jay drawled.

"If I catch you driving again before you get your licence back, I'll have you in court, I swear." And with that, she waved them on to the pearl farm turnoff.

Xan huddled in her seat. On the one hand, she wanted to stick her head out the window and shout to Naomi that Jay was lying, but then who would be the liar? Sure, she hadn't been sick, but she had been incapacitated. If he hadn't forced her out of the driver's seat…she might be dead.

Jay pulled the car to a halt in the pearl farm's staff car

park.

Not a moment too soon. Xan threw open her door and lurched out of the car, staggering toward the oasis of green lawn shaded by palm trees. She made it to the bottom of the steps before she was forced to double over, vomiting up her breakfast until nothing but bile came up.

FOURTEEN

Erica found Xan on the grass, her head stuck between her still shaking knees. "Jay sent me out here to see if there was anything I could do for you," Erica said, after staring at Xan for some time.

"Water would be nice," Xan croaked. Water to extinguish the blaze still crackling in her mind every time she closed her eyes.

"Yeah, I already thought of that. Here."

Xan raised her head to accept the glass Erica offered. Her mouth was so dry she wasn't sure any of her first gulp made it down her throat, but by the bottom of the glass, enough had trickled down for her to dare clear her throat. "Thank you."

"Pleasure. I'll get you some more, if you like. I just refilled all the coolers in the garden, so it's nice and cold." Erica offered her hand to help Xan up. "You know, you'd be better off inside in the air conditioning. It's coolest in the showroom. You could even stretch out on the couch – no tourists yet today until the tour group this afternoon. And you could see Kenji's latest creation – inspired by you, he says."

Xan accepted her assistance and staggered to her feet. "Who's Kenji?"

"Shou's brother. He kept going on and on about that time you took him snorkelling in the resort's lagoon, until Kenji decided to design some jewellery to match what Shou saw in the water. He wanted to name it after you, but Issie talked them out of it. So now it's the Island Romance Collection, or it will be, if Kenji's designs sell. There's only the one so far, but she's a beauty. We put her in the cabinet in the foyer, right beside our highest quality pearl strings." Erica grabbed Xan's arm. "Do you need me to help you inside? You don't look so good."

"I'll do it," said a new voice. Jay.

"Why aren't you sick?" Xan snapped at Jay before her brain caught up with her. Too late.

"Because I didn't eat that dodgy sashimi. Told you not to," Jay lied easily. "Now, you want me to carry you inside like a bride, or be a gentleman and just let you lean on my arm as much as you need to?"

"I'll go get some more water," Erica said, excusing herself.

"I can walk," Xan said. "If you really want to be helpful, just…walk next to me, and catch me if I look like I'm going to fall over." She wouldn't fall, she swore, but it wouldn't be a bad idea to have a quiet word with Jay about what he'd done while no one else was in earshot. Not out here, though – inside the pearl showroom, once she was comfortably ensconced on the couch.

Jay held the mother-of-pearl-handled door open for her, releasing a blast of cold air into the humid garden. Bliss. Xan shuffled inside, closing her eyes to relish the instant coolness as the door closed behind them.

"So that's what Shou thinks you look like, is it? Bit abstract, if you ask me," Jay said.

Xan opened her eyes. Riveting her gaze just the way it was supposed to, sat a pearl ring. Bathed in spotlights from several angles, the small circle of gold managed to outshine even the perfect necklaces on either side of it. Except…it wasn't a circle, not really. Crafted of heavy gold, the ring curled into a wide band made up of coral branches, all twisted together to cradle an enormous silvery-white pearl so lustrous Xan fancied she could see her own reflection in it. "Beautiful," she breathed, walking forward to take a closer look.

Like the pearl strands, this piece was priceless, meaning only people like Jay or the resort's other celebrity guests could possibly afford it. No surprises there. The detail the jeweller had crafted into every unique strand of coral must have taken hours to get just right. A work of art like this didn't deserve a name as ordinary as hers. No, Island Romance was a much better name. Some rich couple who came to the island, fell in love and spotted the design in the neighbouring pearl farm would snap it up, along with the rest of the matching collection, whatever that was.

"So you like pearls?" Jay asked, interrupting her train of thought.

Xan shook her head slowly. "Not really. But I love that."

"If you're good, I might buy it for you for Christmas," Jay said.

"No. That ring belongs on the hand of someone who falls in love out here, and wants to remember the island forever. It's not something you give your employee for Christmas," Xan insisted.

"So what book are you reading now?"

Xan would never understand how Jay's mind worked. "What book am I what?"

Jay leaned over one of the cases in the next room. "It sounds like you gave that ring's story quite a bit of thought, so I figured maybe it was something out of the latest romance book you're reading. What are you reading?"

Xan refused to blush. She could read whatever she damn well pleased. "If you must know, it's a series about shipwreck hunters. Treasure divers."

"So you're reading thrillers now?"

As if she needed reading material to keep her awake at night. Her tossing and turning over what to do about Jerome would now be replaced with dreams of roaring flames. "No. It's romance. Just...with scuba diving. And good food."

Jay stretched out on the couch. "I like good food. Not sure about diving, though."

"It takes practice, and you have to be more careful about things like narcosis and the level of air in your tanks, but diving can be much better than snorkelling," Xan began. "Snorkelling in the lagoon, you only see the surface, but there's a little cave at the southern end that you don't even see unless you dive right down to the bottom. Some of the biggest lagoon fish hide in there, so you never know what you'll find. Once there was one of those big, blue Queenslander things. Can't remember what they're called. You know, big and blue…?"

Jay shrugged. "I wouldn't know. I've never seen one."

Xan laughed. "You swim in the lagoon every day and you've never seen a fish that's as big as a sea turtle? There must be at least three in there!"

"It's not like I wear the sort of gear you do when I swim in the lagoon. You've seen how I swim."

Naked. Not just no clothes, but no mask or goggles. She'd never thought about it before. "You've never seen under the surface of the lagoon, have you?"

Jay shook his head.

"Why don't you join one of the snorkelling tours? Rita's been running them almost daily at the resort since the start of the dry season." Then Xan remembered. "If she hadn't finished up for the season, I'd tell you to tag along today. She's working the summer season at Rottnest now, so she won't be back until May."

Swimming. Diving. Submerging in the lagoon and not leaving it until it felt like there was seawater in her very blood. That would banish the flames from her head. Nothing refreshed her like the ocean could.

"I didn't know we had them," Jay replied. "You never tell me anything about the resort, except to stay away from the guests, especially when I'm swimming."

Ah. That's why she'd neglected to tell him. Guests goggling at Jay's bare body under the water wasn't a tourist attraction she wanted to promote.

"I could take you one day, maybe, when I have time," she offered reluctantly. "You'd have to wear some sort of swimsuit, though. I don't do snorkelling tours for nudists."

"I might be able to manage. For you, of course." Jay smirked. "I think that girl forgot about your drink. I seem to remember promising you one, though, so how 'bout we head to the bar to grab a cold one before Baz brings the boat around to take us home?"

Home. Romance Island was home, and soon she'd be back there. Xan sighed in relief. Maybe it was the air conditioning or the distraction of pretty jewellery, but she felt better already.

FIFTEEN

Jason kept a careful watch on Xan as she climbed into the
Argo. She seemed perfectly calm and collected again –
nothing like the shaking, sicking-up mess she'd been on the
pearl farm lawn, and there was no trace of the frozen panic
she'd shown in the car when that bloody bird had set fire to
the bush on both sides. He hadn't thought she was afraid of
anything, but he had to admit, he'd never seen her around
fire. She was more of a water woman, after all. And if there
was ever a fire to be afraid of, it'd be the one he'd just
driven through.

Take that, Angel's creepy-arse stalker, he thought grimly.
He wasn't the only one who could save a woman from
dying in a fire.

Xan let out what sounded like a strangled scream and
Jason's gaze darted back to the pointy bit at the front of the
boat, where Xan had claimed a seat.

Behind Jason, Baz laughed. "Been a while since she's been out on a boat. If I was twenty years younger…"

"There's another big one over there, Baz. See if you can skirt it without falling in!" Xan called over her shoulder, her face alight with happiness as she pointed at a big-arse hole in the water.

Water didn't have holes. What the fuck…?

"Another whirlpool for the lady. Yes, ma'am!" Baz shouted, swerving the jet boat into a tight curve.

Jason hung on as the trip turned into an unexpected rollercoaster ride. He forgot about the fire. He forgot to worry about Xan, who was obviously enjoying every minute of the ride. He whooped like a little kid at his first Royal Show.

Why hadn't anyone told him the boat trip was better than the helicopter flight to the island?

Xan. Keeping all the fun for herself, probably. By the time they reached the relative calm beside the Romance Island Resort jetty, she looked exhilarated. Like she'd just been fucked to within a hair's breadth of nirvana. He'd never seen a woman look so happy with her clothes on.

Fortunately, his phone beeped with an incoming message before Xan caught him staring at her.

Not a message – an email, he found, swiping at the screen. "Fuck yes!" he cried.

"Language," Xan said.

Jason thrust the phone at her. "Look! They accepted my offer. Now we just have to do the…do…the due diligence."

"What did you make an offer on?" Xan asked.

"A bunch of hotels going bankrupt in Vietnam and Singapore. The record companies are offering a shitload of money for me to sign with them, so I figured I might buy something useful with it. Seeing as this place turned out okay and all." Because of you, he thought but didn't say. "Can you…can you take a look at it? Do the diligence thingy?"

Xan shook her head. "I'm a hotel manager, not an accountant. Your sister, Jo, would be the one to ask."

"Don't tell Jo," Jason said instantly. "She can't know about this until it's a done deal. I've been watching it for a while, waiting until it went up for sale. I just need someone to check the books. I know who I want, but…"

"But?" Xan prompted.

Jason didn't want to say her name. Every time he mentioned something even vaguely related to her, Xan's face would clam up like she was dying to tell him off for the whole mail order bride fiasco, but she didn't say a word. He swallowed. "I want…Phuong."

Xan's eyes widened in shock, before she lowered her gaze and nodded. "She's good. She's also in prison."

Jason's heart sank. "You mean they found her guilty? Even with my lawyers?"

"I don't know. All I do know is that she's still in prison," Xan replied.

Poor Phuong. She'd been through so much, only to end up languishing in prison. She wasn't tough enough for that. "I still want her to look at the figures."

"So ask her." Xan strode away.

Jason took a deep breath. "I can't. Jo made some sort of deal with her not to have any contact with me if she wanted her legal bills paid. If she's still in prison, I can't talk to her."

There was also the matter of her having tried to kill her

previous husband, but Jason still found it hard to believe she'd been capable of murder. It had to be self defence, or something. He wanted to see her, but he couldn't. Had to know if she'd really planned on killing him, too, or whether he'd been right about her. And he'd never know.

"So you want me to take a company's confidential accounting documents into a prison so your ex-wife can check them?"

"It sounds so bad when you put it that way," Jason complained. "But…yeah. I guess."

Xan bit her lip. "Send me what you have. I'll see what I can do."

Jason cheered.

Xan held up her hands. "Calm down, rock star. I only said I'd try. She might not be allowed visitors, or mail. She might not want to do it, either."

Jason knew all that, but still, he prayed she'd agree. And maybe…maybe he would get to ask her if she wanted him dead. Or alive. He grinned.

"Thanks, Xan." He sauntered up the jetty to his villa, whistling happily. What a fucking day. He hadn't felt this alive in months. He should do shit with Xan more often.

SIXTEEN

Next time, instead of inviting the idiot to things like the hotel opening, Xan should avoid the rock star like the plague, she fumed, as she tapped her fingers impatiently on the scored table. Three other tables were occupied by groups of women and children, but the women all looked alike. It wasn't a matter of colour or race – they all hung their heads in the same way, as if anticipating a blow. They looked like the women she'd seen at the shelter in Broome, all abused by men until it took all of their strength just to get up in the morning and live another day.

Except Xan, of course, who'd only agreed to do a man a favour. But she had to admit a certain curiosity about the mail order bride turned black widow.

The security door buzzed and a prisoner walked out, flanked by a guard. The girl wore the same prison greens as every other prisoner in the room, but that's where the similarity ended. Phuong's dark, glossy hair was pulled back from her face, tied in a simple ponytail that trailed down over her immaculately pressed green shirt. Her pants were ironed with equal precision, from the well-fitted waist to the toes of her equally green shoes.

Ignoring the guard, Phuong inclined her head slightly to Xan, then crossed the room to Xan's table.

A chorus of scraping chairs sounded as every prisoner made a point of turning her back on Phuong. Some of the other visitors stared curiously, but were quickly persuaded to look away.

"You're popular," Xan remarked as Phuong sat across from her.

Phuong smiled faintly. "You'd be surprised. I have very little to do in here now I've finished my business degree, so I've been running a few classes in budgeting and basic accounting for the other prisoners. I don't get visitors often, so when I asked for a little privacy for today's meeting, they were happy to help."

Already settling in to her position as queen of the prison, Xan thought. Phuong was craftier than Xan had given her credit for. Jay had had a lucky escape – she'd have killed him in a heartbeat, if she decided he was worth more to her dead than alive. Good thing murderers didn't get short sentences.

"How much longer is your sentence?" Xan asked.

A look of surprise crossed Phuong's face. "Don't you know? I haven't even been to court, aside from the preliminary hearing, which was postponed pretty much indefinitely. You see, they can't find my ex-husband, and without a witness, they can't hold a hearing."

Xan was horrified. "You mean you've been stuck in prison for almost a year for no reason?"

"Well, there was the fact that Norman nearly died because of me, and it's just gone nine months, so it hasn't been a year yet. My lawyers tried to get me bail, but as I'm apparently a flight risk, the judge wouldn't allow it, so here I am." Phuong spread her hands. "Easy for you to find me if you need some number checking done." She nodded at the file on the table in front of Xan.

Reminded of the reason for her visit, Xan pushed the file across to Phuong, then added a memory stick from her pocket. "It's the due diligence for a possible acquisition."

Phuong nodded. "Yours or his?"

Xan laughed. "His. Do you think I could afford to buy a hotel, let alone a whole chain of them, on my salary?"

"Not unless you're finding an illegal way to supplement your salary, no," Phuong said, leafing through the papers. "This will take some time."

"Well, you look like you have it," Xan joked, then closed her mouth when she realised Phuong looked hurt.

"My lawyers had hoped to find Norman by now, so I'd be out by Christmas," Phuong said. "From what I hear, even if they find him today, there won't be any available hearing dates until next year, so I should have time. If not, is there some way I can contact you?"

Xan pulled out her business card. "You can call or email me at the resort."

Phuong held her hands up, refusing to take the card. "Give it to the guard over there before you leave, so she can add it to my list of approved contacts. They monitor everything here."

But they didn't listen to the conversations, Xan thought, noticing for the first time that the families clustered around her provided a noise buffer between Phuong and the guards.

Phuong rose, as if to leave.

But she hadn't agreed to do it! She hadn't said yes or no, and Xan couldn't leave until she had her answer.

"Thank you," Xan said hurriedly, hoping she'd guessed right. "He asked for you especially. He'll be so happy to hear you'll help him."

Phuong smiled sadly. "Whatever I give you won't be official, as I won't have my degree until next year, even if I have finished the coursework. And if I'm convicted, I'll never be allowed to practice in an official capacity, so you'll have to go to some other accountant for an official report, no matter what I find."

Xan's heart ached for the girl. Why would she work so hard for her accounting degree if she truly was a cold-blooded killer, about to be locked away for life? Had the police made a mistake in arresting her?

"I understand," Xan said, hesitating. Then she blurted out, "Did you really try to kill him?"

Phuong leaned forward, dropping her voice to a whisper as she said, "My ex-husband was an obsessive, power-hungry, abusive prick who deserved to die horribly for keeping me as his private slave. He saw me as a thing, not a person, and I believe he would have killed me. It was only a matter of time. I'm sure if you were trapped in his house like I was, you'd be willing to fight against him or maybe even try to kill him, purely out of self-defence."

Xan's mouth went dry. He sounded like a right bastard.

"And Jay? What about Jay?"

Phuong's face went blank. "I don't know anyone by that name." She tucked the files under her arm. "I'll be in touch." She signalled to the guard that she wanted to leave the room, and the door buzzed open.

Before Xan could say another word, Phuong was safely on the other side of the firmly closed security door.

Flustered, Xan left the visiting room to collect her things. The less time she spent in that prison, the better. Just as she closed the door of the locker, she remembered to give her business card to the guard, with a request that Phuong be allowed to contact her.

She hoped the girl would find something to dissuade Jay from buying any more hotels. It was enough trouble just running the resort. If he owned a whole empire…he'd drive her completely insane.

SEVENTEEN

"Don't you know who I am? Closed to the public doesn't mean closed to me!" a familiar, plummy female voice blared as Jason reached the door of the building the charter pilots used for a passenger waiting room.

He peered through the glass, swearing as he recognised Gaia. "Let me just go through the gate to the carpark," he said to Shou. "If she's trying to get to the resort, I don't want her to see me."

Shou smirked as if he knew all about the things Jason and Gaia had gotten up to. Jason doubted he had any idea that the bossy billionaire adored being abased in private. Jason had tried, but the kinky billionaire thing just wasn't for him. Especially as it made him feel like an obnoxious arse, ordering her around and being called 'sir'. Now, if it'd been the other way 'round, with a different woman, maybe he'd have been happy to offer up a, "yes, ma'am" as he did his rock star best to give her a good time. Gaia, though…no. Just no.

He hailed a taxi, but he didn't manage to close the door before he heard, "Mr Felix! Wait for me!"

He ordered the driver to head off as fast as possible, making sure they weren't followed, until taking him to the brewery for a drink. He needed one to banish the thoughts of Gaia from his brain before he did the last minute Christmas shopping he was in town for.

Once he was safely inside the brewery, he ordered a pint of beer and the first item off their lunch menu. Drink in hand, he scanned the room for an out of the way place to sit. Even if Gaia did follow him here, he didn't want her to be able to find him. He found what he wanted in the beer garden outside, tucked behind a tree. Jason strode to the table, only to find it already occupied.

"I'll give you a hundred bucks if you pick another table," he said, throwing the money down.

"I won't accept your money, Jay," a familiar voice replied.

Thank fuck, it wasn't Gaia.

She'd cut off her blonde curls, leaving a sort of pixie cap of hair, but Jason still recognised her. "Flavia?"

She flashed a brief smile that died all too quickly. "Don't say it too loud. Your bitch of a fiancée is out there and if she hears, she'll probably try and set reporters on me again. Are you trying to hide from her, too?"

"She's not my anything, and…maybe. Can I sit here?" he asked urgently as he spotted Gaia on the street outside.

"I should say no and leave you to her, but that wouldn't be fair. Sit down. We can hide here together." Flavia pushed a chair toward him with her foot.

Jason hesitated. "Last time we talked, you weren't this nice."

"Last time we talked, I was in the middle of a media shitstorm that I thought you'd called down on me. It wasn't until later, when I had time to consider everything, that I realised you weren't in any of the stories. They knew about me and the auction, but none of the media companies knew about you. So it couldn't have been you who tipped them off." Flavia's eyes narrowed. "My friend Violet worked it out. The billionaire bitch did it. I can't believe you agreed to marry that woman."

"Didn't you see the TV show?" Jason demanded. "Everyone knows I'm not marrying Gaia!"

"What TV show? The only job I could get where people didn't know about the auction was as a tour guide, doing remote outback tours. Kakadu, Uluru, the Gibb River Road, Karajini…everybody's too busy looking at the landscape to notice the tour guide. Especially when we're all dusty and dirty from camping." Flavia took a long pull from her drink, which looked like one of the brewery's ciders.

"Oh, I signed up for a reality TV dating show. They usually find brides for farmers, but they agreed to help me find one," Jason said.

Flavia choked. "You actually believed they could? And I thought dating that billionaire was stupid!"

Jason frowned. "It was worth a shot. I'd tried everything else. And even if they didn't, I figured it'd squash the rumours about me and Gaia. There was never anything between us. You and me, well, that was…we really had something, didn't we?" He couldn't keep the desperation out of his tone. He hoped she didn't hear it.

"We did," Flavia said slowly. "While it was just us, we did. Until every reporter in Australia got wind of the auction and made my life hell. What would they do if they knew about us?"

"I can protect you," Jason insisted. "You could stay at the resort or at any of my houses. You could hide from the media as long as you have to."

Flavia shook her head. "Forever? I don't think so. They hacked my email account. They would find out one day, and it would start all over again. I'd get called a whore again, and all your fangirls would join in, hating me for having you. Just like that TV anchor when you were younger. You dated her for a bit, and she got death threats all over her social media. You'd have to protect me from the whole world, locking me away without any access to the internet. I can't do that, Jay."

Though he didn't want to, Jason understood. He'd heard Angel and even Jo complain about the band's constant media attention, so he'd taken it on himself to steal the spotlight as much as possible. It had worked for the girls in the band, but it wouldn't work for any other woman in his life. Not once the media circus found out who she was.

"Fuck," he said finally.

"I'll drink to that," Flavia agreed, raising her drink to clink it against his.

Jason drank deeply, not stopping until he'd drained his glass. It would never end. He could never have just one woman, or the media would eat her alive. Not as long as he wanted to be a rock star.

Maybe that's why Angel had broken up the band. Not

because she was sick of music, but because she wanted to settle down to a normal life. Or as normal as life could be for someone like her, with the man she intended to marry.

"Another one?" he asked. "I'm buying."

Flavia nodded, and Jason waved over a waitress to order two more drinks. Lunch arrived not long after, and it occurred to him that Flavia was a tour guide who'd seen places in the Kimberley where he hadn't been.

"So, the Gibb River Road and Uluru," Jason began. "Worth seeing, or just something we sell to tourists?"

Flavia smiled mischievously. "You really should see them for yourself. Uluru's awesome, but Mount Augustus is bigger. Everyone wants to see Uluru, though, so that's where the tours go. You should see it in the wet season. The waterfalls…"

Jason sat and listened, caught up in the wonders of places he planned to visit. Next year, he promised himself. After the wedding and everything was over. Before he signed the recording contracts and had to get back to work in the studio. But not with Flavia.

EIGHTEEN

Xan loaded the last bag into the resort's four-wheel-drive just before the skies opened up. She'd bought too much, she knew, but it was better to be safe than sorry. Besides, it was nice to have the time to experiment in the kitchen again. She hadn't done that since her last Christmas at home, almost three years ago.

If she stayed here much longer, Australia's hot, summery Christmas would seem normal, Xan thought as she bumped along the track to the boat ramp through the driving rain.

The boat was there, but Baz wasn't, so she left the car by the water's edge and sprinted up to the pearl showroom for some shelter.

A harried-looking Erica was on duty at the reception desk today, nodding wearily as she listened to someone on the other end of the phone line. "No, ma'am, I'm afraid I can't do that," Erica said for what sounded like the umpteenth time.

Xan offered Erica a grin of greeting, which the other woman returned, and settled in to wait.

After a moment, Erica beckoned to Xan, then put a finger to her lips. Next, Erica pressed a button on the phone.

"You're not listening. I said to get the resort manager on the phone, now. She knows who I am, even if you don't! Wait until your boss hears about this!" blared a familiar voice through the phone's speaker.

Xan pulled a face as she recognised the unmistakable tone of Gaia Vasse at her most obnoxious.

Erica smothered a sigh. "No, you're not listening, ma'am. I know who you are, but that doesn't change the fact that the resort is closed for Christmas. There's no one left on the island. No one to call, so no visitors are allowed out to the island."

"But I'm not a visitor. I'm a friend of the owner," Gaia insisted. "Put me through to Jay Felix. I know he's around. I saw him in town earlier this week!"

Xan signalled to get Erica's attention, then patted her own chest. "Say you'll put her through to me," she mouthed silently.

Erica nodded. "Ma'am, I'll try one more time to put you through to the hotel manager. Please hold. Transferring you now." She pressed a couple of buttons before sagging in her seat in relief. "Thank you. She's been calling all week, and every time we give her the same answer, but she just won't stop!"

Xan slipped behind the counter and picked up the receiver. "How do I take her off hold?"

Erica pointed.

Xan took a deep breath and unleashed the mining magnate. "This is Xan Lane, manager of Romance Island Resort. How can I help you?"

"You can tell me where Jay Felix is!" Gaia barked.

"I'm afraid our guests' privacy is very important here at Romance Island Resort," Xan said smoothly, crossing her fingers as she hoped Gaia didn't know she wasn't on the island at all.

"He's not a guest! He's the owner. And he invited me up here for a private Christmas celebration, he said."

Gaia was a good liar, Xan decided, but not quite good enough. "Then he must have forgotten. Mr Felix is not currently on the island. I suggest you take the matter up with him."

Gaia audibly ground her teeth. "He's not answering his phone! Damn it, don't you know who I am? I'm Gaia Vasse. I have a right to know where he is!"

More lies, but Xan heard the edge of desperation in the other woman's tone. Gaia had been bitten by the fangirl bug. Badly. What had Jay done to the billionaire to make her into his biggest fan? Jay didn't care a fig for her, but she evidently still held a torch for him. Xan felt sorry for her. "I think if you did, he'd have told you, Miss Vasse, but he's spending Christmas and New Year with his family. And with no one on the island, the resort is closed to guests. Even guests of the owner, seeing as he's not here."

Gaia made Xan repeat her explanation several times until it was Xan's turn to grind her teeth, but she eventually got the message and ended the call.

"Good riddance," Erica said. "I just came in to close up,

and made the mistake of picking up the phone. I thought I'd be stuck here all day!"

"So who are you spending Christmas with?" Xan asked.

Erica shrugged. "Baz and his family have invited me to theirs, seeing as my family's all on the east coast. I figure it's better than spending it on my own. What about you?"

"Actually, I decided to be the island's caretaker while the resort's closed, to give all our staff a proper break. I'm looking forward to having my own private island for a whole two weeks."

"Oh wow." Erica's expression turned dreamy. "So you're not celebrating Christmas at all?"

Xan smiled. "I am. I'm going to try my hand at a roast pork I saw on one of those cooking shows. I got the smallest one they had, but I still think I'll be eating leftovers into next week. All my supplies are down by the boat ramp, waiting for Baz to take me back to the island. Then my holiday starts."

"No presents, though," Erica said. "Or a tree."

"My family sent some presents from the UK, and I have my eye on the little fibre optic tree that's sitting on the reception desk in the foyer. No one will miss it for a few days." Xan winked. "Then it's just me and the fish until next year."

Erica pulled down the shutters, sealing off the reception desk. She reached for the door to the pearl showroom and rattled it to make sure it was locked.

Speaking of fish and pearls…

"Is there any chance I could see that ring before you close up?" Xan asked wistfully. "If I could put one thing on my Christmas list, it would be that."

Erica shook her head. "Sorry, Xan, it sold right after I showed it to you. The next day, I think. Kenji's already started work on the rest of the collection. Maybe I could let you know when another piece is ready for sale?"

Gone. Xan would never know the couple's story, or whether they'd fallen in love at Romance Island. She'd never afford anything bigger than the ring, either. Too good for her.

"Sure, why not?" Xan said, forcing a smile. At least she could admire it and dream.

NINETEEN

By Boxing Day, Xan was sick of roast pork. Oh, sure, it was delicious, but for every meal, two days in a row? She wanted something else for dinner.

A faint thumping sounded outside. It took her a moment to realise that it was the sound of a helicopter. One that was approaching the island, when it was closed.

Gaia, Xan fumed. No matter who the woman had bullied into flying her here, she wasn't staying. She could climb right back into that helicopter and fly back to town.

Xan marched up to the helipad, intent on giving the billionaire a piece of her mind, but by the time she reached it, Shou was already lifting off. Xan shouted and waved, but Shou didn't hear her over the sound of his aircraft.

Swearing, Xan quickened her pace. Gaia wasn't leaving the helipad without a talking-to.

She slammed into a body bigger than her. Harder, too.

Not Gaia.

"Watch where you're going!" Xan shouted at Jay, glaring.

He beamed. "Merry Christmas to you, too. Fuck, it's good to be home." He enveloped her in a hug.

Xan shoved him off her. "What are you doing here?"

"Escaping from my family," he admitted.

"I thought you liked your family." Xan would give anything to have her parents here with her instead of on the other side of the world.

Jay ran his fingers through his hair. "Yeah, I do. Most of the time. But when they spend three days taking it in turns to tell you off for doing that reality dating show, or breaking up with the girl I'd chosen…fuck. Why'd the network have to air the interview with Penelope just before Christmas? Mum was full of hints on how to get her back. Dad just kept warning me about marrying a girl I barely knew. And Jo…she just ripped into me about it. Said I was playing with all the girls' feelings, degrading them…fuck, she made it sound like I was the lowest form of life on earth. When I tried to tell her the girls had signed up for the show and they knew what it involved, she said I was exploiting vulnerable…vulnerable…victims, I think she called them. Like I was some kind of creepy predator dude! Fuck me…having you shout at me's better than that." Jay slung his backpack over his shoulder and headed for his villa.

Swearing under her breath, Xan made her way back to her unit. Before she'd taken four steps, the rain started again, punctuated by thunder and lightning in a proper tropical storm. Xan broke into a run.

She wasn't surprised at Jay's family's reaction. She'd watched *The Rock Star Wants A Wife* herself, marvelling at the budding romance plot Paige had constructed between Jay and Penelope.

By the time she reached her veranda, she was soaked to the skin, which didn't matter so much in the heat, but she hadn't been struck by lightning or hit by falling branches or coconuts, which was more important. The hazards of living on a tropical island in the wet season.

The thunderstorm continued for the rest of the afternoon, keeping her holed up in her house instead of swimming in the lagoon like she'd planned. Not that she really minded. She had a whole stack of books from the resort library, and no one to interrupt her reading.

At least, until someone hammered on her front door.

She found Jay dripping on her door mat. "What is it?" she asked, folding her arms.

"Do you have anything to eat?" he asked, sounding sheepish. "I don't have anything in the house, and there's no one in Catering. Where is everybody?"

"Off enjoying a Christmas break with their family and friends," Xan told him. "We agreed that the extra time off would be better than a Christmas bonus, especially when we had no bookings until next year."

"Oh." Jay scrunched up his face. "So what am I supposed to eat, then?"

It was on the tip of her tongue to say he should have thought of that before he returned to the island, but it would be completely out of character for Jay to think about anything before he did it. So she sighed instead and said, "I have some roast pork."

His face lit up. "Seriously? I haven't had a pork roast in…forever. Christmas is for seafood and all the cold things, not roasts and stuff, Mum says. You are a fucking legend." He squinted at her. "You look like you need a holiday, Xan. Try to relax more. It's still Christmas somewhere in the world!"

"I was on holiday until you turned up," Xan said before she could stop herself.

His grin died, but he held her gaze. "You're right," he said quietly. "You were…enjoying some peace and quiet before I got here. I won't bother you again, Xan. I'll go raid Catering instead. I'm sure I'll find something I can make sandwiches with. Or I'll call Shou to fly in some supplies. You enjoy your roast. Maybe you could write the recipe down so I could try it one day."

Before Xan could think of a fitting reply, Jay took off through the palm trees down the track he'd made uniquely his own.

She wasn't sure what to do. She wanted to call him back and apologise. It's not like she actually wanted any more of the pork. But he was right — she did deserve a holiday. Somehow, she suspected her holiday was over before it had barely begun, all thanks to Jay Felix.

TWENTY

To Xan's surprise, Jay was true to his word. She didn't see or hear him for three days. No, not even his usual morning swim: the wet season had well and truly set in, with the first cyclone of the season forming off the coast. The cyclone was to blame for the week-long storm, someone had said on last night's news report. It sat off the coast, brooding, like it was choosing its target carefully as it built up its strength. Last report she heard, it was a Category Three, but they'd predicted it would intensify to a Category Four if it stayed out at sea much longer. The resort had been on blue alert – the lowest level of cyclone watch – for almost a week now, but that didn't mean anything unless the cyclone moved. At Divers Tavern in town, the regulars would be placing bets as to whether it made landfall at Hedland, Dampier or Exmouth. Cyclones never actually hit Broome. They just sort of cruised past and made a few waves, before sweeping through some other town and causing flooding inland.

Still, she should check if anything had changed. Once the cyclone was gone, the storm-tossed lagoon would be safe to swim in again. Xan was dying for a swim.

Xan pointed the remote control at the TV, but all she got was a blue screen. She flipped through the channels – all blue. That meant something had taken out the satellite dish again. The internet would be down, too, and the security system. Not that it really mattered right now – she and Jay both had access to every building on the island with a swipe of their wristbands.

Last time this had happened, Jay had jumped out of a helicopter and crashed it into the satellite dish. She wouldn't put it past him to do something that stupid again.

Sighing, she found some shoes and headed out into the downpour to his villa.

A long, wet walk later, Xan hammered on Jay's door. After a moment, she heard him shout, "Yeah, I'm coming!"

He took his time, but Xan waited on the veranda until the door whooshed open. Jay leaned against the doorframe, drinking her in. "You know, I think you're the only woman I've ever met who could make it through rain like this without looking like a drowned rat. Come in and get dry. I might even have some spare women's clothes in here for you to change into."

Xan followed him inside and accepted the towel he offered. "Thanks, but I'll only get soaked again on the way back. It's the closest I'll get to a swim until this storm passes."

"Yeah. I miss my swim." Jay sighed and perched on the

couch. "So, to what do I owe the honour of this visit?"

Xan remained standing. "What did you do to the satellite dish? The TV link is down."

"Wasn't me this time. I've been reading."

A likely story, Xan thought.

"I was watching TV last night when we lost reception," Jay continued. He held up his hands as if to calm her down. "It's not just TV that's down, but internet, too. I made a few calls, and managed to get someone to fly out here to fix it today." He looked inordinately proud of himself.

"Who?" Xan demanded.

"The IT guys. Seb and Cameron. Shou said he'd fly them in. They'll check everything out, fix what they can, and head back this afternoon. If they can't fix it, they'll call someone who can."

Wow. He'd actually done the right thing for once. Except that those boys were supposed to be on holiday, not working. "How'd you talk them into coming in to work on their days off?"

Jay shrugged. "Easy. I swore it'd only be one day, we'd fly them in and out, and they'd get an extra day of time in lieu at the end of their break. They agreed."

Xan didn't know what to say. Jay Felix, being responsible? Doing her job, of all things? "Thank you," she said finally. "Can you let me know when they arrive?"

"They're already here. Been holed up in their office for the last hour now."

"I should go find out if they've made any progress," Xan said reluctantly. Damn it, she deserved an extra day off, too. Maybe she'd just take it.

Jay shook his head. "Nah, don't worry about it. They

said they'll tell me when they're done, or when they give up. I got the impression they didn't want an audience. Look, when they turn up at my place, I'll bring 'em round to report to you, too. In the meantime, enjoy your holiday, Madame Hotel Manager." He executed a courtly bow.

Xan smiled. It wasn't like the hotel would fall apart without internet or TV today. There weren't any guests to complain, and she did have a stack of books she'd borrowed from the resort library, courtesy of the rash of Christmas functions they'd hosted in December. As long as neither of them got hit by a falling coconut and needed emergency medical attention, the lack of communication felt…liberating. Like really being on holiday.

New books, the house to herself, bad weather outside…now all she needed was a nice cup of tea to make her day perfect. Xan headed for home to turn the kettle on.

TWENTY-ONE

As Xan debated whether to brew a third cup of tea or prepare an early lunch, she heard another knock at the door.

"Is it fixed?" she called as she opened the door.

"Nope," Jay replied, looking far too cheerful for someone bringing bad news. "Seb says it's the dish, damaged in the storm. We'll have to get the repair guy out again. Baz should have his number, seeing as he did all their upgrades. One of the guys will call him when the get back to the mainland. I called Shou, who'll be here soon to pick them up." Jay's brow creased. "I'm not sure if I heard him right, but Shou said something about an alert for Cyclone Rose. It's been upgraded to yellow in the Buccaneer Archipelago, or something like that. He said if we want to evacuate, bring a bag to the helipad."

Xan's jaw dropped. Yellow alert? That meant they were

in the cyclone's direct path. They had to evacuate. But cyclones never came to Broome.

"Are you sure?" she asked carefully.

Jay shrugged. "That's what he said. He should be here soon, so you can ask him yourself. I'm going back to my place to grab a few things. See you on the helipad."

Jay believed it, then. If the fearless rock star wanted to evacuate his precious island in the path of an oncoming cyclone, then she should, too.

Xan grabbed her toiletries bag from the bathroom and stuffed it into her overnight bag, followed by two changes of clothes. Considering, she added another set of underwear and a dress. Three days' worth of clothes would be enough to wait out a cyclone, surely. If she needed anything else, she could buy it in town. Besides, she wouldn't be staying at whatever evacuation centre Emergency Services had set up. Steve would have rooms free at the Mangrove Hotel, she was certain of it. She probably wouldn't even have to share a room with Jay again.

She paused in the living area to pack the library paperbacks, then zipped up her bag. Xan refused to feel guilty about taking the resort's books offsite. She'd bring them back within the week, which was more than most guests did. She still hadn't found that virginity auction book she'd started reading and never finished. She should probably order a copy online, or see if it was available as an ebook. After the storm.

Xan listened for the sound of the helicopter, but she hadn't heard its arrival this morning over the rain, thunder and other assorted noises of the wind playing havoc with her hotel. Best to be on the helipad early, she decided, hefting her bag onto her shoulder.

At least she didn't have to worry about locking up. There wouldn't be anyone left here to lock out.

Xan hurried along the path, marvelling at the break in the rain. It wouldn't last long, but if she was lucky, they'd be in the helicopter and away before the next squall hit. She sure hoped so.

The skies had started to spit by the time Shou's aircraft cleared the palm trees and started its descent, but Xan held her ground by the helipad fence. Jay, Seb and Cam were laughing about something outside the gate. Once the helicopter touched down, all three men moved to join her.

It was a good thing Shou had four seats, or he'd have to make two trips, Xan thought. She glanced around, uttering a fervent prayer that the cyclone wouldn't harm her hotel while she was away from home.

TWENTY-TWO

Seven words were all it took to make Gaia's day: "Mr Felix will be in town today."

Her hand tightened around her phone, as she wished she could reach down it and haul the pilot out to give her more information. "When? Where? How is he arriving?"

The man was addictive. When she'd first flown away from Romance Island Resort, Gaia could still feel the ghost of Jay's touch on her skin. She'd revelled in it for a few days, before it had faded. Except…it didn't fade entirely. Instead, it left behind an all-over aching that made her want him more every day.

She'd busied herself with work, waiting for him to call and summon her back to his bedroom. To the glorious cocktail of pleasure and pain that sent her body into heights of euphoria ordinary people needed drugs to reach.

The only drug she needed was Jay Felix, rock star lover

extraordinaire. The only man she'd ever take orders from.

But he hadn't called. Maybe he was busy. Maybe he'd forgotten about her.

Then that travesty of a reality TV show had gone to air, with her lover as its eligible bachelor. She'd tried to get the show cancelled, but she didn't own the network, and she hadn't been able to negotiate the purchase before the show went to air.

Nightly she'd watched him dating those common girls who obviously meant nothing to him. They stole kisses, unaware of the masterful man they were courting. None of them could give him what he needed. No one but Gaia, and she knew it.

She bided her time, waiting for the inevitable end of the show, when he'd pick one girl he wanted to be his wife. Gaia had Stephanie prepare background checks on all the finalists. Every sordid photograph they'd posted on social media. Every bit of dirt from their past that could be dug up was unearthed, and held in reserve for bringing the little bitch down.

Penelope left an interesting trail of poisoning cases in her wake. Lorelei's embezzlement was old news to Gaia by the time the show had aired the episode about her arrest. And Calais...the farm girl's sister had died in suspicious circumstances only a few months before the show started.

But in the end, Gaia hadn't needed to use any of her ammunition. A weeping Penelope had admitted on live TV that after watching the show herself, she didn't believe Jay loved her as truly as he'd said, and she could never marry a man without love.

Gaia hadn't believed a word of it. Jay had probably

revealed where his true tastes lay, and their relationship had dissolved before he'd finished her first spanking. What would a cook know about a man's needs? Especially when the man was a powerful alpha male like Jay Felix.

That's when Gaia made up her mind. Someone needed to comfort him. Someone who understood him.

Gaia took the first flight north.

And she'd been stonewalled at every turn. Jay wasn't in Broome. Or he was, but no one knew where. Jay was on his island. Jay wasn't on his island, and no one could tell him where he'd gone. He was staying with his family, or some other silly excuse.

But now she finally had the truth, wrung from the helicopter pilot who'd helped her take pictures of her first date with Jay. Jay would be in town today.

She glanced at the suitcase full of sex toys she couldn't wait to show him. Every bit of her body screamed for his touch.

The pilot had said something, but Gaia had missed it.

"He's where?" she barked.

"He's at Romance Island."

Ha! As she'd suspected all along.

"I'm to pick him up as soon as possible and bring him to town," the pilot said. "I'm about to take off, as soon as I'm off the phone."

"No you're not," Gaia snapped. "Not without me."

"Miss Vasse, there's an emergency and I need – "

"If you lift that bird off the tarmac without me, I'll tell everyone you took the photos of me with Jay Felix. The resort won't work with you again if they know you violated guest privacy and sold those pictures to the press." Gaia smiled. She had him, she knew.

"I never sold any pictures to anyone!" the pilot protested hotly. "I just held your phone and took pictures at your request. I had nothing to do with private pictures going public! I never even saw them! I…"

"By the time I'm done suing you for your breach of privacy, you won't be able to show your face in public again," Gaia said smoothly.

The pilot swore in a language Gaia didn't understand, before he said, "Your helicopter is waiting for you, Miss Vasse. Please be quick. There's a cyclone coming in and it's not safe to fly in those wind speeds."

"Oh, I will be." She ended the call, wanting to scream for joy. Later. Later tonight, as she writhed in ecstasy beneath Jay's naked body.

Christmas might be over for this year, but it was going to be Gaia's happiest new year ever.

TWENTY-THREE

The helicopter door cracked open and a woman stuck her head out.

"Mr Felix, I've come to save you," Gaia said, in a voice Xan decided was probably meant to be sexy, but just came out sounding ridiculous.

"Oh, for fuck's sake," Jay muttered, so softly probably only Xan heard it. He stepped forward and gestured to Seb and Cam. "Get in, guys." He glanced at Xan, gritting his teeth. "You, too."

Xan could count, too. "No. I'm the manager of the hotel, I should stay behind. Shou will come back for me once you're safe on the mainland."

Her heart sank as Shou shook his head. "Sorry, Ms Lane. I already shouldn't be flying in these conditions. It's only going to get worse. If I'd known you were here…" He shot a pained glance at Gaia. "I wouldn't have brought passengers. Please, do what Mr Felix says and get in."

"No," Xan insisted.

"We could draw straws," Cam volunteered. "To see who dies a hero to save everyone else." He paled at the thought.

"No one's dying," Xan snapped. "There's a perfectly good cyclone shelter on the island. I'll just have to spend a couple of nights camping out there, is all. I'll be fine."

"You're leaving with everyone else. I won't put my staff at risk," Jay said. "I'll camp out with my guitar and maybe write a song for the storm." He managed a ghost of his usual cocky grin.

He didn't believe a word he said, Xan realised. No. She couldn't leave him on the island on his own. Gods only knew what sort of trouble he'd cause. Even without a cyclone coming in. "Get in the bloody helicopter, Jay."

Gaia leaned out further. "I'll keep you company through the storm, Jay," she purred.

"No fucking way. You stay in that helicopter, or else," Jay said.

"Or else what?"

The two IT guys looked as eager as Gaia to hear the answer to her question.

Jay scrubbed a hand across his face. "Fuck, I can't do this. Get off my island, Gaia."

As if she hadn't heard a word he'd said, her face lit up. "I don't want to go," she pouted.

Jay's eyed narrowed. "Well, you can't fucking stay. I know what I want and you sure as fuck can't give it to me. And I know for fucking certain I can't give you what you need."

Gaia looked positively thrilled. "Goodbye, Jay."

"Gaia...goodbye," he responded. More quietly, he added, "And good fucking riddance."

"I gotta go, guys. Who's getting in?" Shou asked.

"Him," Xan said just as Jay said, "Her."

"I'm not getting in any fucking helicopter with that fucked up billionaire," Jay growled. "Just get in."

"I'm not leaving you alone on this island," Xan said. She turned to Shou. "Take these three to safety. Tell Baz to keep someone manning the radio on the mainland. We'll see if the cyclone shelter is up to spec." She smiled bravely, hoping it looked far more brave than she felt. She'd have given anything to fly to safety with the others, but she couldn't. A captain went down with her ship, or something like that. Maybe she'd strangle Jay Felix first.

She and Jay backed away from the helicopter to give it space to take off.

Xan clenched her fists at her sides, wanting to appear calm as her last hope of safety flew out of sight.

When she couldn't see the helicopter any more, she turned on Jay. "Why didn't you just get into the bloody thing and evacuate like a sane person? You're a bloody idiot, Jay Felix!"

He visibly sagged. "You're right. Jay Felix is a fucking fool."

The last thing she needed was to share the island with a madman. "You're Jay Felix," Xan reminded him.

"No," Jay said softly. "Right now, I'm Jason Felix. Not a rock star, not a hero, just a bloke who's as shit-scared of this cyclone as you are. Jay Felix is a persona that's gone too fucking far. I hope he doesn't get me killed, because right now, I hate Jay fucking Felix more than you ever could.

You should've gotten into the helicopter, because you don't deserve to die in this storm. Jay Felix would be okay going out in a blaze of fucking glory, sacrificing himself and shit. If it weren't for his reputation, Gaia Vasse wouldn't have looked twice at me, and she wouldn't have been in my seat. We both would've flown out, and we'd be having a beer together in the brewery by sundown. So until further notice, Jay Felix is a fuckwit. If we survive this cyclone…I'll still hate his fucking guts."

Xan wasn't sure whether to laugh or cry. "Fine. Jason. Whatever. At least we agree on something. But we are not going to die here. That cyclone shelter is rated to withstand anything that storm can throw at us. When Emergency Services call the all clear, we'll still be here, holding the fort."

Jay…no, Jason laughed. "The two musketeers. Yes, ma'am. We might need some supplies, though. Meet you in the cyclone shelter by sundown. I'll bring the beer."

"And I'll bring the radio," Xan replied. Someone had to think about practical things.

TWENTY-FOUR

They stayed on yellow alert for the rest of the day, so Xan announced that she was sleeping in her own house until someone sounded the red alert. Morning found her back at the games room, checking the cupboards for emergency supplies. The shelter doubled as a pool hall and games room for the rest of the year, with a bar and kitchenette in one corner, a rack of beach towels at the end and an ablutions block tacked onto the ocean side of the building. On the sheltered lagoon side, a back-up generator nestled under the veranda with enough fuel to last a week.

There was a whole cupboard full of torches and lanterns, but food seemed to be in short supply. Even the fridges under the bar were empty.

Jay wandered in, whistling, dragging a trolley behind him. "Figured I'd get us some supplies."

Xan squinted at the trolley. "Four cases of beer? We're

not going to be in here long enough to drink all that."

He shrugged. "Yeah, but it was easier to just grab the boxes than try to juggle a few loose bottles. Not like we'll be able to just go out and grab another six pack when the storm rolls in tonight."

"So it's tonight then?"

"That's what Baz said." Jay lifted the cartons onto the bar, then tore one open to stack the bottles in the fridge.

"Did you raise him on the radio this morning?" Xan asked.

"Nah, called him on the satellite phone." A long ripping sound, followed by more clinking.

They had a satellite phone? Huh. Xan had never seen it. "How long ago?"

Another shrug. "However long it took for me to get from my villa to the bar, load up this trolley and bring it here. Twenty minutes, maybe?"

So his information was current. Still, she should switch the radio on in here. And make sure they had food.

"Can I take the trolley?" Xan asked.

"What for?"

"Food. I'm not drinking on an empty stomach." Xan didn't intend to drink any alcohol at all, but there was no point telling Jay that. He could probably demolish a fair bit of that beer by himself.

"Good idea. I'll come help." He flashed a…no, not a cocky grin. This one seemed sort of nervous and on edge, just like she felt. Not like the Jay she knew at all.

"Thanks, Jay," she said.

"Jason," he corrected.

Right. Jason. "What's the difference, anyway?" she

asked.

"I get to be as scared as you about this storm, instead of laughing like a madman and pretending I'm not. I'll help you get supplies, because only a rock star would live on beer for two days. If we survive this, I want you to tell everyone that I was drunk when the red alert hit, and I didn't sober up until after the all clear."

"Will you be?"

He laughed mirthlessly. "Maybe. If we get all this sorted by then. That's the secret to surviving a disaster, though. Get drunk and somehow you'll make it through. When the *Titanic* sank. Same with the *City of York*. And the *Batavia*. When it looks like your ship's sinking, break into the best booze and get absolutely blotto on it, and hope when you wake up it's all over."

Xan didn't believe it. "Seriously? It sounds like bullshit to me, Jay…son."

He held up his hands in surrender. "It's the honest truth. They even stuck the drunk guy in the *Titanic* movie. Watch it, if you don't believe me. Just…not with me, please. Jo had a thing for it when we were in high school. She watched it way too many times."

"Okay." If she made it out of this cyclone alive, and to an internet connection, she'd investigate. If he was right, maybe that was why sailors throughout history drank so much rum. Or wine. Or whatever they'd had available.

"So, what do you want for dinner?" Jason asked, levering open the door to the walk-in freezer in Catering. "We're all out of fresh lobster, but I think they have frozen tails in here. I don't know how to cook them, though."

Xan laughed. "You're cooking tonight?"

Another shrug. "It'll have to be one of us, and I wasn't game to ask you, seeing as you outrank me and all. So it's easier to assume it'll be me. And I don't know how to cook lobsters, so I thought I'd put that out there before I get volunteered for shit I don't know."

"All right." Xan considered the limited kitchen facilities she'd seen behind the bar. "We have a sink, a kettle, a microwave and an electric frypan. Whatever you think you can cook with those, I guess. It's only one night. There should be some bread or cereal for breakfast tomorrow. Is there anything we can just heat up in the microwave?"

Jason laughed. "If there was, I'd have eaten it by now. Our chefs run a proper kitchen, with everything made in-house. I did find some blue cheese gnocchi in here the other day. There might be some left..." He rummaged around in the freezer, then held up a frosty vacuum-sealed bag. "Eu-bloody-reka! And a tub of that cream sauce, too." He found a frost-rimed cardboard box and loaded it with his finds.

"I'll take care of breakfast," Xan said, heading for the dry store room. She grabbed a box of her own and filled it with coffee, long-life milk, a couple of boxes of cereal and some sachets of jam and honey. She rejected the Vegemite at first, then wondered if Jason might want the vile black spread. After a moment's consideration, she added those, too. From the fridge, she claimed a tub of yoghurt, but there was very little else on the shelves. There'd be a big supply order when the resort reopened next week.

If it opened next week. The chilling thought forced Xan out of the fridge and into the much warmer kitchen. Even with a cyclone coming in, the Kimberley had tropical heat to spare.

Jason had almost filled a second box when Xan laid hers on the trolley.

"If the power goes out, and we're on back-up, the desalination plant and the water pumps might not work. Did you find any bottled water back there?" Jason asked.

Xan's jaw dropped. How come she hadn't thought of that? "I'll go check." She returned with a flat pack of bottled water, wondering if Jason really was as stupid as he'd always pretended. Or was that part of the rock star persona, too?

He was her boss, yet she barely knew him.

"Are you all right with the trolley?" she asked. When he nodded, she added, "I'll go get us a couple of folding beds from Housekeeping."

She swiped open the door to Annette's office, but there wasn't a single bed in sight, folded or otherwise. Xan checked both store rooms, but found none there, either. Stymied, she marched up to the hotel proper, swiping her wristband against every door that wasn't marked with a room number. She found electrical switchboards, firefighting equipment, linen stores and a pungent cupboard full of cleaning chemicals, but no beds until she reached the corridor that housed the library. There, she discovered a store room almost as big as the neighbouring library, filled with portable cots, folding beds and what looked like enough folding tables and chairs to seat a small army. Or a wedding, she thought. Well, that was one less thing to worry about for next May.

Satisfied, Xan wheeled two beds out of the room and let the door hiss closed behind her. She pushed her charges as far as the hotel lobby before glancing outside. Rain battered the path to the games room, with no sign of letting up.

Xan wasn't one to let a little rain stop her, but she didn't want to sleep in a soaking wet bed, either. She grabbed some garbage bags from Housekeeping and used the tape dispenser from Reception to shroud the beds as best she could. Then it was out into the rain, shepherding her wayward charges through the wind until she reached the games room veranda.

Where she found Jason shoving something huge, white and inflatable through the door.

"Just leave those here. I'll get them in next," he said, waving her away. "Better get whatever else you need, because Baz said they just put us on red alert. That means take shelter now."

Clothes. She needed clothes. Xan ran to her unit, snatched up her overnight bag, and sprinted back to the shelter. If she hadn't been well and truly soaked before, she definitely was now. The waterproof bag should have protected her belongings, though. And the resort library's books.

Now there was nothing more to do except find a spot to settle down to wait out the storm. Preferably a comfortable reading nook. And hope that Jason would leave her alone with her book.

Where was he, anyway?

Jason burst through the doorway with a splatter as his dripping raincoat sent water everywhere. He kicked the door shut before shrugging off the coat. "It is officially not safe for humans out there," he announced. "But I hope I brought enough entertainment to see out the storm." He unwrapped the plastic-shrouded bundle in his arms and laid a pile of books on the bar, looking proud of himself.

Aw, how sweet. He'd brought her books. Xan sidled over to the stack, tilting her head to read the titles. "Are all of these for me?" Every single one was a romance of some sort. "Thanks. You could have brought along a few thrillers for yourself, too, you know. These don't look like your style."

Jason opened his mouth, but no words came out. Finally, he shook his head and said, "I'll manage. I brought my guitar. With the storm outside making so much noise, you probably won't even hear me playing, so it won't annoy you."

Annoy her? "I like music," Xan protested.

"Just not mine," he replied, walking behind the bar.

"What makes you say that?"

"At that party in town, where I got up and played with the band. I've never seen you drink as much as you did that night. And you usually only look that pissed off when you're talking to me." Jason shrugged. "It's fine. Not everyone likes Chaya's style of music. As long as enough people like it to buy the music and keep the band in business, was always what mattered. And me, too, I guess. I had to appear in the media enough so they didn't forget about me."

What to say to that without spilling her guts? "I do like your music. I even have a couple of Chaya albums on my playlist on my phone," Xan admitted. Not guiltily. Half the civilised world could say the same. Chaya was that band you went to when your heart was heavy. When something was wrong and you needed the sort of angsty poetry they used in their lyrics, set to growling, snarling rock music that matched your mood. When you wanted to hit things, but belting out a song felt almost as good.

"So it's just me you hate. Figures." Jason cracked open a beer.

"You're drinking already? You'll be drunk as a skunk by the time the cyclone hits!" Xan exclaimed.

He shrugged. "That's the plan. Too drunk to be terrified." He downed half of the beer, gulping it like a drowning man gasping for air.

Xan checked her wristband. To her surprise, it was a few minutes past noon. Not too early to drink, after all. "Can you pass me a ginger beer?" she asked.

Jason pulled one out of the fridge, flicked off the cap and handed her the bottle. "To surviving the storm," he said.

Xan clinked her drink against his, happy to toast what she thought was pretty much a certainty.

"We've got sandwich stuff for lunch," Jason said. "Bread and whatever else I could find. Fuck, if Gaia hadn't been in that helicopter, we could be having the brewery's lunch special brought out to us, instead of making our own."

Xan drained her beer and figured she may as well ask the question burning her tongue. "What was that exchange about, anyway? The bit where you said goodbye and stuff. It sounded familiar. And why on earth did it make Gaia look like Christmas had come again?"

Jason snorted. "It's a bit from her favourite book. A romance, she says, but it doesn't have a happy ending, so it can't be. Not really. The couple break up at the end."

"Which book?"

"Can't remember the title. *Fifty Lashes* or something like

that. The one they made into a movie recently. All about some kinky billionaire getting obsessed with someone who thinks that sadism and masochism sucks."

Xan coughed out a laugh. "I think you got the title wrong. But did you actually read it?"

He shrugged. "I may have watched the movie."

"So you haven't read the books, and you don't know what happens after the first one," Xan said slowly, understanding dawning.

"More kinky shit, probably," Jason said. "Not my thing."

"You really should have read them all. I bet Gaia did. Romance books in a series don't need to all end happily, just as long as the last book does. I hate to spoil it for you, but in this one…well, the couple get back together."

"Fuck! Really?"

Xan hid her smile as she nodded. "Yeah. So Gaia probably thinks you two have your own happy ending in the works."

"Fuck!" Jason wailed, dragging his fingers through his hair. "I'm going to need more beer, so I forget you said that."

Sharing a cyclone shelter with a drunk rock star. Xan couldn't imagine a worse thing to do with her New Year's Eve.

TWENTY-FIVE

Xan set up her camp bed near the bathrooms, far from all the external windows and doors. Everything was shuttered against the storm, but she wasn't taking any chances. The wind had started whistling, then outright howling, and the metal sheeting on the roof rattled almost constantly. She'd turned the radio up, but the only sound it emitted was static. Normally this channel was alive with chatter between the local boat-owners, but today's forecast had grounded even the most rabid fisherman. No one was out in this storm. No one except them.

Jason stood at the kitchen bench, fixing himself a sandwich. Xan had prepared hers already. Now, she stretched out on her bed, flipped open her book and took a bite of bread, bacon, sundried tomato and lettuce. Between the book and her BLT, she hoped she could forget the weather for a little while.

TWENTY-SIX

"Hey, Xan," Jason called. "Are you hungry yet? Dinner's ready."

Dinner? But the book was just starting to get hot and heavy, and the heroine had resisted the hero for so long even Xan had gotten frustrated waiting for them to surrender to the chemistry. It couldn't be dinner time yet. She'd barely finished lunch.

Xan glanced at the plate she'd set on the floor several chapters earlier. Only an hour at most. She took a deep breath and inhaled the rich-smelling, cheesy goodness of whatever was going on in the kitchen. Jason could cook?

She climbed carefully off the folding bed, pausing to stretch her stiffened muscles. Maybe she had been reading for longer than she'd realised.

"Good book?" Jason asked.

"Yes," she responded, allowing her curiosity to drag her

to the kitchen.

A colander full of gnocchi sent up a curl of steam from the sink draining board, beside an electric frying pan full of what looked like vomit at first glance, but it sure didn't smell like it. She spotted mushrooms swimming in the sauce, amid lumps so smothered in the stuff she couldn't identify them. "What's that?" she asked, pointing.

"Chicken, I think," Jason said. "It was frozen, so I didn't see it had stuff in it until I'd heated it up. By then, I already had the can of mushrooms open, so I added them anyway. You don't mind mushies, right?"

Xan assured him that she didn't mind them, hoping the incredible smell meant all this was actually edible. She popped one of the gnocchi in her mouth and bit down. "Oh my god," she groaned. "What did you do to it?"

"Microwaved it in some hot water until it was cooked," Jason said. "It said it was stuffed with blue cheese. Maybe there's something wrong with the cheese?"

The cheese tasted like it had been crafted on Olympus and gifted by some culinary deity. Xan needed to know the name of the chef who'd made the gnocchi. The stuff was seriously good.

Xan shook her head and searched through the cupboards for crockery so she could have some more. She loaded half of the gnocchi into a bowl, then eyed Jason's sauce. Though it wasn't really his sauce at all – he'd just heated it up and added stuff. She speared a gnocchi with her fork, skimmed it through the sauce and collected a mushroom. Xan transferred the dripping morsel to her mouth. It was even better with the sauce, mushrooms and all.

"Is it all right?" Jason asked.

Xan used a spoon to drown her dinner in sauce. "Mm-hmm." She had better things to do with her mouth than talk.

Behind her, Jason dished up his own dinner. After a long moment, he said, "Hey, this is actually good!"

Silence reigned inside, while the storm shrieked outside. Probably jealous, Xan thought, surprised to find how quickly she'd eaten. She should have savoured it, but it had been so good that she just couldn't stop.

Reluctantly, she forked the last bite into her mouth. After she'd swallowed, she said, "When the resort reopens, I want to know who made that gnocchi. We need to keep that chef here."

Jason smiled sadly. "Always working, aren't you, Xan? I guess that's what you want in someone who manages your investments. Don't you ever have fun?"

"I've barely done any work since the resort closed for Christmas," Xan protested, setting her bowl down. "And I have plenty of fun. My favourite thing in the world is diving and snorkelling. Here, I get to do that every day." She paused. "Well, every day it's not blowing a gale outside. I swear I know every coral bombie in that lagoon, and I still see new things every time I go for a swim. And if that's not enough, I can always take a ride in the jet boat with Baz through the whirlpools. Beats any rollercoaster ride, anywhere."

He looked lost for words.

"Actually, I want to keep that chef here so I can eat that stuff again sometime. I can't afford a personal chef, so the next best thing is to employ great ones for the hotel." Xan found herself reddening. "Okay, it's selfish, I know, but I'd pay for my special dinners. I'm not Meier."

She took a deep breath. "And if this is about how I've never taken a holiday in the time I've been working here, you're right, I haven't. I've been saving them. Look, I've been living in Australia long enough to apply for citizenship. Or permanent residency, at least. I like it here so much I want to be able to live here indefinitely. But the deal is that I have to keep staying here until the paperwork gets approved. When I'm officially a citizen, I can travel again. I'll actually be able to hug my parents instead of seeing them at the other end of a video call."

She dropped her empty bowl in the sink. "You know what? You're wrong. I don't hate you, but sometimes, when you make some stupid, arsehole comment like that, I really don't like you. I think you like your rock star image so much that there is no separation between the persona and the person any more. I hope you do sign a contract for more concerts and albums and whatever else is part of the package. Your rock star antics are wasted on me. I never have been, and never will be, one of your fangirls."

Xan felt an inexplicable urge to cry, but she forced the tears back. "I'm going to bed. Please turn the lights off over that side of the room, and keep the noise down."

TWENTY-SEVEN

As Jason washed the dishes as quietly as he could, he racked his brain to work out what he'd done wrong this time. He'd made dinner, and Xan had liked it, so it couldn't be the food. He was even doing the washing up, so it couldn't be that, either. He'd let her read without interrupting her.

He still had all his clothes on, and he hadn't played golf, slept with anyone, crashed anything, broken anything or thrown up. Yet.

But even on his best behaviour, he'd still fucked up somehow.

"Are you angry about what I said to Gaia?" he asked.

No answer.

"Or that I'm here with you instead of recording my next album?"

In Xan's dark corner, bedsprings creaked. "I don't care about your career, or whether you ever choose to record another song. I don't care what you say to your girlfriend, either."

"You know she's not my girlfriend."

Xan snorted. "Fine. Fangirl, then."

This was about Gaia. "You're the one who told me to be nice to her, back when she was trying to buy the island. From the moment I first met her, I wanted to tell her to fuck off and not come back. I still do." Jason snatched up a tea towel and rubbed it furiously against the electric frying pan.

"Do you hate all the women you've slept with?"

What kind of question was that? "No. Not a single one. Not even…well, okay. Maybe I do hate Gaia for what she did to Flavia. I wouldn't sell someone out to the press. And she never wanted me. She wanted a fucking gigolo. Someone who'd do everything she wanted in bed, not…not…what I usually do with women. Women who want me."

"The rock star." Xan made it sound like an insult, instead of the awesome job it was.

"Yes, the fucking rock star. Which I was, and I will be again one day, when everything's signed." What he'd do without Angel to write the songs and both Jo and Angel to make sure everything went smoothly at concerts, he didn't know. He'd play with other musicians if the girls didn't want to go onstage any more, but how the fuck was he supposed to be Chaya's front man, rock star extraordinaire, by himself?

"Why haven't you signed? Your agent or manager or whatever she is calls a couple of times a week. I've heard Philly talking to her at Reception, saying you're not taking calls. You never take her calls. Is it because you're too lazy to work, now you have your private island?"

Jason glared into the darkness where he knew Xan could see him, even if he couldn't see her. "You wouldn't understand."

"Try me."

He moistened his dry mouth. "You wouldn't. You only see the face of the band. The albums, the concerts, the media coverage. You see me, all over everything. But I never...I was only..." The words spilled out. Stuff he'd never said to anyone, because who would listen? Who would even believe him? How it was Angel's band, not his. How the girls only tolerated him because he was the band's pretty face, the one they could hide behind. They relied on him to bring in the fans, all the while laughing behind his back about how he did it. How he couldn't stand to disappoint his fans, couldn't say no, but that only meant there were more girls trying to get into his hotel room the next night until it was everywhere he went. That tantric sex course...

"What?" Xan demanded, rearing back in her seat. Somehow, while he'd been talking, they'd ended up sitting together at the bar. "You did a tantric sex course? With who?"

"By myself!" Jason snapped, setting down his empty beer. "I gave a fake name, because I didn't want anyone to know I was doing it. Didn't want people knowing the big rock star didn't know the first thing about giving a girl a good time. It's not fucking instinctive. It takes practice. Lots of practice."

Xan laughed. "Oh, so that's what you call it. You weren't

just sleeping with anything in a skirt. You were perfecting your tantric sex skills."

Stung, Jason protested, "It wasn't like that! Not for them. Even the instructor said I was good."

"So, you became a tantric-trained rock god, which no girl could refuse. Such a hard life." Xan drained her ginger beer.

"I never asked them." Jason's voice was barely audible above the storm.

Not loud enough for Xan to hear, evidently. "What?"

He considered just shaking his head and not telling her. But what did it matter, anyway? "I never asked them," he repeated, much louder. "They all propositioned me."

"You've never asked a girl to sleep with you?" Xan's eyebrows shot up so high, they vanished into her hair.

"That's right." Jason needed another beer. No, he needed a whole bottle of bourbon, but he hadn't grabbed any. Yet another stupid thing to add to the endless list of things he had and hadn't done.

"Afraid you'd be rejected?"

"Maybe." More like yes, but Xan would only laugh at him if he admitted it. "The few times I asked girls out, they refused."

"Before you were a rock star," Xan said slowly.

"Well, yeah. Afterwards, I was so busy I couldn't really ask anyone."

"Or you'd disappoint your fans." The way Xan stared at him, it looked like she pitied him. She shook her head. "It's usually women who have to do that kind of thing for fame. I never thought…I'm sorry, Jay. Jason. No wonder you like to hide out here, instead of going back to that life. I couldn't do it."

Jason summoned a grin. "It wasn't all bad. I mean, it was hard work, making sure every night I was giving a girl the best night of her life. It's every guy's dream, really. And on concert nights, when I was so high on the adrenaline after the performance…it was more than one girl those nights. Fuck, I'd go back to that life just for the concerts."

"And the orgies afterwards." Xan slid off her bar stool and headed for the kitchen. "Another drink?"

Jason nodded. He found himself facing a glass of water.

"Drink that first, and I'll get us a couple more beers." She drained her own water and opened the fridge.

Jason obediently did as he was told, then wiped his mouth with the back of his hand. "I'd be all right without the orgies, I think. I mean, it was great at first, but you get tired of doing the same thing every night. And it's not like I need sex every night."

Xan cracked open two beers, passing one to him. "That's not what I heard when I arrived. There was the receptionist, the tour guide, most of the maids…to hear HR tell it, you cut a swathe through the female staff from the moment you arrived."

"It was only two maids," Jason said. "And the rest were because of the tour guide. She took me out on the boat for a private tour of the lagoon. We went out on the lagoon, all right, but we spent most of the day exploring positions that worked in a boat without capsizing us. She must've told the story to everyone in the staff room that night, because the following day, there was another girl in uniform on my doorstep, and it wasn't just my room she wanted to service."

Xan pulled a face. "Gods, Jason, can you ease up on the details? The mental images are going to haunt me for weeks."

"Well, you already know what I look like naked in the lagoon," he began helpfully, "so just add in a naked woman and a boat and —"

"Jason!" She smacked his arm, making him spill his beer.

"Good thing tattoos don't come off that easy," Jason said, swiping at beer-drenched arm with the tea towel.

"What is your tattoo, anyway? I've always wondered," Xan said.

Jason extended his arm, angled so she could read it.

"All the world's a stage," she read aloud. "Shakespeare. Huh. Not what I expected at all. Were you drunk when you got this?"

Jason almost spat out his beer. "Fuck, yes. I had to be, or I'd've passed out from the pain. I couldn't look at it, either, but I was so shitfaced that everything was too blurry to see. I had a bottle of bourbon in my other hand to keep things that way, too."

Xan drank deeply, then set her bottle down. "So you don't remember why you chose to have these words permanently carved into your skin."

"Yeah, I do. I picked the quote sober, then blew through the bourbon so I could get it done. It's the only tattoo I've got, too. Couldn't face another one. Didn't need another one, anyway. This was enough to remind me…remind me that my world was a stage. I entered and exited where I was told, playing the part they gave me. I knew it would end one day, but just like life, you always want the good parts to go on forever."

"Do you know what play it's from?" Xan asked, tracing the letters with her finger.

It was the first time she'd ever willingly touched him, and Jason was surprised to admit to himself that it felt good. Not that he intended to admit that to Xan – it'd probably qualify as sexual harassment, or at the least, piss her off again. He didn't want to piss her off. He liked her company. She was…honest. Not afraid of him or his reputation, or awed by it, either. And she listened, which was more than most people did. Maybe too well, given all the comments she'd made tonight, but she understood discretion, too. It was pretty much an essential part of being the manager of Romance Island Resort.

"*As You Like It*," he responded. "I did my first year in Fine Arts at university before I bombed out. I'm not entirely stupid."

"I never said you were," Xan protested.

"But you thought it. Everyone does," Jay said.

Xan sighed. "So if rock stars aren't stupid and hotel managers aren't boring workaholics, where does that leave us?"

Jason had the answer to that. "In a cyclone shelter in the eye of the storm, on a private island we both call home."

Xan smiled, right at him. "Yeah. Well said, rock star."

This time, it almost sounded like a compliment.

TWENTY-EIGHT

Xan wasn't sure if she was just getting used to the noise, or if the cyclone was finally dying down. Either way, it was time to make an executive decision before Jason talked her into another beer. "I'm having a shower," she announced, sliding down her bar stool. She made it to the floor without incident – she was slightly tipsy, not drunk. The ginger beer had some alcohol, but not enough to make her stupid. Besides, she'd only had two. Maybe three, if you counted the one with lunch, but that was hours ago. Probably out of her system by now. And speaking of getting things out of her system…there were other facilities she needed to visit in the bathroom, too. Rather urgently.

She snatched up her bag and headed for the bathroom block. Here, she could hear the wind whistling around the building, rattling the roof sheeting. No, the storm wasn't spent yet.

Fortunately, the showers spouted hot water, which Xan was happy to use to her advantage. Who knew how long they'd have power – or hot water? Normally, hot water wasn't a worry, as the sun took care to turn any cold water into lukewarm at the very least, but sunrise was a long way off – if the sun could break through the thick cloud cover at all tomorrow. She took her time for once, not limited by the three-minute quota allotted to the staff showers. If her staff had to take short showers, so did she, but tonight there was just Jason, who didn't live by the same rules and restrictions in Villa Penguin, the smallest of the Pearl Villas. He'd never know she'd snatched an unaccustomed luxury.

Except…she'd forgotten to bring a towel. Luckily, some kind person from Housekeeping had left a stack next to the washbasins, probably assuming that most hotel guests wouldn't have brought one, either. Wrapping a towel around herself, Xan swore she'd thank Annette and her team for their foresight when she saw them next. Yes, when. She'd survived the worst of the storm. Now it was only a matter of time before Emergency Services announced the all clear over the radio, and she could go outside to assess the damage to the resort.

Was it just her imagination, or had the wind picked up again? Maybe it just sounded louder because she didn't have the shower on any more.

Xan pulled on her shortie pyjamas and headed back to the games room, combing her wet hair.

When she caught sight of Jason, she dropped the comb in surprise. "What on earth are you doing?"

"Making my bed," he replied cheerfully, laying a hand on the side of the fully inflated boat. For some reason known only to crazy, drunk rock stars, he'd stuck it on top of the covered pool table. And, true to his word, he had made a bed – he'd taken the mattress off his folding bed and placed it in the bottom of the boat.

"In…a….boat," Xan said.

"Well, yeah. There's space for you, too – that's why I grabbed the big RHIB."

"The big…what?"

"RHIB. R-H-I-B. Stands for…rigid hull inflatable boat, one of the maintenance guys told me, last time they took it shark fishing in the lagoon. Baz said to make sure we had one at the shelter, just in case." Once again, Jason looked terribly proud of himself.

Baz had told him to sleep in a boat? When? And why? Xan said, "You're not making any sense. The storm's dying down. We should just try and get some sleep. In bed, not a boat."

Jason shook his head. "The storm's not over. Baz said this would happen – it's the calm, the eye in the middle of the storm. When it gets quiet for a bit, but the other half of the cyclone's still to come. And the worst of it. Most places, the biggest danger is the wind, strong enough to blow a man away, or rip off the roof. This cyclone shelter's strong enough to protect us from the wind, so that's all right, but Baz said the real danger is the storm surge. When the wind and the swell and the low pressure system all combine to make bigger waves than usual. Waves that could wash over the whole island, taking the buildings with it. Just like that little cyclone last season did to the sea wall over on Lorikeet Island. The real danger's not the wind, but the water. High tide's still a couple of hours away. I figure if we're going to wake up in the lagoon, better to be floating in it than drowned." He gestured toward the boat.

"The island could flood?" Why hadn't Xan thought of it? She'd seen the sea wall collapse at Lorikeet Island. Sure, this cyclone shelter had held up well in the storm so far, but how well would it protect them if it was underwater?

"That's what Baz said. Bad combination, really, like Cyclone Rose deliberately picked a full moon to come visit us."

Xan itched to go outside, to see if Jason was telling the truth, but the wind's wordless howling told her it would be suicide. She didn't need to check the tide times to know he was right about those – island life revolved around them, so it was second nature to check the tides along with the weather forecast.

"I'm not letting some bitch of a storm end me. And not by drowning. That's the worst insult ever, for someone with a name like mine." Xan jerked her chin at his mattress. "Shift that over to make some space for me. And you better stay on your side of the boat."

"Yes, ma'am." Jason grinned, grabbed her mattress and lifted it into the empty side of the boat. "You okay with the port side?"

"Fine," she said, wondering how she was supposed to climb into bed now. The sides of the boat were chest height, sitting on top of the table. No harder than hauling herself out of the water after a dive, though, really, she thought. She took a deep breath and launched herself into the boat, rolling over the side to land on her mattress. Sleeping in the boat was softer than the folding bed, she decided, making herself comfortable.

"I'll get the lights. I might leave the bathroom ones on, though, yeah? So we can see where to go if we need to get up in the middle of the night," Jason said.

Xan nodded, closing her eyes. Would she even hear the waves licking at the shelter, with the wind shrieking so loudly? One thing was certain: she wouldn't get much sleep tonight, what with new things to worry about and all. She never wanted to be caught in a cyclone again.

The boat rocked as Jason climbed in. Xan heard the rustle of sheets in the dark as he settled into bed before he said, "Xan? Why is it an insult?"

"What is?"

"You said drowning is an insult to your name. What is your name?"

It was pitch dark, but Xan felt his eyes on her anyway. What did it matter if he knew? He could wheedle the information out of Human Resources, if he really wanted to. "Xanthe."

"Kssss…what?"

She sighed. This is why she shortened it. "Kssszanthee," she said, drawing out the sibilance. "It's the name of a deep sea nymph in Greek mythology. Dad said I was born to dive."

"Xanthe," Jason repeated. "I like it. I've never met anyone called that before. Why don't you tell people your real name? Zzzan just sounds so flat in comparison. Like a droning blowfly."

Xan smiled into the darkness. "And have to explain how to pronounce or spell it every time I introduced myself? No, thanks. It's easier this way."

"But not as pretty. It even sounds like waves crashing on

the shore. Xanthe."

Xan didn't want to think about what waves did right now. Not waves or tidal surges or anything to do with the ocean. "Enough using my name in vain. I want some sleep," she said.

"Sure thing, Xanthe," Jason said. He paused, then added, "And…thanks for staying here with me, when there wasn't space for both of us in the helicopter. I think I would've freaked out a lot more without you here. You're a life saver. Really."

Xan didn't reply, but she did allow herself a small smile. Maybe Jason wasn't so bad, after all. At least he could pronounce her name, which was more than Jerome had ever managed.

She had to do something about Jerome. Get rid of him, one way or another. Maybe one day she'd forgive his misguided attempt to help a girl out, but that wouldn't change the fact that he was a lying, cheating paedophile and she'd be happier to marry Jay Felix than him.

Xan smothered a laugh at the thought of what Jason would say to that. He'd probably propose, like he did to all the other girls she'd seen him with at the resort. He wanted a wife for Angel's wedding, but he also wanted to be a rock star again. What if…

"Jason, all the women you've been trying to persuade to be your wife, so they'd attend this wedding with you. What did you intend to do after the wedding's over?" she blurted out.

"What do you mean?"

"Well, you're only marrying them for the wedding, right? So if you're going back to the rock star life again, you'd want a divorce, so you could go back to romancing the fangirls every night, right?"

A sigh. "I don't know. I never really thought about it. I mean, that's what I'm famous for. That's the image they want when people buy my albums. But if I had a wife…would anyone buy my music?"

Xan tried not to laugh. "I didn't buy it because I wanted to sleep with you. If there wasn't a cyclone outside and a king tide threatening to drown the island, I certainly wouldn't be sharing a boat with you, let alone a bed."

"Yeah, but…you're just one person. There are millions of girls out there who…want me. Or they used to."

This time Xan did laugh. "Even I don't believe you've slept with millions of girls. And what about those guys at the Mangrove Hotel? They were absolutely in awe of you. You didn't sleep with any of them. I remember, because you shared a room with me."

"Well, yeah, but…"

If she could see his face, she probably wouldn't say it, but in the dark it was so easy to not hold back for once. "I think you're scared to stand for something you want. Afraid you might fail. You never chased after any of those girls when they left you because you were scared they'd turn you down. Same with all this talk of being a rock star. You were a rock star, and you could be again…but you might have to go for a solo career instead of with the same band. You can't play it safe if your dream is bigger than normal, Jason. It's what I did, coming out here. I wanted to wait until I was married and do the trip as our honeymoon, but then Jerome started talking about settling down straight after uni, so I knew the only way I'd get to travel was if I went on my own. And this job, too…my visa was about to expire, but I wanted to stay in Australia, so I applied for the job at the resort. For the job as a tour guide, the one I eventually hired Rita for, not Meier's job. He tricked me into signing the contract for his job. He said it was the same as the original with some mistakes corrected, so I didn't read it properly. When I found out he'd made me the hotel manager, I freaked out a bit…but I also figured it was too late to back out. You all looked to me to manage the place, so…I just got over being scared about how much I might suck at the job, and I did it."

Jason swore. "Seriously? I had no idea. You just seem so perfect for the job. I never thought…and you, scared? The first time I saw you, you managed to scare the shit out of my hangover, you were that menacing. I don't think anyone except Angel and maybe Trevor could do that. You're perfect, Xan."

And Jason had to be drunk, saying stuff like that. "Good night, Jason."

"G'night, Xanthe."

Even drunk, he'd managed to say the right thing. For once.

TWENTY-NINE

Xan roused from her dream, feeling unusually hot. Had she somehow turned the air conditioning off? And that crackling sound, overlaid with static, like a bad home video recorded on a really windy day. Wind. Storm. Cyclone Rose.

She blinked the sleep from her eyes, trying not to laugh as she realised why she'd overheated. Somehow, Jason had cuddled up to her as she slept and thrown an arm over her, and the man was just as hot in bed as his reputation said he was. Ha, with his clothes on, thankfully.

How long had they slept like that? Xan had never shared a bed with anyone. Not even Jerome. Oh, sure, they'd fooled around – she'd left her virginity behind a long time ago – but sleeping in the same bed was one of those intimate things she'd never done. To trust someone to sleep beside you while you were unconscious was just…asking a lot, Xan felt. Yet somehow she'd managed a peaceful night's sleep in her boss's arms, of all people.

Oh gods. Technically, she'd just slept with her boss. Xan clapped a hand over her mouth, trying to stifle her laughter before she woke him up. Carefully, she edged away from him, hoping to get out of the boat before he realised what had happened.

The radio gave a decisive crackle. "Emergency broadcast, all channels," a man's voice said. "Cyclone Rose has been downgraded to a Category Two. King Sound south to Derby, you are all clear. Repeat, all clear. The cyclone has passed, and is moving inland. Cyclone warning for the Buccaneer Archipelago, Dampier Peninsula and King Sound has been cancelled."

"Well, woohoo," Jason said softly. "Did you hear that? We survived the cyclone."

Xan clambered out of the boat, trying to hide her reddened face. It's not like they'd had sex, but…

"Romance Island Resort? Are you receiving, over?" the radio blared.

Xan dived for the radio, fumbling for the microphone. "Romance Island Resort receiving," she said breathlessly. "Um, over."

"Satellite tracking shows your island as the hardest hit. Do you need medical assistance, over?"

Xan glanced at Jason, then down at herself. "Uh, no. We're fine. The cyclone shelter held up through the storm. We're not sure about the buildings on the rest of the island, though. We haven't been outside yet. I'll get started on the damage report. Over."

"No hurry, Romance Island Resort. Let us know if you need emergency assistance. Oh, and happy new year. Over and out."

Happy new year? Was that what day it was?

Xan found herself grabbed from behind and spun around, before Jason planted a smacking kiss on her lips.

"Happy new year! We survived a cyclone! How's that for an awesome new year?" He released her before she could gather her wits enough to push him away. This time, he didn't apologise.

"We should go outside and see what's left of the hotel," Xan said, striding toward the nearest exit.

Jason ducked under the bar to get something out of the fridge. "Nah, it can wait until after breakfast. It's not going to get any better if it waits half an hour or so. And you can't tell me you don't want coffee."

Once again, the rock star was right.

The radio erupted in more chatter, so Xan turned the volume down before joining Jason in the kitchen. "Unless you're offering to make pancakes, I'll take care of my own breakfast," she said.

Jason grimaced. "I don't know how to cook pancakes. If I order the ingredients from the mainland, want to come over to my villa for breakfast one day, so you can laugh at me while I make a mess?"

Xan laughed. "Tempting, but no." She dug out the yoghurt, then hunted through the cupboards for a bowl and a spoon. She served herself a generous portion, figuring that she deserved it this morning. Xan clicked the lid back onto the tub and bent to put it back into the fridge.

Something tapped on the door. A pause, then a series of louder taps, like someone was knocking on it. But they were the only people on the island, weren't they?

Jason laughed. "Sounds like someone's at the door. What's the bet that it's a tree branch that – "

"Hello?" a man's voice called. "I heard you on the radio, but when I hailed you, you didn't respond."

Xan and Jason exchanged glances. They weren't alone on the island any more. How had this man arrived, though?

"Look, we were planning to head for Broome, but with the storm system offshore, we moored up near one of the oil platforms for a while. I got a voicemail message from someone called Sebastian, saying you needed repairs to your satellite dish. I figured while we were in the neighbourhood, I might as well stop in. We're a bit low on fuel and supplies, though, so if it takes more than a day or two, we might have to head round to Broome and come back."

"Who's we?" Xan called through the door.

"I'm Joe Fisher. I fixed your dish back at Easter, when we were staying at the pearl farm. My wife and son are still on the boat. We tied up at your jetty, so I could come ashore to find you."

The name sounded familiar, though Xan would have to go to her office to check. Instead, she opened the door, yoghurt bowl in hand, and found herself face to face with a bloke who could've been Jason's older brother. Ten years older and definitely leaner, Joe Fisher wore a t-shirt and shorts, with thongs on his feet.

"What sort of supplies?" she asked.

Joe stared at her bowl. "I know my wife wouldn't say no to yoghurt." He looked past Xan to where Jason was toasting bread in the electric frying pan. "Or fresh bread. Me, I'd kill for an iced coffee."

"We're not due a fresh milk order for another fortnight,"

Xan said with relief. "There was bread in the freezer, though. This is the last tub of yoghurt, but there's still a bit left."

"I'll tell her," Joe said, heading up the path. "How about I send her up here, while I go see what I can do for your dish?"

If they still had a satellite dish. Xan didn't even know that for sure. She took a deep breath, then followed the bloke's scraping steps to the jetty.

Palm fronds and seaweed carpeted the paths. A dead rat floated in a puddle between two palm leaves, which Xan stepped over, hoping Joe hadn't noticed. A section of tortured roof sheeting, contorted into a flattened cylinder instead of its usual flat expanse, curled around a palm tree that was now nothing but a severed trunk.

When Xan dared to raise her eyes to the hotel proper, she saw where the roofing sheets had come from. Two more were loose, but still attached. She'd need to get a tarpaulin up there before any more rain got in. There were guest rooms beneath the breach – ones that were probably now filled with water and storm debris.

The lobby looked mostly intact, protected by the storm shutters on all sides. The cyclone had woven leaves and seagrass through the shutters, but Xan was sure a clean up crew could take care of that. She rounded the main building, crossing her fingers as she hoped the jetty would be undamaged. Joe had said he'd tied a boat up there, but if the boat wasn't any bigger than the overgrown dinghy she and Jason had slept in last night, then maybe...

Xan lifted her eyes, taking in the lines of what was clearly a luxury yacht. Or was it a yacht – didn't it need a sail to qualify? This sleek vessel didn't have a sail, though it had several storeys. It was longer than she expected, too — the back deck looked like some of the dive boats she'd worked on. Elaborate calligraphy identified the craft as the *Siren* — a fitting name for such a beautiful temptation. You could live on a boat like that for the rest of your life, sailing the world and only coming into port for food and fuel.

If she ever had as much money as Jason, she wouldn't buy an island. She'd buy a boat like this. A ship meant freedom. It was a line from some Disney movie, she was sure of it, but that didn't make it any less true.

"She's a beauty, isn't she?" Joe asked, like he knew what she was thinking.

Xan nodded fervently, then turned back to the boat as movement caught her eye. A woman — the wife Joe had mentioned, presumably — leaped lightly onto the jetty and glided toward them, clutching a white bundle to her chest. She trod the jetty like a model might saunter along a catwalk, but there was something otherworldly about her that set alarm bells off in Xan's head.

Venus rising from the foam, was the first thought that came to mind. Like a goddess among mortals.

"This is my wife, Vanessa, and our son, John," Joe said.

Venus indeed, Xan thought, as she smiled and introduced herself to the woman.

Vanessa stared at Xan's breakfast even more intently than her husband had. "Is that yoghurt? I haven't seen any in months. I would pay quite a bit for whatever you have on hand."

Xan itched to ask her if they'd run out of ambrosia, too, but she managed to swallow the urge. Instead, she said,

"Sure. Seeing as your husband's giving us a quote on our repairs, that makes him staff, so that would include staff meal privileges. We don't have a chef on the island at the moment, because the resort's closed for the holidays, but you're welcome to what we have." Xan led the way back to the cyclone shelter, where she found Jason chomping on some charred toast. "This is Vanessa," she told him. "I said she can help herself to breakfast."

Jason's eyes fixed on Vanessa. "Anything you want," he said. "I'll make you toast, coffee…"

Coffee. Xan stayed long enough to make herself a cup, then left them to it. Surely Jason couldn't get himself into too much trouble with a married woman whose husband was just outside?

THIRTY

Xan found Joe crouched at the base of the satellite dish. "I think I found your problem," he said. "I might even have the parts you need in the hold."

Now that sounded like some sort of miracle. If the wife was Venus, did that make this man Vulcan, the smith, in a much more modern guise? He didn't look particularly godly, even if he did have a nice backside.

"It's like you knew you'd be paying us a visit," Xan said, watching him to see his reaction.

"Nah, not really. I did some upgrades on the system on our island, when I finished up with yours at Easter. Ours is pretty much a smaller version of yours now. I keep spares on hand, just in case. So not that much of a coincidence." He laughed. "I'll have to hope we didn't take any damage from the storm, otherwise I'll be waiting weeks for replacements to arrive for ours."

If he owned an island like this one, no wonder they could afford the yacht. "Which island is yours?" Xan asked.

More laughter. "Oh, it's not really ours. We just lease a bit of it, with a bunch of other fishing families. Our operation's based down at the Abrolhos, near Geraldton. Bit of tourism, a lot of fishing, and a bit of pearling, too. At least, that's my wife's latest project. It'll be years before we get any pearls out of her oysters, but she's got the patience for it."

"You should talk to Baz and the other guys at the pearl farm on the mainland here," Xan suggested. "They've been farming pearls longer than almost anyone else."

"So she said – she came up here at Easter, too, and took a good look around then." Joe straightened. "Want me to take a look at your generator, too, while I'm here? It'll be quicker than getting an electrician out from the mainland, and we can fire your system up properly to check if I missed anything."

"Sure." It would be weeks before Xan could bring a contractor from the mainland, and if he really was the same bloke who'd repaired the dish when Jason decided to jump out of a helicopter onto it, no wonder the IT guys had called him again this time. A miracle worker, indeed.

She followed him to the power plant, where he estimated it would take him a couple of hours to have the hotel up and running as usual. They agreed on price – no need to haggle, seeing as he suggested they waive the normal callout fee in lieu of breakfast – and Xan was torn between watching him work and taking her empty cup back to the kitchen to wash it...and see how Jason was going.

"Can you tell my wife how long I'll be?" Joe asked.

That decided matters. Xan headed back to the shelter. She found Vanessa seated on a deck chair on the veranda, breastfeeding her baby as she stared out across the lagoon.

"Where's Jason?" Xan asked.

"Inside, washing up," Vanessa said. She lifted her arm to point at the water. "Do you know you have a rather large shark in your lagoon?"

Xan glimpsed the fin before it sank under a mess of palm fronds. She swore. "It must've swum in during the storm. I'll have to get the maintenance guys to fish it out when they get back." That might be another week, during which she couldn't swim in the lagoon. Damn, damn, damn.

"He's too big to fish out. You'll get in trouble with the Department of Fisheries boys if you catch him. And the longer he stays, the more of your reef he'll eat. Right now, he's crunching through your shark nursery like they're a bowl of chips."

"Oh no!" All those baby black-tipped reef sharks. What if the monster shark started going after some of their older residents, like the Queensland groper?

"If I have time, I'll go for a swim and see if I can persuade him to leave," Vanessa said.

Xan stared. Who persuaded a shark to do anything? Only Venus, maybe.

"It's no big deal. Sharks are instinctive predators. If he finds another predator in this lagoon he can't hold his own against, he'll head somewhere else."

Xan had dived with sharks before, and while she usually wore her shark shield, she knew the drill if you were ever caught in the water unprotected with a shark: make yourself look bigger and scarier, and don't back down. If you did, and they took a nibble of your thigh while you swam away, you could bleed out before you made it back to the boat. But to go into the water deliberately, to take on a shark? Not even Jay Felix was that crazy.

"Do I have time?" Vanessa asked.

"Joe said to tell you he'd be a couple of hours," Xan said.

Vanessa nodded, glancing down at the baby, who'd fallen asleep while nursing. Not bothering to do up her top, she simply pressed the child to her chest and headed inside the shelter.

She placed the baby in the boat-bed that Xan and Jason had shared. Vanessa removed her shirt completely, then shimmied out of her shorts before she tied her bikini top properly over her breasts. Well, sort of. The stringy top covered her nipples, but left plenty of flesh still exposed. The perfect breasts of the goddess of love, all right. Xan looked away, embarrassed, but Jason just kept staring at her.

"Are they real?" he breathed.

Vanessa's eyes flashed dangerously. "Watch him for me," she ordered.

Xan opened her mouth to protest.

"Yes, ma'am," Jason replied, drying his hands on a teatowel. He took up his post at the stern of the boat, where he could see the sleeping child.

Xan waited until the woman left before she hissed, "You can't ask a woman if her boobs are real!"

Jason shrugged. "The only women I've seen with boobs that big had implants. You can tell when they bounce, or if they don't. Either hers are real or she has a cosmetic surgeon so good you can't tell the difference."

"Of course they're real!" Xan said. "She's a breastfeeding mother. They get bigger when they're full of milk."

"So yours will look like that, too, when you have kids?" Jason asked.

Xan's mouth opened, but no sound came out. She wasn't sure whether to laugh or tear him a new one. "If I ever have kids, then yes, I imagine so. But seeing as I haven't met anyone I'd like to have kids with, who might actually make a good father, it's not bloody likely, is it?"

"Do you want kids, Xan?"

Maybe. She'd never really thought about it. Definitely not with Jerome. If anything, she'd be worried that he'd turn paedophile properly. If she had kids, she wasn't letting Jerome within ten miles of them. She had her answer then, didn't she? Jerome could rot in hell before she'd ever forgive him, let alone trust him again. She was staying here in Australia, taking that citizenship, and building a life in the sun.

"Do you?" she blurted out.

Jason's face lit with a beaming smile. "Fuck, yeah. I'll never be as good a dad as mine was for me, but I'd still fucking try. I could watch them play and learn and discover shit all day. Maybe even teach them to swim in the lagoon. Wouldn't this be an awesome place for a kid to grow up?"

With sharks and cyclones and Jason's irresponsible tendencies to do stupid things, like rooftop golf? Not that he'd be playing golf up there for a bit, with the cyclone damage and all. Still, the island was dangerous. "Older kids, maybe, but not a baby," Xan said.

"He's spent all his life on a boat, she said." Jason nodded

toward the sleeping baby. "All two months of it. They've been out at Cocos, then here, and they're headed south next to where they have a fishing shack. No life in the suburbs, just going to an ordinary school, for him. I want my kids to have a life like that."

"You don't have kids. Or a wife who'd consider having them with you," Xan reminded him.

Jason's face fell, and Xan's heart twisted. An apology for her cruelty floated on her lips.

Jason raised his head and met her gaze. "Not yet, but I will," he said. "Call it a new year's resolution, if you like. I'm going to sign a new recording contract, and after that, I'm going to look for a woman who'll want me forever. Who I'll want forever. With kids and all that comes with that." His eyes dared her to disagree. "What's your new year's resolution?"

She toyed with the idea of saying she didn't believe in such things, but that would be a lie. "I'm going to break it off with Jerome for good, even if I have to beat it through his thick head, so he goes back to the UK and leaves me alone," she found herself saying. "And I'm going to become an Australian citizen because I like living here."

"I'd drink to that," Jason replied. "But, you know, I'm watching the baby. Here's to a good new year, Xan. You deserve it."

"After the disastrous year you've had, so do you," she said. She meant it, too.

THIRTY-ONE

Xan stood with Jason on the jetty to wave goodbye to the Fishers, or whoever they were. Even if she received Joe's invoice for the work, she'd still wonder. Their arrival seemed too fortuitous to be coincidence. Like something out of a romance novel. Did that make the baby Cupid, then? Or one of Venus' other kids? Xan couldn't remember if Vulcan had any children. She'd have to look it up on their newly-restored internet access.

Right after she went for a swim in the lagoon. Vanessa had assured her the tiger shark was gone, though not before he'd gorged himself on their fish.

The damage report was better than Xan had expected, but it still wasn't good. Villa Maxima had taken the brunt of the cyclone, given its elevated position on the north-east corner of the island. Fallen palm trees had smashed through the storm shutters and the windows all along the north side, and most of the roof was gone. The staff accommodation had come out almost intact, with just a bit of flooding in the lowest lying rooms. The hotel roof and the rooms below the breach were on the list, too. Both jetties had survived the storm without damage, though the swimming platform from the Penguin Jetty was now floating at the southern end of the lagoon.

Trees were down all over the place, with so much stuff floating in the lagoon that it was hard to see the surface. A particularly big frangipani had gone through the shutters at The Jungle, so the pub looked like it had hosted a bad brawl, with the furniture thrown everywhere and wind-blown debris covering everything.

With power restored and both of their houses intact, both she and Jason would be sleeping on their own tonight, instead of in the cyclone shelter.

"I should put the boat back where I got it," he said, as if reading her mind.

"I'll return the beds to Housekeeping," Xan replied. "Look, about last night…"

"Two people taking shelter in a storm, sharing the available resources," Jason said smoothly. "We shared a boat, Xan. Not a bed. Even if we had, I don't talk about that sort of stuff. You know that."

She did. Despite his troublesome reputation, she knew she could trust his discretion. The man could keep a secret. "Good," she said. "I don't want the staff thinking…"

"They wouldn't believe it anyway," Jason insisted. "Their fearless rock star and unruffled hotel manager so freaked out by a storm that they slept in a boat on the pool table? Sounds like fiction no one would believe."

Xan relaxed. No, they wouldn't. "Thanks, Jason."

"I have one condition, though," he continued.

"Mm?"

"You still owe me that snorkelling tour in the lagoon."

She did. "Once we fish out all the palm trees and coconuts, and check if there are any more big sharks hiding in there, sure," she said.

"It's a date, then." He grinned.

Xan laughed. "No, it's not. But we'll do it. The owner of a gorgeous resort like this should see all of it. Otherwise, you're missing out."

"Can't have that. And I won't." Jason headed for land. "I better go deal with that boat. Disposing of the evidence and all that shit."

Speaking of disposing of rubbish…if communications were back, she'd better call Jerome and tell him they were finished. The sooner the better, so she could enjoy her new year.

THIRTY-TWO

The call to Jerome was awkward and painful and all the things Xan hated. It wasn't until she told him she'd sold her engagement ring and given the money to a women's shelter that he finally agreed to go back to the UK. If only all her communication left her feeling so liberated, but of course it didn't.

Xan spent most of the next week on the phone, organising repairs and reassuring staff that the resort was still standing. The maintenance team came back early, eager to clear the lagoon in the hope that they'd find another shark.

When they found nothing bigger than the resident groper, Xan kept her counsel, not sure how to explain to the men that the monster shark they were hunting for had been driven away by the goddess Venus in a string bikini. She still wasn't sure she believed it, though the shark had definitely departed.

The lagoon was the least of her worries, though. She couldn't get construction crews or building material until April, they all told her – citing everything from the weather to Christmas to a building boom in Perth. It was enough to make her scream.

At this rate, repairs wouldn't be complete before the wedding. Xan waited in daily dread for a phone call from the bride, asking for an update.

Xan buried her face in her hands. Sometimes this job was just too hard.

Jason wandered into her office without knocking. "Sleeping on the job, Xanthe?"

"I wish," she replied, smoothing her hair in the hope that it would calm some of the turmoil in the brain underneath.

"Have you heard back from Phuong on the due diligence stuff for those hotels?" Jason asked.

"I got a voicemail from her about it a couple of days ago, telling me to call her, but I haven't had time to follow up on it. I'm too busy getting quotes for repairs."

"So when is the repair crew coming to sort the roof at Maxima and the main building? Jo keeps calling, wanting an update for Angel. I told them both not to bother you because you're busy enough dealing with the mess."

Xan's dread drained away. "Thank you. I don't know, though. The earliest date I can get is April for any of it."

Jason frowned. "Three months away, when another cyclone could come through? And Angel's wedding is in May. Fuck that. Give me the quotes and I'll see if I can do any better."

It was a testament to her frustration that Xan handed over the file with no hesitation whatsoever. "Good luck."

She busied herself with the million and one other things screaming for her attention. Morning passed into afternoon as she worked steadily. Five o'clock approached when Jason returned to her office and threw the file on the table. He collapsed into the client's chair, looking as exhausted as she felt. "No luck?" she asked with sympathy.

"Depends what you call luck. The materials will all be delivered next week. Not sure if they're coming from Perth or Darwin, so I don't know what day. The roofing crew's coming in the week after that. I didn't manage to get a hold of the painter, though."

Xan's jaw dropped. "How?"

"I told them who I was, and how I've got a wedding coming up. Then I said I'd promised her everything would be perfect. Most of them started talking about March or February at that point. That's when I remembered what Angel does to get what she wants." Jason's eyes met Xan's worried ones and he quickly explained, "No, not the knife. She offers an incentive. The steel supplier is getting a couple of cartons of beer, and the construction team is getting a weekend at the resort once everything's complete. With a bar tab."

Xan pressed her lips together. "Why didn't I think to offer blokes beer and a rock star to hang out with?"

Jason shrugged. "Because you're not a bloke? I dunno."

Maybe he was right. Sexism was rife in the world, and probably always would be. At least she'd used the right man for the job.

"Thanks," Xan said. "That's a weight off my mind, for

sure. I'll call Phuong first thing tomorrow and set up a meeting."

Jason rose. "Thanks. And any time you need help, just ask. Especially with Angel's wedding stuff. It all has to be perfect for her, and if it's not, it'll be my fault."

"But she knows you're not responsible for the resort or the wedding, right?"

"Doesn't matter. If anything goes wrong, it'll be my fault," he repeated. "It always is. You'll see. Anyway, if you need me do to anything for the wedding, say so. Not like I have anything else to do."

"What about your recording contracts?"

"Negotiations take time, my agent says. Mostly, the record companies take a while to come back to me when I turn down their offers. They want the whole band, and I told her they can't have that. But if they want me…I don't know what they'll pay."

Xan nodded. "So while they deliberate, you're stirring up trouble by dropping hints to random contractors that you're getting married soon? Guys gossip just as much as girls. I know that much. The press are going to come sniffing after you and the name of your bride. What do you want me to tell the media if they call?"

Jason grinned. "Give 'em the hotel's standard line about guest privacy, and how you can't say. They'll make shit up, I'm sure of it."

"While the recording companies' bids increase in line with the media coverage?" Xan guessed.

"Hey, I'm a good investment. What's it matter how much more they offer? I'm worth it!" He tried and failed to flip his hair – it was much too short – and strode out of

Xan's office.

THIRTY-THREE

Once again, Xan found herself sitting in the prison visiting room, her table an island amid a sea of families. But this time, Phuong wore a smile.

"You look pleased with yourself," Xan said as Phuong sat down.

"I've had a particularly good week," Phuong said.

Xan nodded at the file Phuong had placed on the table between them. "Are you going to tell me this is the best investment money can buy?"

Phuong's smile faded slightly. "I'm afraid not, though the price is good."

Xan smothered a sigh. "What, then? Have they finally set your trial date?" She'd have gone mad waiting. Phuong must have the patience of a saint to put up with the delays.

"No. In fact, there won't be a trial at all. They've finally located my ex-husband, so the committal hearing was yesterday. The magistrate decided to dismiss the charges. All of them."

Xan managed a smile. "No wonder you're pleased. But…doesn't that mean you're free to go? Why are you still here?"

Phuong laughed. "You've watched too many American legal dramas, I think. It doesn't work like that here. There's paperwork to be filled out before the prison releases me from remand, and that takes a few days. Seeing as it's Friday now, it looks like I'll be in for the weekend. If I'm lucky, I'll be free on Monday."

Free to pursue Jason again. Suddenly, Xan didn't think that was such a good idea. He might still want a wife, but this girl wasn't right for him. Too risky.

"So what will you do next?" Xan asked.

"My degree arrived in this week's post, so I'm a qualified accountant now. My Australian citizenship application was held up because of the charges, but now I have no criminal record, it's been approved. I had planned to look for a job, but this," Phuong patted the file, "changes things. I may have to visit Singapore to take care of some family business."

Now Xan was definitely lost.

"You do know this is my father's hotel chain, don't you?" Phuong asked.

Xan shook her head.

Phuong flipped open the file. "It all looks fine, except that the company isn't making anywhere near as much money as it should. In fact, if you believe this, it's been running at a loss for the last four years. Unlike Meier, though, the drain's hard to identify, because it looks legitimate." She tapped a highlighted line in a table. "See this name?"

Xan peered at the string of Chinese characters. "Yes, but I can't read it."

"It comes up a lot, along with two other consultants. One of them is my brother's wife's brother, who I know audited my father's accounts. His fees have increased significantly over time, particularly after my father's death, but that might just be because my brother never had a head for business, so he called his brother in law to do his job for him. The second one is my sister in law – my brother's wife. Now, I know for a fact that the only consulting she does is to check her manicure for chips. The woman hasn't worked a day in her life. Yet she's getting paid a lot of money to do nothing. The third one…well, that's my Chinese name."

Xan digested this slowly. "So, you're saying that you bankrupted your father's company?"

Phuong shrugged. "That's what the numbers say. It's what my brother believes, too. It looks like my father took money out of the company every month to pay for my university expenses. But…he didn't. He paid every semester in a single payment – and it definitely didn't cost as much as these monthly withdrawals. Someone's been salting money away in my name for three years, and then it stops. The money drain didn't stop, though – right about the time my father died, the company started buying back its privately held shares. Starting with mine." She looked pained. "I don't have any shares in the company, or I didn't before my father died. If he gave me any in his will, I never heard about it. And I never would have agreed to sell them without even looking at the company's financial statements.

That's just plain stupid, like something my brother would do." Phuong bit her lip. "I worked out how much I estimate the company is worth, as well as how much money has been stolen from it over time. Factoring in a reasonable interest rate over the last four years, I think someone's set aside just enough money to buy the company, knowing no one else will want something so unprofitable, and once they do…all the accounts will mysteriously vanish, so no one knows where all that money went."

Phuong looked Xan in the eye. "Tell him thank you, but if he buys this business, he'll be buying stolen goods, and he'll lose his investment when I speak to the right people in Singapore. My report cites losses and mismanagement as the reasons, but I'm telling you that he needs to back out of this deal."

"Why don't you tell him yourself?" Xan asked.

Phuong dropped her gaze to her clasped hands. "Because that was the deal, and I'll honour the contracts I signed. Maybe one day I'll be able to repay him for what he did. He's the reason I left Norman, and if it weren't for his lawyers, I'd be facing the rest of my life in prison. He's an amazing man, who deserves…love at its most passionate, with someone who deserves him and loves him like…something in a fairy tale. I'm not sure I'm capable of that sort of thing, and as for marriage…I'm swearing off that for life. I won't steal his chance at happiness. Besides, I have my own quest. I'm going to catch the thief who stole my father's company from me instead."

Xan believed her. She rose, clutching the file to her chest, and thanked Phuong for her time. They said their goodbyes and Xan soon found herself walking out to her car in the afternoon sun.

The last bride standing had turned him down. Xan would have to attend Angel's wedding with him for sure, now. Funny how she didn't mind as much as she thought she would. Perhaps Jason was growing on her.

Like the fungus on the couch in Villa Maxima. She had to find a replacement for that before she left Perth tomorrow.

THIRTY-FOUR

Roofs repaired – check. Windows fixed – check. Damaged storm shutters replaced – check. Lagoon no longer looked like a Palm Sunday parade – check. Villa Maxima completely refurbished – check. Everything that could be cleaned or repaired had been, so why did Xan feel so nervous, waiting for Angel to arrive? She'd spent so much time with Jason lately, checking everything twice, that she automatically used his name for the girl.

When the helicopter landed, Xan was pleased to find that the hulking security specialist hadn't come along this time, but Angel wasn't alone. She introduced her companion as Liv, her photographer, who had come along to advise on possible spots for the ceremony, the reception and photographs throughout the day.

"But aren't you doing it all in the function rooms?" Xan blurted out.

"Only if it rains, which you've already told me it doesn't during the dry season," Angel said. "I want to do things outside as much as possible. I don't like being confined. I want a beach ceremony, and the reception somewhere by the water, too. I want to be able to see the stars when we dance our bridal waltz, so we must have an outdoor dance floor."

"We don't have anywhere like that. This is the Kimberley, where it gets hot, so all our public areas are shaded. You can't put a dance floor out in the blazing sun — you'll roast your guests."

Angel smiled thinly. "Dancing is for after dark, of course, just like the rest of the wedding reception. Perhaps you could remove the roof from one of your existing public areas?"

She'd just spent the last month putting roofs back on buildings! Didn't the girl understand?

Angel continued as if she hadn't expected a response, "I'm still not certain that would be enough. Nothing you have is close enough to the water. What I really need is a large expanse of decking, extended across the lagoon."

Build in the lagoon? The wildlife on the reef had barely recovered from the cyclone and its hungry shark visitor. Sinking concrete pylons into the water would cause immeasurable damage to what was a unique and quite delicate ecosystem. "You can't," Xan said firmly. "The island is a nature reserve, and building a structure like that in our protected lagoon would never get approval. Even if it would, you'd never get a response from the Shire planning office in time."

Thunder clouds lurked in Angel's eyes. "Call Jason. We'll

see what he says."

Xan used her wristband to send an urgent page for Jason, who appeared promptly less than five minutes later. Probably lurking, listening in on their conversation, Xan thought.

Angel repeated her proposal for Jason' benefit, then folded her arms across her chest, waiting for his response.

"I…I guess we could," he said, looking from Angel to Xan and back again. "Do you think we could get one of the construction crews back in time to build it before the wedding?"

Jason probably could, but Xan might have to wait until April. Still, constructing decking couldn't take much longer than removing and replacing a cyclone-warped roof, and that hadn't taken more than a week.

"It's not about the construction, it's about the lagoon life," Xan explained. "There are fish species in our lagoon found nowhere else in the world except here. The resort has a responsibility to protect them, not build a bloody great big platform over the top of them."

"It wouldn't be across the whole lagoon, right? Just a small bit of it, in the shallows. If we picked a spot where there aren't any fish, we wouldn't hurt any of them. Maybe…" Jason babbled on, looking increasingly desperate.

He couldn't refuse Angel, Xan realised. The longer she held out, the more miserable he became. And if it came down to it, Jo would probably weigh in on Angel's side, too. None of them knew how amazing the lagoon was. None of them had ever been under the surface, to see the life teeming in the reefs, the natural aquarium just begging to steal your attention for hours at a time. There was just so much to see.

"You need to see it," Xan blurted out, interrupting Jason. "You need to dive in the lagoon to understand what I mean when I say it's unique."

"Absolutely not," Angel said.

"I've never been scuba diving before, and I don't have the gear," Jason said.

Xan didn't let up. "Snorkelling, then. We have plenty of masks and snorkels here for the tours we run in the dry season. I'll personally take you on a snorkelling tour of the lagoon, so you see what you'll put at risk by disturbing the seafloor."

Angel waved dismissively at Jason. "Take him. I didn't bring any swimwear. And while you're in the water, find a spot where I can have my deck. The whole lagoon can't be precious coral reef. I know for a fact that part of it gets dredged out to keep it from silting up entirely. If that isn't disturbing the seafloor, I don't know what is." She headed in the direction of the pub. "I'll be sitting somewhere cool. With a drink."

Xan waited for the girl to disappear from sight before she grinned at Jason. "Ready for that snorkelling tour I promised you?"

"If it keeps me away from her for a couple of hours, then fuck yes," Jason breathed. "You know we're going to have to do what she says anyway, right?"

"It'll cost a fortune," Xan replied.

Jason shrugged. "Tell her that. I don't think she'll care. It's her wedding, and she can afford it. Fuck, she could buy my share in the resort if she wanted, and still have money to burn on her precious deck."

"I'm not sure I'd want to stay on as manager if she took over as the owner," Xan said.

"You mean you like me better?" Jason asked eagerly.

Xan snorted. "I wouldn't go that far." She sighed. "You better go get changed into your swim gear. I'm only taking you on this tour for as long as you keep your pants on. I'll meet you back here in fifteen minutes."

"Yes, ma'am." Jason sketched a salute, then strode off down the path to his villa, whistling.

THIRTY-FIVE

True to his word, Jason returned wearing a pair of board shorts. Xan felt unusually self-conscious in her bikini. The memory of Vanessa Fisher was still clear in her mind, and Xan came up short when compared to the goddess of love.

Not that she was after love here, Xan told herself. She wanted to share her love of the reef with Jason, that's all. Better that his eyes were on the fish and not her boobs, anyway.

On the shore, his gaze was fixed on her face. His whole face lit up like a kid at Christmas when she held out his mask.

She explained what to do if his mask or snorkel filled with water, as she would for any novice, and Jason nodded gravely. For once, he seemed happy to do as he was told.

Together, they knelt in the shallows, letting him get accustomed to breathing through the snorkel.

He let out a shout and pointed at something, raising his head so the top of his snorkel dipped below the surface. While he spluttered, the turtle that had attracted his attention paddled into deeper water, out of sight. There would be more, Xan knew, but she thumped Jason on the back and waited for him to recover so they could set off after the turtle.

High tide was an hour away, so the lagoon was still as a millpond, ruffled by the slight breeze, but otherwise calm. The perfect time for a beginning snorkel. Xan had considered bringing fins, but with no current to speak of, she'd decided against it. Jason was a confident swimmer. The mask and snorkel were enough to get used to on this first trip. Another time, if they spent some time on the southern reefs, when the tide was on the way out, they could try a more strenuous swim with fins.

Observing Jason's progress now, she knew she'd made the right decision. He shouted and pointed to something else, dunking his head under the water again. This time, he trod water while he cleared his snorkel, looking to Xan for what to do next.

"If you see something you want to share, just pat my arm and point. Most creatures don't like a lot of noise. It scares them away. And you'll see more if you're not splashing around with your snorkel on the surface all the time," she said gently.

Jason nodded.

"Shall we go?" Xan pointed in the direction of the first coral bombie, home to anemones and their resident striped anemonefish.

Jason set off slowly, assuming the same leisurely pace

he'd used while swimming naked past her window this morning. Xan kept pace with him this time – unlike this morning, when only her eyes had followed him. It had been envy and longing she'd felt. Not for him. Of course not. She'd wanted to swim, but known she wouldn't have time for that luxury until after Angel's visit. That made this swim an added bonus, hours earlier than expected.

Xan glimpsed a flipper on the far side of the coral – Jason's elusive turtle, perhaps. She tapped his shoulder, pointing the way, and found him following her lead.

Rounding the bombie, a tumbled mass of calcified coral that stretched several metres from the sea floor almost to the surface, Xan waited for Jason to see her favourite coral garden.

He gurgled something and pointed, but his eyes widened further behind his mask as he saw more and more. Anemones drifted lazily as striped black and white fish wove between the hydra-like fronds. A couple of bright blue parrotfish rasped their rosy beaks across the hard coral, dislodging sand in their search for food. A small green turtle, perhaps the size of a dinner plate with flippers, floating above the bombie, like the strangest angel she'd ever seen on a Christmas tree.

Xan glimpsed movement in the shadows of a crevice in the side of the coral, but she was too slow to see if it was a fish or an eel. Or maybe even a lobster, which grew quite large in these protected waters, where fishing wasn't allowed. Well, except for the odd invasive shark.

Jason grabbed her arm, gesturing furiously with his free hand at something in the deeper water.

Xan peered in the direction he indicated. Ah, the bulky

shadow ahead could only be the grandfather groper, a giant, blue Queensland groper that probably weighed more than she did. Not that he would ever know the indignity of a fishing hook, or a set of weighing scales, while he ruled the lagoon. He wasn't afraid of humans, either, so Xan pulled Jason toward the huge fish.

He hung back a little, reluctant to get too close, so Xan did something she normally wouldn't. She dropped down, right in the fish's path, removed her snorkel and pursed her lips at the fish.

Not that she wanted to kiss the animal's thick, blubbery lips, but Xan was pretty sure she wasn't the fish's type, either. Jason got the message when the fish simply swam by her, so close his scales brushed her skin: despite his size, this fish was nothing to fear.

Jason circled the groper for a few minutes, before Xan led him away through the shark nursery. There weren't many sharks in there now – the tiger shark had eaten too many of the babies, and the next generation of black-tipped reef sharks wouldn't be born for months yet. The sheltered cove was empty but for a few small rays, which flew from their shallow, sandy hiding spots as Xan approached.

Something brushed against her chest, leaving a mild sting, and Xan waved her hand to encourage whatever it was to swim away from her. The last thing she needed was one of the anemone branches stuck in her bikini again. That thing had left welts behind that took days to heal.

Where to next, she wondered. There were more turtles on the other side of the cove, grazing the algae that grew in the shallows. Jason might like more turtles, so she cut across the cove, gesturing for him to follow.

Yearling sharks swam below them in the deeper water, fish as long as her arm and probably about as round, too. Barbeque sized, she'd heard recreational fishermen call them, and they were right. Scaled and gutted, you could fit a whole black-tipped reef shark yearling, wrapped in foil, lengthwise on a barbeque grill. Not that she intended to tell Jason that. Like all the other life in the lagoon, these sharks were protected.

Sure enough, there were turtles aplenty having their mid-morning munch, including a scarred leatherback that had to be older than she was, it was so big. She could've sat on the creature's shell with room to spare.

They must have spent at least half an hour drifting through the algae meadow. Jason was fascinated by the turtles, and Xan didn't want to rush him.

Her lower back gave a sudden twinge and Xan rubbed at it absently. Perhaps she shouldn't have helped move the new furniture into Villa Maxima yesterday, but she'd wanted their most luxurious villa to look perfect, and that couch had been half a metre off where it belonged. The pain became more insistent and Xan wondered if maybe it was that time of the month again. It didn't usually hurt this much, though, or come on so suddenly.

Reluctantly, she told Jason they should start heading in.

He grinned and pulled out his mouthpiece. "Race you back," he suggested.

Actually, that might not be a bad idea, she thought, as she set off across the lagoon. Her tummy twisted, and for a moment Xan thought she was going to be sick. Not in the lagoon. Not now! Gritting her teeth, she concentrated on her strokes, working with a powerful kick to carry her to shore where she could throw up all over the sand if she needed to.

She heard Jason call something from behind her, but Xan didn't slow. He wouldn't distract her from her course. She needed to reach the shore.

Xan's chest felt like there was a steel band wrapped around her ribs, not letting her breathe, even as she dragged air in through her snorkel. She must be unfit, from not swimming for a few weeks through the bad weather, she decided, pushing herself to go faster. Jason hadn't swum for about as long, so he was no fitter than she. She could still win this.

Her knees grazed sand, and Xan leaped to her feet, stumbling as the water slowed her strides up the beach. Her chest hurt even more now, and her back felt like someone had hit her with a cattle prod, or stabbed her, maybe. Xan fell face-first on the sand, gritting her teeth against the pain. Why wouldn't it go away?

Water splashed against her skin, every droplet like a rubber bullet, painful but bouncing off without penetrating. She wanted to say something, but couldn't seem to unlock her jaw to get the words out.

"Xan! Xanthe! Are you okay?" Jason panicked.

She squeezed her eyes shut as he touched her, grasping her shoulders to flip her over onto her back. The slight impact as her back hit the sand jolted her teeth apart, and a pitiful moan escaped.

For a moment, she saw Jason's face, his mouth and eyes wide with horror. "I'll go get help," he said.

Gone. He was gone.

Her back hurt. Her chest hurt. Every damn muscle in

her body hurt. She'd heard about pain scales, where one was barely hurting and ten was practically unbearable. Childbirth was meant to be a ten. She wondered what happened if you hit eleven. Was that when you died? Your body just shut down, unable to process the pain, so it gave you relief the only way it could.

That'd be real nice, right now. If someone would just switch off the electric current running through her whole body, that would be wonderful.

A new face swam into view. Angel. The last person Xan wanted to see right know, while she was lying helpless on a beach. Hardly the capable hotel manager she was supposed to be.

"Can you hear me?" Angel asked.

"Yes," Xan managed to whisper.

"Where does it hurt?"

"Ev…everywhere. Chest. Can't…breathe," Xan gasped.

"There's something here, on her chest. Caught under her bikini top. I'll get it out. You get that first aid kit open."

Sunlight glinted on metal. A knife. A huge, sharp knife that looked like a more lethal version of Xan's diving knife. The blade came down, scraping across her skin.

Xan whimpered. Would it hurt less if the girl stabbed her? At least the pain would stop.

"Get the Flying Doctors out here!" Angel bellowed. "Tell them I need fentanyl, oxygen and we needed it fifteen minutes ago. Jason, do you want her to die or not?" A sharp prick seared Xan's arm.

Xan didn't care any more. Darkness enveloped her, dragging her down, and it was good.

THIRTY-SIX

Xan woke to the worst hangover she'd ever known. Worse, she couldn't remember drinking anything. And it wasn't just her head aching, either – her whole body hurt, like she'd been hit by a road train. Except there weren't any vehicles at Romance Island Resort, unless you counted the electric golf cart Maintenance now shared with Housekeeping. Xan definitely hadn't left the island – she had too much to do in preparation for that woman's wedding. The one who wanted to dance on top of the lagoon.

The crazy woman who'd also pulled a knife on her, Xan remembered now. Which would make her either dead or in hospital. She forced her eyes open and took a look around. Beeping machinery. Foam panelled ceiling with old-school institutional fluorescent strip lighting, above a single bed that she'd been pinned to with bedsheets tucked in so tightly there would be no escape. And in the visitor chair beside her…

"Stay away from me," Xan croaked at Angel.

The girl raised her eyebrows. "Most of my patients thank me for saving their life."

Patience. Bridezilla didn't have any patience. She wanted to build over the lagoon.

Angel tapped a name badge clipped to her shirt. Dr Alana Miller, it read.

A thought niggled in the back of Xan's mind. Yes, the girl had been introduced to her by that name, not Angel. "Not a real doctor," Xan rasped.

Angel…Alana…whoever she was, poured a cup of water from the jug on the table and handed it to Xan. "I am, and even Jason knows it. He might have panicked when you collapsed, but he came straight to me. He grabbed my arm and dragged me halfway across your island, too. I honestly think he would have carried me if I hadn't come to your assistance. Definitely not normal behaviour for him, but then…he's been different since he met you, Jo said, so I shouldn't be surprised. He even pulled some strings in the Health Department and got me transferred up here from Fiona Stanley Hospital, just to take care of you. As though the doctors here can't handle an irukandji sting."

"A what?" The word sounded vaguely familiar, but Xan's head was too fuzzy to make sense of it.

"A tiny box jellyfish. About this big." She held her finger and thumb an inch apart. "It had hitched a ride in your bikini top, splaying its tentacles over your heart. And speaking of your heart, it appears to be fine, despite some tachycardia overnight. Your blood pressure's back to normal, too. In fact, if you don't develop any further complications, you could be home within the week, making plans to drain the lagoon and turn it into tennis courts."

Xan drained her cup. "You're not touching the lagoon," she growled.

"That was my poor attempt at a joke, I'm afraid." The doctor tossed the empty cup in the rubbish bin. "I said you'd want to fill the lagoon in when you found out you'd nearly been killed by one of the resident jellyfish, but Jason said you wouldn't want it changed, no matter how many killer jellyfish lived there. For once, I guess he was right."

"They don't live there," Xan insisted. "We swim in that water every day. We never saw any jellyfish."

Angel shrugged. "Well, I know I did. The one that stung you. Good thing I had my knife on me – if I'd touched it, I'd probably be in the bed next to you. The doctors here sent it down to the museum in Perth to see if the staff there can identify the species. Not that we need to know that to treat you, thank goodness. It's not like a snake – we don't have an antivenin for these things. Wish we did. Jason might not have been pacing the corridors all night, upsetting all the staff."

Xan fixed her gaze on Angel. "I don't believe you. Jason hates hospitals. He'd rather jump out of a helicopter than be here."

Angel shrugged. "I didn't believe it either. I've only seen him willingly enter a hospital once before, and even then he didn't stay very long. Now, I can't get him to leave."

"Where is he now, then?" Xan asked.

"Probably getting more coffee, or using the bathroom. He's been stomping up and down the corridor outside your room, waiting for me to tell him you're awake."

If he cared so much, why wasn't he here?

Angel coughed. "Ah, I think I hear his footsteps again. He'll stick his head in shortly. You might want to cover that up." She pointed at the cannula taped to Xan's wrist with a blood-spotted dressing.

Xan blinked at her arm for a moment before she remembered why. "Oh, of course. Don't want him fainting in here." She stuck her arm under the sheet, then looked up to find Angel staring at her in surprise. "What?"

"He told you. He doesn't like anyone knowing, except, well, family." Angel coughed again. "Well, that explains a lot." She rose. "I'll go put him out of his misery." She crossed the room and cracked open the door. "She's awake, Jason, and asking for you."

Xan opened her mouth to contradict her, but she was distracted by Jason bursting into the room. He beamed at her for a moment before he grabbed Angel around the waist and lifted her off her feet in a crushing hug.

Angel struggled free, shoving him away much like Xan might have. The knife didn't make an appearance at all. "I'll leave you two alone for a bit, okay?" Straightening her clothes, the grumpy girl left.

Jason didn't seem to notice, or to care. "You're all right!" He dived forward to hug Xan, too, though a lot more carefully than his hug with Angel. "I was so scared."

Xan's heart rate picked up, and was amplified by the beeping machinery behind her. It was the surprise at Jason's hug, she told herself fiercely. Not because she enjoyed being cuddled by her boss. Even if he had sort of saved her life.

Jason threw himself in the visitor's chair. "Jo said she'd

kill me if you didn't wake up. She's the one who sent the flowers." He waved at a display of orchids beside the water jug. "I'd have gotten you flowers, too, but I didn't know what you like."

Nor did she, really. No one had ever bought Xan flowers. And they probably never would. Jason's worry wasn't for her so much as his own precious skin – if his sister said she'd kill him. Good thing she hadn't enjoyed being in his arms, then, seeing as the contact meant nothing to him.

"All my favourite plants grow in the ocean, and they don't really have flowers," Xan said.

"I can see why. That coral looked so cool yesterday. All those colours, and the turtles! I can't wait to go snorkelling with you again." Jason's smile slowly faded as his brain caught up with his mouth. "When you're okay and if there aren't any more killer jellyfish in the lagoon, that is," he added.

Xan wanted to know about the killer jellyfish situation, too, before she went for another swim. "Yeah. I guess you'll be giving up your morning swims now, too, after that."

"Uh, yeah. Yeah," Jason replied, looking like his thoughts were back at the resort. Definitely not in the hospital room, anyway.

Xan hid her smile. If she could be anywhere else, she would be, too.

THIRTY-SEVEN

Jason couldn't take his eyes off her. He'd nearly lost her. Fuck it, she'd nearly died. He couldn't lose Xanthe. Couldn't. She was the only friend he had. They'd survived a fucking fire together. And that cyclone. Losing her to a fucking jellyfish smaller than his thumb? Fuck that. He'd begged Angel to help her, and even that hadn't seemed like enough until now. Now, that Xan was finally awake and talking and looking at him like he'd lost his mind.

Maybe he had, a bit. Without her.

That's why he couldn't lose her.

"Marry me," he said, or he tried to, but the words didn't come out. He cleared his throat and tried again. "Marry me."

"What?"

He seized her hand, the one on top of the sheet. The other one was still tucked into bed at her side. "Marry me,

Xanthe."

She eased her fingers free and shook her head. "Don't be silly."

"I've never been more serious in my life," he replied, wishing he'd brought the ring. That one the pearl farm's jeweller had crafted just for her. Then she'd know how serious he was.

"But you're still being silly. I've told you, you don't need to bring a wife to your friend's wedding. I've already agreed to go with you. Just because she thinks there's something going on between us when there isn't, doesn't mean you have to marry someone when you don't want to."

But I do, Jason wanted to say. Xan was the one woman he'd do anything for. He'd done Gaia, and that whole reality TV thing, all the while realising that the woman he really wanted was right there. And he couldn't say anything because the first time they'd met, she'd threatened to take him to court for sexual harassment if he so much as breathed a word of his attraction to her. Did a marriage proposal count?

"You're still coming to the wedding, aren't you?" Jason said instead.

"Yes, as long as they let me out of hospital before then." Xan glared at the machine beeping behind her. "But there's no point in pretending there's something between us when there isn't. Because there isn't, right?"

He stared at her for a long moment, and she didn't blink. Jason looked away first. "No, there isn't," he mumbled.

Good thing he hadn't brought the ring. If friendship was all she had to offer him, he'd grab it with both hands, and try not to fuck it up any more than he already had.

Too bad if he wanted more. Even rock stars couldn't have everything.

THIRTY-EIGHT

By the time Xan returned to Romance Island Resort, almost a week later, she already knew what the museum had said about the jellyfish that had nearly killed her: it was an irukandji species usually found in northern Queensland, which they'd never seen west of Darwin before. They'd sent an excited staff member up to drag a net through the lagoon, looking for more of them, but after two days of finding no jellyfish at all, the poor woman went back to Perth, complaining that the turtles had probably eaten them all.

Armed with all the advice she could stomach about stinger suits and proper first aid for box jellyfish stings, Xan flew home, wishing she'd never heard about the bloody irukandji, let alone been groped by one.

Shou helped her out of the helicopter like he thought she was an invalid, and Jason waited on the helipad to keep an eye on her, too, Xan assumed with a sigh. She wasn't ill. Both Angel and the hospital doctors had given her a clean bill of health, yet here she was, being coddled.

It didn't stop there, either. She wasn't allowed to work for a week, even if she was living on the island. Jason had arranged for Catering to provide her with room service to her unit for her first week back, so an apprentice chef appeared on her doorstep as soon as she'd managed to get rid of Jason, asking her for her menu choices for that night's dinner and the following day.

Xan protested that she was perfectly capable of showing up in the staff dining room for meals, but after a lot of "Mr Felix says" from the apprentice and the chef she called in Catering, Xan gave in. Sadly, that blue cheese gnocchi wasn't on the menu. No one could remember who'd made the batch they'd eaten, and none of the resort chefs said they'd ever made gnocchi with blue cheese before.

At lunchtime, just as Xan was about to head to the staff dining room, Jason showed up with a picnic basket from Catering, insisting on sharing it with her. She suggested they sit on the Penguin jetty with it, but Jason tried to talk her out of exerting herself by walking so far. It was enough to make her scream.

In the end, Xan rummaged through the basket, found something that looked like a sandwich, and marched off with it.

It only took Jason a moment to catch up, with the basket bumping along at his side. "You're supposed to rest!" he hissed.

"I've spent a week lying in bed, doing nothing, while I feel fine," Xan snapped. "I'm sick of rest and sick of staying inside. I have work piling up that no one's doing. If I rest this week, there'll be twice as much waiting for me next week!"

"There shouldn't be," Jason said slowly. "I mean, there'll be some stuff, but I told everyone to direct all your communications to me, like you did when Gaia was here and you were in Perth. I couldn't handle everything, but it's been pretty quiet. Most of it's wedding stuff. Angel still wants that decking and I think it's a good idea. If we had a platform that went from the path to the Jungle out into the dredged part of the lagoon, it's all sand under there. I talked to the environment officer, who found some old aerial photos of the island before the resort was built. That bit was actually dug out to make a beach that wasn't there before."

"I've changed my mind. I don't want to go back to work yet," Xan grumbled.

Jason laughed. "Think about it, though. On clear nights, we could open it up as a sort of beer garden extension to the pub. If we angle it right, the guests could even watch the moon rise over the lagoon. And I kind of like her idea about dancing under the stars. They're so clear out here."

The first night he'd met Jason, he'd shown her the stars. Then, she'd found him strange but compelling, the odd drunk man who wanted to share so much beauty, but asked for nothing from her in return. There'd been so many shooting stars, she'd run out of wishes while he babbled about fairy tales that didn't come true.

She'd wished for a fairy tale then. The same thing Phuong had wished for Jason, who said they were nothing but bullshit. Who knew? She couldn't have predicted her life would lead her here.

"I still don't know any of the Southern Hemisphere constellations," Xan admitted. "Maybe we should see if we can get someone to run astronomy tours here once a week in the dry season."

"I know just the guy. I'll call him later and see what he thinks." Jason turned to her. "So, we're on for Angel's dancing deck?"

Xan sighed. "As long as it doesn't damage the rest of the lagoon, yes. We should try and get the same guy who did the new pool deck at the pearl farm."

Jason cheered. "Then you'll dance with me under the stars. I'm looking forward to it, Xanthe."

Xan wasn't sure what to say to that, so she said nothing.

"Philly gave me the list of confirmed guests, too. I didn't know what to do with it," Jason admitted.

"Give it to me. I need to arrange their accommodation. Angel's booked the whole island, but she left the arrangements up to the resort. I'll go through it later to see if there's enough rooms for everybody." For a moment, Xan considered changing her mind and agreeing to rest for another week. But all the work would still be there waiting when she got back. Best to deal with it now.

"After we have a picnic on the Penguin jetty," she finished.

"It's a date," he responded.

"No, it isn't."

THIRTY-NINE

When Jason wasn't looking, Xan sneaked into her office and turned on her computer. As she'd suspected, the list of emails was into the hundreds, and growing as she watched. One popped up with a red flag marking it as urgent, so Xan clicked on it.

She read it once, then a second time, just to make sure she'd understood it properly. It purported to be from a major international hotel chain, offering her a job managing a new boutique hotel on the east coast. The salary they offered was almost double what she was earning at the moment. It had to be a joke, she decided, ready to delete it.

As if right on cue, Jason sauntered in. "Caught you! I'm going to ask the IT guys to revoke your access to this office until next week. A week off means no working, Xan!"

She shut down her computer before he saw the email. It wasn't as if she was even considering the offer, but it still didn't feel right to tell Jason someone had tried to headhunt her. Through her work email, no less. It left a sour taste in her mouth.

Xan rose. "You're right." She wanted to laugh at his wide-eyed surprise, but instead, she turned to grab a few sheets off the printer. "All I'll work on today will be the accommodation arrangements for Angel's wedding. Nothing else."

"I'll help you," he offered. "Come over to my place. I have a bigger dining table than you do. We can lay it out there, and if we're still working on it come dinner time, Catering can bring our meals to mine."

Xan was happy to agree. Better to receive room service at the villas than at her unit in the staff compound. She'd never allocated herself special privileges like Meier had, because she truly believed she was no better than the staff she worked with. She didn't share every meal with them in the staff dining room, but that's because she had her own kitchen, where she could prepare her own. That was different to room service, though.

She followed him back to the villa and spread the pages across the table. Right, match the guests to rooms, she thought. Go.

She ran out of people before the hotel was even half full. That couldn't be right – Angel had booked the whole island. Yet the empty lines in her spreadsheet told her there weren't any more names on the list.

"Can you check if I'm missing a page?" she asked Jason. "This can't be all of them."

"What do you mean?" he asked, claiming the chair beside her. "You've got…all her family, me and Jo, plus his family and friends. It was never going to be a big wedding."

"But...surely this can't be all of them. She said she's paying to fly everyone here, and she's already paid for the island, so it's not like people aren't coming because of the cost. The new decking, all the extras she's asking for...for less than forty people?" How could anyone have that few friends?

Jason shrugged. "She's lived in witness protection for years, and rock star life doesn't really let you make many friends, either. She's not like you. If you got married, most of Broome would want to be there to cheer you on. You know everybody."

"Good thing I'm never getting married, then. It'd cost a fortune," Xan muttered.

Jason said something that Xan didn't hear, but two names on the bottom of the list had drawn her attention more than anything Jason might have to say.

"Why are there ASIO agents on this guest list?" She pointed at the names of the two anti-terrorist agents who'd interrogated her last year, when Jason had made that stupid comment about being happy to host terrorists at his hotel.

Jason shrugged. "That's where he used to work. I guess they're his friends, being old workmates and all."

Xan allocated them hotel rooms at the opposite end of the hotel from her unit. She wanted to see as little of the agents as possible.

"I gave the couple the honeymoon suite, but there's a note next to these names, asking for our best accommodation." Xan peered at the paper. "Mohsen...I can't even pronounce the rest of it. Sounds Arabic." ASIO agents and Arabs. Now that sounded like trouble before they'd even arrived.

"Probably is. Her mother's family is from the Middle East. Angel was born there." Another shrug. "So give them Villa Maxima. And don't put Angel in a hotel room. Give her the villa next to mine. And give Jo the one on the other side."

"Why? You don't want to be next door to them on their wedding night, do you?" Xan couldn't imagine anything worse than hearing honeymooners on their first night together, when you'd been in love with one of them. Torture, surely.

"Not really, but…that's the way it's always been. Whenever we were touring. Me on one side, Jo on the other. Just do it," Jason said shortly.

"So who gets the other villas? We still have Pinctada and Albina."

"Her family and his. Stick her father in one and his family in the other one. Albina's the one with the extra bedrooms, right? Give that one to his family, seeing as Angel's dad will be by himself. Allocate one of the extra bedrooms in Albina to the groom, so his parents can keep an eye on him the night before the wedding. Don't want the bachelor party getting too out of hand." Jason smirked.

Xan stared. "They haven't mentioned anything about parties the night before the wedding."

"Well, she wouldn't, would she? Most brides don't like bachelor parties, though they're no worse than hen's nights. Jo will take care of the hen's party, though, so she'll let you know if she needs anything. Us blokes are easy — as long as there's food and drink, we'll be fine." A wicked grin. "Don't worry, I'll take care of the bachelor party."

Of course Xan worried, but she had so much to worry about, one more thing on the list didn't make much difference. At least she had the room allocations sorted.

"I got the quotes back on the deck, by the way," Jason said, swiping his finger across his tablet screen.

"Oh?"

"Looks like we'll be dancing under the stars sooner than we thought," he replied. "Baz's carpenter says he's free next week, and the lumber yard in town had everything he needs."

"Let's take a look, then," Xan said, taking Jason's tablet.

The sooner they got that decking done, the better.

FORTY

"Hi, and welcome to Romance Island Resort. I'm Xan
Lane, the hotel manager here. And you are?" Xan repeated
for what felt like the hundredth time. She handed the
helicopter load of guests to Philly and Rita, who escorted
them to Reception, where they'd receive their wristbands
and directions to their assigned rooms.

Dennis was doing duty on the jetty, mostly dealing with
the contractors delivering things for the wedding. Both Baz
and Shou checked their IDs against the list of people
allowed on the island, before they were allowed to board a
boat or an aircraft, but Angel's strict security measures
called for everyone to be double checked, so Xan did as she
was told.

As Xan sent this group of guests on their way, Dennis
came running up with a huge grin on his face. "We've
solved the drone problem!" he cried.

Now that was good news. Dealing with uninvited guests was easy when you controlled access to the island, and everyone in town had spread the word that the island was off-limits to charter pilots and boats for the weekend, but Xan hadn't considered anyone would send flying drones equipped with cameras to spy on the island until she'd seen one hovering over the lagoon a week earlier.

Reporters used remote-control helicopters to take their pictures now?

Apparently they did, Trevor the security specialist had told her. Somehow word had leaked to the media that the rock star wedding of the year was at Romance Island this weekend, and everyone wanted a glimpse of Jay with his bride. No one had bothered to correct them that it was Angel's wedding, not Jason's, so more reporters arrived every day, filling up the hotels in town.

"How?" Xan demanded.

"Baz enlisted the local shooting club."

Great. Solving a problem with guns. That could go wrong in so many ways.

"No weapons on the island," Xan said flatly. "We've made that pretty clear."

Dennis waved away her concern. "And they won't be. He invited the local shooting club to the pearl farm for the weekend, and offered to sponsor a competition. Shooting aerial targets." His grin widened as Xan caught on. "And a special bonus prize for anyone who can take down an aerial drone he's bought specially for the competition. They're now fully booked with shooters from Perth to Darwin, from farmers with rifles to professionals who've been to the Olympics and Baz is talking about making it an annual thing."

Xan couldn't help laughing. Only in the Kimberley could you do something like that. "I hope he does well out of it. Angel should be pleased. Has she arrived on your end yet?" The girl definitely hadn't been in any of the helicopters, and the wedding was tomorrow.

Dennis shook his head, hurrying to take shelter with Xan as Shou took off.

Five minutes later, another helicopter took its place.

Finally, Xan thought, recognising Angel, though she didn't know the pilot or the man beside her.

One of the porters helped load their bags onto a trolley while Angel and the man headed for Xan.

"Hi. At Jason's request, I've given you Villa Akoya, over the other side of the lagoon," she told Angel. "As you probably saw as you flew in, the decking you asked for is complete and the dance floor is in one of the function rooms, ready to be laid out for tomorrow night."

Angel nodded, then glanced at the man at her side.

Xan introduced herself, holding out her hand to shake his.

"Nathan Miller, otherwise known as the groom." His handshake was a quick press, before he released her. Dark circles under his eyes said he hadn't slept much lately. He didn't seem like the sort of brute Jason had described, but that didn't mean Jason was wrong. After all, she'd only just met the man.

Xan said, "I've set you up with a suite in the hotel, but if you'd prefer to share with your family, they're in Villa Albina, which is – "

"He's staying with me," Angel interrupted. She snapped

her fingers at the porter. "Take all our gear to Villa Akoya."

Xan was lost for words. "But...the bride usually...I mean, the morning of the wedding...it's bad luck to..."

Angel's mouth smiled, but her eyes turned cold. "Oh, there'll be much worse luck if anyone tries to separate us. We'll take the villa." She tugged Nathan's arm, and he followed her obediently away from the helipad.

Xan stared after them, but not for long. The helicopter was soon ready for takeoff, with another buzzing beast waiting to take its place.

FORTY-ONE

It was nearly dark by the time the final flight arrived. Xan recognised the sound of Shou's helicopter, and switched on the landing lights to help him find his way down.

Shou must be tired, Xan decided, as she watched him land the aircraft at a ninety degree angle to his usual position, with his tail pointed away from the gate. Very tired, she amended as a small, dark shape slid out of the pilot's seat and onto the ground. Shou didn't let anyone pilot his aircraft. Ever.

Xan stepped forward to challenge the figure with her standard greeting. "Hi, I'm Xan Lane…"

The girl unwrapped the scarf covering her head. "Yes, I know." Even in the dim lights, Xan could see the similarity between her and Angel. Family, she supposed.

A man landed heavily on the helipad, then crossed the concrete to stand beside the girl. "You are the hotel manager, yes?"

Xan gave a curt nod.

"I am Mohsen Rezaei," he said grandly.

The Middle-Eastern man, Xan thought, glad to tick the final name off her list. "And this is your wife…?" Xan wasn't sure she could pronounce the woman's name.

"My niece, Parisa," Mohsen said smoothly. "My wife is in Rome, looking after some business interests."

Alarm bells rang in Xan's head. "Ah, I'll have to check. You see, her name isn't on the guest list and only approved guests are allowed on the island. Shou should have told you this before you…" Stole his helicopter, Xan realised, as her heart sank. This was exactly the sort of thing the resort's extra security measures were supposed to prevent.

"I did," someone croaked. A third figure clambered out of the helicopter, somewhat stiffly. "I checked before they boarded. She's a relative of the bride. Just send them to their rooms, Xan." Shou's eyes implored her to cooperate.

Xan sighed and sent them with Rita to Reception. Once they were out of earshot, she turned on Shou. "Why weren't you flying?"

"She's an assassin. She's got more knives under that jacket than I've ever seen one person carry. Guns, too – the kind that aren't legal here in Australia. She said she was flying the helicopter, not me, but she'd let me live to fly home if I kept quiet until they'd landed. You watch out for her. I'm going home before she changes her mind." And with that, Shou hopped into the pilot's seat, closed the door behind him and lifted off in record time.

Bugger. Xan pulled her phone out of her pocket and called Trevor, Angel's security specialist. "I have a problem," she said after he'd answered. "Mohsen didn't bring his wife. He has someone called Parisa who he says is his niece, but my pilot says is an assassin. An armed assassin. They're headed for Reception now."

"Dr Miller is at Reception, sorting out an issue with her wristband, I believe. I'm on my way." Trevor ended the call without another word.

Xan broke into a run. Maybe she could catch up to them and persuade them to come to Villa Maxima with her. The last thing she needed was something getting injured or worse, killed, on the island.

Xan took a shortcut through the jungle, arriving at the lobby door just as Mohsen did. The lobby looked empty, without even Philly manning the Reception desk. Thank goodness. "Let me get that for you," she panted, summoning a professional smile. She wrenched open the door and stood aside to let them in.

Her timing couldn't have been worse. Philly walked into the lobby, followed by Angel and Dennis.

"Kiana!" Mohsen beamed.

Angel inclined her head. "You made it. I thought you said you'd had some trouble with airport security."

Mohsen's expression darkened. "Yes, I did. My bodyguards weren't allowed to enter the country. They detained me, too, but your country's security personnel can't tell a terrorist from a businessman. Women, they are much more lenient with. That's why I brought my niece, Parisa, instead."

"Niece." Angel's tone turned deadly. "That would make her...?"

"Lilupar's daughter," Mohsen said smoothly. "I forget

that you haven't met. Parisa, this is Kiana, Fatima's daughter."

The two women faced each other, mirror images of the same deadly threat. Angel's fingers lingered on her arm, where Xan knew she kept a knife, while Parisa's hand hovered over her own arm. Parisa had a slight height advantage over Angel, but that was about all the difference between them. The girls could have been sisters. Ones who wanted to kill each other.

Parisa was the first to relax, dropping her hands by her sides. "Kiana. I believe I owe you a debt."

Angel didn't relax at all. "She deserved what she got."

"My father's killer deserved much, it is true. That is why I waited, and trained, so that I could do the job properly when the time came."

"You waited too damn long," Angel snapped. "She killed my mother. The woman who would be my sister in law. And she tried to kill me. You owe me, all right."

"Indeed."

A long moment passed while both women stared at each other. Xan wanted to scream in frustration. Philly had fled, but Trevor and Dennis hovered by the exits, looking for a chance to de-escalate matters, Xan hoped.

Mohsen clapped his hands, the sound echoing loudly in the tiled lobby. "Excellent. I'm sure Parisa would like to hear your memories of her mother, Kiana, when time permits. Perhaps over a high tea?"

Angel's hands dropped to her sides. "Perhaps." She nodded to Parisa, Mohsen, then Trevor, before turning on her heel and leaving the lobby.

Well, this wedding just got interesting, Xan thought.

Rock stars, security, a possible terrorist, and now an assassin? She'd prefer another round with the jellyfish. With a cyclone thrown in.

FORTY-TWO

Xan couldn't believe how nervous she felt. Anyone would think she was tomorrow's bride, not the girl sleeping in Villa Akoya tonight.

Yet here she was, pacing the length of the Penguin jetty again, wishing for some sort of inner peace that swam just out of reach in the waves below as the tide rushed in.

The helicopter was safely on the pearl farm landing pad, with the *Argo* moored nearby. All the guests who were attending tomorrow's wedding had arrived and there would be no way on or off the island until Sunday. The only communication with the mainland was via the radio in Dennis' office, now the satellite uplink and mobile phone tower had been disabled for the event, as per the bride's imperious instructions. The kitchen had closed for the night, though one chef remained on call, in case of any late night room service requests. The Jungle was open for a few more hours, but it'd looked like the guests were saving themselves for tomorrow, so they'd all gone to their rooms early. Xan hadn't seen a single soul since she'd left Marcel at the bar. Even Jason seemed on his best behaviour.

Speak of the devil…

"I bet tomorrow's will be the most organised wedding in the history of weddings, no matter what fuck-up has you pacing. Go on, tell me. What's gone wrong?" Jason called from the head of the jetty.

"Nothing," Xan admitted, not wanting to mention the assassin in their midst, then added, "Yet. Nothing's gone wrong yet, but that's the thing about weddings, isn't it? Something has to go wrong, because it can't be perfect."

"Sure it can." Jason strode out to her. "You're organising it. If anyone can hold the perfect event, it's you, the patron saint of hotel management and weddings."

Xan snorted. "You're laying it on a bit thick, aren't you? I thought only the Pope could name saints, and then only after they're dead. I'm still breathing and I plan to be for a long while yet, though that could change tomorrow if I mess up this wedding. It's my first, so I'm bound to."

Jason reached her end of the jetty, and wrapped a reassuring arm around her shoulders. "You won't. If anything goes wrong, it won't be your fault. She'll blame it on me," he said blithely, nodding at the dark shadow of Villa Akoya.

Xan shrugged off his arm. "I take it all the lights out means she's going for maximum beauty sleep tonight?"

"Maybe." The way Jason said it, it sounded more like a *no*. "First night in a new place, she usually gets an early night. Jo and I would take it in turns, staying up, waiting.

Because…well, it was better than getting woken up by it."

Xan squinted at the villa. "Woken up by what? Do she and her boyfriend have noisy sex on the first night? That's hardly unusual behaviour for a hotel. At least hotels like this one have soundproofing. At the backpackers where I used to work, you could hear – "

A piercing scream came from the villa, followed by another, louder than the first.

Frogs in the bathroom. Xan would wager a week's wages on it. She marched up the jetty, intent on rescuing the bride from her uninvited guests.

The back of her shirt snagged on something, pulling her up short.

"What the…?" She twisted around, trying to unhook it, but Jason held her fast. "Let go!"

More screaming issued from the villa. This time, it sounded like there were words in the screaming, most of them abusive.

"Jason, let go!" Xan insisted. "I need to help!"

"Let him do it," Jason said darkly.

Xan's blood ran cold. "You mean he's in there with her? And she's screaming like that? What if he's trying to kill her? I can't just stand her and let some prick – " She wrenched free of Jason and set off again.

This time, he grabbed her, not her shirt. Both arms clamped across her middle. "You can't! If you go in there, you'll get hurt."

"So come with me. I'll page security, and between us, we'll get him away from her." Xan lifted her wristband to tap the emergency code.

"NO! No security. No one goes in there."

Bloody coward. Xan stomped on Jason's foot and he released her. "You mean to tell me, you'd let some arsehole beat up your friend because you're scared of him? I thought you had more balls than that, Jason Felix, but maybe I was wrong. I'll break it up on my own. You just watch me."

The screaming had stopped, shrouding the villa in eerie silence.

"She sleeps with a knife and a taser. If you burst into her room, she'll hit you with one or both. You know there's a character in the Harry Potter books that did bad things to people if you woke him up? Well, that bloke's nothing to her. We had a security guard once who was too stupid to follow orders. He got a knife in the chest. He was lucky to survive."

Xan stopped. "Your friend would stab me?"

"Probably not. She threw the knife at the guard from the other side of her hotel suite."

Not particularly reassuring. "So if it's quiet now, that means…?" Xan ventured.

"She's awake, most likely. I hope she tased him. She got a real heavy-duty taser. The aftershocks can seize your muscles up for hours afterwards." Jason's teeth flashed white as he grinned.

"You sound like you have first-hand experience," Xan said.

"Nah, not personally. She's used it a couple times, though, and she paints a pretty fucking clear image when she wants to. She can knock a guy out with that thing."

Xan didn't feel comfortable standing here when anything could be going on in the villa. "Still, I should go and at least knock on the door to ask if she's all right." She thought a moment, then added, "Or if he needs medical attention."

As if on command, the lights clicked on in the villa and one, no, two figures came into view, walking through the living area to the veranda.

"Aw, I really wanted her to hit him," Jason said softly.

Nathan swept Angel up in his arms. "C'mon, it's time for that sex on the beach."

Angel laughed, sounding younger and more carefree than Xan thought possible. "No, it isn't. Plenty of time for that sort of thing after the wedding."

"We're awake, and the beach is just down this path. We've got time now," Nathan insisted, carrying her down the steps and out of sight.

A long moment later, they heard a shriek mingled with a deeper shout.

Angel's voice was clearer. "I told you! The tides up here are huge. The beach will be back in the morning."

The couple walked back into view, hand in hand as they ascended to the veranda.

"I've seen enough," Jason muttered, marching back to his villa.

Xan watched the pair head inside their own villa, then share a cup of milk before ambling down the corridor to the bedrooms. Despite all the security measures and Angel's celebrity status, these two looked like any normal couple, about to be married in the morning. Two people who planned to share a happy future.

For a moment, Xan envied them. To be so sure of someone that you wanted to spend the rest of your life with them…no, it was a crazy risk to take. One she never would, she vowed, as she followed their example and headed off to her own bed. Tomorrow would be a long day.

FORTY-THREE

"I can't do this without you." Six simple words that were the reason Xan found herself standing on North Beach, beside a white carpet, with Jason clinging to her arm like a terrified toddler. A toddler with a very firm grip.

She should have been sorting out details, decorations, last minute menu changes or whatever else needed to be done, but she kept her promise and stood at Jason's side while the woman he'd loved for most of his life walked down the aisle in a ruby-coloured wedding dress. Its Middle-Eastern style, heavily embroidered in white and gold, suited the diminutive bride. She wore no veil, so her dark hair gleamed in the sun, pinned and curled so that it fell to just above shoulders.

Her fingers rested on her father's arm as he walked beside her, but her eyes were fixed on her grey-clad groom. Out of respect for Broome's tropical climate, he wore no tie or jacket, just a white shirt with a pale grey vest and pants. Nathan looked like he was going to cry, Xan thought, as he stared at his bride. He wasn't the only one, either.

Angel passed her bouquet – a carefully sculpted cascade of frangipani flowers – to Jo, where it blended with the flower print of her dress. Deliberately, Xan was sure.

Xan let her mind wander as the wedding celebrant said things she probably repeated for every wedding. She was brought back by a particularly violent squeeze from Jason that nearly crushed her fingers.

The wedding vows, Xan realised, curious to hear whether the couple had chosen to be boring and traditional, or if they'd written their own, to be parroted after the celebrant when they forgot the words.

Traditional be damned, it seemed. They said their vows in unison, their words simple but poignant enough for Xan to remember them days later:

"I am yours, and you are mine; to love, care for and protect. I will share your pleasure and your pain. I will stand with you through anything life has in store for us."

Rings, kisses, signing the relevant paperwork…none of that was anything out of the ordinary, and Jason seemed to relax, or at least grow resigned to the marriage. Xan's heart ached for him, though her throbbing fingers weren't quite as sympathetic.

FORTY-FOUR

The rest of the day felt like an anticlimax, after all the work she'd put in. Not even a peep out of the assassin – though Trevor and Dennis kept a careful eye on the girl the whole day.

When someone's father stood up to make a speech, Xan took the opportunity to do one final check on her staff. All the food had been served, so the only duties that remained were clearing away the dessert dishes and serving drinks to guests until the wedding reception ended. She could relax, drink a glass of champagne and maybe even take a turn on the dance floor.

Xan had expected a live band, given Chaya's reputation. After all, all but a handful of musicians in the world would have jumped at the chance to perform at this rock star wedding. Angel or Alana or whatever her name was would only have needed to ask, Xan was sure of it. But the bride had chosen a DJ instead, a sound guy Jason evidently knew well, judging by how happily they were talking together as the DJ set up his equipment.

Jo's voice blasted through the sound system, bringing Xan's attention back to the speeches. "I've known Caitlin since primary school and I could tell you some stories..." she began. Xan listened as Jo described her friend's budding talents as a doctor, musician and MMA fighter, making everyone laugh. Jo continued, "But there are three lessons she taught me that I'll never forget, and Nathan, as her husband, you'd better not forget them, either. Lesson one: size matters!"

A roar of laughter echoed across the lagoon, fading as Jo explained that she meant the size of hearts and love and other non-R-rated things, then launched into a second rambling point that Xan didn't quite catch.

"And last but not least, lesson three. Love conquers all. I've played to packed stadiums right alongside her. I've shared a coffee with her the morning after she's worked all night to save a patient's life. All exhilarating, awesome moments in anyone's life, and we've celebrated them all. But I've never seen her as happy as she is today, when she married the man she loves. So I'd like to propose a final toast tonight to the bride and groom, Mr and Mrs...whoops, Dr Miller!"

Xan raised her glass and drank the lot. Yes, she deserved a whole glass of champagne to celebrate a job well done. She'd never seen a wedding proceed so smoothly.

The DJ called the guests to assemble around the edges of the dance floor for the bridal waltz. The bride and groom hung back, sharing a kiss while everyone's attention was elsewhere. Everyone except Xan.

A sharp crack rent the air, followed by three more in quick succession.

The newlyweds dropped out of sight too quickly for Xan to see whether the gunman had hit them or if they'd simply taken shelter behind a table. She glanced around, noticing several others doing the same thing, but most of the guests stood on the dance floor decking, staring out over the lagoon.

Xan reached the couple first. The bride was barely visible beneath the groom, a deliberate move on his part, Xan decided, as he covered both his head and hers.

"There! Can't celebrate love without fucking fireworks!" Jason shouted somewhere over on the deck. "Congratulations!"

"It's just fireworks, Nathan," Angel said, rolling him off her. She straddled his hips, her skirt pooling out like blood over them both. "Look up."

Four more reports sounded. Seconds later, colours bloomed in the sky to the oohs and aahs of the guests.

"I thought…I thought…" Nathan began.

"I know," his bride soothed. "But I'm fine. You're fine. We're both safe and no one's trying to kill us here."

"I'm sorry – "

She placed her hand over his mouth. "Say it. We're safe."

"We're safe," he repeated. "You're safe."

"Yes." Angel smiled. "I love you. And we're going to spend the rest of our lives together. A long, long time. Because I married you. Because I love you. Now, kiss me."

"Because you told me to?" he asked.

"Because you love me. Because you want to. Because today's our wedding day." She paused, then finished with, "And because I'm your wife, and I told you to."

He sat up, wrapping his arms around the blood-dipped bride on his lap. "Because you love me," he said slowly. Their kiss was slow and sensual, passionate in the extreme.

Xan found she had to look away as her insides flooded with heat. How long since someone had kissed her like that? Had anyone ever kissed her like that? Passion so hot it burned her, several metres away, watching…

She shouldn't be watching, Xan told herself, hurrying to join the guests on the deck. Jason would be there, and she'd promised him one dance.

The newlyweds finally made their way to the dance floor. The music started and the pair twirled across the deck in their first dance as a married couple amid the strobe-like flashes from everyone's cameras. None of the pictures would make it onto social media tonight – all communications with the outside world were down, as per the bride's instructions.

Xan scanned the crowd, looking for Jason, who was nowhere to be seen. But he had been here not long ago, watching the fireworks with the rest of them.

Fireworks. That the couple hadn't expected. That no one had expected. Xan sure as hell hadn't organised them.

Jason must have. Had he seen the newlyweds' response? If he had, he'd have slunk off to sulk, most likely, she decided. Before she'd really thought it through, her feet had already started along the path that led to the villas. If he was sulking, he'd let her off that dance and she could go to bed after a very long day.

The music followed her around the lagoon. Good thing there weren't any non-wedding guests on the island, as no one would be sleeping with that noise going on. Xan had to give the DJ credit, though – the music wasn't bad. And every track was worth dancing to. Maybe if she couldn't find Jason, she'd head back and join the party. After all, she did have an official invitation.

She strode past the house and toward the jetty. It was pitch black out there, but she knew by now that's where he'd be. If she'd thought about it, she'd have brought a torch. Or even her phone, but that was sitting on her kitchen bench, switched off like the useless device it was out here.

"Jason?" she ventured, stepping onto the boards.

"I'm not even sure of that any more. This week, I'm nobody. Definitely not a rock star. And now, uninvited to the wedding." His voice came from close to the end, but it grew louder as his thumping footsteps brought him into view.

Xan managed a smile. "You'll always be Jay Felix the rock star to me."

"Is that because you think I'm a dick, too?" His eyes glistened in the path lights. No, surely not with tears.

With anyone else, Xan would have tried to be diplomatic, but there was no use hiding her opinions from Jason. And she wanted to know the truth, which he'd respond with if she was honest. So she said, "That depends. Did you do it on purpose? Did you know how he'd react?"

Jason shook his head. "Fuck no. Like I said, real love has fireworks. I wanted it to be a surprise, my gift to them. I brought up one of the pyrotechnic guys who does the

Australia Day fireworks. She always loved fireworks. She'd come down to the foreshore or Kings Park with us every year, and we'd have a picnic and watch the sky show. No idea he'd go psycho. He knocked her down. Bastard knocked her down. And instead of taking a knife or a taser to him, like she would anyone else, she just got up and pretended it was nothing. Then she threatened me if I didn't leave her wedding. So now I'm here." He waved at the jetty. "Got two bottles of champagne, though. The good stuff. Want one?"

The man owned the whole hotel, but he'd stolen two bottles of champagne from one of his guests. A girl who was crazier than he was. Xan shook her head. This was all too much for her.

"Yes, please," she said.

Jason disappeared into the dark and returned a moment later with an unopened bottle of champagne, which he popped with gusto. All without spilling a drop. He handed it to her. "Sorry, didn't bring glasses. I didn't expect…"

To share. For anyone to notice he was gone. Anyone who cared, anyway. Xan blinked back tears. Impulsively, she threw her arms around him in a hug made awkward by the champagne bottle she still held. "I'm so sorry, Jason."

Jason returned her hug, not the slightest bit awkward. "He's going to kill her, isn't he? Fuck, how am I supposed to just stand by and wait for it to happen?"

Xan thought of the strange couple she'd watched all day – not the man who held her in what was a surprisingly comfortable embrace – and shook her head. "I don't think he will. There's something not right there but it's not…I know she's scared of something. They both are. But…I don't think the danger's him. Even if it was, there's nothing you can do about it, except be willing to help if she asks for it. She's an adult and she married him. She gets to make her own decisions, and her own mistakes." Like Xan nearly had with Jerome. Bloody hell.

Squirming out of Jason's grasp, she brought the champagne bottle to her lips and gulped some down. When she looked around, she found Jason had disappeared. The pop of a champagne cork in the darkness pinpointed his location as he returned with a second open bottle for himself.

Drinking champagne – the genuine French stuff – out of the bottle, on a jetty with the rock star owner of an island resort. Shit, but her life was crazy. Xan raised her bottle in a toast. "To adults who do crazy stuff."

Jason clunked his bottle against hers and they both drank. Crazy stuff, indeed.

FORTY-FIVE

Some time later, Xan set down her nearly empty champagne bottle. She couldn't have drunk all of it. Jason must've helped, she told herself, peering at the starlit waves beneath her swinging feet. It wasn't all that dark, not really, with the Milky Way shimmering across the sky.

"I should go home to sleep," she said, struggling to her feet. Bloody hell, she had drunk more than she'd thought. Xan wobbled as she fought to get her feet into her shoes for the walk back to her unit. Jason might have fallen asleep on the jetty, like so many nights before, but it wouldn't do for the hotel manager to imitate the rock star. Double standards, she thought muzzily.

"Why did you come out here, Xan?" The shadow that was Jason sat up. "You weren't uninvited. I'm sure you could've stayed at the reception until the end, when one of the psycho's buffed-up mates would offer to show you his incredible stamina for the rest of the night. Or is the helicopter pilot more your type? I forget."

"His buffed-up mates are ASIO agents who interrogated me last year. Not my type." Xan's voice turned cold. "And not all of us look for the next person to pull into bed. Some of us have standards and integrity and self-respect, and we expect the same from anyone we choose to have a relationship with. A relationship, not a one night stand. Not to mention, that would be unprofessional and against hotel policy."

"Fair enough," Jason replied, sounding completely unfazed. "So why did you come out here?"

Xan sighed. He probably hadn't heard a word of what she'd said. In one ear, out the other. Bloody overgrown teenager. "Because when I agreed to go to the wedding with you, I promised I'd dance with you."

"And that's what I love about you, Xan. Standards and integrity and all that shit. You keep your promises." Jason unfolded to his full height. "Let's have that dance and we can go to bed."

Xan frowned. "Our own beds. Alone."

It was Jason's turn to sigh. "Yeah, that. Some of us are just destined to be alone. At least we have each other, right, Xan?"

"That dance?" she prompted.

His arm was warm around her waist as his hand clasped hers. As if on command, the music across the lagoon morphed from a fast track into a much slower song. Her head was filled with champagne froth, making it hard to remember the steps.

"Let me lead. Just this once," Jason breathed in her ear,

pulling her closer.

It felt like the most natural thing in the world to have her body moulded against his, just the thin fabric of her dress and his shirt between them. Rock stars didn't do ties, or jackets, for long. But they could dance.

"Where'd you learn to dance like this?" she mumbled as he guided her effortlessly across the boards, not stepping on her toes at all.

Laughter rumbled through his chest. Bloody hell, she was so close she could feel it.

"Jo did ballroom dancing all through high school. She needed a partner, so she bribed me into it. It paid off, though." His breath was warm on her neck.

"What with? Alcohol? Girls?"

"No. She agreed to be the drummer in my band, and she persuaded Caitlin to join as our guitarist. Before she was Angel, she was Caitlin. And now she is again, or so she says. But none of this would have happened if I hadn't agreed to dance."

Xan laughed with him. "People have done worse for fame."

"Yeah, I have. But not tonight. Tonight I get to share one dance with you."

"Yes." Xan rested her head against his shoulder, just enjoying the moment.

He was the only man she could dance with, without him expecting more. No obligations. No expectations. Just Jason.

"The music's stopped," Jason remarked, but he didn't let go of her.

So it had. Across the lagoon, the party was over.

So why did she want to linger a little longer here with him?

"Xanthe," he breathed in her ear, drawing out the sibilance. "Kisssss-zanthe…"

Yes. Kiss me.

Xan turned her head so she could feel his breath on her face. Just once. One dance, one kiss, and she'd go home. In the morning, she'd say she was too drunk to remember, but she wasn't. She wanted to know what it was like to kiss Jay Felix. Why so many girls had fallen for him. How he'd charmed all those girls into his bed. It wasn't just his dancing skills, or his celebrity status. Something more…

Her lips brushed his, burning like that first gulp from the bottle of Moet.

"Xanthe, you're drunk," Jason murmured. He didn't move away, though.

Maybe she was. Maybe she wasn't. But for a moment, she wanted to pretend…

Xan grasped his shoulders and kissed him properly.

For a moment, he stood as still and hard as a statue. Not moving, not responding. Then he melted, and the whole world moved.

Once again, Jason took the lead, like the expert he was. Their tongues danced, and it didn't matter that Xan didn't know the steps. He held her like he didn't intend to let her go. And she didn't want him to.

Her blood fizzed with champagne bubbles, then warmed, sweeping her higher like one of the geysers she'd seen in New Zealand. In the distance, the music began again. One final song. In Jason's arms, she moved with him, dancing to a rhythm he knew better than she did. And still they kissed, because she couldn't bear to tear her lips from his.

But he could. "Yeah! Fireworks! Just like in the books!" Jason cheered.

"What books?" Love and kisses and fireworks…those sort of metaphors only happened in romance books. Realisation dawned. "All those girls. The books that went missing. You getting drunk in the library. You've been reading romance books!"

"Fuck yeah. What women want, right?"

Romance books. A rock star who read romance books. Xan's shoe caught in the gap between the boards and she stumbled. Jason caught her, but not in time. Together, they tumbled off the jetty.

FORTY-SIX

Thank fuck it was high tide and not low, was all Jason had time to think before he hit the water. Remembering his high school surf lifesaving classes, he dragged Xan to the surface so she could breathe, and headed for shore.

"Let go of me, you bloody fool. Have you forgotten I can swim better than you?" Xan snapped, tearing out of his grasp. Jason wasn't sure if the kick she delivered to his thigh was accidental or deliberate.

"But the deadly jellyfish…" Jason began.

"They prefer calm water, like the lagoon. Not rough waves with the tide coming in. Believe me, I checked. I don't want to meet another one." Xan paused. "But sharks feed at night, and I don't have my shark shield on. I swear that tiger shark's still hanging around, looking for a way back into the lagoon. Race you to shore?"

Tiger sharks? "Fuck yeah. You're on."

But as Xan pulled ahead, Jason didn't have the heart to try and beat her. He'd kissed her. He'd fucking kissed her. And for a moment, one really long, blissful moment, there'd been fireworks and lightning and toe-curling and every fucking metaphor in the book. In the whole fucking library. He hadn't imagined it that first time, wishing her a happy new year after the cyclone. It wasn't the adrenaline-fuelled, we-just-survived-certain-death euphoria that he'd felt. It was full-blown love. For the one woman he couldn't have.

Doomed love. Fuck. It was almost like some bitch was writing a book about them. One who hated his guts. What had he ever done to her? Well, no hoity-toity writer got to control his life. He'd take matters into his own hands.

He waded out of the water, to where Xan already stood, dripping, on the beach.

"Good thing the nights are warm and the water's warmer," he said. "Come back to my place to dry off."

Xan shook her head. "No, I'll head back to mine, thanks. Like you said, the night's warm. And all my clothes are there." She glanced down. "Well, all except the shoe I lost in the water." Moonlight winked in the water droplets falling from her bare toes.

Jason turned back to the sea. "Want me to go get it?"

"No. It's just a shoe. I'm sure I can get a new pair from Target in town tomorrow."

Every girl he'd ever been with before had prided herself on her fashionable wardrobe. But Xan... "You seriously wore Target shoes to a celebrity wedding?" Jason couldn't stop laughing.

Xan shrugged. "Nobody noticed. Everyone's eyes were on the bride, like they're supposed to be. No one even glanced at the hotel manager, unless they needed something."

"I noticed," he corrected. "I noticed the way that dress is the perfect colour for you, showing off your curves without showing too much. The way the heels made your legs look longer, and you walked in them without tripping or stumbling, as if you were just as comfortable wearing those as the flat shoes you usually wear to work. You look beautiful tonight, Xanthe. And anyone who didn't notice is a fucking idiot."

Xan snorted. "With one shoe and a soaking wet dress. That's one hell of a compliment, Jason. Thanks. Now I know you're drunk. And on that note, good night." She marched up the beach and the darkness swallowed her.

Every instinct Jason had told him to follow her, but he knew she'd only kick him again. On purpose this time.

Somehow, he'd fucked up again, and he didn't know how. With the one woman he couldn't afford to lose.

Shouldn't have kissed her, he told himself, stumping along the sand to his villa. Shouldn't have had that dance and kissed her and…

But fuck, it had been worth it. Fireworks and all.

FORTY-SEVEN

Xan was adrift in her dreams, feeling the blissful roll of a boat under her feet as she walked the deck of a yacht just like the one the Fishers owned. Instinctively, she knew this was her home, though how she knew it, she couldn't say. She called a name as she searched for someone, a vague sense of unease growing in the pit of her stomach.

But there was no one else aboard.

Laughter drifted up from the waves, and Xan turned to look. On the dive platform at the back of the boat sat a tiny toddler of indeterminate sex, dangling its feet in the water as the fish rose up to kiss the child's toes.

Relief flooded through Xan. This was the child she was searching for. Her child, though she had none.

She climbed down the ladder, stretching her arms out. A pair of much larger arms lifted the kid up, pressing the toddler to her chest in a three-person hug. Warm lips melted against hers, giving and demanding in equal measure. Better than a book. Better than any book.

"I love you, Xanthe," Jason said, before he kissed her again.

Bloody hell! Xan jolted awake. Thank all the gods and anyone else who was listening: she was home, alone in her bed, with no sign of Jason in the house. She still felt the heat of his lips on hers. Somehow, that kiss on the jetty was seared into her memory so deeply it had invaded her dreams.

She should never have done it. Danced with him, kissed him…any of it.

She needed to leave before she was tempted to do something stupid. Again.

Time to travel. Time to go. Time to look for something new.

She hadn't told him, but her citizenship papers had come through this week. She'd been too busy with the wedding to do more than glance at them, but she was free to leave the resort and take any job she wanted now.

Xan thought of her dream. It would be wonderful to feel a boat deck under her feet again. Diving expeditions didn't pay well, but she didn't need them to. It might take weeks or even months to find another job on a dive boat, though. The summer was over, and the wet season wasn't. Nowhere in Australia would be hiring right now.

That headhunting hotel chain. If they still wanted her, she might be able to do their job for a little while until something better came up. If it was still available.

It was four in the morning, but Xan itched for action, so she switched on her laptop and found the email. She read it through twice, before typing a short reply:

Yes, I'm interested. Can you give me further information about the position or the hotel?

She hit SEND before she could reconsider. A request for information was hardly a signed contract, she told herself, as doubt crept in.

She didn't want to leave Romance Island. She loved the place.

She loved its owner, a man she couldn't have, because he didn't love anyone but himself.

That's why it was time for a new adventure.

FORTY-EIGHT

A tentative knock on the door dragged Xan's attention from the lagoon, where no naked rock star swam this morning. Maybe he'd slept in, after all the drinking and dancing last night. If she was lucky, he'd have forgotten all about their kiss.

After waiting half an hour for a response that evidently wasn't coming, she'd switched off her laptop and stuffed it back in its bag. She'd check her email again later, but today she deserved a rest. The wedding had been hard work.

She squeezed past the dining table and unlocked the door.

Jason stood on the door mat, a strange intensity in his eyes that Xan couldn't remember seeing before.

"I'm looking for the lady who owns this rather remarkable shoe," he said, holding out one of her heels from last night.

Another line he'd stolen from a movie. Or a book. Xan couldn't remember. Were all the charming things he said and did borrowed from the books he'd read? Maybe none of it was him at all.

"I don't have any use for a single shoe. I have two feet."

"That's why I brought them both." Jason pulled his other arm from behind his back, showing her the pair she'd worn yesterday.

No wonder he hadn't been in the lagoon this morning. "You went swimming for my other shoe?"

He grinned. "Nah. The heel was caught in the jetty, like Cinderella was too busy fleeing the scene to free it before she took off. The other one was still on the beach where you'd left it, too. So I figured I'd bring them back to you. Especially as neither of them is a Target shoe." He held them up so she could see the brand name clearly on the insole.

Xan sighed. "No, they're not from Target. I bought them in Melbourne at one of those designer outlet places. They suited my dress, so I wore them."

"I didn't come here to talk about shoes, Xanthe. I'm here to talk about last night."

Last night we danced and kissed and it was so potent it infused my dreams, Xan thought but didn't say. Instead, she said. "What's to talk about? Your friend got married, we all drank too much, did things we regret and would like to forget, and now it's time to clean up the mess and go back to normal life. I should go see what the damage is to the new deck."

"You want to forget last night?" Hurt hooded Jason's eyes.

"Of course I do. Don't you? Weddings are like fireworks. One night when everything seems to burn a bit brighter, but it's just an illusion. In daylight, there's nothing there." Xan forced herself to shrug. She couldn't look at him. One more moment of looking into those eyes and she'd give in and kiss him again. She had to get away from him. And the resort. But mostly from him.

"Bye, Jason. Thanks for the shoes."

She pushed the door shut, then sank onto the sofa, her head in her hands.

Only an idiot fell in love with her boss. Last night she'd become that idiot. But she wouldn't stay that way for long. She'd run far and fast, somewhere he wouldn't come searching for her. Because that was what Jason did – he just forgot about his girl of the moment and moved onto the next. He didn't chase girls. Didn't even ask them on a date.

She'd be crazy to consider a relationship with him. That's why she was considering a job on the other side of the country instead. Much smarter.

FORTY-NINE

Xan hoped the coffee she clutched to her chest would be what she needed to cure the worst case of Monday-itis she'd ever known. She'd barely slept all weekend. Since…

Since she'd stupidly kissed her boss.

She slammed the cup down on her desk and woke up her computer. Was it too soon to hope for a reply from Sydney? It was almost lunchtime over there now, and if they were really as eager as they'd said to have her manage their hotel…

But the email hadn't sent yet – it was still sitting there in her outbox, waiting to go. What in hell?

Communications were still down for that bloody wedding, Xan realised, closing her eyes. She'd have to call Villa Akoya and hope the honeymooners answered the phone. Like that would happen. But she'd agreed to keep the satellite dish switched off until the bride gave the all clear. Now there was another stupid thing she'd done. She should have insisted the bride's father or someone else who wasn't engaged in a marathon sex orgy right now be able to call off the communications blackout. How could she possibly get any work done without internet and phones? She'd thought last week was bad. Five minutes in and today was already shaping up to start the week from hell.

"Good morning," an impossibly cheerful voice announced.

Xan stared. What was the bride doing out of bed? Wasn't she on her honeymoon?

The grinning girl in a singlet top and shorts didn't seem fazed by her silence. "I thought you'd like to know that my cousins flew out at dawn, so all your phones and internet should be working again. At least, that's what your IT department told me. You might want to follow up on that yourself, of course."

Xan found her voice. "Thanks. I will."

"You'll probably be pleased to know that most of the wedding guests will be flying out today, so you'll only have Nathan and I here for the rest of the week. In case you want to reduce your staff numbers or anything," the girl continued. "Oh, but I'd appreciate if you kept the kitchen open. Damned if I'm cooking on my honeymoon."

"All right," Xan ventured. She'd heard so many names for the bride that she wasn't sure which one to use any more. It was like watching *Kill Bill* for the first time. Idly, she wondered if this girl owned a samurai sword. It wouldn't surprise her at all.

"Thank you." The girl stuck out her hand. "Truly, thank you. I know this wedding wasn't easy for you to host, but you've done a masterful job. Except for the hiccup with the fireworks, which I'm assured were entirely Jason's idea, everything ran almost perfectly. Both my cousins and my security consultant were impressed, and it takes a lot to do that. I'm sure they'll be recommending your hotel to other high profile clients, so be prepared for more unusual bookings."

Don't touch her. Jason's warning rang in Xan's head, making her hesitate when normally she'd have shaken the girl's hand. Now, she eyed the outstretched fingers, wondering whether the girl's other hand was wrapped around her hunting knife.

The girl gave a little snort of laughter, her dark eyes reading Xan's soul, or so it seemed. "I'm unarmed today. There's no threat on your island I need a knife for now, or so my security assures me."

Her hand felt so delicate in Xan's, though Xan's hands were hardly huge. Xan was scared to exert too much pressure or she might crush the delicate bones.

"Good to know, Doctor," Xan managed to say.

"You can call me Caitlin. My friends and family do."

Xan nodded. She doubted she'd see the girl again after this week, but it was nice to put a name to her.

"And this is yours. A more…material thank you than words can convey." Caitlin lifted a gift bag onto the desk. One of the big, expensive ones from the pearl farm.

"I can't accept this," Xan insisted, pushing the bag away.

"Of course you can." Caitlin's eyes darkened as her voice hardened. "The rest of your staff will receive cash bonuses as a token of my thanks, but Jo and Jason insisted you wouldn't accept money, even though you did more than anyone else. Jason said he'd take you into a jewellers to find something suitable that you would accept." Her voice turned more frightening still. "If he's lied to me and you don't like it, let me know. I'll write you a cheque for the value so you can spend the money on something you do like."

Great. If she didn't like it, Jason would be in trouble. "I'm sure I'll love it," Xan said hastily, racking her brain to work out when she'd ever been in a jeweller's shop with Jason, and what she'd seen that she liked. She stifled a gasp as she realised there was only one item Jason had ever seen her admire.

The ring. Gold and coral and pearls, like something plucked from the lagoon. Holding her breath, Xan peered into the bag. No, the box was much too big to be the ring. Surely they hadn't bought her a string of pearls? Those things cost a fortune. She couldn't accept a gift like that.

She withdrew the box, closing her eyes as she opened it. She had to find a diplomatic way of refusing the girl's gift. Without getting Jason killed or maimed or whatever Caitlin had threatened him with.

"It's certainly unusual, but I like it," Caitlin commented.

Pearl strands weren't unusual.

Xan's eyes snapped open. Her jaw dropped, too. "Wow."

Not the ring. This made the ring pale into insignificance.

The necklace glowed in pale gold, shaped into delicate coral strands much like the ring or the bombies in the lagoon. Where the ring had only one pearl, this had more than a dozen, set among the coral like the jewels they were. The earrings were smaller versions of the ring, inset with pearls like the necklace.

"It's beautiful," Xan breathed, wanting to touch it but not sure if she should. Her hand hovered over the masterpiece of jewelcrafting that she'd never seen in the pearl farm's showroom.

"So you like it, then?" Caitlin asked.

Not sure of her voice, Xan nodded.

"Good. That's settled, then. Now, another matter." Caitlin crossed the room and closed the door, before returning to perch on the client's seat across from Xan. "While I understand your hotel has a reputation for respecting guest privacy, what I'm about to say now cannot leave this room. Do you understand?"

Xan wet her lips. "Will I get to leave this room?"

Caitlin laughed. "Yes. But if you ever repeat what I tell you, you may wish you hadn't."

"Because you'll have to kill me?" Xan quipped.

Caitlin shook her head. "Oh, not me. You're not a threat to me, and I'd hate to see someone who Jason cares about so deeply hurt for being careless. My past is bigger than just me, and others who are involved…are more…ah, risk-averse than I am."

Xan put the vague statements together. "You're about to tell me things that could get me killed, if other people know I know them."

"Perhaps. I suspect Jason has told you enough misinformation to place you in danger anyway, though. Allow me to set the record straight?"

Surreal. Like something out of a spy movie. Yet Xan found herself nodding. If she was in danger already, what did she have to lose?

"First, remove your wristband. There will be no recording of this conversation," Caitlin instructed. She took both her and Xan's ID bands and shut them in the bottom drawer of Xan's filing cabinet. Then she returned to her seat and said, "I saw you watching us on our wedding night. During the fireworks."

"I did," Xan admitted, not sure what else to say.

"What did you see?" Caitlin enquired.

"He didn't know. Jason thought he was doing you a favour, because you liked fireworks. He had no idea what effect it would have on your husband." Xan took a deep breath. "Honestly. He was gutted that you didn't like them."

Caitlin blinked, her face blank, not giving anything away. "I meant when you looked at us, not Jason."

Xan closed her eyes, trying to remember the scene. Before champagne had clouded her judgement. "I saw you both startle as the first fireworks went off. Then he pushed you to the ground and shielded your body with his until you managed to persuade him to get off you."

Caitlin nodded slowly. "Accurate, or mostly. Do you know why he did it?"

"Post-traumatic stress disorder, I imagine, from some violence in his past. Does he do that often?"

"Throw me to the ground? No. This was the second time." Caitlin closed her eyes. "The first time he took a bullet for me."

Wait…what? The words must have been written on Xan's face, because she didn't need to voice them before the girl continued.

"Nathan and I have a shared, violent past. One where we both have blood on our hands. Him more than me, but only because he got there first. Did Jason tell you that I'm a killer?"

Xan nodded. Why lie?

"He's right, though he knows nothing about it. About me or Nathan. Did he call Nathan a psycho?"

"Yes," Xan whispered. Caitlin's husband wasn't psychologically sound. Even Xan could see that.

Caitlin nodded grimly. "He wouldn't dare say it in front of me. Not any more. I know Nathan's not perfect, but then, neither am I. So on Saturday, when you watched two damaged people commit their lives to one another, were you envisioning our end?"

"I did consider offering you a card for the national domestic violence hotline," Xan admitted. "I still think – "

"You're wrong," Caitlin interrupted. "I'm not like Phuong, Jason's mail order bride. If Nathan ever tries to hurt me, he won't survive the day. He – "

"Wait. You know about Phuong? Jason swore everyone to secrecy, that we wouldn't mention a word to you."

Caitlin shrugged. "Of course I know. About her, and all his girls. The names of every staff member who lost her job here because of him. The maid, the mail order bride, the virgin, the heiress and every reality TV starlet he slept with along the way. Phuong's husband was a real piece of work, by the way. He deserved to die far more painfully than he did."

"He's dead?" Xan blurted out. "But I thought..." She stared at Caitlin. A killer, she'd said. But...

Caitlin smiled. Sharks looked friendlier. "Men who abuse women don't live long around me."

Xan swallowed. She didn't think she was getting out of

this room alive. No wonder Jason was scared of this girl. "So what's your husband's life expectancy, then?"

"Hopefully another fifty years or more. When we're both old and grey and have to keep our weapons strapped to our walking frames." Suddenly Caitlin looked like a bride again – smiling radiantly like a normal newlywed. "Nathan will never hurt me. I know that for certain."

Said every domestic violence victim ever, Xan thought but didn't say.

Caitlin seemed to read her mind anyway. "Sometimes life has moments you can't afford to forget. Now, most men, if someone held a gun to their heads and told them that they had to hurt someone or they'd die…most men would consider it. Some would do it. How many men you know would risk their lives for you?"

Jason, Xan thought. First in the fire. Then during the cyclone. And again with the jellyfish…and this girl.

"None, right?" Caitlin continued, as if she hadn't expected Xan to answer. "Nathan saved my life, though he didn't expect to survive. And he's done it more than once. When life gives you a man who loves you and truly would die for you, you don't ask for perfection. You take that gift however he comes and you hold onto him. Help his scars to heal because he's worth spending the rest of your life with. Whatever the future holds."

Worth spending the rest of your life with. No need for perfection. Hold onto him. Not throw his peace offering back in his face.

"Then I wish you all the best for your future together," Xan said hoarsely.

"Thank you," Caitlin replied, and left, shutting the door

behind her.

Xan buried her face in her hands. Jason. How had she been so blind? Had he seriously considered her as more than a night's conquest, all this time? If so, she'd screwed up so royally she could never look him in the eye again.

Bloody hell.

FIFTY

Jason pushed himself to swim twice the length of the lagoon that morning, same as yesterday. He was angry, he was frustrated, he was fucking pissed off at himself for fucking up so royally after the wedding and worst of all, Xan hadn't been watching him swim from her kitchen window, like she did every morning. Every morning until the morning after he fucked up, that is. Now it was two days in a row he hadn't seen her.

Where was the point in having your own private island with a lagoon you could swim naked in every morning, if the one woman you wanted to admire your arse as you swam past wasn't looking? It was enough to make him stop swimming altogether. Or to wear something while he did it.

Or maybe it was time to leave the island for a while, and go to the east coast while he was recording the album. Find replacement band members over there. Do a few shows, then maybe head overseas. Angel had never wanted to tour much, so they hadn't. Funny, that the songwriter and guitarist could call the shots for the whole band. But she could and she had. That was something else he'd need – a songwriter. Everything he'd tried to write the last few months was shit. Especially that song he'd given up on that night of the wedding. Definitely not good enough to play in public.

Maybe he should try asking her one more time, while she was still basking in her honeymoon glow…

Or maybe not, seeing as the last time they'd spoken had been at the wedding reception, with fireworks exploding overhead as she told him exactly how many seconds he had to get out of her sight before she rendered him incapable of fathering children.

Fireworks were what had fucked up his night. First the ones in the sky, then the ones with Xan. Should never have kissed her…

"Why is your hotel manager looking for jobs on the other side of the country?" a voice enquired.

Ang…no, Caitlin. That's what she wanted to be called now, after so long as Angel. She sat on his veranda, enthroned on one of his outdoor chairs. Normally, he'd be worried about her cutting bits off, especially after what she'd said the other night, but the thought of losing Xan stopped him dead.

"Bullshit. We pay her plenty here." Jason wished his voice didn't sound so weak.

Her eyes filled with pity. "She has a job interview next week in Sydney. I saw it in her email inbox when I dropped off her gift. She liked it, by the way."

Who cared about the necklace and earrings if Xan was leaving?

"What did you do?" Caitlin asked softly.

"I kissed her," Jason snapped. "On the night of your wedding, I kissed her."

"Must have been a really awful kiss if that's why she's leaving."

"It fucking wasn't, okay? It was an awesome kiss. So awesome we fell into the water. And now she doesn't want to talk to me. Even look at me." Jason stomped up the steps to the door. "Aren't you just the bad news fairy? First the band's breaking up, then you're engaged to Dr Crazypants who tried to break my face the day we met, and now Xan's leaving. Fan-fucking-tastic." He swiped open his front door and strode inside.

Caitlin followed him. "So you're just going to let her go? Not fight for her?"

"You think I should turn all crazy stalker and follow her? That's rich, coming from you." Jason refused to look at her. Fuck, of course he wanted to fight for her. Run up to her office right now and beg her not to go.

"Of course not. There's a big difference between stalking a girl and asking her on a date, or for something more. You hounded me for years, but you were never a stalker."

"No, I paid someone more qualified to follow you around and keep you safe. Or so I thought. That's what you want me to say, isn't it? That I'm sorry I fucked up? Then with the security guard, and now with the fireworks? I'm sorry, all right? I fuck up. I'm human. Not as perfect as you. Or Xanthe." Jason wished she'd leave him alone to his misery, but he didn't dare say so. "Why aren't you enjoying your honeymoon bliss with your new husband? Doesn't he have the stamina to satisfy you?"

Caitlin laughed. "There's nothing wrong with his stamina. His family fly home tomorrow, so he's taken the helicopter to town to do some sightseeing with them. And his little sister…well, you know how much you hate Nathan? She likes me a lot less than that."

Staring at the girl he'd fallen in love with about the time he'd learned to read, Jason found that hard to believe. Everyone fell for Caitlin. It was something about the big eyes and how delicate she looked that somewhere in between you just couldn't help yourself.

"Anyway, don't change the subject. We're talking about Xanthe Lane, hotel manager extraordinaire. When I treated her in March, she definitely meant something to you. And you've kissed her, what? Once?"

"Three times," Jason admitted grudgingly.

"Three kisses, then. Why haven't you slept with this girl?"

He couldn't lie to her. She probably already knew, anyway. "Because the day I met her, she said if I ever propositioned her again, she'd take me to court for sexual harassment. And she threw a bucket of water over me. I was hungover as all hell from the night before and in no state for anything, but I do remember that."

Caitlin laughed. "I like her."

"So do I."

"So you've never asked her again?" Caitlin pressed.

No way was he telling her he'd proposed to Xan in hospital. "No. Because no means no, right? You taught me that."

"Yeah, but…no a year ago to a stranger lying in a pool of his own vomit is different to if you asked her now. You know, sober and clean and not really a stranger any more."

Jason frowned. "I don't want a one night stand with Xan. Not any more."

"No," Caitlin said thoughtfully. "I guess you don't. So offer her something you do want to share with her instead."

"And if she says no?"

Caitlin shrugged. "Don't ask her until you've given her a bloody good reason to say yes. But ask her. Tell her how you feel. Don't just let her walk away without trying something. Nathan and I…we walked away from us, without saying everything that needed to be said. It cost us six years. Six years I'd take back in a heartbeat if I could, no matter what we did in that time. Nothing can make up for lost time."

Jason's heart froze. "You'd have given up all of Chaya for him?"

Caitlin squeezed her eyes shut. "To save him from the pain of those years, yes. Oh, that reminds me. I didn't just have a thank you gift for Xan. I have one for you, too." She pulled a USB drive out of her pocket and held it out. "Jo said you're considering signing a new contract. A comeback tour, with a new band to front, if need be. I want you to know that I'm happy to sign over the rights to the band name, just like Jo will. You can call it Chaya if you want. And if you do…that drive has every unreleased song I've ever written on it. Some are pretty rough, but that should keep you going for the next decade or so."

Jason closed his fingers around the drive. Such a tiny

thing could ensure his rock stardom for the foreseeable future. Caitlin, as Angel, was always the heart of the band. "Are you sure I can't persuade you to…?"

Caitlin shook her head. "No, my performing days are over. But if you decide to record any of those…I wouldn't say no to a royalty share."

Worth it at twice the price. "Of course. Thank you."

She patted his shoulder. "Good luck, Jason. Now I'm settled, I'd like to see you and Jo happy, too."

"I'm not marrying her!" Jason squawked in mock-horror. "She's my sister!"

With a wave goodbye, Caitlin left.

So, a trip to Sydney was in order. He could do that. A few phone calls and he'd have accommodation and flights sorted, no worries. Maybe Caitlin was right. What did he have to lose? Only Xan. And there was no fucking way he wanted that. If any woman was worth fighting for, it was Xanthe Lane.

FIFTY-ONE

As she climbed into the helicopter, Xan congratulated herself on managing to avoid Jason all week. It had meant spending more time at home and less in the lagoon, but she had been busy preparing for this interview. All her citizenship papers were in order, so she was allowed to stay in Australia no matter what job she held now – no being tied to the resort. Or the too-tempting man who owned the place.

Admittedly, she hadn't managed to avoid the honeymoon couple, who spent an unusual amount of time outside their bedroom together. They couldn't keep their hands off each other, but it wasn't in that get-a-room way other honeymooners did it. Maybe things were different when the girl was as hands-off as Caitlin. The honeymoon was over, though – the couple had flown home yesterday, laden with their luggage and a pile of wedding gifts.

Xan's only luggage was a carry-on case, containing a couple of interview suits and a dress. She figured she'd spend a day shopping in Sydney, taking advantage of the number of stores that the tiny town of Broome just didn't have. Maybe even splash out on a new pair of shoes. She'd need them, if she worked in Sydney. No more resort style clothing for work. It would be formal suits every day.

"What are we waiting for?" she asked Shou.

"Another passenger," he replied.

Xan's heart sank as the door cracked open. Jason stood framed in the doorway, an uncertain smile on his face, before he climbed into the seat beside her.

"Where are you headed?" she asked before he could question her.

"I have to discuss terms and sign some contracts with my agent. We need to work out the schedule for recording the next album, and touring afterwards." Jason reclined in his seat, folding his arms behind his head. "Fuck, it'll be good to be back behind the mike again."

"How long will you be gone?"

"As long as it takes, I guess," Jason replied. "Can't rush these things. And on tour, everyone wants a concert or two. Can't disappoint the fans."

Xan breathed a sigh of relief. If this interview went badly, then she might have a reprieve at the resort for a while, if Jason was away. She'd still look for another position, but she wouldn't be under as much pressure to get away from him.

Shou fired up the rotors then, making the cabin too noisy for talk. Jason put his headphones on, but Xan left hers on the seat, not wanting to hear any more. Instead, she contented herself with the view out the window. This might be one of her last opportunities to see the Kimberley laid out below her. Funny to think of all that red rock as home. Not to mention she'd miss the opportunity for daily snorkelling. After just a week out of the lagoon, she was already missing her afternoon swim with the local wildlife.

Maybe she was being too quick, taking the first job offer she'd seen. Sydney had never been her scene. She'd have been better off waiting for a position on another island resort, maybe on the Great Barrier Reef or somewhere in the South Pacific. Or even Mauritius. No, she didn't speak French, so Mauritius was out.

She risked a glance at Jason. He was just enjoying the ride, as usual. Was there anything about life that could upset the man for long? A week ago, he'd been as down and depressed as a man could be as he watched the girl he loved marry another man. Now, he looked like he was planning mischief. Knowing Jason, he probably was. Thankfully, she'd be too far away to deal with it until she got home.

All too soon, the helicopter circled in to land. Moments later, a familiar jet with a kangaroo adorning its red tail dropped onto the runway. Xan's plane to Sydney.

She bade the boys a curt goodbye and headed for the main terminal building, wheeling her case behind her. Xan waited patiently in line to pick up her boarding pass, trying not to look impatient as the family with far too many suitcases in front of her took forever dragging their luggage to the counter. One of the check in staff signalled to Xan that she was free, so Xan strode to the counter, holding out her passport.

"Flying to Sydney?" the woman asked.

"Yes," Xan replied.

"Luggage?"

"Just my carry-on."

The woman nodded, her red and white striped nails ticking on the keyboard. Xan wondered who did manicures like that. Surely painting all those little lines took forever, and what if you chipped one? If the woman did them herself, she must have the patience of a saint. Or perhaps nail art was her thing, her mindfulness exercise, for when her job got too boring or too stressful or –

The last voice in the world Xan wanted to hear said, "You've given her the wrong seat." Jason tapped Xan's boarding pass. "This says economy class. My staff fly business or first."

The woman looked flustered. "But she's only paid for – "

Jason produced a credit card. "Fix it, please."

Xan felt her face grow hot. "It's fine. I'm not flying for business. This is a personal trip."

"Doesn't matter. You're the manager of a high class resort. It's a matter of reputation." Jason shoved the credit card at the woman. "I can't allow you to fly economy. If it bothers you, you should find a job managing a less exclusive hotel."

If anything, Xan's blush deepened. He couldn't possibly know about her job interview. He couldn't. "Fine," she muttered, taking the new boarding pass and heading for the security scanning station. He couldn't follow her through there.

She stuck her laptop in one of the plastic trays and pushed her bag with it toward the conveyor belt. Behind her, a wallet and phone thumped into another tray, alongside a handful of tinkling keys. Why was Jason following her?

"What are you doing?" she hissed.

"Emptying my pockets to go through security, or they won't let me fly," Jason replied, stepping through the scanner. The bastard didn't even beep. He shoved his belongings into his pockets before they'd even scanned her bag.

"You're not flying anywhere. You don't have any luggage!" Xan said, ripping open her bag so she could dump her laptop inside.

Jason shrugged. "Don't need it. I have plenty of clothes at my place. Just need the keys." He dangled them from one finger.

For a moment, Xan had forgotten that Jason owned more properties than just the resort. To be fair, she hadn't really thought about it before, but it made sense. He probably had a place in every major city he visited often. A beachfront villa in Queensland, something overlooking Sydney Harbour, an inner-city bachelor pad in Melbourne, a penthouse in Peppermint Grove in Perth...but they couldn't compare to the resort, or he'd be living at one of them. Romance Island was the best.

Or it would be, if she didn't have to share it with him. She could barely look at him now, without thinking of his searing kisses on the jetty, how they'd danced, and how she'd dreamed...

That's why she had to leave. To take this job, wherever and whatever it entailed.

Xan headed straight for the bar.

"Where are you going?" Jason asked.

"I need a drink."

Jason jerked his head. "But the business lounge is that way. I'd take you as my guest, but I don't need to. Your ticket is invitation enough."

For the first time, Xan glanced at her boarding pass. Business class, not first. Not that she'd complain. "Where is it?"

Jason lifted his chin, eyeing what Xan thought was the airport control tower. "Up there." He wove through the crowd, headed for the stairs at the base of the tower.

It wasn't until they reached it that Xan noticed the sign pointing the way up to the business lounge. The rock star was right.

FIFTY-TWO

She managed to avoid him during the flight, as her seat was on the other side of the business class cabin to his, but he found her again at Sydney Airport while she was trying to get a taxi.

"I have a car, and I can give you a lift to your accommodation, if you like."

Xan shook her head. "I've seen you drive. You might have your licence back, but I'm not getting into a car with you. I remember what happened last time."

He actually laughed. "It's not bushfire season any more. And I mean, I have a car with a driver. My car's in my garage here."

"I'm sure you're not going anywhere near where I'm going," Xan said, hoping to discourage him.

"Where are you staying?"

She didn't remember. Somewhere cheap she'd booked at

the last minute, not far from where her interview would be held. "Somewhere in the CBD," she said, knowing it was a nightmare to drive through.

"Perfect. My place is in Kent Street."

Bugger.

"You know, you could just save your money and stay with me. I doubt any city hotel can beat my place," Jason continued.

She could imagine. "Let me guess. A penthouse with views over Sydney Harbour?"

His brow wrinkled. "You've seen it?"

Xan laughed. "No, just a good guess. This isn't my first time in Sydney."

"What are you doing here?"

Such an innocent question, but Xan didn't want to answer it. "Some shopping, maybe meet up with a few people. I just wanted…a break. Something different, after all the worries of that wedding."

"My place would be perfect for that. Close to everything, really. I won't be home much, either – I'm here to meet with my agent and the record company."

"So you're really doing it? Going back to the rock star life?"

Jason frowned. "I guess so. Yeah. Uh, car's waiting. You coming or not?"

The taxi drivers didn't seem to want to know her, so Xan grumpily agreed.

She sat in the back seat in silence while Jason chatted with the driver all the way into town.

There hadn't been many accommodation options for her, what with so many conferences on this week and the short notice. If she'd known, she would have accepted the initial offer of a hotel room in the place she was being asked to manage, but she'd turned it down, thinking to take a few extra days to make it a proper break, just like she'd told Jason. It didn't help that the only direct flights between Broome and Sydney ran twice a week, so she'd be here almost a week, whether she liked it or not. That didn't come cheap.

For a moment, she wished she could take Jason up on his offer of a place to stay, but it just wouldn't be right.

"Xan?"

Xan looked up to find both the driver and Jason staring at her. "What?"

"I said, would you like to at least see my place, so if your accommodation isn't as nice as you expect, you'll know what your other options are?" Jason said patiently.

"Sure." The word was out of her mouth before she'd really thought it through, and then it was too late. Jason grabbed her case and she followed him out onto the footpath. The car sped off and out of sight before Xan could change her mind.

"So, you're coming up?" Jason asked eagerly.

"As long as you don't want me to see your etchings or whatever, yes," Xan said.

"Etchings?" It took Jason a moment, then he burst out laughing. He was still laughing as he led the way through the lobby and into the lifts. He swiped his passcard, keyed in a PIN and pressed the button for the twenty-second floor. "Nah, I don't do those. Give me some credit, Xan. I don't deal in euphemisms. I'm offering you a place to stay. As a friend, because I figure that's what we are." There was a challenge in that last bit. One Xan felt compelled to answer.

"I'm here for a job interview," Xan blurted out. "You're my boss. I can't stay with you while I'm trying to find another job." There. She waited for her words to hurt him.

He shrugged. "I'm not your boss. I just own the island where you work. In case you've forgotten, you're the one in charge of the island, not me. And you do what you have to do. The room's still yours, if you want it. At least wait until you've seen it."

The doors dinged open, so Xan followed Jason to his door. Not quite the penthouse, as there were several other apartments on his floor, but they weren't set that close together.

Jason unlocked the door and let Xan enter first. It didn't look much different to Villa Penguin, really. Roughly the same size, though a lot higher up.

"Here. This is the best view," Jason said, beckoning her through the dining room.

Xan couldn't keep the smile off her face as she beheld the promised harbour views, from the balcony, no less. Wherever she'd booked wouldn't have a view like this.

"The bedrooms are through this way. Mine's the first one, but there's two other guestrooms, plus a bathroom I don't use, so you'd have it to yourself. You can take your pick."

Xan peeked into Jason's bedroom, which looked about as lived-in as a hotel room, but then, so did both of the guestrooms. "You aren't here very often, are you?"

"I like my island better. I stayed here whenever we did stuff in Sydney. Concerts. Recording in a studio. Some of the media interviews. New Year." He ventured a smile. "I used to spend every New Year's Eve in Sydney for the fireworks and concerts and stuff. You want to know my best New Year's ever?"

Probably headlining a concert in the Opera House, followed by fireworks and a night filled with fangirls. "Probably not."

"You were there. Cyclone Rose, blue cheese gnocchi, and Xanthe in a boat by my side. I'll never tell anyone else that, because I promised you I wouldn't, but it was a New Year to remember, right?"

"Yes. Yes, it was," Xan said, her eyes darting from one guest room to the other. She wanted the one with the balcony. Even if it was next door to Jason, it was a million times better than the shabby-looking hotel room she'd booked. But she was trying to distance herself from him, not further their friendship. Damn it, if she shared a house with him, she'd kiss him again for sure.

Jason closed his eyes. "Look, I told you then that deciding to go back to music, especially with a solo career, is a big thing for me. Fucking scary, really. It'd be really great to be able to share that with someone. Someone I can talk to about it, so I don't do anything stupid."

Xan swallowed. Anyone else, she'd have agreed to help. Damn it, she wanted to help him so much. Instead, she forced herself to say, "But what if I come back from my interview, thrilled because I got the job, and I want to celebrate?"

His eyes met hers. "Then we get some fucking champagne and celebrate, if that's what you want." He meant it. He really meant it. "We'll already have plenty of bugger-the-whole-world bourbon in the house for bad news."

Xan couldn't help it. She laughed. "When did you hear me call it that?"

"One of the nights we spent talking on the Penguin jetty. Probably with a bottle of bourbon," Jason admitted. "Please stay. It's fucking lonely here by myself. I'll even make you pancakes."

Those warm honey eyes had won her over, and she knew it. "You don't know how to make pancakes."

"Fuck, you're right. Maybe I'll buy a cookbook or something so I can learn."

Xan just shook her head. "All right. I'll stay."

He hugged her. "You're a fucking legend, Xanthe. Thank you."

This time, she didn't push him away. She'd have to do that for good soon enough.

FIFTY-THREE

"Are you an Australian citizen?"

"What do you think is the biggest challenge facing the hotel industry today?"

"What's your view on diversity in the workplace?"

And so it went, until Xan was sick of answering questions. Job interviews weren't the worst thing in the world, and she'd done enough of them to be good at them, but she'd never like them.

This time, though, she was the only candidate, and she knew it. Which meant that while she was trudging back to Jason's apartment, exhausted by the interrogation, they called her to offer her the job. Wary of being duped like Meier had managed to, she asked for them to send her contract and job description through for her to peruse at her leisure. She also asked for a tour of the hotel they wanted her to handle before she gave them her answer.

The documents were emailed through almost instantly, while the tour was arranged for the following day.

Xan found herself almost breathless at their efficiency. So different to the laid-back resort life in Broome. Was she even up to that kind of pressure?

She wasn't sure, and the next morning didn't offer her any answers, either. It was a lovely hotel, but it was a lot like the apartment block where Jason lived. Big apartments with grand views of the city and the harbour, but not much else. It didn't have any of the unique attributes that made Romance Island Resort pretty much sell itself as an ideal holiday destination. The tropical aquarium in the lobby only made her homesick.

In fact, when she returned to Jason's apartment that afternoon, she was determined to find somewhere to snorkel, even if the weather wasn't looking good. All she needed was a wetsuit and she'd be fine.

Except Jason had arrived home early, too. "How'd it go?" he asked.

"Great."

"So you got the job?"

Xan took a deep breath. "They offered it to me. I have until the end of the week to make a decision."

"What do you want to do?"

"Go snorkelling," she answered. When he looked stunned, she explained, "I always feel better after a swim with some fish. With snorkelling, I don't have to worry about dive tables or tanks or anything. It's just me and the fish."

"You want to go out in that?" Jason pointed out the west-facing window, where storm clouds massed, waiting to attack the city.

"It's all water," she replied, though the sensible part of her balked at the thought of swimming in a storm.

"Give me half an hour, and I'll see if I can sort something for you," he said.

As if rock stars had the power to call off storms, Xan thought, grabbing a bottle of juice from the fridge to take to her room. At least she'd brought a book to read while she waited.

Within twenty minutes, Jason stood in the doorway to her room, almost bouncing in excitement. "I got you a sheltered snorkelling spot. We've only got half an hour, but the visibility's better than anywhere else, and there aren't any jellyfish."

Of course. He would check for jellyfish, even if Xan knew box jellyfish didn't come this far south. "We?"

"I'd like to come, too, if you don't mind."

How could she say no? "Let's go, then."

Jason led the way toward Darling Harbour, mystifying Xan even further. It wasn't until he walked into the aquarium building that she understood.

"You figured taking me to the aquarium would let me spend some time with fish? That's sweet, Jason, but it's not quite the same. Walking through glass tunnels isn't sharing the ocean with them. It's – "

He grinned. "We're getting in. In the tank, with the fish and the sharks and stuff."

It was the best she could expect, if she decided to move to Sydney this winter. All the ocean snorkelling spots wouldn't be warm enough until spring.

But for half an hour, she forgot all about buildings and

hotels and everything else, while she swam through the aquarium with Jason. Later, when they'd dried off and dressed, and were watching the dugongs through the glass, she thanked him.

"Any time," Jason replied, and Xan's heart sank once more.

Every moment she spent with him, she wanted more, but she knew she couldn't have it. It was better this way.

FIFTY-FOUR

On their way back to the apartment, they ordered pizza. While they waited for it to be delivered, Jason offered to open a bottle of champagne to celebrate her new job.

"I haven't accepted it yet," Xan protested.

"Job offer, then," he said, popping open the bottle and pouring her a glass anyway. They drank it in the living room, watching the storm clouds roll in from the west, glad to be in out of the rain. The wind speeds of this storm matched those of a Category One cyclone back on the island, so Xan was doubly pleased she hadn't gone swimming at the beach in this weather.

The pizza arrived, smelling so good that Xan stuffed half a piece in her mouth before she'd even found a plate to put it on. Jason just laughed at her, helping himself to a slice.

"I saw you wore the necklace Caitlin gave you to your

job interview yesterday," Jason said between bites. "So you really do like it, then?"

"It's beautiful," Xan replied. "I'd hate to think how much it cost, but she wouldn't take no for an answer, so I had to accept it. I figured now I have it, I may as well wear it." It had felt like a piece of home around her neck all through the interview.

They chewed in silence for a while, until they'd finished the pizza between them.

Jason headed to the kitchen to wash his hands. "I have something else you might like," he said. He dried his hands on the tea towel and disappeared down the passage to the bedrooms.

Restless, Xan got up and washed her hands, too, but she couldn't seem to sit down again. She knew she had to make a decision.

If only Jason could've stayed an arsehole. If only the Sydney hotel had a tank big enough for her to snorkel in every day. If only she hadn't fallen in love with Jason, slipping deeper every moment she spent with him. He truly would do anything for her, wouldn't he?

"Please don't leave."

Xan turned to find Jason staring at her. "I wasn't. I just got up to stretch my legs." Too late she realised she'd been pacing in front of the door.

"I know I'm going to fuck this up, but can you promise to hear me out, and if you're going to leave, please don't do it until tomorrow?"

Now he wanted a promise? "I already said I'm not leaving."

He wet his lips. Swallowed. Wet his lips again. "Okay. I

want to ask…have wanted for a while now…I don't want to lose you. Please, Xan, will you marry me?"

Xan's breath caught in her throat. It was her turn to stare, to see if he was serious. It truly looked like he was. "This is because of the job, isn't it? You don't want to lose me as your hotel manager."

Jason snorted. "Right now, I don't give a fuck about the hotel. All I can think about is you."

"Why?" was all she could say.

He dragged his fingers through his hair. "Because you're incredible. Awesome. The one, perfect woman for me. The one I'd do anything for. The one who makes me want to do heroic things instead of just fucking up all the time. Because I don't know what I'd do without you. If I lost you. Because I love you."

Xan's mouth turned desert-dry. "I bet you say that to all the girls."

He shook his head slowly. "Nope. No one. Not until you. I swear, Xanthe. You're the only woman I've ever truly loved."

"You're my boss."

He shook his head again. "I'm not. Never have been. The boss of Romance Island Resort is you, since the day you arrived. If I want to stay at the resort, I have to do what you say, and I have. Mostly."

Except when it came to putting pants on.

"What if I want to leave the resort, to take the job here? What if I want to travel?" Xan persisted.

"Then I'll come with you. Wherever you want to go. I can record music anywhere, give concerts anywhere. You can come on tour if you want, or we can plan a tour to all the places you want to go. Whatever you want, Xanthe, I'll give it to you. Just say you'll be mine." He dropped to his knees and flipped open the ring box. "Marry me, Xanthe. Please."

Somewhere between the way his voice caressed her name and the way his honey-coloured eyes lured her in, Xan's heart melted. He loved her. He wanted her. He was the one man who'd do anything for her, who she'd be crazy to let go. Who cared if he owned the resort? He wasn't really her boss. Nothing else mattered but him, and her, and love.

Tears sprang to her eyes. "I will."

He leaped to his feet. "You will?"

"Yes. I will."

"Thank fuck for that."

Xan's laughter died in her throat as he kissed her, just like on the night of Caitlin's wedding. And maybe there were fireworks, or thunderstorms, or curling toes and clenching cores. She didn't care, because right now she was kissing Jason and he was kissing her, and no romance book could compare or even describe it, because this was real and theirs and no one else could share it.

The next morning, Xan woke alone in her bed, her lips tender from so many kisses the night before. Her memories were perfectly clear, though they felt like a dream: last night Jason had asked her to marry him, and she'd agreed.

That was all he'd asked, though, which was why she'd slept in the guest room. After lying awake half the night, second-guessing herself, of course. No wonder her dreams had been filled with him – some of them erotic enough to make her blush when she saw him next.

It hadn't been like that with Jerome, of course. The night she'd said she wanted to travel the world while he finished his studies, he'd demanded that he agree to marry her, so she'd come back. Then he'd insisted they have sex to seal the deal. That hadn't been anything to write a book about – a few minutes of fumbling in the back seat of his car with her head against one door and her knees hiked up to give him room to move, before he'd groaned, stilled and then thrown the used condom out the window. Sex with Jerome had felt like a chore.

What would it be like with Jason? Like something out of her dreams, a re-enactment of every steamy romance book he'd read? He'd mentioned some sort of tantric sex course he'd done, which meant he had to know more than just the theory of what goes where. He'd definitely had enough practice, even during the time Xan had known him.

She headed for the kitchen and coffee, hoping for a few minutes to straighten her head out before she had to face Jason.

Xan drained her cup, but her thoughts were still tangled. She wasn't sure how she could go back to the resort and tell everyone she and Jason were now together. The ring still sat in its box on the dining table – she'd shied away from wearing it.

Now, with no one watching, she pulled it out and slipped it onto her fourth finger. As luck would have it, it fitted her perfectly.

Xan stared at the ring, the gold reflecting the sun streaming through the window as the pearl glowed with hidden secrets, including the biggest one of all: Jason loved her, had asked to marry her, and she'd said yes.

She didn't want it to be a secret. She wanted someone to shout it from the rooftops until the whole world knew, because that would make this all the more real.

"Good morning. It suits you," Jason said, bending down for a kiss.

Yes, it did. But it didn't feel right to wear it yet. A ring this grand screamed of victory, of love so firmly established that no one could tear them apart. A marriage of souls as well as hearts. It wasn't an engagement ring. It was a wedding ring.

At the thought of planning another celebrity wedding, even her own, Xan's heart sank. All the security and the stress and the planning for a single day?

"I don't want a big wedding," she said, slipping off the ring to nestle it back in its box. "I always liked the stories where the couple eloped to Las Vegas and just…did it."

Jason nodded. "Definitely a rock star thing to do. When do you want to go to Vegas?"

Flummoxed, Xan floundered for a bit. "I…don't want to go to America. If there was a way to do it here and now, I would. It's just…a long engagement, when I could be here while you're off recording or touring or whatever, or if I'm at the island…would you forget about me, like all the other girls? Would you spend every night with fangirls again, like you used to? Jerome cheated on me with a teenager. I don't think I could forgive you if you did the same."

"Xanthe, all I want is you. I don't need any fangirls, not if I have you. Besides, you'll be with me, if you want. Fuck, I'll find a way for us to get married today, if that's what you want."

"If we wait too long, I'm scared I'll back out, or get cold feet, or realise just how crazy this is, me marrying a rock star. It doesn't feel real yet." Xan couldn't seem to find the right words. What was she saying? She never second guessed her decisions. "It's time for a new adventure. I want to sign something. I want to do something. Today."

Jason nodded like he understood. "I'll make it real. Today, or tomorrow. Before we leave, anyway. We'll sign the papers and say the words and I'll be yours, Xanthe. Officially." He swallowed and flashed a shy smile. "And you'll be mine."

"Yes."

FIFTY-SIX

And that's how, at four o'clock that afternoon, Xanthe Lane stood beside Jason Felix in the waiting room of the registry office. She wore a new dress she'd bought only that morning, a summery style fit for a garden party in shades of violet, lavender and white. When Jason had seen her cutting off the tags, he'd laughed and brought out a shirt that matched the violet perfectly. He wore it now, fiddling with the buttons on the cuffs like he wasn't used to wearing long sleeves. And he wasn't – it was novel to see him wearing a shirt at all.

The receptionist called their names, and Xan's knees went weak. She was going to do this. She was going to marry the man she loved, who loved her.

"I hate Sydney traffic," grumbled a familiar voice.

Xan spun, to find Jo and Angel…Caitlin in the room with them. She stared at Jason.

"I called them," he said sheepishly, staring at his feet. "We're supposed to have two witnesses and I thought it'd be nicer to have people we know instead of strangers."

"We stopped for flowers on the way from the airport. I think we got the colours right. It was hard to tell from Jason's phone photo," Jo said, holding out a bouquet of purple blooms.

"Thank you," Xan said, overwhelmed. "You both flew in from Perth for this?"

"Wouldn't miss it," Caitlin answered. "I knew there was something between you two, but Jo didn't believe me. Now she does."

"I'll believe it when I see it," grumbled Jo. "They're here, but they're not married yet."

The impatient receptionist called their names again, and Jason led the way into the tiny room where ceremonies were held. Xan didn't even know the celebrant's name, or what he'd say, but it didn't matter.

Jason coughed and pushed a piece of notepaper into her hand. "After Caitlin's wedding, I wrote this. I tried to make it into a song, but I suck at songwriting, so it's just the words for now. I figured we could use them as wedding vows, if you want."

A quick glance told Xan all she needed to know. "Sure," she said, and Jason beamed.

The celebrant galloped through the preamble, so that all too soon, it was time to read the vows Jason had written.

Xan cleared her throat, raising the paper in one hand while Jason held fast to the other. "Through fire and water and storm and sea, I will love and cherish you. Through it all, you will be my happily ever after, and I will be yours."

Jason repeated the same words, his eyes shining as he didn't take his gaze off her.

Next, he produced two rings – her pearl and coral creation, with a simple gold band for him. She pushed the band onto his finger, repeating the celebrant's words.

Then it was her turn. Jason slid the beautiful ring onto her finger, breathing the words like a blessing. Or a fervent prayer.

The celebrant said something about Mr and Mrs, and kisses.

Kisses. Jason's lips caressed hers, a promise of more to come, before he pulled away.

Xan caught sight of Jo shaking her head before the celebrant demanded her attention again, this time for paperwork.

All five of them signed the certificates, and it was done.

Xan handed the bouquet back to Jo. "Thank you for bringing those. I wouldn't have thought to."

"Hold it!" Caitlin commanded, holding up her phone for a photo. Xan had been aware of both girls taking pictures throughout the ceremony, but only now did she realise they held the only records of her wedding.

"Can you send those to me?" Xan asked.

"Sure thing," Jo said. "Mine will probably be better. Caitlin doesn't take many photos, but I've had plenty of practice."

The receptionist had gone by the time they reached the waiting room, her window shut for the day. There was a crowd waiting for the lift, though – all tired-looking office workers, staring at their phones and tapping their feet.

Jo and Caitlin moved in close to Jason, who now wore a

pair of huge, ugly sunglasses. It took Xan a moment to realise why.

Disguising him, so he wouldn't be recognised. They might be married, but their wedding was still a secret.

They all bundled into a taxi to take them back to Jason's place, where both women hugged her and wished her the best. Jason invited them to dinner, but the girls declined. They had a flight to catch, and work tomorrow.

A whirlwind of polite goodbyes and sisterly kisses surrounded Xan for a moment, and then she found herself alone with Jason. Her husband. On their wedding night, the thought of which turned Xan into a bundle of nerves.

"What do you want for dinner?" he asked without the slightest hint of lust in his tone. Didn't he want her?

"What about sex?" Xan blurted out, then blushed. "I don't mean for dinner. I just thought…with your reputation, you'd be ready to tear my clothes off right about now."

Jason laughed ruefully. He wrapped an arm around her waist, pulling her against him. "Xanthe, I will never rip your clothes, unless you ask me to. I've wanted you from pretty much the moment I met you. I've dreamed about you so many times I can't remember a night I don't think about you." His eyes burned. "Fuck, if you say you want me now, I figure it'll take me less than three seconds to be balls deep inside you, and in about five minutes, it'll be over. I've waited so fucking long."

His kiss seared her lips, caressing her tongue with far more fervour than he'd shown in the registry office.

She wanted more than five minutes, though most men didn't last that long, in her experience. Jason was a man, after all.

She slid her hands under his shirt, stroking the rock-hard abs she'd admired through her window every morning. Hers to caress now. "I want you," she admitted.

"Fuck. And I want you, Xanthe. So fucking much. But I don't want to give you five minutes. Shit, I don't think five hours will be enough. I want you all night."

Pressed against his body, melted by his kisses, Xan murmured her agreement.

Jason pulled away. "That's why we need to get dinner first. Once our clothes come off, we're not going to be doing a fucking thing except make love until morning. I don't want to fuck this up."

"You won't," Xan reassured him. "I'll make sure of it." She wasn't sure how, but she could work that bit out later. After dinner, if he insisted on it.

"Hey, there's a whole box of spring rolls here that we missed. You want one?" Jason asked.

Xan didn't even glance at them as she shook her head. She just wasn't hungry any more. Nerves writhed like snakes in her belly, leaving no room for anything else.

"I've fucked up again. I should have taken you to Sydney's finest restaurant, not ordered a bunch of stuff from the local Chinese. I'm sorry, Xanthe. I'm just so fucking euphoric about today that I wanted to keep you to myself for a bit longer." His eyes beseeched her. "Tomorrow, I'll take you out to dinner wherever you want. I'll find something with Michelin stars or something."

"We can have all the fancy dinners we want at home. The resort's chefs are as good as any you'll find in Sydney, or anywhere in Australia."

Jason ran his fingers through his hair, like he always did

when he got nervous. "Right. Of course. What about dessert, though? We forgot to order sweets."

He was as jittery as she was about tonight, Xan realised. One of them would have to take the initiative, of they'd be dithering all night. "I think it's time for the taking our clothes off bit."

"You're sure?" he enquired.

Xan laughed. "Now that has to be a first. I've never seen you hesitate about getting naked before, least of all around me."

He grinned. Off came the pants, followed, one button at a time, by his shirt. He turned his back before he took off his undies, flashing his taut backside before he rotated around to show her the goods. Jason struck a Priapic pose, his hips thrust toward her so he jutted out impressively. "It's all yours, Xanthe. Every inch."

She'd only ever seen him during or after a swim, and she'd thought him big then. But she'd never seen him properly turned on, like he was now. The man wasn't just big. He was huge.

Xan swallowed. "You might have to go easy on me with that thing," she said. "I haven't had sex for three years. I might be a bit out of practice."

Jason nodded gravely. "Three years? Seriously? We better start practising tonight." He eyed her dress. "I could bend you over the table right here if you want to keep that on, but I really want you to take it off. I've dreamed about you naked for a bloody long time."

Xan rose and held out her arms. "Take me bed, Jason."

He lifted her like the bride she was and carried her to his bedroom. He set her on her feet, pulling her in close for a kiss. Now, her pretty dress got in the way. Too much fabric between his skin and hers.

Xan reached for her zip, but found his hands already there, undoing the back of her bodice in a steady purr. The straps slid down her arms, so she stepped away from him to allow the dress to puddle at her feet.

He closed the distance between them in a moment, making her gasp as his body pressed against hers. Now, the only obstacle between them was her underwear. She didn't have time to think about it, though, because Jason was kissing her again. Devouring her lips, then pressing feather-light pecks along her throat to her chest. His deft hands slid her bra off so smoothly he didn't even pause in his path down her breast. She sighed as he took her nipple in his mouth, gently sucking for just a moment before he turned his attention to her other breast.

Warm satin landed on her foot. Her knickers, she knew, removed by Jason's hands, which now cupped her bottom, pressing her firmly against him.

All thoughts about size faded away as Xan hooked a leg around his hip, wanting nothing more than to feel him inside her. She murmured something to that effect, but she wasn't sure if he heard her, what with him so focussed on her breasts and all.

Evidently he had, because the next thing she knew, Jason lifted her effortlessly so she sat in the middle of his king-sized bed with her knees bent up and everything between on display. She didn't have time to feel self-conscious, as Jason knelt between her legs, one hand lifting his length as the other stroked her thigh.

Fear returned. Gods, it looked even bigger than before.

More aroused than before, by her. Sure, she wanted him, but how in hell was he going to get that thing inside her?

"Go easy on me?" Xan squeaked.

Jason laughed gently. "Don't worry, I'll take it slow. We have all night." He took hold of her thighs, pulling her legs toward him so she lost her balance and her head hit the pillows. Her eyes never left his. "So you want to feel me inside you?" Jason murmured.

No longer sure of her voice, Xan nodded.

He gave her no warning, driving into her so sharply that she cried out. She clenched around him, but he withdrew as quickly as he'd entered her.

Jason held up two dripping fingers. "Fuck, Xanthe, you're wetter than the ocean down there. And smooth as silk." He pushed his fingers slowly back inside her. And again. He'd angled his hand perfectly to hit all the right spots, and his eyes told her he knew it.

His name became a breathless moan on her lips as he stroked her all the way to Elysium and back. She found herself shaking as he leaned in to kiss her, while his fingers maintained their relentless rhythm.

She was no longer Xanthe, a woman of flesh and blood. She was a nebulous cloud of sensation, spun by Jason's skilful hands until she saw stars. Then she screamed, and Jason's face swam back into focus. Triumphant, grinning, as he lifted his dripping fingers to his lips.

"You taste like the sea, too."

Another orgasm like the last one would blow her apart, Xan was sure of it. She reached for him. "Make love to me, Jason," she implored.

"I'm not done kissing you yet," he said. He moved down

the bed, away from her, and Xan raised her head to see where he'd gone. He sat between her knees now, lifting her legs up higher.

"Yes. Oh, yes," she murmured, bracing herself for his first thrust.

His fingers parted her, the rough callouses on his fingertips rasping over sensitive skin until she let out a low moan. He knew exactly where to rub her just right so that she writhed in his grasp, plunging helplessly toward another rush of pleasure.

Just as she peaked, he plunged into her, so that she came hard around him. It wasn't until she came up for air that she realised he was only teasing her with his tongue. Xan stared as Jason licked his lips, then lowered his head to run his tongue over her, inside her, again.

And once again, she was lost. So completely out of control. And his, by all the gods, his.

FIFTY-EIGHT

Xan's body trembled all over, like a little lightning storm played across her skin and everything inside it. Jason's lips touched her thigh and lightning struck again, overwhelming her with sensation once more. She'd never felt so alive. So unearthly. Like a goddess made flesh for the first time. A goddess who'd married a sex god.

She opened her eyes to the sound of Jason's laughter. "All night," he said. "We've had all night, and I still can't get enough of you."

"All night?" No one lasted all night. Not outside of fiction, anyway. Xan raised her head to peer at the window. "It can't be dawn already."

"It is. Our wedding night's over, Xanthe. I hope you enjoyed it." Jason flopped onto the pillow beside her with a blissful look on his face.

It couldn't be over. "But we didn't…we didn't…"

He'd spent the whole night pleasuring her. With his mouth, his hands, and the rest of his body. Except for the bit that mattered.

"We didn't have sex," she said.

"Plenty of time for that. When you're ready."

Xan rolled onto her side so she could meet his eyes. "You've spent the whole night on foreplay and you still don't think I'm ready?"

"I was waiting for you to ask. I didn't want to fuck up."

Xan bit back her frustration. "You've given me more orgasms in one night than I've had in the decade before last night. That's the opposite of fucking up. More like…fucking awesome. Legendary, even." She climbed on top of him, so she could feel his arousal between her thighs. "Finish what you started, rock star."

He barely hesitated. "Condoms are in the top drawer," Jason said, waving at the bedside cabinet.

Xan took a deep breath. "I hate them." Nasty, sticky things. "I haven't slept with anyone for years, and I'm clean. Are you?"

Jason stared at her. "Of course. I haven't slept with anyone for a year, and never without a condom."

Xan found that hard to believe. "It can't be that long. Penelope was here until September, wasn't she?"

Jason bowed his head. "I never did it with her. Not last year, anyway. I didn't sleep with any of the reality show contestants. The last time I had sex with a woman was…Gaia. A year ago."

"And she made you swear off sex?"

"For a week or so, yeah. Fuck, I had nightmares about her screaming for me to spank her harder, when it stung my hands as it was." Jason shuddered. "But when she left, you got out of that helicopter and it was like dawn breaking through the clouds. You let me hug you and it was like…home."

Xan swallowed. He'd been in love with her that long and she hadn't even noticed? "But…a year? How did a rock star like you manage to keep your dick in your pants for a whole year?"

"You were the one telling me to wear pants."

She laughed. She might have told him to, but he'd rarely listened.

"So what with being a good boy so long and all, the first time we do this, I'll be lucky to last five minutes."

Xan ground her hips against him, making him groan. "Then I'll ask you for an encore later," she said.

Honey-coloured eyes stared at her, filled with longing. "You really mean it?"

She was aching for it. "Give me my five minutes, rock star."

He shifted and they rolled together until he was on top.

At least he hadn't picked doggy style, she thought as she relaxed beneath him like a proper missionary, ready to let him do all the work.

Jason shook his head, lifting her legs up so high, her toes pointed toward the ceiling. "They might only be five minutes, but they'll be five fucking awesome minutes, I promise." He knelt so close to her that she could feel his knees behind her bottom.

Before Xan could protest that she'd never heard of a sex position like this, she felt the heat of his tip parting her folds. Jason eased inside her, inching his way over skin so sensitised it sang at his touch. She closed her eyes in bliss.

This. This was what she'd craved, longed for, dreamed about. Hot and hard and filling her so perfectly he felt like a part of her.

But Jason had stopped moving. "Are you all right, Xanthe?"

"Yes," she said, clenching lightly around him just to see if she could. Oh, that felt incredible. "Keep going."

He chuckled. "Oh, I'm all in. Balls deep in my wife. You know what it feels like when you do that? Like coming home to the heat of a roaring fire, gliding through silk and that little clench thing you did there? That's a fucking welcome home hug right there. It even makes my toes curl."

Home. He was right. Comfortable and yet toe-curlingly incredible, all at the same time.

"Xanthe?"

"Mmm?" Now she had him inside her, she didn't want to think about anything else.

"What if I want more than five minutes?"

She held her breath as he slid out of her just as tortuously as he'd glided in. No, almost out, before he resumed his slow thrust into her depths. "Take as long as you like," she breathed.

"I want forever, Xanthe. Forever with you."

"Then take it. I'm yours, and you're mine. Forever."

When his triumphant shout harmonised with hers, a considerable amount of time later, sunlight streamed through the window, haloing them both as it bathed their bodies in light.

"Is this what happily ever after feels like?" Jason

murmured, his honey eyes sweet with love.

Xan laughed. "Yes. And it's better than anything I ever read in a book, because it's ours."

FIFTY-NINE

Xan shifted uncomfortably from foot to foot in her new shoes, wishing she'd worn a different pair. Her body still ached from their lovemaking marathon, even after a stint in the spa. Or maybe it was the multiple encores that were responsible. Somewhere in her head, she'd made a mental note that slow and steady in a position Jason had called the anvil made for unbelievable sex. Part of her ache was a desire for more, she knew, though they'd have to wait until they reached the island for that. Then, in the privacy of his villa or her unit or maybe even the honeymoon suite, she'd surrender and let him worship her body all over again.

At least she wouldn't be returning to Sydney for a while. She'd taken the time to call the Sydney hotel and tell them she wouldn't take the job. No, not even if they increased the salary. When they'd asked her why, she'd said it was because she loved island life too much to move to the city.

Jason finished reading the recording company's prepared statement, and invited questions from the assembled crowd of reporters at the airport media conference.

Xan should have predicted the first one, but it took them both by surprise.

"Where's your bride?"

Jason hesitated for a moment, then repeated what he'd said in the statement about his plans to tour Australia.

His hand shook slightly as he pointed to another reporter for the second question.

"Everyone knows you got married at a secret ceremony on Romance Island Resort a few weeks ago, and this is the first time you've been seen in public since then. But the one thing no one seems to know…who is the bride?"

Jason fixed a smile on his face and launched into a paean of praise for the resort. Not once did he mention a wedding, or Caitlin, or his own bride. He finished with, "Romance Island Resort is the most romantic honeymoon destination you can imagine."

He'd promised to show her, when she said she'd prefer to return to the island instead of staying another week in Sydney. Xan did her best to hide her smile, though she didn't think anyone was looking at her. All their attention was fixed on Jason, who continued to ask for questions he didn't actually answer. The reporters began to complain about Jason's stupidity, which Xan thought was particularly unfair. This was a press conference called to publicise the news of his comeback tour, not his personal life.

"When will we get the wedding photos so we can publish them?" an irate reporter demanded, digging her long nails into her phone case as she strove to record his response.

Probably never, if Xan had any say about it. And she did, seeing as she was in them. She'd had enough, anyway. She stepped up to the microphone beside Jason.

"As always, Romance Island Resort respects the privacy of its guests, and I'm sure Mr and Mrs Felix are grateful for your discretion. Perhaps when they are ready, they will release photos to the press, but I understand Mr Felix is eager to return to the island, to continue their honeymoon. I'd like to take this opportunity to thank him for sharing his momentous music news, and wish him every happiness with his new wife." And with that, she called an end to the press conference.

Now the whispers sounded like her name, as those who didn't know her were quickly filled in by those who did. Not a single one of them tried to ask her about his wife, though. None of them seemed to realise the truth – that Jason's bride stood before them, and they hadn't asked her a single question, or tried to snap her photograph. So nothing had changed, really. They all still worshipped Jason the rock god, while she was…no one.

And not important enough for Jason to introduce to them as his wife, either, Xan thought sadly, grabbing her carry-on case and wheeling it behind her.

Jason hurried to catch up. "Thanks," he panted. "I thought they'd want to know more about the tour. Not…Caitlin."

"Why didn't you distract them by telling them about me, then?" Xan asked.

"I wouldn't throw you to the wolves like that. They'd eat you alive," Jason hissed, glancing back.

"I can hold my own against a press crew. I did just fine back there," Xan reminded him.

"Why didn't you tell them, then?"

That brought her up short. "Because…well, you didn't. I figured you didn't want them to know. I mean, what sort of rock star marries a hotel manager? It's not the sort of thing people write romance books about."

"Fuck the books," he growled. "This is real. I love you and I don't care what they think. I think you're fucking awesome."

Xan wet her lips. "Tell them, then. Tell the world."

Jason glanced back. "You want me to spill my feelings to those vultures?"

"No," Xan said patiently. "Just tell them I'm your wife. We're about to hop on a plane to Broome, where we'll hide out at the island for as long as our honeymoon lasts. By the time it's over, they'll have run out of stories to spin about us, and moved on to the next celebrity crisis. Someone's boobs or bottom or baby."

He stared at her for a long moment. "I'm not going to tell them anything. A picture tells a thousand words, right?" He grabbed her hand, the one with the ring. "Stick your hand on my shoulder, here. Now, hold on and look like you're enjoying it."

He let out a piercing whistle, so every eye in the airport turned to him.

Jason took a deep breath, wrapped his arms around her, dipped her low, and kissed her.

Camera flashes strobed, people clapped and someone let out a wolf whistle louder than the noise Jason had made, but Xan didn't care. She didn't have to pretend to enjoy anything. Jason's kisses were a promise of the bedtime bliss that would come later.

Eventually, he let her up, still not letting go of her. "Do you think we made that clear enough?" he asked.

"I think so," Xan said softly. "Can we go catch that plane now?"

"Yeah. It's time to take my wife home."

A loud voice from behind shouted, "Where are you going, Mr Felix?"

Jason stopped. "Wait. I'll answer this one." He turned to face the crowd, pulling her so she could see them all, too. "We're going home. To the home of romance – Romance Island Resort!" he roared.

Xan waited until they'd gone through the boarding gate before she said, "You might be a rock star, but you're still crazy, Jason Felix."

"Yeah, but you like it. You're a bit crazy, too. I mean, you married me."

"Yeah," she sighed.

"Speaking of crazy stuff, want to join the mile high club with your husband on the way home?" he asked eagerly.

"Jason!"

The next book in the
Romance Island Resort series is
Maid for the South Pole

ABOUT THE AUTHOR

Demelza Carlton has always loved the ocean, but on her first snorkelling trip she found she was afraid of fish.

She has since swum with sea lions, sharks and sea cucumbers and stood on spray drenched cliffs over a seething sea as a seven-metre cyclonic swell surged in, shattering a shipwreck below.

Demelza now lives in Perth, Western Australia, the shark attack capital of the world.

The *Ocean's Gift* series was her first foray into fiction, followed by her suspense thriller *Nightmares* trilogy. She swears the *Mel Goes to Hell* series ambushed her on a crowded train and wouldn't leave her alone.

Want to know more? You can follow Demelza on Facebook, Twitter, YouTube or her website, Demelza Carlton's Place at:

www.demelzacarlton.com

Books by Demelza Carlton

Ocean's Gift series
Ocean's Gift (#1)
Ocean's Infiltrator (#2)
Ocean's Depths (#3)
Water and Fire

Turbulence and Triumph series
Ocean's Justice (#1)
Ocean's Trial (#2)
Ocean's Triumph (#3)
Ocean's Ride (#4)
Ocean's Cage (#5)
Ocean's Birth (#6)
How To Catch Crabs

Nightmares Trilogy
Nightmares of Caitlin Lockyer (#1)
Necessary Evil of Nathan Miller (#2)
Afterlife of Alana Miller (#3)

Mel Goes to Hell series
Welcome to Hell (#1)
See You in Hell (#2)
Mel Goes to Hell (#3)
To Hell and Back (#4)
The Holiday From Hell (#5)
All Hell Breaks Loose (#6)